BELLS OF REDEMPTION

DAVID MARTYN

BLUE FORGE PRESS
Port Orchard ❂ Washington

Blue Forge Press is the print division of the volunteer-run, federal 501(c)3 nonprofit, Blue Legacy (EIN 83-4307421), founded in 1989 and dedicated to supporting artisans marginalized due to race, age, disability, economics or other factors. We strive to empower storytellers from all walks of life with our four divisions: Blue Forge Press, Blue Forge Films, Blue Forge Gaming, and Blue Forge Sound. Find out more at www.BlueForgeGroup.org

Blue Forge Press
7419 Ebbert Drive Southeast
Port Orchard, Washington 98367
blueforgepress@gmail.com
360-550-2071 ph.txt

To the tens of thousands *of brave Belgian and French citizens, helpers, who rescued, hid, fed, clothed and guided allied airmen out of World War II occupied Europe to England to rejoin the fight against Nazism. Many were young women, students, and children but also, doctors, train station agents, even police chiefs.*

They fought without arms. Thousands were captured and sent to the concentration camps and thousands more were executed. They sacrificed their lives so that thousands might fight again.

You are bought with a price.
I Corinthians 6:20

ALSO BY DAVID MARTYN

THE HALL OF FAITH

The Praise Singer:
A Disciple of Melchizedek

The Oak of Weeping:
The Story of Isaac, Rebekah, and Deborah

The Epistle:
A Story of the Early Church

ROBERT CURTIS MYSTERIES

Called Into Service
Soldiers of the King: The Bramshill Affair
Lords and Ladies: The Banqueting House Plot
For God and King: The Deadly Pamphleteer

NOVELLAS &
SHORT STORY COLLECTIONS

Huldah and the Last Righteous King
A Light in the Darkest Night

www.BlueForgePress.com

PREFACE

Many who are familiar with the World War II British Special Operations Executive know that their squadron of small planes, the Special Duty Squadron 161, used to support MI6 and MI9 intelligence operated from RAF Tangmere. They used small planes to parachute and land teams, money, and material to the French resistance and the unarmed *helpers* behind the German lines. Their story has been well documented and told by historians and an excellent museum has been established at Tangmere.

A key figure in this book, Karel Kuttelwascher, an RAF ace and a Czech citizen scored his victories with RAF Squadron One also based at RAF Tangmere. His biography is a great read. I moved and separated out the MI9 operation—charged with establishing escape lines with the French *helpers* to RAF Churchstanton and the fictional Special Duty Flight 545 to create a fictional hero and not deviate from biographies of the heroes of Tangmere. They are credited in the book.

My fictional hero, Major Montclair 'Ike' Curtis, is a descendant of my hero in the Robert Curtis Mysteries series. He represents many men caught up in the war, burdened with a past and stressed by the unrelenting turmoil of combat. The story also draws from some of my other works of historical fiction and bridges my past work toward the present day and may introduce new readers to my others series and short stories.

I have dedicated this book to the Belgian and French Helpers, but remembering their heroism and sacrifice is not enough. So many who went before us bought us our freedom and a period of unusually long peace in the West. We must dedicate ourselves to act as they acted, to be willing to make sacrifices, to love others as God loves us.

BELLS OF REDEMPTION

DAVID MARTYN

CHAPTER 1
NIGHT MISSION

Blackout curtains covered the windows. A small, well-shaded desk lamp cast its beam on the nameplate below: Major M. I. Curtis, US Army Air Corps. A folder was open, spilling its contents, photographs of woods and fields, barely visible in dark shades of gray but well-marked in yellow. Major Curtis reached for the cigarette burning in the ashtray. Muscle memory of an old habit guided it to his lips. Sitting back, he took a deep drag and slowly sent a column of smoke up into the blackness of the ceiling, its destination hidden in the darkness above unlit overhead lights. At last, he took his eyes from the status board at the end of the room. An attractive young British RAF Women's Auxiliary Sergeant sat quietly beside the lit board. Her tired eyes were fixed somewhere between the phone and the silent teleprinter-waiting.

"Check the line again."

"I checked it not ten minutes ago, Major. And the teletype as well. There is no report."

"What time is it? He asked. Curtis stood up and instinctively walked to the window. He stopped at the thick black curtain. "I need some air. And coffee. You know where to find me."

"It's nearly zero-five hundred, Major Curtis. I'll find you when the report comes in."

Major Montclair Isaac Curtis, US Army, Ike to family and friends, and Mic or Mickey to the Officer's Mess, stepped outside and breathed in the cold, damp English predawn air. His thoughts escaped on his tongue. "No word. Can't be good. It could be radio problems, but nothing from the resistance either."

The distinctive sound of a Hawker Hurricane returning to RAF Churchstanton caught the Major's attention.

"Kut!" Curtis sprinted back inside. "Sergeant, get me the duty officer of Squadron One on the phone ASAP!"

Sergeant Dorothy Barkley reached for the phone to dial and mumbled, "The Czechs. I hope this fellow's English skills are better than most."

Hearing a slow, struggled "Squire drone wone, how low?" She replied, Major Curtis, RECON 1 calling for the duty officer." She handed the phone to Curtis."

"This is Major Curtis, RECON 1. Has Flight Lieutenant Kuttelwascher returned? I need him to make a quick pass near Honfleur."

Curtis shook his head. "I know what time it is. Yes, Honfleur, Normandy. You tell Kut to call me. ASAP!"

Curtis hung up and said, "Get a pot of coffee and cups. I'll babysit the coms until you get back."

Back at his desk, Major Curtis began leafing through the folder of photographs and uncovered the map. "Hmm. He'll want coordinates from reliable lighted marks. No gyro, on the Hurricane, he'll want compass courses. Hope his deviation chart is up to date."

Hot coffee was on the table when Flight Lieutenant Karel "Kut" Kuttelwascher strode into RECON One office. "You got something for me, Mickey? It must be juicy. I told them to refuel my plane and reload ammo. They're on it as we speak. No luck yet tonight, so maybe something juicy, yes? A bomber squadron? I would like that very much—juicy, many sweet kills!"

"Not tonight, Kut. You'll need a camera...."

"A camera is mounted on my plane. You should know this."

Curtis replied, "Not like this one. Different film. Infrared. Different light spectrum. As I was saying. we landed a Hudson transport near Honfleur," Curtis punched the map on his desk with his index finger. "Here. Four agents, radios, weapons, explosives, and cash to set up a new operation."

Kut leaned over and studied the map. Curtis continued. "No word from the pilot or the resistance team on the ground. I'd like you to drop in and take a look. I know RECON is not your game, but what the hell, you can fight your way back. Just give me eyes on the landing site before you begin the hunt."

Kut nodded as he scanned the map. "Yes, I know this area. There is an airbase here, not twenty miles away. You were cutting it close, my friend." He looked up and said, "Ja, Ja, I can do that, not an hour's flying time. Give me the camera. I can be in the air in twenty minutes."

"You are comfortable with the handheld camera? Get as much of the surrounding forest as possible."

Kut laughed. "Comfortable? The cockpit is my home, the only place I am comfortable! I will take your photos and bring back your special camera. Yes, and I will take photos of my kills!"

Kut was out the door. Curtis stood up and stretched his back. "You heard him; an hour and twenty minutes, and we will know something. Have some coffee, Barkley, Sergeant—it's Dorothy, right? May I call you Dorothy? I don't want to trample on your British formality, but we have been working together for a week...."

"It must be true. All Americans are, are so...."

"Are what? Do I make you uncomfortable? Have I offended you? You feel unsafe sitting here at night?"

She smiled. "No, not at all. You may call me Dorothy, Major, but better not let the Group Captain hear you."

Curtis chuckled. "Call me Ike. No, Group Captain Hastings would not approve. I am a guest here and will heartily endeavor to remain on my best behavior. So, Dorothy, you were about to confess that you find us Americans a rowdy and unwholesome lot."

"Ike? Not Mickey?

"I hate Mickey, you know, Mickey Mouse."

Dorothy nodded. "Okay then, Ike. Forward, I was about to say forward. Open with your views and your words."

"It's this war. Who knows what tomorrow brings? Why bottle up your emotions inside? Say your piece—act now, don't wait. Tomorrow is not guaranteed."

"Is that why you like Flight Lieutenant Kuttelwascher? He seems to relish the fight."

"Kut? It would be a shame if he didn't survive the war.

But this war will take our best men. What's his count now? Fourteen? Fifteen kills? He is good—very good, but he is not invincible. Kut has good reason to fight, to hate. Czechoslovakia is lost. Who knows what has become of his family? Hunting Nazi planes keeps him sane. It buries the pain. Give Group Captain Hastings credit. He swallowed his up-tight English pride and let a Czech become an ace night hunter. I only wonder if he will sacrifice Kut or do the right thing and rotate him out before it's too late."

Dorothy sighed. "You think it's too late for our agents?"

"I pray not. O, how I pray they are safe." *Lord, Save them. I don't even know their names. They will never forgive me. I chose the landing site. Forgive? How could they? I will never forgive myself.*

"Are you going to report Flight Lieutenant Kuttelwascher's mission to the Group Operations?"

"Every Brit thinks all Yanks are cocky. So, call me guilty as charged! I overstepped my authority. Let Kut get in the air over the channel first. Then I'll call."

"Is that why you wait here in this office and don't join the others in the Operations Room?"

"I don't need them to see me second guess myself. And yes, I like having a plan B, even if it's been disapproved. Quiet phone and teletype. We haven't heard any action on their part."

An hour later, Curtis called Group Operations and reported Kut's mission. "I'll hold for the Group Captain." A few moments later, he spoke on the phone. "Yes sir, yes sir, I know that, but, no sir, I didn't.... yes sir, at once sir."

He hung up the phone. "I am to report to the Group

Captain at once. You may call it a night, Sergeant."

Dorothy replied, "Yes, sir. Good night, Major."

Curtis forced a smile and walked out the door.

In the OPS Room, the OOD, Officer of the Day, greeted Curtis, "The old man is livid, Mickey. Waiting for you in his office."

"Thanks. I know he doesn't like to reprimand in public."

"I hope for your sake it is only a reprimand."

Curtis stepped across the hall and knocked on the Group Captain's door. "Major Curtis reporting as requested."

A voice from the inside replied, "Come through, Major."

Curtis opened the door. Group Captain Hastings was seated at his desk. Without looking up, he said, "Close the door."

The door closed. Curtis stood at attention in front of the Group Captain. Hastings continued to read from a folder in front of him. Finally, the Group Captain looked up and studied the officer standing before him. After what seemed an eternity to Curtis, Hasting spoke. "Bloody Yank! What the hell were you thinking?"

"I, we needed to know…."

"You will speak when I say you can speak, Major. You risked our most valuable pilot, a top ace, needlessly. You know the plan, the rules—yes, orders for the operation. Our agents meeting enemy resistance are trained in escape procedures. Any survivors will make their way to French resistance forces. Damn, impatient, bullheaded Yank. Orders. Follow orders! You are not a one-man show!"

Hastings sighed. "Look, Curtis, I know you were not

satisfied with the landing site reconnaissance. But we made a decision to go with what we had. The war will not wait for us. I knew the risk, and I approved the plan."

Hastings shook his head. "What's Kut's ETA over the target?"

"May I speak freely, Group Captain?"

"Let's hear it, Major."

"Yes, I know the risk. Kut should be over the target within the hour. He's a man on a mission. He can't be kept on a leash, and before you reply, I gave him an infrared film camera. The plane-mounted cameras are no match for German camouflage. Our cameras can't see their positions, and they move often, frustrating resistance spotters. Let's see what he finds."

Hastings stood up and paced the room. "It will be dawn before he leaves occupied France, a good target for their anti-aircraft guns."

"Yes. He knows the risk better than we do. He was not hesitant."

Hastings sat down. "Of course not. He never is. It had to be Kut. I have orders to pull him from combat. After his action against the Bath raids, hell, the night hunters, the Czechs of Squadron One decimated the Luftwaffe bombers—after two nights of heavy losses, the Jerries had second thoughts. Have you missed that burned-out hangar at the end of the runway? One of Kut's kills crashed there. The bodies of the bomber crew are fresh in their graves at the parish church. Look, London doesn't want a dead ace. He's become a hero. A delegation is coming on Monday. There's even talk of sending him to recruit his countrymen in the US."

Hastings looked into Ike's eyes. "Are you a praying man, Major? You better get on your knees and pray Kut makes it back." Hastings shook his head and sighed. "That will be all, Major. Stay in the OPS Room until he returns."

After a quick knock on the door, the OOD popped in and announced, "Group Captain, we have Flight Lieutenant Kuttelwascher on the radio. He's over the landing site."

Hastings and Curtis rushed to the OPS Room. As they entered, they heard Kut's voice over the squawk box crackling and broken, but unmistakable. "I have the transport in sight. Appears intact at the end of the field. Will take a turn around the surrounding woods before going in for a closer look. Tell Mickey the camera is easy to operate with one hand. No lights—can't see into the woods going in."

Thirty long seconds of silence later, Kut transmitted again. "Taking small arms fire. Scheis! Anti-aircraft fire! Good thing I'm low. The Hudson is pretty shot up. No one is visible. Wait! Sorry, gotta go. I got company two, no three Messerschmidt Bf 109s coming at me. Later gentleman, Night Hawk out."

Hastings took the microphone. "Disengage Night Hawk and return to base. Return to base. Night Hawk?"

Static was the only sound in the room.

"Night Hawk, do you acknowledge?"

"Night Hawk, acknowledge orders, over."

The squawk box just crackled with static.

CHAPTER 2
THE BELLS OF SAINT PETER AND SAINT PAUL

A half-hour passed. The morning sun was still hidden behind the blackout curtains. A teletype machine came alive, clattering as it spewed a thin single-line tape of code, groupings of four letters. The tape was fed into another machine, and soon, another teleprinter—a new automated typewriter, joined the teletype and began to type methodically. The rapid typing, the carriage returns, and the movement of the paper continued in a staccato rhythm.

A one-armed officer walked to the teleprinter and tore off a page. With surprising dexterity, his thumb quickly fed the page through his hand as he read. When he finished, he looked to Group Captain Hasting and said, the team is believed all dead. The Resistance team was destroyed. One survivor, wounded, escaped to make the report. Ambush suspected. Enemy forces had the field surrounded."

Hastings asked, "Any word on Night Hawk?"

Another officer pulled a sheet of paper from the

teleprinter. "A spotter reports a low-altitude dogfight over the area. Appeared to be three-on-one. Two aircraft hit, and one crashed. No further information on the incident."

Hastings nodded. Turning to Curtis, he said, "It's been a long night, Major. Get some sleep. Nothing more that can't wait until the debrief."

Curtis could only manage a sigh and a nod. His knees felt wobbly as he turned to leave. The one-armed officer followed him out. "Major Curtis, a word, please."

Curtis turned and stared at the man. On his shoulder, a unit patch above the pinned-up sleeve read *Cold Stream Guard*. The captain continued, "Haven't seen you at the mission pre-brief or in the OPS Room last night. Heard you were unhappy with the reconnaissance. They say you're reclusive. Even when you appear in the Officer's Mess, you keep yourself to yourself. Is it true you sent out Night Hawk on your own?"

Curtis stared for a moment and then replied, "Have we met Captain? Seems I would have remembered you."

"Oh, you mean this," he said, moving his shoulder. "Dunkirk. Enough for a Vichy French doctor to declare me unfit for military service and approve repatriation home. I won't lie. It's a damned nuisance, but others fared far worse."

"I've heard of the Coldstream Guard—serious soldiers. You newly assigned or a guest for last night's failed operation?"

"Something like that. Tell me, Major, would you do it again?"

"You mean standby while a high-risk site is approved?"

"I mean, would you initiate action on your own without command approval."

"What can they do? I'm a rented-out RECON officer. They needed one. Worst-case scenario—I'm sent packing back to the US Observers. They'd just chew me out and send me to another unit. Yes. Yes, I would do it again. Dunkirk Captain, would you leave a comrade behind?"

"I'll see you at the debrief, Major. Don't sit this one out. Good day."

The captain turned to go back in. Curtis called out, "Captain, what's your name?"

Without looking back, the Captain of the Coldstream Guard called out, "Captain Langley, James Maydon Langley."

As Curtis walked to the Officer's Quarters, he heard church bells calling the faithful to Sunday worship. A highly trained team of men and women lay dead in a field in Normandy, brave French resistance fighters sacrificed, and the church bells of Churchstanton were ringing as they did every Sunday morning.

The bells pealed in unique cadences, their different pitches countering each other, not in harmony but in joyful, spontaneous voices in praise. Curtis's mind went back to his hometown on Washington's Puget Sound. *Not one church bell, but many! And not an old favorite hymn, but spontaneous joy! Without words, they affirm the old song, 'God is not dead, nor does he sleep.' They call me. Solace, yes, they bring solace. It's like God calling me. I need to know He still cares. Yes, Lord, I hear the bells. I will come.*

Though the Air Station was close to town, the gate was opposite the village for security reasons. Curtis drove the short distance to Churchstanton and joined the parishioners already in worship. He quietly found a seat near the rear as the congregation sang from the liturgy:

> "Send out thy light and thy truth, let them lead me;
> Oh, let them bring me to thy holy hill.
> Send out thy light and thy truth;
> Let them lead me to your holy hill.
> Lead me, O LORD, in the way everlasting:
> O lead me and guide me to thy holy hill."

The Anglican liturgy was new to him, though it reminded him of his wife's Lutheran church. *Linda would be happy to see me in church. I wonder if they really do look down upon us from heaven. The creed and the Lord's Prayer are universal. Even so, Dad wouldn't approve, 'Three hymns, a prayer, and a sermon. Anything more is prideful.' It took Mom's pleading to get him to the Lutheran church for our wedding. Linda, I miss you so much.*

At the end of the prayer for the congregation, the vicar invited the congregation to add their prayers aloud or silently. After several prayers for healing or safety of family service members, Curtis found himself silently praying for the team of agents likely dead, wounded, or captured in France. Then, a new thought and a new prayer. *I warned against the landing site, but Kut, Kut's loss is on me. Only me. I sought him out and urged him to go. A combat pilot with a hand-held camera? It was crazy, and I knew it. Oh, Lord, please keep him alive—safe and return him to England. Amen.*

As the worship service continued, Curtis surprised himself. He stood and joined the congregation in a hymn. Voices all around him sang out, "Now thank we all our God, with heart and hand and voices...."

I know this song. Curtis sang: "…who wondrous things has done, in whom the world rejoices, who from our mother's arms has blessed us on our way with countless gifts of love, and still is ours today."

Curtis stopped. *I don't feel blessed. I don't see countless gifts of love.* He stood still, staring at the cross over the altar. Slowly, the words captured his heart:

> *"O may this bounteous God through all our life be near us,*
> *With ever-joyful hearts and blessed peace to cheer us,*
> *To keep us in his grace and guide us when perplexed,*
> *To free us from all ills of this world in the next."*

The Anglican recessional means the vicar is at the door to greet departing parishioners. An American officer in attendance added fuel to the rumor spreading throughout Churchstanton: "There's a yank at the air base—you can be sure many more are coming."

The vicar politely asked, "Welcome to Saint Peter and Saint Paul. Just visiting? Or will you be with us for a while? I heard talk of an American Officer. Can we expect more of your countrymen soon?"

Curtis smiled. "It was good to worship with you today. I feel somehow refreshed."

A young woman stopped as she was about to walk past. "You're Major Curtis! Uncle Hugh, you know he can't say, even if he knows."

The vicar nodded. "I leave you, then, to my niece, Miss Osbourne, Major. Come worship with us again."

The surprised Major Curtis asked, "Excuse me, have we met, Miss, Miss…."

"Osbourne. Sorry, I should have introduced myself. "I'm Rose Osbourne, Dottie's sister. Surprised you're here. Dottie came home at dawn totally fagged and went to bed."

"Dottie?"

"Ah yes, she said you were all business. Dottie, Sergeant Dorothy Barkley."

"Of course, Dorothy. Very conscientious, I'm pleased to have her help. Your surnames…."

"Yes. Dottie is married. But she is living at home while she waits for word."

Curtis' blank stare prompted Rose to continue. "You don't know? Dottie's husband is missing over France. RAF. Shot down a couple of months ago. Last seen parachuting over Normandy. No word from the RAF or the Red Cross. But she clings to hope."

"No, I didn't know." *I sensed she has an inner strength.*

Rose asked, "If you were up all night, what brought you to church this morning?"

"The bells."

It was Rose's turn to want more.

"It was a hard night. Bad news. I heard the bells, and it seemed God was calling me. I needed to know He is still there and cares."

Rose was surprised. "Every church in England has bells and bell lovers—the bell ringers. Not often hear say they called to you."

"Well, they are beautifully rung. It must take practice— and the melody—that can't be the right word—the composition so joyfully independent in their unity of praise. Not like the bells of my hometown. Yes, they have reopened my heart for the first time since… the first time in, I can say in years."

Rose smiled. *He is holding onto a secret, yes, a painful secret. Dottie sees something in him. I trust her judgment.* "Well, you must join us for practice. See how it's done. Yes, Major, come by on Tuesday evening. Dinner, just local fare, and then the bell tower."

"I'd like that. Yes, very much. I will see if I, that is, Dorothy and I can manage the schedule. Thank you. Now, if you will excuse me, at once, I am incredibly tired and must return to the base."

In the quiet solitude of the dark black night of the small quarters of Major Curtis, words, first only quiet mumblings but growing loud and clear, a nightmare tore apart the peace of sleep. "We're going ahead. We must. Of course, we'll be fine. Honey, you know I would never let any harm come to you. Trust me. You can always trust me. I love you more than life itself."

Curtis tossed in his bed. Unseen sweat poured from his brow. He screamed out, "No! No! Get down! Brace, for God's sake, please, God, no!"

Shaken awake, he sat up in bed. Startled eyes searched the darkness for any hint of light. A deep sigh rose from his diaphragm and streamed from his mouth. *The dream, different than before, but still with Linda. I pray she at least has found peace. I don't deserve peace.*

CHAPTER 3
THE BRIEFING

Curtis looked at his watch. "Zero one thirty. Good Lord, I'm thinking in army time! One thirty? Could I have slept over thirteen hours? Should I get up? And do what? The mess doesn't open until six. I could read."

Another sigh, softer this time. *I'm still tired. Yes, I'll try to go back to sleep.*

Two hours later, Curtis got up, dressed, and went to the Officer's Mess. Somehow, there was always coffee. He took his mug from its hook beside the urn, held it under the tap, and let the thick black potion flow in. The aroma of old coffee scalded for hours flowed through his nose and alerted his brain. The smell of the caffeine brew alone was enough to bring him to full consciousness. As he made his way to the magazine rack, he heard whistling. *Who in the world whistles at four a.m.?*

The Officer's Mess door opened. The whistling grew louder. Kut stepped through the door. "Mic! What are you doing up at this hour? But I am glad to see you, my friend! I have you to thank for another kill and a probable. Probable? Good only for bragging and war stories to grandchildren."

"Kut! You made it! We lost contact… I didn't know… thank God, you're safe!"

"It will take more than three green Krauts to down me. Though a couple of lucky shots killed my radio, not in the cockpit—good armor—no, just the antenna and cable. And then the flak took out half my tail, but England is a big Island—not easy to miss. No problem, I was out again tonight but came up empty."

Kut went to the coffee pot. "Gonna stay up. I want to see the pictures. Briefing at zero eight hundred. Hope your special camera got a clear picture of my kill."

As Kut manned the spigot on the urn, he asked, "Why are you up, Mic? No special mission last night."

"No. No special mission, overslept then couldn't sleep."

Kut replied, "I hate sleep. I force myself because my body needs it. But I hate it."

Curtis gave a slight shake of his head. "You too? It's like everything I bury during the day haunts me at night. Dreams. Dreams are the worst. Do you dream, Kut?"

Kut turned to Curtis and swallowed his coffee before answering. "Dreams, no. Nightmares. Not knowing is the worst. I have a different nightmare every night. Their faces, always in shock. I pray they are only my fears, and somehow, they survive."

Kut took another gulp of coffee, smiled, and said, "So, you see, my friend, I intend to kill every Nazi I can until the day I join my family in the hereafter."

Kut sat next to Ike Curtis at the morning brief. "So, my friend, we will see if your special camera can see more than the belly-mounted one. I hope so. I could direct it much better."

Curtis replied, "It can't be worse. I still don't know how you can fly your plane and handle a camera. Autopilot? Flying requires two hands. The camera meant flying straight, and level made you an easier target for…."

Kut laughed. "Two hands? Mic, I wear the cockpit! Yes, two hands and two feet, but also legs and knees, elbows, shoulders, and arms. They all connect through the cockpit controls to my wood, canvas, and metal body. My Hurricane and I are one! The camera was strapped over my neck. Only one hand. My greatest concern was the viewfinder. I didn't use it. I couldn't risk my peripheral vision. My eyes are the eyes of a raptor! They are alert to any movement, any change. They are my advantage."

Curtis chuckled, "Your eyes, elbows, and knees. You have become the perfect night hawk, the hunter in your Hawker Hurricane."

Group Captain Hastings stepped forward. "Gentlemen, our sources in France have confirmed the loss of our assets inserted into Normandy Saturday night. The team is missing and presumed dead. This is a hard blow for those who have trained and worked hard, but we know the risks. Those lost knew these risks and willingly put their lives on the line. This loss will not deter future efforts. I'm certain each of us will step up when we are called upon, and many more of us until this war is won."

Hastings bowed silently, looked up, and said, "Flight Lieutenant Gordon, you may proceed with the brief."

Gordon stepped forward. "We have something new for you this morning. Please turn off the lights."

As the room darkened, images appeared on the screen behind him. The forest, its trees distinct but in a strange red color, surrounding an open field in a lighter red shade, revealed distinct images of vehicles also in shades of red. "Gordon directed a pointer at an aircraft at the far end of the field. "This is our Hudson that carried our team. These tanks and personnel carriers are visible through both darkness and camouflage covers. Notice the small, scattered light blotches around them. German troops."

A low murmur rose from the assembled men. Flight Lieutenant Gordon continued. "Kut took these photos upon arrival over the scene before dawn. He used a common handheld camera with a new American infrared film. What you are looking at, gentlemen, is heat. The heat of warm engines and the body heat of enemy soldiers are captured in a higher light spectrum. Thanks to our resident Yank, Major Curtis, we have a new tool, a camera that sees through the darkness and even the cover of camouflage."

Gordon paused as the briefing room erupted in a dozen conversations. He banged the pointer against the podium and continued. "Your attention! There is more." New photos were on the screen. Side by side, taken in the early morning light. On the left was a photo taken by the belly-mounted camera; on the right, an infrared taken by Kut. A German column of tanks, artillery, trucks, and personnel carriers traveled on an open road. "These photos provide us with a key. Not that infrared was beyond interpretation, but these photos show the infrared signature of a dozen distinct German field pieces."

Another set of photos appeared on the screen. German Messerschmitts. "Kut has given us the signature of the Bf 109 fighter."

A new photo appeared of a Bf 109 on fire in free fall. "Kut's kill was confirmed by French resistance in addition to the photo. And…" Another photo appeared of a burning Bf 109 flying low into the sunrise. "Another probable kill for Kut."

The lights went back on. An officer stood and asked, "Heat? You say the infrared captures heat signatures but as the engines cool…."

Group Captain Hastings stepped to the podium. "As the target cools, the image fades, but an image will remain. The infrared spectrum gathers more light—from any ambient source, the moon, stars, or man-made source. Major Curtis, would you like to add anything to the brief?"

Ike Curtis stood. "Come forward, Major."

Curtis joined the Group Captain at the podium. "As Group Captain Hastings said, the heat signatures will remain for quite some time and reappear. Large man-made objects take a very long time to reach an equal temperature with their surroundings, and even then, they warm and cool at a different rate than the surrounding forest or field. Of course, humans exhibit body heat as long as they live and only slowly dim after death."

A RECON pilot questioned Curtis. "Why Kut? And when will these cameras be installed on our aircraft?"

Curtis answered. "Kut was immediately available. Kut volunteered to try something—a test, a desperate attempt…He used a handheld camera. There is no need to replace the current mounted cameras. We need infrared film in the size and format of our cameras. These photographs demonstrate the utility and urgency of infrared film. And not just film but infrared scopes and signaling devices for our in-theatre teams.

Hastings interrupted, "Thank you, Major. That will be all. Mic was trying to say that he took the initiative to try something new, something which has shown great possibility. I'm sure the Major would affirm the importance of proper procedure and chain of command in pursuing new strategies, especially when risking men and materiel."

Hastings turned to the briefing officer and said, "I'll let Flight Lieutenant Gordon continue with the weather and today's missions."

Ike Curtis followed Hastings to the rear of the room and asked softly, "You say presumed dead. There was no human signature in their plane."

"No, but they would not be taken alive. Training, you see."

Curtis went to return to his seat. Hastings said, "Tell Kut to see me immediately after the brief. Immediately, that's an order, Major."

"Aye, Group Captain. Flight Lieutenant Kuttelwascher to report to the Group Captain immediately following the morning brief."

Curtis sat next to Kut and whispered. "The Old Man wants to see you right after the brief. Even said it was an order."

Kut shook his head and said, "It's the politicians. He's going to pull me from combat. But thanks to you, I got number eighteen."

After the brief, Kut sighed. "I can't blame the Old Man. He put them off as long as he could. But I am glad for the last mission. That camera—it will help kill many Nazis. I'll see you in the Officer's Mess later."

When Curtis reached the door, Captain Langley was waiting for him. "Major Curtis, a word with you. Somewhere private."

"My office? It's only me and my sergeant."

Langley replied, "Lead the way, Major."

Curtis went through the door first. Sergeant Barkley quipped, "Should I pack my things, Ike? Word is the Group Captain was livid…."

Captain Langley followed Curtis inside. Ike said, "The Captain and I have something to discuss. Sergeant, why not take fifteen minutes for coffee or tea, whatever Auxiliary Sergeants do on break."

Sergeant Barkley stood. "Yes, sir. Messages are on your desk. Fifteen minutes."

As Dorothy Barkley walked to the door, Ike Curtis said, "Knock before entering when you return."

She nodded as she closed the door behind her.

Captain Langley stood in front of the status board. "Three RECON planes. Not much of a squadron. Armed?"

"They're good men. Planes are unarmed. Twin Beechcraft Expeditors. All crew carry standard small arms. Pilot and spotter on each. Extra set of eyes and hands for onboard equipment come in handy."

Langley nodded. "They'll have to do. Can you get the

infrared film for the cameras?" "Actually, it's more than cameras."

Langley turned and faced Curtis. "Major, you'll be working with me. The team we lost Saturday night was one of mine. New program. Separate from Special Operations Executive. Military Intelligence operation. Escape routes for downed airmen and high-value locals. Your camera proved my concerns were justified. We dropped the team into a Nazi trap. Those troops were not there two days before. My man walked the woods. There must be a leak. I need your help laying a trap for the Nazi infiltrator in our operations."

"Of course."

Captain Langley continued, "You'll need a cover for the operation. Group Captain Hastings has been briefed. No one else."

Curtis was surprised to hear himself ask, "My Sergeant. Capable and keeps a secret. Stood by me when I—when proper procedures were not...."

Langley smiled. "When you took the initiative when the plan unraveled. Initiative is something we value in my business. Your Sergeant will be here with you during the operation. I'll look into her background and let you know."

He walked to the large wall map of the continent. "Close to the failed Normandy operation. I'll coordinate the same ground team or what is left of it. I want you to choose the site. Here's what we need...."

Chapter 4
Goodbye and Hello

At lunch, Curtis was surprised to see Kut sitting with two other men in suits at the Group Captain's table. Just the cut of their clothes and how they carried themselves told Ike the men were not English and certainly not American. It was clear that Kut wasn't happy. When Kut slammed his fist onto the table, the whole Officer's Mess noticed. Group Captain Hastings said, "It's settled, Flight Lieutenant. Report to my office at 0800 tomorrow for your orders."

Hastings and the two men in suits stood to leave. Captain Langley stepped over and whispered in the ear of the younger man. While Hastings and the older stranger left together, Langley and the younger civilian found an empty table and sat down.

Once Hastings and his guest had made their way out, the curious faces of the officers returned to their meals, and the din of conversation resumed. Ike Curtis stood up, grabbed his plate, walked over to Kut, and said, "Mind if I join you?"

Not waiting for a reply, Curtis set down his plate, sat

across from Kut, and said, "The news you dreaded, no doubt. When?"

Kut sighed. "You heard him. Tomorrow. London tomorrow for 'protocol and diplomacy' training. In a few weeks, I will be in America. A trained monkey for the Czech President."

Ike asked, "Was that him? The older one?"

"Yes, Edvard Benes. President of Czechoslovakia in exile. He can't get any more from England, so he sends me to America."

"And the other man, sitting with Captain Langley?"

Kut stared coldly at the man across the room in conversation with the one-armed British Captain. "Frantisek Moravec, Benes' chief spy. A holdover from our Military intelligence."

Kut nodded as he stared. "He is a crafty one. A true soldier and spy, not a politician." Kut looked into Ike's face. "I tell you this, Mic, I only go because Moravec says I must. But I told them I will go only if I can fly again when I return."

Curtis smiled. "Your story is worth more than 18 downed planes. But the US has a draft and is enlisting millions to fight."

"That's what I told them. They believe Czech and Slovak Americans still need to be recruited.

Ike replied, "The Moravians resist the draft. It is their religion. The Moravian Brethren are pacifists and German."

Kut nodded. "It is a point Benes made. But it is also true that they would rather be identified as Czech than German. Czechoslovakia was never one people: Moravian Germans, Poles, Czechs, Slovaks and Silesians. It is the plight of Czechoslovakia. Benes' true intention is to bring attention to our cause and our needs. Money and equipment first for the resistance, troops, and aircraft to take the fight to our homeland."

Ike sighed. "I will miss you, my friend. But I am glad you will be safe."

"They are preparing a speaking tour for me to cities with large Czech and Slovak populations. They say Bethlehem, a great city in Pennsylvania, was founded by Czechs and others in Texas, Iowa, Minnesota, and North Dakota... say, Mic, where are you from? Perhaps I can speak in your hometown."

"Not likely, Kut, I'm from Washington...."

"Washington? We start in your capital, Washington."

"No, Kut, Not Washington, DC but Washington State. Far across the country on the Pacific Coast. I'm from a small fishing village founded by Croatians but overrun with Scandinavians. They won't be sending you to Gig Harbor."

"We Czechs view Croatians as brothers. We endured centuries of the same Habsburg boot crushed against our necks. You must give me your family information. One never knows. And we shall write. We will meet again, Mic. I shall see to it."

"Call me Ike. It's what my friends and family call me."

"And I am... I was Karel to my family. We shall save our goodbyes for later."

As the lone American on a British Airbase, Ike Curtis could not access a better-stored American base exchange. The RAF didn't eat much better than their countrymen. A carton of cigarettes, two cans of Spam, and a box of powdered eggs didn't seem like much to give in return for a home-cooked meal. So, Ike stopped by the Officer's Mess where liquor smuggled in by the arriving U. S. Eighth Air Force was in good supply. He chose a good Bourbon to take to the Osbourne house.

Ike carefully followed Dorothy's instructions. The last turn took him down a one-lane dirt road with gravel-filled potholes to a large farm cottage of honey-colored limestone glowing in the setting sun. The house with a barn and several smaller outbuildings was set in a small dale. Not another structure was in sight. Several acres of paddocks, fields, and a small orchard surrounded the house. The enchanted valley was surrounded by thick forest. Memories of a small farmstead in narrow Crescent Valley near Gig Harbor flooded Ike's mind.

Rose answered the bell and opened the door. "Welcome Major Curtis. Come through. Dottie is in the kitchen. Hope you like meat pie—well, if you consider spam meat."

Rose read Ike's face and looked down at the sack he held. "She laughed, Spam. Everyone brings it home from the base."

Ike grinned. "I'm afraid it's even worse—powdered eggs."

He reached into the bag and said, "But this may save the evening." And he pulled out the bourbon.

Rose nodded. "I knew inviting you was a good idea! Uncle Hugh will be glad you came."

"Ahem." A man cleared his voice across the room.

Rose turned, "Major Curtis, you remember my uncle Hugh, vicar of Saint Peter and Saint Paul."

Ike walked across the room as Hugh Osbourne stood. Good evening, sir, er, vicar."

"Call me Hugh, Major…"

"Ike. Ike Curtis."

Hugh put down the pipe in his hand and said, "Why not a taste of the bourbon while Rose helps Dottie get our dinner on the table."

"After dinner, Uncle Hugh!" Dorothy shouted from the kitchen. "Supper is on the table."

Ike followed Hugh to the dinner table. He noticed a framed picture of a smiling RAF Pilot Officer as he passed the mantle. Rose pointed to a seat. "Major, you may sit here. Uncle Hugh sits at the head of the table. Dottie likes to be close to the kitchen."

Dorothy came from the kitchen, carrying a large baking dish, filling the room with the aroma of home-cooked goodness. "Just a simple shepherd's pie, Major." She said.

Hugh inhaled the aroma. "Just simple pie, she says. Best in the county. You're in for a treat, Major."

Dorothy smiled. Ike watched her as she took her seat. *I don't recall ever seeing her smile before—warm and open. With her hair down, wearing a dress—and makeup, why, she is beautiful. Yes, strikingly beautiful.*

Uncle Hugh continued, "Grow all our own vegetables, potatoes, onions, peas, and carrots. The secret is the stilton cheese and sliced potatoes crusting the mash. Even with diced spam, it's a great treat."

"Dorothy, we agreed you would call me Ike. But you were holding back. It's not Dorothy, it's Dottie."

Dorothy blushed. "Here, among family, you may call me Dottie."

BELLS OF REDEMPTION

Ike smiled. *She hasn't shared her nickname at the base, not even with the RAF Women's Auxiliary.*

"I couldn't help but notice the picture on the mantle. Your husband. Rose mentioned he was missing. Waiting for the reports from our returning pilots must be hard for you. The agent insertion operation that failed—I didn't know—I would not have asked you to…."

Dorothy turned to look at Rose, who sank in her seat. "My sister has many virtues, but privacy is not among them. Charles. His name is Charles. We met at Oxford. The day after war was declared, he enlisted. We married—he was given only a two-day pass after training before joining his squadron. A bombardier. It was only his third mission."

Ike replied, "I'm sorry. I didn't mean to…."

"No, Ike. It's all right. It is never out of my mind anyway. It's why I joined the Women's Auxiliary RAF."

Ike asked, "Oxford?"

Uncle Hugh replied, "Incredibly bright! Our Dottie is more brilliant than the lot of them."

"I had no idea Oxford accepted women."

Hugh nodded. "Home students. Not permitted in the Men's colleges. But matriculated nonetheless."

"From here, little Churchstanton to Oxford."

Dorothy smiled. "Connections. We Osbournes, my grandfather and father, worked at Otterhead House. Estate manager and head gardener. During a sale of the property, Dad was given the opportunity to buy this, the estate steward's house and ten acres…"

Ike interrupted, "Your father won't be joining

us tonight?"

Rose replied, "Dad is in Gibraltar. Works for the MOD. When the army took over Otterhead estate, they had no need for an estate steward. But Sir William found a job for Dad. He's an appraiser and works for the MOD appropriations of houses and estates. Afraid he won't be visiting anytime soon, not after the Germans have made the Med their lake."

Dorothy smiled patiently for Rose to finish. "Dad tries to come home every few months or so. As Rose said, there's no, telling how long it will be now. As I was saying, Otterhead House—the owners and tenants always treated us well. We were given access to the library. Dad was an avid reader. The classics, mostly. Urged us to read as well. Sir William Goshen was the last tenant. He treated us more as friends than children of the estate manager. Why he arranged for Uncle Hugh to attend Cambridge and then granted him the beneficence of St. Peter and St. Paul. Sir William wrote letters challenging the Association for the Education of Women to find a better woman prepared for studying the classics than me. I'm certain there are many more qualified, but based on his letter, I was admitted. I met Charles at a lecture by Doctor C. S. Lewis on the value of myth. Enough about me, eat. Don't let the pie go cold."

Uncle Hugh commented, "Rose fancies a good legend— or Christian myth, earlier than King Arthur. The Holy Grail and the sword of Saint Peter."

Ike smiled at Rose, who was grinning at him. He said, "Wasn't King Arthur himself merely a legend?"

Hugh replied, "Likely, as you say. But the whole legend of Arthur revolves around the search for the grail. Goes back to

Glastonbury and the legend of Saint Joseph of Arimathea. Brought Christianity to England. Said to have brought the grail, the very cup used by our Lord Jesus at the last supper. Missing long before Glastonbury Abbey was destroyed by Henry VIII. Churchstanton has its own legend—the grail and the sword of Saint Peter were brought here before the Normans built Saint Peter and Saint Paul. An older church—just a chapel for a small monastery. Legend has it they're still here."

Rose put down her fork. "Uncle Hugh, they must be somewhere. Churchstanton's legend is as valid as any other."

Ike turned to Dorothy and asked, "What would the famous Doctor C.S. Lewis say on the matter? What is the value of myth and legend?"

Rose quipped, "Dottie isn't one for legends. I bet she only remembers making eyes at Charles that night."

Dottie didn't look up. "I do recall quite well, Rose. I wasn't making eyes for Charles. He returned my pencil after I dropped it, and it rolled under his chair. I thanked him, and he invited me to join him after the lecture."

Turning to Ike, Dorothy continued. "Lewis would say, 'What flows from myth is not truth but reality. Truth is always about something, but reality is that about which truth is; therefore, every myth becomes the father of innumerable truths on the abstract level.'"

Ike paused. "What you are saying is truth is about facts, but myths speak to reality—to our core understanding of life— our worldview, so to speak."

Dorothy nodded. "That's right. Lewis said, 'The heart of Christianity is a myth that is also a fact. The old myth of a Dying

God, without ceasing to be a myth, comes down from the heaven of legend and imagination to the earth of history. By becoming a fact, it does not cease to be myth: that is the miracle."

Hugh smiled. "Sir William was right, not a brighter woman at Oxford."

Dorothy blushed. "Better finish if you want to get to the bell ringers on time."

Rose asked, "Ike, can I call you Ike, Major Curtis? Dottie does."

"Of course."

"You haven't told us about yourself? Do you have a family? Are you married?"

Dorothy interrupted. "Rose! Where are your manners?"

Ike replied, "No, it's okay. My family is in a small town in Washington State, in our Pacific Northwest. I'm married. I mean, I was married. My wife has passed away…."

Dorothy thought: *He's haunted by his wife's death—poor soul.*

Rose said, "I'm sorry. I didn't mean to pry."

Ike continued, "No, really, it's a fair question. You've been so open with me. I have a son, Earl. Eight years old. He lives with his grandfather in Gig Harbor on the Puget Sound."

Dorothy, surprised, said nothing. Rose replied, "You must miss him terribly."

"I do. Yes. Now, perhaps we should go on to the church for the bell-ringing practice. I'm curious to learn how it's done."

Dorothy said, "You and Rose go ahead. I'll stay and clean up."

Hugh added, "Stop by afterward for a nightcap, Major."

Ike looked at Rose, "I guess it's just you and me."

Ike held the door as Rose climbed into the car. "No chaperone? Uncle Hugh trusts me to drive off with his pretty young niece?"

He called me pretty! Was he just being nice? He seems so nice, so different.

Rose chuckled. "Uncle Hugh isn't our chaperone. We look after him. He would be lost without us. Truth is, he is lonely. He never got over the death of Aunt Jane. She and their child died in childbirth. Left alone, he drinks. Don't misunderstand; he is a good man and a caring vicar, but no one can replace Aunt Jane. I'm sorry, Ike, you must understand—losing your wife, I mean, well...."

Rose stopped talking. Her blushed red face unseen in the darkness.

Ike broke the silence. "Where is this Otterhead Estate?"

"You're on it. That is, it's all around us, over two thousand acres. The house and gardens are just over the hill. We'll go by the house drive on the way to the church. There's a guarded gate. You can't go in without a pass."

The lights were on in the church when Ike and Rose arrived. Rose led the way to the belfry. They climbed steps to a room larger than Ike expected. Six men and two women stood in a circle, each behind a red velvet-covered rope. A man spoke as they entered, "Ah, Rose, we were about to begin. Is this the yank, er, gent, come to learn bell ringing?"

"Tommy Jenkins, this is Major Ike Curtis, yes, an American come to help England fight the Nazis. The Major remarked how the ringing of the bells of Saint Peter and Saint Paul spoke to him—they led him to worship with us. You always say bellringing is a ministry to God; well, here is proof. Thought you'd be honored to share your skill—ministry with him."

Tom Jenkins nodded. "Can't be denying the parish secretary, seein' as she is the vicar's niece. You're welcome to watch us practice, Major. Just don't be interruptin' and save your questions for our breaks. If you behave, Major, perhaps we'll let you give the bells a tumble yourself."

CHAPTER 5
COLLATERAL DUTY

The next morning, Ike greeted Dorothy as he walked through the door. "Morning Dottie, it was nice...."

Dorothy interrupted him, "Major Curtis, a visitor, Captain Langley is waiting." She motioned with her eyes to Langley seated behind the door."

"And Group Captain Hastings requests you see him first thing this morning."

Ike turned to Langley, who stood and said, "Good morning, Major. Let me walk with you to the Group Captain and explain what's about to happen."

Ike nodded. He turned to Dorothy and said, "You know where to find me, Sergeant."

Outside, Langley spoke. "A bit of formality, but you'll need command signoffs. We draw the line at kidnapping Allied officers. Good opportunity to meet the senior staff. Get a feel for the outfit. Ask questions but be discreet. Better to listen than speak but answer honestly."

Group Captain Hastings gave Ike his full attention. "You're a good officer, Curtis. I'm not giving you up—just a collateral duty, understand? You will accompany Captain Langley to London to be interviewed by Colonel Z, SIS. I expect you will confirm all orders with Major General Chaney, Commander of the US Army Special Observers Group. This collateral duty should fall right in line with your Observer role. Right. Safe travel. Here are your pass and travel orders. Report to me as soon as you return. Good day, Major."

On the road, Ike asked Langley, "Colonel Z? Can't even say his name?"

Langley laughed. "Few know his real name. Colonel Z is his codename. To insiders, he is Haywood or Uncle Claude. Don't let him hear you say that. He'll know more about you than you know yourself, but never expect to know anything about him. I will say he is an uncanny judge of character. It's like a sixth sense with him. You wouldn't be with me today if he hadn't already made his preliminary decision."

In London, Langley drove to 54 Broadway. A sign read: "Minimax Fire Extinguishing Company." The tall building was in the heart of London, halfway between Parliament and Buckingham Palace. Langley presented a pass and was permitted to park in a reserved spot. Colonel Z's secretary greeted them as they entered. "He's expecting you. Go right in."

An officer wearing the uniform of a Lieutenant Colonel was seated behind a large mahogany desk in the sumptuous wood-paneled office. "Major Curtis, I presume. Thank you for carving out time from your important work and accepting my invitation. Please sit. I'm sure Langley has filled you in. Will be good to have an American observer on the team. Helps run interference with your Commander."

"You're a bit of a puzzle, Curtis. Black sheep of the family, as you Americans like to say. Father and brothers were in the ferry boat business—Gig Harbor, Washington. But you chose a different path. The University of Washington, a rower. Yes, your eight put the Nazis in their place in '36. Double major, Geographic Information Systems and Engineering. ROTC. Air Corps Pilot but turned down flight duty. I suppose your wife's death influenced your decision. Was it your wife's religion that prevented your father from accepting her?"

Ike's jaw dropped. But he said nothing. Colonel Z continued, "Group Captain Hastings finds you a bit of a loner. Conscientious but stubborn and opinionated. Stepped on a few toes, but your initiative paid off. The question is, Major, can you balance initiative with obeying operational orders and respecting the chain of command."

"Knowing initiative is valued, I can trust my superiors and the chain of command."

"That's good to know, Major, but can I trust you?"

Colonel Z stared at Ike. "It's a rhetorical question, Major. As for your relationship with Sergeant Barkley, tell me, has it become intimate?"

Ike bit his lip and let his anger cool, but it was only a moment before he replied, "The Sergeant loves her husband, an RAF pilot missing over France. We are co-workers—both outsiders. Friends yes. Caring, yes, but…."

Colonel Z cut him off. "Pilot Officer Charles Barkley is listed as missing. There have been no reports from our agents. Likely, he is dead, but that is not our determination to make. Extraordinary academic record and a favorite of Sir William

Goshen. I will approve her participation in your duties, Major."

Z handed him an envelope. "Take this letter to General Chaney for his approval. You'll receive your orders from Captain Langley. We will inform Group Captain Hastings what he needs to know. Husky. Your code name is Husky. Good day, Major."

Captain Langley stood. Ike followed his lead. Colonel Z added an aside, "Give my regards to General Chaney. I pray he will have a safe crossing back to Washington, DC. Initiative, Major. Expected of Generals. Better to learn it as a Major."

It was a short ride to General Chaney's headquarters. Ike took out a cigarette and held the pack towards Langley. The one-armed man took one and laughed. Ike lit his and spoke as he blew gray smoke. "What's so funny? I thought you Brits enjoyed a good American smoke."

Langley mumbled as he lit the cigarette. "Pall Mall. We're on Pall Mall here in London."

Ike exhaled another cloud of smoke. "Really? They're named after a street in London? Best kept secret in the States!"

"Not any street, a boulevard from the palace along Saint James Park. Royalty used to parade Pall Mall. Now it's home to the finest shops in London."

"Even worse. We threw all that royalty out over 150 years ago."

Langley let blew a stream of smoke before asking, "What do you know about General Chaney?"

"Chaney is Commander US forces in the European Theatre in addition to Commander of the US Special Observer Group. He's well-regarded in the Army Air Corps. Flew in the last war. He remained in Germany with the occupation forces and served as a Military Liaison to Italy. In addition to his extensive experience in Europe, Chaney was a pioneer in Army Aviation training. In the Air Corps, only Hap Arnold is better regarded."

When the staff car pulled up in front of the Chaney's Headquarters, Ike tossed the half-empty pack of cigarettes to the driver. "Should've offered you one earlier. Have a smoke while you wait."

A staff car bearing a red flag with three stars drove to the front of the building. The driver stepped out and stood by the door as four officers exited the building. Ike came to attention and saluted as the officers approached. "Good afternoon, General Arnold," Ike said as the Senior Officer returned his salute. "What's your unit, Major?" Arnold asked.

"Special Observers, General, assigned to RAF Churchstanton—Air Reconnaissance."

"Churchstanton? Very Good. Well, keep the faith, Major. Many more of us are on the way. Soon, you'll be doing more than observing."

The Major General alongside Arnold was silent but studied Ike Curtis carefully as he waited for General Arnold to climb into the staff car.

Ike and Langley climbed the stairs to the top floor and presented their orders from Colonel Z. The staff officer replied, "Make yourselves comfortable. I'll tell the General you're here. General Chaney has a full schedule."

Ike asked the officer, "I just saw General Arnold leaving. Who was the Major General with him? What's going on? Air Corps coming at last?"

The adjutant looked before replying. "We're coming in

force, Air Corps, Infantry, Artillery, Engineers, the lot. That's for sure. As for the two star, that's General Eisenhower, Marshall's golden boy. Two stars in less than two years. Not afraid of getting his hands dirty. He'll be reporting to General Marshall on European Theatre Operations. Wasn't happy with what he found."

The adjutant stepped into the General's office. Langley whispered, "Who's General Marshall?"

"Army Chief of Staff. Senior US Army Officer—reports to the President."

The adjutant returned. "Major Curtis, General Chaney will see you now."

Langley waited as Ike went in. Chaney stood by the window, watching the street below. "That was Hap Arnold."

"Yes, General, I passed him on the way in." General Chaney stepped back to his desk and sat down. He read the note from Colonel Z.

"I heard about your stunt at Churchstanton, Major. I shouldn't be surprised SIS wants their hooks on you. We're finally joining this war. Everything I have prepared for if Eisenhower doesn't ground me with Marshal. Uncle Claude didn't say anything to you, Curtis, did he?"

"He sends his compliments and…"

Ike hesitated. "Spit it out, Major. And what?"

Ike mumbled, "He wishes you a safe trip back to DC."

"Son of a bitch! How did he know? Eisenhower made up his mind before coming."

General Chaney signed the orders and gave them back to Ike. "Good luck, Major. Take this to G2, Intel, downstairs. Colonel

Fields will instruct you regarding restricted information and need-to-know contacts. That will be all, Major."

Late the next evening, Ike and Langley returned to RAF Churchstanton. Ike was surprised to see the lights still on in his office. Entering, he saw Dorothy arranging folders on his desk. "Dottie, er, Sergeant Barkley. Didn't expect to find you here this late."

Dorothy looked up and saw Langley follow Ike into the RECON office. "Much has happened since you left, Major. I wanted to organize things for you. It's good that you are here. You'll be able to get a head start on tomorrow. You meet with the Group Captain immediately following the morning brief. There's been quick progress on the infrared film. You are to present a plan of action to take it operational. He requested plans for training, developing, and installing infrared technology. Also, there are new reports from Normandy—the deaths are confirmed, and well, there appears to be more, but it is restricted. I haven't seen it. I just thought you might want to— you should—well, intel has it. And then there are the new aircraft coming."

Ike walked to his desk and looked at the folders. "Thank you, Sergeant. I'll get right on it. I think Captain Langley has something for you."

Dorothy blushed and turned to Langley. perplexed, she stared at the silent British officer. Langley handed Dorothy an envelope and said, "Sergeant Dorothy Barkley, you aware of the Official Secrets Act? Read these orders and sign them."

Stunned, Dorothy sat down in Ike's chair, opened the envelope, and read. She stopped and stared at the two men standing silently before her. She exhaled a deep sigh and bit her lip. She picked up a pen.

Ike spoke. "Before you sign and Captain Langley briefs you, I want you to know what this will entail. You don't have to do this. It may have been presumptuous of me to request you for this assignment. It may not be what you intended when you joined the RAF Women's Auxiliary. Simply stated, a small team is being gathered…"

Ike looked at Langley, who nodded.

"A small team dedicated to locating and assisting downed airmen—any allied personnel or valuable civilian personnel, in escaping Nazi-occupied territory. It may be painful for you, considering…"

Dorothy quickly signed the pledge. "Major, this is exactly why I joined the Women's RAF."

Langley walked to the map on the wall. "Right. First order is establishing corridors, safe routes, so to speak…"

"Like the underground railroad for American slaves to freedom in the North," Ike interjected.

"Yes, railroads, if you will, with depots, safe houses, and supplies along the way. Communications, documents, food, and clothes. But separate from resistance saboteurs. Better to separate the missions. Different objectives, different risks, different motives. Safer all around. Intel and coordination from here. Your duties with the team are restricted—need to know. Only Group Captain Hastings here at Churchstanton. I will be his point of contact. Let me run interference if conflicts of duty arise. The Group Captain will be tasked with assuring that this does not happen. For now, focus on your RECON duties. I must leave. I'll be back in three days. More then."

Langley stopped at the door and turned around. "Major, give your highest priority to the equipment. When I return, I expect your earliest go date for Operation Mongoose. We don't want Cobra to slither away. Right. You may brief the Sergeant as necessary. Three days."

Ike and Dorothy looked at each other.

Langley said, "Good, no questions, three days." And he was out the door.

Dorothy looked up at Ike. "Mongoose?"

Ike replied, "Identify and eliminate Cobra—the Nazi informant who betrayed the team."

"Good."

Dorothy stood up. "It's late. Did you get anything to eat, Ike? If we hurry, we may be able to get something at the pub."

The York Inn in the parish village of Churchinford was still open. The Whitewashed brick pub was a warm and welcoming beacon on a dark, damp evening. Most of the locals had called it a night. The innkeeper was gathering empty mugs and wiping down tables as Dorothy and Ike came in. "About to close. Time for the last call."

"Now, Archie, you wouldn't send our American friend home without supper. What have you got back there that's still warm?"

"Drinks first—won't be havin' no report of late drinking at the York Inn."

"Ale for me, Ike said."

Dorothy smiled. "Two mugs, Archie. And the best the kitchen can provide."

"I can do a quick rarebit. Warm you up and sit well with you to bed. Er, not to imply...."

Dorothy laughed. "No offense, Archie. The rarebit and the ale."

They found a table near the dying fire. Only a few red embers remained atop the white ash. "It's good to see you smile, Dottie. You have a beautiful smile."

Dottie beamed. Ike continued, "I don't want you to get your hopes up. We do as we are told on this one. We help who we can and pray others help those near to us."

"I know, Ike. Just being able to do something, anything. It's all I could hope for. Thank you for including me."

"Don't thank me, I have it on good authority—the cleverest woman at Oxford."

Archie set two mugs of ale on the table. "Rarebit with the best local stilton toasting in the oven."

Dorothy smiled. "Thanks, Archie."

Archie nodded. "It's nice to see a smile on your face again, Dorothy."

Archie gave Ike the look a father gives a boy dating his daughter for the first time. "I expect you'll be a gentleman with our Dorothy, Yank."

Ike smiled and nodded. Dorothy shook her head. "Major Curtis is the perfect gentleman. You treat him well. Archibald Pelfry."

Archie walked back to the kitchen. Dorothy turned her smile to Ike. "You know the story of my Charles. I could see how troubled you were when you spoke of losing your wife. Has it been long? And you mentioned a son with his grandfather."

Dorothy sat back. "I'm sorry. Now, I'm the one being forward. You don't need to tell me anything."

Ike sighed. "No. It's okay—really. I feel I can tell you. Telling someone might help. Linda. Her name was Linda. We grew up together in Gig Harbor. Went to the same small school. She was a tomboy. Loved to fish, hunt, and climb trees. I remember one day, we saw a half-tied pile of logs over by Donkey Creek. She decided we should make a raft. I bet her it wouldn't make it to the sandspit at the mouth of the harbor before breaking up. Never dare Linda! She guided it past the sandspit and out into the sound."

Ike laughed. "Out in the sound, the tide caught us, and we were off to the races. Thank God, my dad's ferry was coming across. He saw us and rescued us. Got a good lickin' that night."

Ike smiled; his eyes focused on the past. "Well, she grew up. The prettiest girl in town. Lightest of blonde hair—beautiful blue eyes, and a figure that coveralls couldn't hide. Ole, Mister Olson, her dad, a fisherman, took a shine to me. Don't know why. The Olsons were good Lutherans—the Swedes in the Pacific Northwest stuck together. They picked on the Norwegians, but both went their separate way from the Croatians—Catholics, you see. We were the real outsiders, though the town was barely fifty years old. A lifelong Baptist, Dad didn't trust anyone not baptized only after being saved. That meant Lutherans and Catholics were lost souls. Dad only set foot in a Lutheran Church twice. The day Linda and I married, and the day she was buried."

Dorothy whispered, "I'm sorry. Your son. Tell me about him."

Ike wiped his eye as a tear began to form. "Earl. Thank God he wasn't with us when it happened. I worked for Weyerhaeuser, a lumber company. Geographical systems. I prioritized lumbering operations based on terrain and infrastructure development. It's how I ended up in RECON. I learned to fly while at the University of Washington. Got my wings with Army ROTC. Three years ago, is it really three years? I took Linda along for a ride in the company seaplane. The weather was a little iffy, with fog over the water but clear over the Olympics. It happened during the landing. Bullheaded pride. I came down in the fog—a deadhead. A log floating in the current. It took out the starboard sponson, or float. The plane flipped, and the right wing broke—a beam came through the overhead."

Ike bowed his head. "Earl was with my dad. Thank God he didn't watch his mother die."

Ike looked up. "Earl is eight now. A great kid. Sweet, like his mom. A towhead. Curly blonde and blue eyes. When I look at him, I always see her."

Archie returned with the meal.

Ike took a sip of ale and picked up a slice of the toasted rarebit. He blew on it lightly as the tip burned his tongue. "Still hot."

Ike gazed back into the past. "Earl has two grandpas that love him. Dad and Ole have become close. Marge Olson, Linda's mom, dotes on him. I think Dad might even find room in heaven for a few Lutherans. Earl can't wait to join Ole on a fishing trip—though with the war, it's mostly Salmon or crab inside the Puget Sound. Even the Strait of Juan de Fuca isn't safe from the Japanese subs. A new bridge over the Tacoma Narrows nearly put Dad's ferry out of business. They called it Galloping Gertie. Seems it spectacularly danced in the wind during a strong breeze before it fell to the bottom of the sound."

"That sounds terrible, so frightening!"

Ike nodded. "A miracle, really. The only casualty was a dog who bit the hand of a stranger who crawled out to rescue him. I have a younger brother. He works at the Navy Shipyard in nearby Bremerton."

Conversation punctuated by light laughter continued as they ate. When Ike drained the last of his ale and wiped his mouth with the napkin, he smiled contentedly at Dorothy, "This has been a memorable evening. Thank you for inviting me."

Dorothy grinned. "I feel like I've known you forever. I thank God he has sent you to us—Oh, and before I forget, Sunday. Rose insists you come for dinner after church. She has something she claims you must see. The vicarage, right after worship."

"After worship? Are the two of you trying to make a churchgoer out of me?"

"Ike, you're the one who said the bells called to you. Worship, then Sunday dinner. Now, I think it is best if you took me home so Archie can go to bed."

Ike dropped Dorothy off and made sure she got in safely. As he drove off, he thought: *Yes, the church bells did call to me.*

CHAPTER 6
THE PARISH SECRETARY

Ike was walking from the car park as the bells of Saint Peter and Saint Paul began to peel. He thought of the ringers putting their weight into pulling the ropes, like members of a dance troupe intent on keeping in step with the rhythm and the ring order. Rose and Dorothy met him at the door.

Rose chimed, "I spoke to the ringers. You're welcome to join them again at practice."

Ike smiled. "I was impressed. It takes much more skill than I imagined."

Dorothy took his arm. "Come. The family box is near the front where Uncle Hugh can keep an eye on us."

They walked past the acolytes and the choir queuing for the procession and sat in the second box on the right below the raised pulpit. As they settled in, the bells ceased tolling, and organ music filled the nave. The congregation stood for the processional. Voices in song filled the church with the call to worship. The altar candles were lit as the procession followed a white-robed acolyte carrying a cross. Congregants turned and faced the procession, bowing as the cross passed. A curate followed, holding a Bible above him with outstretched arms. Next, the choir marched by, singing as they made their way to the choir stall. The Reverend Hugh Osbourne was the last to enter, bowing at the altar before finding his seat behind it.

Ike found himself singing along, his mind strangely at peace. *Majesty and order. God is majestic. He is the ruler of all created order. I should never forget that. Even in these times.*

Rose opened the Book of Common Prayer and handed it to Ike, and he followed along, reciting the ancient liturgy. The words came alive and spoke to him, and with each 'amen,' his heart responded, 'Yes, Lord.'

During the prayers for the congregation, he heard Dorothy say, "Protect my husband Charles and return him home safe."

Others prayed for husbands, sons, brothers, and friends. Prayers for those lost, injured, or now homeless from the persistent bombing. Prayers for healing and an end to the war. Ike heard his own voice, "Lord, comfort the families of the brave team lost in Normandy last week."

When it was time for the sermon, Hugh rose from his seat and climbed the steps into the pulpit. He opened the Bible in front of him and looked out over the congregation. "Dear friends, we gather here to worship and beseech Almighty God. For some time now, years, we have been searching for comfort and guidance, for God's truth to sustain us. But we seek even more. Answers—God's answers. Why? How long? Do you hear our cries, Lord? Will you ever answer our prayers?"

Ike listened as Hugh preached. "This has been a continuing search. There is no one sermon, one teaching, one lesson that will make us understand. Like God's servant Job, we journey along, not so patiently, wondering and waiting while God above watches."

Ike watched as the gentle Reverend Osbourne sought the words to assure his congregation, clearly people he loved, to make sense of the incomprehensible misery engulfing the world. *There's much more to Hugh Osbourne than the kindly uncle with a love for myths, legends, and bourbon. He has a pastor's heart and a shepherd's grasp for leading his flock. Is it blind faith? No, not blind, but what does he see that I miss?*

After the service, Ike followed Rose and Dorothy outside. "It's a beautiful place. Don't see anything like it where I'm from. Old—nothing is old in Gig Harbor. I mean the piers and net sheds look old, but only because the price of paint is dear."

Dorothy said, "Why not walk through our churchyard, the cemetery? There are graves hundreds of years old. They connect us to our past—reminders that our ancestors are still with us in worship and communion."

Ike stopped and pointed to six new graves; their mounds not yet settled to ground level. "Recent additions? Victims of the Luftwaffe?"

Dorothy shook her head. "They are Luftwaffe. Killed when their bomber was shot down and crashed at the airfield."

Ike remembered. *Kut's kill that Hastings mentioned.*

Dorothy continued. "Uncle Hugh gave them a funeral, same as any parishioner's. A few gawkers came to scoff—the raids in Bath killed 417, and over a thousand were injured. Fires destroyed half the city. There was little love lost for dead Germans. But Uncle Hugh insisted on a full funeral, even the bell ringers showed. Afterward, he sat down and wrote a letter to each of the dead's families—sent them via the Red Cross—expressing his sorrow for their loss and telling them where they could find their loved one. He urged them to visit once this tragic war is over, promising they would be welcome, and their grief shared."

Ike stared at the graves. *Enemies by circumstance of birth.*

Rose chirped. "Enough of this. We should head over to the vicarage. We shouldn't keep Uncle Hugh waiting."

Over dinner, in the stately stone vicarage, Ike surveyed the priest sitting across from him and asked, "Reverend Osbourne..."

"Please. Call me Hugh."

"Hugh, today's sermon. Did you mean to imply God does not answer prayer?"

"Has He answered *all* of your prayers? You have attended two Sundays. Do you think the prayers of the congregation have changed much since this war began? How many soldiers and sailors are lost despite fervent prayers? How many innocent men, women, and children were killed in the bombings and fires that resulted? Prayers go up to God. Unceasing prayers, and yet the pain, death, and destruction continue. But consider, also, the poor soul fighting for faith or to give up sin—something that haunts his private life and soul—lust of some sort. Burdened by guilt, he prays and prays and prays for God to take away whatever weighs down on him. But the guilt remains with the sin. A dark shadow of condemnation. It is far more common than we admit."

Ike replied, "It's prayers for loved ones—the end of the war and needless death that I hear."

"Yes—and the war continues with no end in sight. Why, God? Why my loved one? Or why me? It plagues the good Christian's heart. But we come to an understanding—or accept the platitudes: God is judging us. We live in a broken and sin-filled world. Others are suffering. Can I really expect to be different? Would it be fair? Platitudes, or shall I say the myth that we accept as reality? I tell you; these times are normal. What generation, what people have not lived through war, or disease, or disaster? No, it is a struggle for faith—the sin we cannot overcome and the resulting guilt, despite our countless prayers, which makes God appear far off. It must be addressed. This struggle is the real veil separating the believer from the comforting joy of Christ."

Ike listened as Hugh explained. "Some, feeling separated from God, rationalize their sin—a spiritual denial. That is why the story of Job resonates. Even a righteous man felt ignored by God. But I will also preach from Saint Paul. He speaks to those who see their sin as insurmountable. The closer they come to God, the greater their sin appears. Paul famously said, 'I do what I don't want to do and fail to do what I desire to do. Who will save me from this wretched state?' We see that sin and prayer are linked but not as we often surmise."

Dorothy interrupted. "I shall not cease praying, Uncle. Never. I shall pester God until Charles is safely home again."

Hugh's face warmed as he said softly, "You are exactly right, my dear. Keep praying. That's our duty. God desires your prayers. Be certain he hears, be certain he cares, be assured he loves you and intends only good."

Ike mumbled, "And to those who have prayed in vain, their loved ones now dead or maimed. What good came to them?"

"Major, we live in a world disfigured and tortured by sin. God does not separate us from this world. We live in it with the fallen. We do not fully see God's purposes, but we have assurance and glimpses beyond the veil of eternal joy to come. I don't suggest we live only in the hope of heaven, rather determined to bring others along with us and, as we do, strive to remake ourselves closer to Christ, our model."

Rose spoke. "I didn't invite Ike to dinner to hear a sermon. I found something exciting in the parish records. Please, let our guest enjoy dinner, and then I will show him my surprise."

Hugh smiled. "Of course. I won't keep you any longer. Major, stop by before you return to the base. Join me for a taste of the fine bourbon you gave us. I promise not to be overbearing. I enjoy conversation with someone free to express a different perspective."

Dorothy's eyebrows were raised. "He means other than female."

Rose stood, and Ike followed her lead. Dorothy looked up. "You and Rose go ahead. I'm tired. I'll stay here. I think I'll take a nap."

Rose chatted happily as they walked to the church. "Parish records—they go back far beyond the building. That's why I studied Latin. Not just church custom—but law. The parish has been the official keeper of records for births, deaths, marriages, and property for millennia—really since Christianity arrived in the British Isles. Parish records were far better protected than buildings and not plundered like silver or gold. What you call myth or legend has roots in records to this day."

Ike replied, "So they're not just a resource for genealogies and identifying unreadable gravestones?"

Rose opened the church door. "Don't laugh. Genealogies are important, not just to family titles, but claims to estates and land rights for generations. But it is the asides and little things that are written that can be the most enlightening. The unofficial records, long forgotten observations. They yield treasure not otherwise discoverable."

They made their way through the nave, past the sacristy to a doorway. As Rose slid an ancient key into the lock, Ike saw the determination in her eyes. He replied, "And these records have never been cataloged or transcribed for recovery."

The door creaked on iron hinges as it slowly opened. "Exactly. I make use of my time searching through visitor records, letters, and all the unofficial correspondence and cross-reference them into files. Yes, I am intrigued by the legends, but sometimes I come across something—something that may be of interest, though I don't know why."

Rose stretched on her toes and blew a tuft of her flaxen hair from her face as she reached for a box. "I found this some while ago, and last week, it came back to me. A name. It was a record of a visit. It's in English, so I will let you read it for yourself."

Ike interrupted. "Let me help you with that," as he reached from behind her and took the box. Ike's chest lightly touched Rose's back. He felt a jolt—nerves up and down his body awoke to a feeling he had not experienced in years. His nose inhaled a feminine aroma, and the tingling ran its course again.

Rose removed the lid and pulled out a parchment from inside. "A visit recorded by our vicar in 1630."

Ike stepped back and took the parchment. Stepping into the light streaming through the leaded glass window, he read aloud. "Visit of Lord and Lady Montclair, the Earl, Sir Robert Curtis, Lord Inquirer to King Charles and his wife Eleanor, seeking ancestral information of the papist priest, Father Robert Philip, late confessor to Queen Henrietta Maria. Aforesaid Father Philip claimed to be the ancestral guardian of the ancient Sword of Saint Peter removed from Glastonbury Abbey to safekeeping at Churchstanton."

Ike paused. "Support for your legend of the Sword of Saint Peter and a strong tie of Churchstanton to Glastonbury Abbey. I suppose all of Glastonbury's legends."

Rose replied, "Yes, of course, that's why I filed it—but look at the names."

Ike nodded. "Curtis is a fairly common name."

"Yes, but tied with Montclair? You said Montclair was common in your family. And your own son, Earl."

Ike scratched his head. "The firstborn sons, as far as we can go back, have been named alternately Montclair and Earl. A strange coincidence. My father was Earl. His father, Montclair. I know we are English. We go back to Virginia—early 1700s. I have to admit, it is a strange coincidence."

Rose turned to face Ike. She leaned against the desk and

brushed her hair from her face. It took a faint red glow in the light. "I'd like to follow up on this. See where it goes."

Ike nodded. "You should—perhaps a trip to Glastonbury…"

"Of course, the sword story, but I meant your genealogy—a search of the Montclair peerage—and your genealogy."

"Me? Why, I don't know. I mean, I have nothing to hide—you think, somehow, I'm connected to these legends?"

"Not legends, Ike. You hold in your hand history—facts."

"Maybe I need that drink with Hugh after all."

Rose was leaning back, sitting on the edge of the desk, her legs crossed, her knees peeking from beneath the hem of her dress—smiling.

Does she know how attractive she is? Confident, warm, and open.

Rose stood, picked up the folder from the desk, and walked over to Ike. Handing him the folder, she rose on her tiptoes and gave him a warm peck on the cheek, "There is more in the diary. Take it. Read it. See for yourself."

Rose took Ike's arm. "Let's go. You look like you need that drink with Uncle Hugh."

Ike blushed. "He is probably concerned for your safety."

Rose laughed. "Uncle Hugh knows I can take care of myself. Besides, he likes you."

As they walked, Ike asked, "Rose, do you struggle with unanswered prayers?"

With a smile in her voice, Rose replied, "I don't want to sound selfish—I do pray for Charles and Dottie.…

Ike replied, "I'm sure you do I mean, your prayers, your desires."

"No, I understand. I just wait. Somehow, I know He will answer—in goodness and blessings—I know God loves me. It's enough."

Uncle Hugh greeted them as they returned. "Ready for that drink, Major?"

"If my company is not growing stale…"

Hugh was already walking to the table with the bourbon and several glasses. "Straight or a little water."

Ike nodded. "It's good Kentucky Bourbon, not Scotch. We don't drown it."

He paused., "Rose and Dottie? Will Dottie join us?"

Rose smiled. "I'll see if she has finished her letter. It is her habit. She writes to Charles every Sunday. She holds the letters for the day he returns."

Ike nodded. "The nap. She didn't want to say. I hope she doesn't feel betrayed."

Rose shook her head. "No. She just doesn't want others to feel sorry for her—to make her their project to help. But Uncle Hugh and I see through all of that. We let her know we're always here for her."

Ike nodded. *I must watch out for her as well. Who knows what lay ahead?*

With Rose upstairs, Hugh picked up a glass. "What should we drink to, Major?"

Ike glanced up to the ceiling, mindful of the two women upstairs. "To happily ever after."

Hugh smiled. "By God's mercy, may they one day live

happily ever after."

Hugh reached for his pipe, struck a match, and puffed in the flame. Ike followed his lead and lit a cigarette. Hugh poured two more drinks. Not looking up, he said, "Major, Rose is a very determined young woman. She knows her own mind and is quite persistent. She has a good heart, and I trust her judgment."

Ike exhaled a stream of smoke. "I can see that. Determination to follow through on her beliefs."

Hugh nodded. "Yes, that, and she is always successful in her pursuits."

CHAPTER 7
OTTERHEAD HOUSE

The orders were sitting on Ike's desk when he walked into the office. Ike read them softly aloud. "From: Commander US Forces Europe, Commander US Observers Group. To: All officers US Observers Group. Report to Command Headquarters 1 July 1942. Briefing with the Commander. Travel and subsistence... Dottie, have you seen this? Of course, you set it out for me."

"I'm already working on the travel orders. Lodging in London is tight, but I think I can get you into a nearby hotel. Two days of meetings. Not to speculate, but I suppose the Yanks are coming in force."

"Major General Eisenhower. Things are going to be different. The Eighth Air Force is on its way. They'll be looking for airfields and logistical support. Probably want RECON officers with local knowledge."

Dorothy was surprised. "You think you'll be transferred?"

"I hope not. The work we are doing—it's important. I almost feel like I've been somehow called to it."

Dorothy chuckled. "Like the bells of Saint Peter and Saint Paul. Should you ask Langley or, better, Colonel Z to put in a word…"

"Well, I have to say I've been ordered. I'll leave it at that and trust his judgment."

In London, General Eisenhower made it clear things had changed. Every observer should expect reassignment. In the meantime, each was charged with reporting on the capability of every RAF airfield to support US B-17s as well as the fighters that would soon follow. In addition, they were to develop plans for hangars and tents until barracks could be built for US personnel. Observers assigned to the MOD were tasked with coordinating with their British counterparts acceptable fielding of US forces. The general's closing words stuck with Ike. "Gentlemen, this is the number one priority. Hit it fast and hard—you're already late."

As the briefings came to an end, and the men were dismissed, the aide called out: "Major Curtis, please come with me."

Eisenhower was leaning over his desk when Ike Curtis was shown in. Ike saluted. "Major Curtis, General, as ordered."

At ease, Major. "The Brits seem to want you where you are, Curtis, though looking at your record, I can't see why. Can I depend on you to give me the report I need—where are you? Oh, yes, RAF Churchstanton. Do that, and you can remain at the disposal of Colonel Claude Dansey in British Military Intelligence."

Ike replied, "Yes, general, I will do my best." *Claude Dansey. Uncle Claude, yes! He's Colonel Z.*

Eisenhower looked up. "I hope your best is good enough, Major, Don't let me down.

Ike found a thick folder on his desk when he returned to Churchstanton. Dorothy was on the phone, "Yes, sir. Right away, sir. I'll tell him, sir." Dorothy rolled her eyes when she caught sight of Ike's stares. She pointed to the pile on the desk, covered the mouthpiece of the phone with her hand, and whispered. "You need to sign for the equipment. Stores Branch requests your immediate attention. They have truckloads of equipment marked 'For your attention only."

She uncovered the mouthpiece, "Yes, Group Captain, he has just arrived. I'll tell him your office ASAP."

Dorothy hung up the phone. "Group Captain Hastings requests your immediate attendance. Then, see the Group Stores Officer. Probably should take the file with you."

Ike's eyes bounced between the thick file on his desk and his sergeant. Dorothy explained, "Infrared film and equipment receipts, and more. Something big coming up."

Ike nodded. "Right. Hold the fort. I'll start with the boss."

Ike found Langley seated in the Group Captain's office. *He's here again—always when I'm called for.* Hastings looked up from his desk. "There you are, Curtis. New orders. You've been transferred to Independent Flight 545. RAF Special Duties Service. Seems Colonel Z has passed you off to MI9, Military Intelligence. New unit. Captain Langley will brief you."

Surprised, Ike turned to Langley, who said nothing. Ike put out his hand to Hastings and said, "It has been an honor to serve with you, sir. When do I leave?"

Hastings stared back, "Leave? The 545 will be based here at Churchstanton. You're not going anywhere, Major. I'm to be your landlord of sorts. Now I understand you have equipment and aircraft that need your attention."

"Aircraft? My attention?"

"The three RECON Expeditors have been reassigned to the 545, as well as a Lysander, and a Spitfire. You are the senior RECON officer and the nearest the 545 has to a Senior Officer— you are the 545 Flight Commander. RAF Churchstanton will provide ground support. Your pilots and noncoms will be provided quarters and personnel support. I'm hoping you can find time to provide RECON for us."

"Of course, Group Captain. We will support you as best we can. Oh, by the way, in London…"

Hastings broke in. "We're already working on General Eisenhower's request. I'll let you sign it when it's done. The priority will be East Anglia, but, as the General probably told you, every airfield in England will not be enough. Churchstanton will see its share, and many more will be built. I believe Captain Langley is waiting."

Outside the office, Captain Langley was the first to speak. "Rank Major, MI9 can't ignore it completely. You're our air recon, so with your rank comes leadership responsibilities."

"Must have been hard on Hastings."

"Major, you continue to underestimate the Group Captain. He understands exactly what we are trying to do. We— you have his full support. Now, let's get the new equipment sorted. Most must be trucked to our field training center."

Ike asked, "Which is where?"

"You'll see. And bring Sergeant Barkley. We're going to Churchstanton Supply depot at Otterhead House, where you'll be briefed on current operations and planning.'

"Including Operation Mongoose?"

Langley paused before answering. "Let's keep Mongoose between us for a while. I don't want unconfirmed speculation of an infiltrator to distract from Operation Oaktree planning."

The new supplies sorted, Langley drove Ike and Dorothy to Otterhead House. Dorothy frowned when she saw the overgrowth and neglect of its famous gardens. Water features were turned off, and the pools and ponds and beautifully landscaped lakes were fouled with leaves, branches, and debris. Even the great house appeared to weep with dirty stains from overflowing clogged gutters and downspouts. *Three years of Government neglect. Will it even last through the war?*

Langley parked at the front steps, unquestioned as the trucks left a dust trail of gravel going around the back. Inside the house, Dorothy glanced into the library as they passed by. The shelves appeared full, but the furniture was replaced by tables manned by ten or twelve clerks.

I hope the library's collection fares better than the gardens.

Langley led them through to the dining room, set up as a council room for senior officers. There were three vacant chairs at the table. Langley headed for the one at the head and pointed to the one on his right. "You're here, Major." Dorothy quietly took the remaining chair. Standing at the head of the table,

Langley continued. "Major Curtis and Sergeant Barkley have joined the team. The Major commands our air reconnaissance arm, Independent Flight 545, at RAF Churchstanton. We now own air RECON. The Major's initiative with infrared technology has rewarded us with new tools and equipment. In all operational matters, his code name is Husky, and Sergeant Barkley, let's see, yes. She is Goldenrod. I shall permit introductions—name and function. They shall meet with you later for briefings."

After a quick round of introductions, Langley spoke, "Gentlemen, MI9 has been tasked with the rescue and recovery of downed airmen and escaped allied prisoners from Nazi-occupied territory. Today, we will focus on Belgium and France. With our friends and *helpers* in France and Belgium, MI9 funds and operates two independent escape lines..."

An American officer with a Russian accent interrupted. "Like an underground railroad with depots, stations, and conductors."

Langley replied, "Yes, thank you, Captain Bouryschkine..."

"I remind you my name is no longer Bouryschkine, it's Williams, Val Williams. I am a good American."

Langley continued. "Right. Underground railroads, if you like, the Comet Line originating in Brussels, through France, across the Pyrenees into Spain, and by available ship to England, and a close sister is the Pat O'Leary or Pat Line headquartered in Paris, also routing our men through Spain. Both lines require support—money to pay the mountain guides, buy food, clothes, and equipment, as well as radios and skilled operators. It takes time, and many brave French helpers are at risk of infiltration by the Abwehr—German Military Intelligence, and informers. Oaktree Line will save time and reduce risk by establishing a new sea escape line from the Brittany Coast to Falmouth. The Royal Navy will provide the boats and sealift. Major Curtis will brief you on infrared technology and operational testing. Then I want you, Val, and Ray Labrosse, to brief Husky and Goldenrod on preparations and planning for Oaktree."

Langley paused. "Oh, and each of you is to familiarize our new members with standard operating procedures for drops, agent insertions, and extractions. Right, Major, infrared technology—urgency. Before you get into the details, when can we begin operational testing?"

A Canadian spoke up. "Begging your pardon, Captain Langley, but what does intel report on the failed SOE insertion? We're thinking there may be a mole, an infiltrator. Seems they were sold out."

Ike turned to Langley, who answered, "Ray, I understand your concern. The operation is being investigated. Appropriate action will be taken. Your focus should be on Oaktree— preparing your radios and honing your skills. You must be able to set up, broadcast, break down, and evacuate in minutes. The Germans are getting faster and more proficient in detecting our transmissions. Now, Major Curtis, your brief."

Val interrupted. "How do we plan for insertion if we don't know who we can trust?"

Langley shook his head and sighed. "Major Curtis will brief you on an operation planned to smoke out any infiltrator. But first, infrared cameras and film."

Ike nodded. "New cameras and film are being mounted and loaded on 545 RECON planes as I speak. I plan on beginning operational testing tomorrow. I will need several days of testing to determine optimal performance. Then…"

Ike got the nod from Langley. "Then we execute Operation Mongoose. Our target is Cobra, the traitor responsible for the deaths of three SOE agents and the capture of weapons, explosives, and 200,000 francs."

Val interrupted. "Tell me we're going to kill the bastard."

Langley answered. "We share real-time intelligence with SOE. We will set the trap and identify Cobra, but SOE will drop the hammer. SOE insists on keeping their field operations close to the vest. Can you blame them? Continue, Major."

"Right. SOE has narrowed it down to three possibilities—teams, or cells expecting the SOE field operators. The Resistance saboteur team, our Paris agent with the French command and finance team, and the *hebergeur,* or host, scheduled to meet them and move them to a safe house. Mongoose is simple, really. Each team received their orders from a different wireless operator. Since every wireless operator has a unique cryptogram and code name known only to MI6, they can be given unique orders and are incapable of receiving orders meant for another wireless operator. Each of the three teams will receive notice of a second attempt to insert a team for the same mission. However, each will be directed to a different landing site. Mongoose will see who is waiting at each site. Any Nazi welcoming party will show Cobra's hand."

Someone asked, "You can't expect to land another Hudson in a Nazi trap?"

Val spoke up. "Better a couple of Spitfires or Hurricanes for ground attack."

Ike tapped the podium with his pointer. "There will be no landings and no attack aircraft. We will do night vision and infrared photography and simulate landings. Each will have Spitfire support overhead. Our job is to identify Cobra's team. SOE and the resistance will deal with him. Now—three sites in Normandy, here, here, and here, But first testing and calibration for optimal infrared camera performance, then preliminary day high altitude and night low and slow over the sites before their locations are given to the wireless operators. Questions?"

Langley stood up. "Thank you, Major. Val and Ray, you will provide Husky and Goldenrod a detailed brief on Oaktree—everything you have to date. Major Curtis will select your insertion site."

Langley paused and looked around the table. "Each of you is here for a reason. We have one goal—to get every Allied airman and every Allied soldier we can out of occupied territory. Yes, pilots have priority—we can build airplanes faster than we can train pilots, and seasoned pilots must take priority."

Langley cast his eyes on Dorothy. "But every soldier is important—to the war effort, yes, but even more so to their family. The nation—yes, but we, too, owe them that. We must open new escape lines—faster and more efficient than the Comet and Pat Lines. This is our mission, our contribution to the cause. That is all. Dismissed."

An hour later, on the ride back to RAF Churchstanton, Dorothy laughed. Embarrassed, she covered her mouth. Ike asked, "What's so funny? Out with it."

"I was just thinking, Val Williams is a Russian American, Labrosse is Canadian, Major Curtis another American, and I am Women's Auxiliary. It appears to me we're ..."

Langley uncharacteristically laughed and said, "And you work for a one-armed chap not clever enough to go home and sit out this war. It's true, MI6—all of SOE doesn't trust the Yanks, the Canadians, women, God forbid the Irish, or anyone lacking an Eton pedigree. That's why they agreed to establish MI9 as the authority for escape routes. We work with unarmed helpers, not warfighting resistance cells. MI6 acknowledges the need but sees it as secondary to reducing Nazi warfighting ability."

CHAPTER 8
SHINING A NEW LIGHT

After briefing Flight 545 RECON pilots on the peculiarities of infrared aerial photography, Ike went to the hangar servicing the ungainly Lysander. The new Spitfire was parked in front. *What a beautiful machine! I must put her to good use before they take it away—too critical for the war effort to sit unused. Experienced pilot—flew maritime RECON before being reassigned. This will be different than hunting U Boats. Was it Langley who pulled this off? More likely, Colonel Z is setting up his one-armed, fair-haired boy.*

The lead mechanic saw Ike coming. "New film loaded. Cameras adjusted and tested. Your birds are ready to go back to work, Major."

"The Spitfire as well?"

"Yes, sir. She's been well-maintained. Engine overhauled before she arrived."

"Thanks. Good to know they're in capable hands. I've got a new problem, hope you're up to it."

Ike walked over to the Lysander and grabbed a wing strut. "I may need a float plane. What do you think? Can we find a couple of floats anywhere on this green and sceptered isle?"

Sergeant Major Brown pulled a rag from his back pocket and wiped his hands. He smiled and raised his eyebrows. "Got something good planned, have ye, Major? Well, the twin Beeches, the Expeditors, common as ants at a picnic in England before the war, came with a float option. I'm sure we could find a set for them."

Ike nodded. "Get on it. But the Lysander, smaller, shorter take-off and landing—anything we could do for her?"

Sergeant Major Brown rubbed his chin. "Any number of small float planes in Britain. Aye, we can find floats. Not a difficult job to fit her. Need to give me time to work it out. But, aye, we can get it done. Where are you intending to fly from? We'll need to install the floats at a ramp we can fly into."

"You find the floats; I'll find the site."

Brown looked at Lysander's streamlined wheel struts. "One last question, Major. Who is your float plane pilot? Not your standard training."

Ike smiled. "You're looking at him."

Ike opened the cabin door and peeked inside the tight cockpit. "Get her ready. I need to get acquainted with all of them. I'll start with the Lysander. Say an hour?"

Brown replied, "She be out front with the engine warm."

Sixty minutes later, Ike returned with the assigned Lysander pilot. Ike climbed into the pilot's seat; the pilot sat behind him. He listened as the junior officer explained the characteristics of the Lysander, and Ike became familiar with the gauges and controls. "Pretty straightforward," Ike said,

"Let's go."

Ike was surprised when the little plane climbed off the ground in little more than 600 feet down the runway. The young officer behind him spoke, "Automatic wing slats and slotted flaps. Gives maximum lift all on its own. Full load, she'll clear 50 feet vertical in 900 feet."

Ike circled the airfield. "Very well-mannered." He pointed the plane south towards the coast. Opening the throttle, he commented, "Not much speed."

"They say 212 mph. I found that only with a tailwind. No sir, she's built for lift."

Ike glanced behind him. "Only two seats."

"Yes, but we're able to squeeze five men inside. It's just a matter of proper packing."

Ike replied, "Enlighten me."

"Pilot, two in the crew seat, one on the floor, and one on the shelf between pilot and crew."

Ike shook his head. "Incredible. Thanks, I'm taking her down."

When Ike returned to his office, Dorothy stared at him in his leather jacket and flight suit. "I thought you gave up flying, Major."

"We all have to sacrifice something for the effort. I can't send other men to do something I refuse to do myself. If I am to command Special Duty Flight 545, I'll do my time in the air. I'm now qualified on the Lysander; tomorrow, the twin Beech and the Spitfire."

"You're qualified? Who…"

Ike smiled. "The Wing or Flight Commander is authorized

to qualify pilots. That's me. Type it up, Sergeant, for the record."

"Yes, sir. By the way, Uncle Hugh is expecting you in church on Sunday. Standing invite for Sunday dinner. I think the bourbon is getting low."

Ike stared at the packages on his desk. "Thanks. I'll pick something to restock his locker. I've been thinking about our conversation last Sunday."

"About his sermon, what was it he said…."

Ike did not look up. "Unanswered prayer. Been stuck on his last comment, 'Our prayers may go unanswered because of sin but not as we surmise."

Dorothy paused and waited for eye contact, which did not come. She pulled out a form and put it into the typewriter. "Well, he'll be happy to know someone listened and someone cares."

Ike sat down and pulled an infrared flashlight from one of the boxes. He turned it on and watched a beam of light turn papers on his desk a light red. He was about to turn it off when he saw something unexpected. Forgetting office protocol, he called out, "Dottie, close the blackout curtains and turn off the lights."

Dorothy turned in surprise and asked, "You want it dark in here?"

"Yes, hurry. Then come and look at this."

In seconds the room was dark except for the red beam from the flashlight. Dorothy stood alongside Ike, "What is it?"

Ike moved the box away and held the light over an open file on his desk. "Look. Rose gave these pages from the parish records for me to read. But look closely. Do you see the writing under the writing?"

Dorothy crouched low. "Yes, there is something. It's not English though, looks like Latin."

Ike nodded. "That's what I thought. Maybe Rose can translate it. This could come in handy with the mission. What do you think? Another layer of code. Every layer will help our agents and their French helpers."

"Do you want to share it with Captain Langley?" Dorothy asked.

"Yes, of course. The records of this old Earl of Montclair, Sir Robert Curtis, is such a strange coincidence, and now he gives me a new tool for my trade."

"New tool?"

Ike was studying the image. "What if...Yes, a great help indeed!"

Dorothy's curiosity compelled her to lean over Ike's shoulder. Feeling her breath on the back of his neck, Ike looked up, smiled, and said, "How do our pilots find their targets?"

"Why they navigate. I suppose they have a flight map on board."

"Yes, and how do they read their map at night?"

Dorothy shrugged, "I don't know, they must have lights."

Ike nodded. "Very dim light so as not to impair their night vision. Dim red lights, to be precise. We depend on the resistance and helpers to find our downed pilots. What if we equipped our pilots to find the resistance? It would have to be secure—safe in case of capture. Maps. Maps of extraction sites air dropped to our agents. Maps overprinted with the escape routes visible only under infrared light. Small flashlights with red lenses—red like the night vision lights in the aircraft. I'm sure there are issues to be sorted, but the concept could work."

Dorothy asked, "Should I arrange a meeting with Captain Langley?"

Ike was talking to himself now, "So many intelligence applications with this technology—codes, drawings, plans...."

"I have Captain Langley on the line, Major...."

"Tell him we're on the way...no, wait—tell him I'm adding a high-altitude daylight RECON flight today, and we're set for the night flights. Tell him we'll be standing by in the OPS room for the flight, and I have something new to show him."

Dorothy gave the report and hung up the phone, "What is it, Ike? What changed your mind?"

"I need more information—Can't get the cart in front of the horse. We have seen what infrared can do on old vellum, but we don't know how to replicate it. Special ink? Maybe. That works with ultraviolet. We don't know how the original ink was removed. Some kind of chemical wash? And I'm still worried about sending our slow, low altitude RECON planes over target areas at night, risking..."

"The ambush of the team was not your fault. This mission is for them. I've prayed about this, Ike, and somehow, I have peace."

"Peace? You have peace? Even with your husband missing?"

Dorothy stood close and looked Ike in the eyes. "I gave it to God. What else could I do? There is a God, Ike, or all is lost. This is not the first war. Hitler is not the first evil maniac to butcher and murder innocent people. It will pass. I trust God. Yes, He is there. I know it. He hears my prayers, and I trust Him."

"Charles Barkley, wherever he is, is a lucky man. Now, I want to see Flight Officer Marley about high-altitude flights."

"You're using the Spitfire?"

"Speed and altitude. A good addition to our unit. I want to discuss camera options with him. Have him meet me at his plane in fifteen minutes."

Marley was waiting beside his Spitfire when Ike arrived. He saluted in the exaggerated British fashion. Ike returned his salute and said, "At ease, Marley. Change in plans. I'm sending you over three RECON sites today. I want your opinion on the cameras. Show me your configuration."

Marley wasted no time. "Yes, sir." He stepped beneath the Spitfire. "Standard belly trimetrogon installation. One vertical and one oblique on each side. Also, this rearward-facing camera. Maritime operations proved it helps overcome some of the jitters of sideways movement."

Ike nodded. "Look like F24 cameras."

"Yes sir, dependable and best camera for night use."

Ike nodded. "Today, you'll be flying high altitude—more challenging for useful photographs."

"Yes, sir. These cameras are modified for anti-fogging and fitted with long focus optics."

Ike was face to face with the belly pod when he answered, "Goddard's Law. There is no substitute for focal length in RECON work. Are they shutter in focal plane?"

"Yes, sir," Marley replied, impressed an American Officer knew the difference.

Ike stepped from beneath the Spitfire. "At altitude and speed, exposure is tricky."

Marley smiled, Something the Yank didn't know. "She has a cockpit-mounted intervalometer. I can key in speed, altitude, and interval, and the cameras do the rest."

Ike sized up the young man before him. "Today. I want you up in the air ASAP. You have the sites. What's your ceiling?"

"33,000 feet."

Maintain altitude 33,000 feet…"

Marley interrupted. "Intervalometer ceiling is 25,000, Major."

"25,000 feet then and maximum speed over the target. I don't want you to take any unnecessary risks. Get in and get out. If the Luftwaffe shows, don't be a hero. Hightail it back here. We're returning tonight anyway, low and slow. Understand?"

"Yes sir, go in high and fast and return to base."

"You know the frequency. Good luck, Flight Lieutenant."

Salutes were rendered and returned. Ike made his way back to the RECON office.

That evening, Ike and Dorothy waited in the OPS room at Otterhead House. At the pre-brief, Ike reported that Marley's photographs clearly captured enemy troops and vehicles at two sites. Ike pronounced the third site as clear of targets. He concluded with his recommendation. "I feel confident we can move forward with Operation Mongoose."

Langley walked to the board where the afternoon's photos were posted. "Good initiative on ordering the high-altitude daylight flight. A margin of safety for tonight's low and slow test, Major. However, your assessment falls short."

Langley went to site three and circled a gray line. "I'll chalk it up to training, Major. We can remedy that. Notice this shadow from the barn. And here, in the pond. A reflection. The out-of-place line—the reflection. It's the barrel of a tank—and this is the turret. And here—my interpreters found an armored personnel carrier. They're encamped not two miles from site three—the same area where our team was trapped last month."

Ike's face flushed. "Do we continue with tonight's low and slow test flight to site 3? And Operation Mongoose?"

James Langley smiled. "This gives an opportunity for a good test. We continue. Send all three low and slows—simultaneous targeting. Let's get a good preliminary look at the targets and flight times. The BBC will broadcast the code messages to the three site teams tonight after your birds have returned. Operation Mongoose is a go in two days."

The two Beech Expeditors and the Lysander approached their assigned sites precisely on schedule. The small RECON planes with onboard spotters, standard night, and infrared film, had no field lights to guide them. They relied on their dead-reckoning navigation skills, and the few distinctive landmarks visible in the dim moonlight. There were risks—margin of error in their navigation, Luftwaffe night fighters—but any enemy presence in the vicinity should be captured on film.

Only minutes apart, the three planes reported their overflights completed, and they were returning to base. No crew reported any visual enemy presence at their target site. When the planes reported over the English Channel, Langley ordered. "Major, I want to see the film, Your office 0800."

Ike asked, "The BBC coded message?"

Langley smiled. "Already out.":

On the drive to RAF Churchstanton, Langley broke the silence. "My apologies, Major. I was wrong to correct you so publicly. I like your initiative and your dedication to the mission. You haven't had the benefit of Wilton Park."

Ike didn't understand. "Wilton Park?"

"Yes, Wilton Park, Beaconsfield Buck. It is the MI9 Headquarters and the training center. I'll arrange for you to visit before the greenlight on Operation Oaktree."

Dorothy interrupted, "They train in interpreting RECON photos, no doubt. But do they develop code and secure communications for agents?"

Langley nodded. "Of course—the whole gamut of covert mission operations."

"Well then, Captain. Major Curtis has found something with great potential. The experts at Wilton Park may want to see."

Langley turned to Ike, "Yes, you were going to show me something."

Ike looked down at the file on his lap. "Another side of infrared. I see utility, but I haven't sorted all the issues yet." Ike opened the file to the Robert Curtis letter. He took a small infrared flashlight from his pocket. "Driver, let me know if the light bothers you. About the same light a pilot uses to navigate at night."

Ike gave the old visit record to Langley. "Keep it low on your lap." Then he leaned over, turned on the light, and pointed it over the paper. "What do you see?"

Langley read silently. "A visit by the Earl of Montclair, Sir

Robert Curtis—are you trying to gain sympathy with a common English name?"

"Look closer, beneath what you just read."

Langley brought the paper closer. "Anno Domina—in the year of our Lord.... What is this?"

"It is an ancient document that has been erased and written over—visible still only under infrared light."

Langley asked, "How?"

Ike shrugged. "I don't yet know."

Dorothy cleared her throat. "Ahem. Perhaps Wilton Park can help."

Ike continued. "But consider the possibilities! Flight maps protected—our pilots provided the escape routes-hidden to all but clear under a small flashlight—looking to all the world like an ordinary red night lens. Leaflets dropped to our agents— the resistance. Any number of...,"

Langley was nodding. "Yes, I need to get you two to Wilton Park."

Chapter 9
Operation Mongoose

The next morning in Ike's RECON office, Langley waited with three of his photograph interpreters. This time, Ike waited for Langley's analysts to give their report. "We find no evidence of enemy troops or vehicles at the targeted areas."

Ike asked, "The earlier sighting, a mile from site 3?"

"Nothing in the photographs, Major, the distance and with potential error in navigation, we cannot confirm one way or the other if they have moved on."

Ike looked off toward the windows. "I'd like to send another daylight high-altitude flyover, just to be safe."

Langley shook his head. "Denied. The landing codes have been broadcast. We don't want to add to the interest with any more flights. There's no telling what reports have already been made by German spotters. No. If there is a Nazi trap set, we must be confident it was the work of Cobra. Tomorrow night, 0330 at each site."

A visit by Group Captain Hastings after the brief took Ike's mind off the unanswered questions of Operation

Mongoose. "Good morning, Mic," Hastings said as he came through the door. "I know you have a lot on your plate, but if my information is correct, a couple of the 545 RECON planes should be available today."

Ike pointed to the chair alongside his desk. Hastings sat down. "I've come to collect on your promise. I need RECON on a train carrying guns—coastal artillery to the Normandy coast. They want to follow it to the coast before my fighters and light bombers take it out. We will follow up on the emplacements afterward. You'll have your birds back in time for Mongoose."

"Did intel mention if the train was armed for anti-aircraft?"

"I'm afraid it goes with the territory. I recommend daylight high over the line followed by night slow and low. No need to stay close. Just keep it in sight. Darkness and stealth, Major. It's what RECON trains for."

After a long night, the two RECON planes returned safely to RAF Churchstanton. The Nazi train was attacked as it moved to a side rail at Grandcamp-Maisy on the Normandy Coast. A coordinated attack by RAF fighters and light bombers struck German batteries under construction.

The following night Ike was surprised to see Ray Labrosse and Val Williams in the Operations Room when he entered with Dorothy. Langley greeted them. "Make yourself comfortable. They're just approaching the channel—radio silence until after they surveil the targets."

Dorothy asked, "What if they get—what if there's an emergency?'

Val Williams answered, "Oh, we'll hear about that. Don't

you worry your pretty little head, Blondie, that is, Goldenrod. They'll squawk like hell. Hopefully, give us an idea of where they are. If we can get one of the standbys there fast, they have a good chance. Time. Time is the enemy. Especially if there is no word."

Langley cut him off. "That's enough, Val! You're here by invitation, Only background for Oaktree next week." Langley turned to Dorothy and said softly. "We can't pick up every downed flyer immediately. That's why these lines are critical. They must be protected and expanded,"

Time, the only resource that cannot be recovered or replaced, passed slowly. She knew how time worked against her Charles' survival. The radio frequency was silent. Only background noise reminded them the radio was working. The large clock read 0332 when a voice broke through the clutter and reported. "Site two landing lights set. Overflew twice, signaled wave-off and departed. No enemy spotted. Returning to base,"

Not thirty seconds later, another voice crackled over the speaker. "All clear site 1. Helpers present. Gave a wave-off and departed safely. No enemy sighted. Returning to base."

The speaker fell silent again. A radioman adjusted the gain. Minutes passed. Dorothy closed her eyes and lowered her head. Ike stared at the speaker. *Say something! Anything. Where are you?*

The radioman adjusted the gain. The crackling squelch grew louder. "Over site..." The voice faded. The radio operator turned down the gain dand increased the volume. "...overflight. Making another pass, a wider pattern. Still no landing lights. No lights of any kind—no contacts, friend or foe observed site 3. Returning to base."

Langley ordered the radioman. "Break silence. Ask, 'Is the mission equipment operating?'"

The room fell silent as the question was asked. This time, the voice was loud and clear. "Got two good low passes in a widening arc and continued as we made altitude. If anyone was there, we'll know."

Ike asked Langley, "If site 3 was a no-show, does it mean the team has been terminated but not penetrated? Or...."

Langley finished the thought. "Or do they have the radio and the code and have decided to use it wisely? We must assume there is a Cobra."

Ray Labrosse asked, "Do we proceed with Oaktree as scheduled?"

"You won't be able to depend on the locals. The risk— well, you heard the risk."

Val answered, "Ray and I have trained for this. We're ready. Hell, we waited long enough."

Langley stared at the silent speakers, sighed, and nodded. "Oaktree is a go on schedule. But I remind you—and this is an order. Make no attempt to contact the resistance. You're on your own. This must be clean—a totally new line. Security—you've seen and heard enough. Trust no one. You need help—you call us—only this OPS room. Is that clear?"

Val turned to Ray before turning to Langley. "Clear. We're on our own. We're ready. We won't let you down."

By the time the planes returned, the film developed, and

the photographs interpreted, the sun was climbing in the east. Ike told Dorothy to take the rest of the day off. He made his way to his quarters, stopping by his mailbox. Besides the usual Plan of the Day and routine base notifications, a thick brown envelope was bent in half and shoved tightly in the slot. The back, lacking any postage stamps, bore a large black ink APO stamp. He smiled as he read the return address: Earl Curtis, General Delivery, Gig Harbor, Washington.

Ike tossed the letter on the desk in his small room. He closed the curtains in the window to the bright morning sun. *I'm tired. I will enjoy it more when I'm awake. Sleep first.* Ike laughed out loud. "Who am I kidding?" He grabbed the envelope and tore it open. A folded sheet of double-line school writing paper was clipped to old newspaper clippings. Ike unfolded the paper and recognized the pencil-printed hand of his son, Earl. The bold pencil strokes stayed between the lines. Capitals precisely spanning two blue bold lines and small letters neatly within a lower bold and an upper dotted blue line.

Daddy,

When will you come home? I miss you. Jimmy and Frankie's dads went away to the army after you, and they came home for a visit. Grandpa says you are too far away to come home. If it was not too far to go, why is it too far to come back? Pappa Ole says you can come fishing with us. We can't go out of the Sound, so you won't get seasick. A lot of the kids' dads have gone, but they come home. Grandpa Earl says you are in England. He showed me it on a map. It doesn't look that far to me. He says you can learn about us being English.

Miss Barrett at school says we are Americans. Can't you come back to America and come home to visit me?

Your son
Earl

Also, I think I will be a pitcher on the baseball team If I can learn to throw a curveball.

Ike smiled, then sighed. *Work on that curveball, little man. I miss you, Earl. How I miss you growing up, learning, and seeing wonders in the world every day. Thank God you're safe from this horror.*

A folded letter on thin onion skin airmail paper slipped from beneath the paper clip. Ike unfolded it and read.

Son,

Young Earl so looks forward to your letters. Please write more often. Hard news—your brother-in-law Gus is missing. His ship was sunk in the North Atlantic—guessing the Murmansk run. Ole is heartbroken, though he keeps a loving face for young Earl. Marge is his solid rock. Ed's boy is off to the Merchant Marine Cadet Corps' new Academy in New York. A town on Long Island called Kings Point. He'll fast-track to Third Mate. Won't be any safer than an Ordinary or Able Seaman, but he'll be paid better. Ed brags he is serving as well as any man but making a lot more money doing it.

I've had these old newspaper clippings in a shoebox. Never shared them with you. Family history—not sure to be proud or ashamed. Not sure if it's true or all tall tales.

Anyway, since we're Earl and Montclair, I thought maybe you could tell me. Little Earl will need to know someday.

Dad

Ike mumbled, "Family history? Really? That can wait. I'm going to bed."

A light knock on his door woke Ike. His eyes opened, but his mind was elsewhere. The knocking resumed. *Thank God, it was only a dream. I could not take it much longer—I saw Linda knocking on the cockpit window, her eyes wide with fear, blood swirling in her hair as it flowed in the cold, murky water. The coroner said she was dead before the cabin flooded. He said it was fast. She didn't suffer. She didn't drown. Why am I tormented?*

The knocking on the door resumed. "Come through. I'm awake," Ike responded. The door opened, and a non-commissioned officer stepped in. "Sorry to wake you, Major. Group Captain Hastings sends his compliments and requests the pleasure of your company at your earliest convenience."

Ike rubbed his eyes and yawned. "Right—what time is it?"

"Past noon, sir. If you're hungry, the mess is open another thirty minutes."

"Tell the Group Captain I'll report at 1300." Ike rubbed his hand over his chin. "That will give me time to shave and wash my face. Thank you, Sergeant. That will be all."

Ike reported to Hastings' office at 1300, shaved, washed, and in a clean uniform. The door was open, and Hastings called out. "Come through, Major. Close the door behind you."

Ike closed the door and sat down as Hastings pointed. "Tough luck last night, Mic—you don't mind me calling you Mic? Seems everyone else does."

"Mic is fine. What can I do for you, Group Captain?"

Hastings smiled. "Right to the point. Has it always been that way with you? You're a hard man to get to know. But, yes, I'll get to the point. I need your help on a mission. I'm aware Oaktree is two weeks away. I'm requesting 545 support before then. MI6 operation. Colonel Z—you owe him, Major. Coordinated attack on a French aircraft factory at Argenteuil. Dewoitine may have fled to America, but his planes are still being built for the Nazis. Need you for reconnaissance and diversion—-and another MI6 insertion. I want you to send the Nazis to their shelters. Resistance will have their shelters booby-trapped. With an MI6-assisted ground assault, we're hoping Nazi anti-aircraft will be silenced before our bombing run. Helps you with reduced Nazi forces in your OPS Theatre for Oak Tree and hits Nazi war production both in factory and personnel. Just an overview, you'll get a full brief tomorrow."

"When will you need 545?"

"Two days before Oaktree. Should keep the Krauts busy in the north for some time."

Ike mumbled, "That's the Paris suburbs! Busy? Busy as angry hornets looking for anything to sting."

Hastings replied, "Angry, yes. But disorganized. And organization is their strength. Right. Insertion will be simple—12 men parachute. Only three coming back. The others will be enjoying the French countryside for a while. You find the landing zone."

Hastings paused before continuing. "And there's another matter. You've been assigned an adjutant. Can't do it all yourself, Major. 'Best I could do was a junior officer. No RAF pilots to pull off flight duty. Section Officer, Women's Auxiliary RAF. You can do the honors with Barkley. Next time I see Section Officer Barkley she is to be in proper uniform."

Ike grinned. "You're promoting Dorothy, I mean, Sergeant Barkley? And what is a Section Officer?"

"Equivalent to Pilot Officer, that's First Lieutenant to you Yanks. Thank Uncle Claude. He arranged it. Can't have an Oxford graduate, an agent he recruited, without a commission. She's proven herself most capable and seems to have earned your trust. Besides, I need a proper Brit on your staff."

Ike was speechless. "I don't know what to say—sorry, I hadn't thought to request..."

"You will introduce her to the Officer's Mess at your convenience. That is all, Major."

Ike stood to leave. Hastings had the last word. "And Mic, begin with immediate RECON over Argenteuil. I want pictures—day and night—lots of photos."

Like every good sergeant, Dorothy was in the office working before Ike arrived. He smiled. "Don't you ever sleep? If Hastings hadn't sent for me, I'd still be in bed,"

Dorothy looked up. "I'll let you in on my secret. Whenever the Group Captain sends a non-com to request your presence, they tell me first. It's something we sergeants do for each other—and with all these night missions, I've come to rely on it."

"We sergeants? No longer. Sergeant Barkley, stand for orders!"

Dorothy was puzzled, but she stood up and stepped away from her desk and came to attention."

The smile drained from Ike's face. "Don't you salute a senior office when called to order?"

Now Dorothy was stone-faced. "Yes, sir," as she saluted Ike.

"Attention to orders. Sergeant Dorothy Barkley is hereby commissioned Section Officer. Royal Air Force, Women's Auxiliary. Section Officer Barkley is ordered to Special Duty Flight 545, RAF Churchstanton, Special Duty Flight Commander's Adjutant."

Dorothy saluted. "Yes, sir. Section Officer Barkley reporting as ordered, sir!"

Ike returned her salute and smiled. "At ease, Section Officer. Congratulations, Dottie. How soon can you be in the proper uniform? Hastings insists you be introduced to the Officer's Mess. And I believe a celebration is in order."

"Give me a day to find the Pilot Officer sleeve striping and sew it on."

Ike nodded. "Good. Now, if the 545 is going to be a proper unit, we need a full complement. You, Section Officer Barkley, shall find us a proper staff—start with clerks. Go to the WAAF. They seem to be a quality source."

"Major..."

Ike looked at her and replied, "It's still Ike in private."

"Ike, I'm grateful for the clerical help, but..."

"But what?"

"But if the 545 is going to be a 'proper unit,' as you say, you need a Number One, a pilot. We are a flying unit. As you would say, an Executive Officer. Properly, he should be next in seniority to you. That would be Flight Lieutenant Marley. He can take most of the administrative load off you."

"Right, the Spitfire. And he is our most experienced pilot. Yes, send for him. But Dottie, for now, regarding Mongoose and Oaktree operations, he is need-to-know only. Just operational orders, unit administration, morale, and good order."

Ike sighed. "Now for the bad news. We have another mission—over Paris, two days before Oaktree. And, as it happens, Marley will provide RECON."

CHAPTER 10
ROSE

Uncle Hugh smiled when he spotted the neck of the bourbon bottle peeking over the top of the bag Ike held. "Always welcome, Ike, but if that's what I think it is, doubly so today! Come in and make yourself comfortable. Dottie is in the kitchen with Rose."

Rose stepped out of the kitchen as Ike set the bag down. "Kentucky's finest for you Hugh, and something for Rose as well."

Rose wiped her hands on a towel, "For me? Really?"

Ike smiled. "That is if Dottie hasn't spoiled the surprise."

Dottie called from the kitchen. "Been quiet as a church mouse, Ike."

Ike pulled out the file Rose had given him. "Those are the records I gave you. I don't understand."

Ike motioned. "Sit down, you've found much more than you thought." Rose sat and stared at the first page.

Ike pulled the infrared flashlight from his pocket and shined a red beam on the page. "Look close."

"What am looking for?" Rose asked.

"Look closely. Very close between the letters, even beneath the letters."

"I see it! Uncle Hugh, come look! Another document—Latin! It's very faint but I can read it even under the in faded black ink. What is?"

Uncle Hugh leaned in close, "It looks like an inventory. It's dated 1048." Uncle Hugh turned a page. "Yes, here it is—the monastery, an inventory, no, an index of sorts, a listing of records."

Hugh looked up. "The document beneath this visit record is 900 years old! Amazing!"

Ike asked, "Hugh, what do you know about the paper—how did they…"

Hugh replied, "How did they write over it? It's not paper, it's vellum. It was the practice to reuse vellum of outdated documents. They merely scraped away the old ink and reused the page."

"Vellum?"

Hugh nodded. "If it were Roman, it would have been paper. Both linen and papyrus were inexpensive and in good supply. But after the empire fell, access to linen and papyrus ceased. Animal skin—vellum came into use here and in northern Europe. It wasn't until the late Middle Ages that rag paper became common."

Rose had been studying the document. "If these are on reused vellum, there must be many more. Who knows what is hidden in the archives."

Hugh took a puff on his pipe. "Certainly, anything written on vellum."

Rose kept staring at the old record. "So, all I need is a red flashlight."

Ike sighed. "Not quite. It isn't any ordinary-colored lens. It's, well, it's infrared, a different light spectrum."

"Where do I get one?"

Ike feared this question. "I probably crossed a line showing you this. You must promise to say nothing about what you saw or this flashlight."

Hugh commented, "Infrared light is well known. We aren't speaking of a military application…"

Ike interrupted, "I don't believe the use of infrared to see through a printed document is in the public domain. I can't take that chance."

Rose looked up and said sweetly, "You can trust me, Ike. I mean you already have trusted me."

Dottie shook her head. "She has you there. You let the cat out of the bag on this one."

Ike sighed. "Yes, but we must be careful. How about I let you use it in my presence? You can find the old vellum documents, and then we can check them together. But the flashlight stays in my possession."

Rose stood up and kissed Ike's cheek. "Thank you! This will be so much fun. I can't wait. I know we will find answers—answers to all those old legends. We can run over to the church now."

Dottie laughed. "No, Rose. Dinner. And it wouldn't be fair to Uncle Hugh."

At dinner, Ike asked, "Hugh, I've been thinking about our conversation—unanswered prayer. We never finished. You said something about sin and unanswered prayer being linked, but not always as we surmise. Did you mean sin as disobedience to God, and therefore, we become unworthy of an answer? Or sin as a sign of weak faith? I haven't been a churchgoer for many years, not since, well, let's just say I didn't see any reward worthy of faith."

"If you are asking does God reward faith? Yes—and always. But His reward does not mean we are immune to all that troubles our broken world. It means He comforts us and comes beside us to see us through any trial or tribulation. No, what I meant was that God calls us and sometimes He calls us to a specific time or task. Now, be sure He will accomplish His will with or without our answer to His calling. A good example was the advice Mordecai gave his niece, Esther, when asking her to confront the king of Persia to save the Jews. He said, 'If you keep silent at this time, relief and deliverance will arise for the Jews at another place, but you and your father's house will perish.'"

"You're saying our prayers aren't heard if we say no to God."

"Oh, He hears them. And there are many reasons prayers can go unanswered, but yes, saying no to God, whether by lack of faith or rebellion, is high on the list."

Ike spoke softly, "I've been saying no to any suggestion of God's comfort for years. I guess I've been a no to His calling."

Rose reached across and put her hand on Ike's. "The bells. You said yes when you heard the bells."

Ike smiled. "Yes. The bells did call to me. Perhaps it was a God thing."

Rose's eyes widened, and she nearly shouted, "I almost forgot! I found something else! Come. I'll show you." She stood, grabbed Ike's hand, and dragged him up. "More records at the church."

"Let me guess. The Earl of Montclair. Rupert Curtis."

"Robert Curtis. And don't pretend you're not interested. Admit it. If you didn't have the papers with you, you would not have discovered the hidden Latin and your infrared secret."

Ike laughed. "You have me there, Rose. I guess I owe it to him and you to have a look. Dottie, are you coming?"

Dorothy shook her head. "I've a letter to write."

Ike turned to Hugh, who shook his head. "I've a date with a friend from Kentucky. Don't be long."

Outside the door, Rose took Ike's arm, looked up into the afternoon sky, and said, "What a beautiful day! Such a simple pleasure. It's hard even to notice the beauty of a sunny day. The war. It's all one thinks about. Is it wrong, Ike, to be amazed by beauty in the midst of war?"

"It's hard. Hard to find peace and tranquility—enough to think, let alone meditate. No, it's not wrong, just forgotten." Ike glanced at the happiness holding his arm and reached around and patted her hand. He took a deep breath of quiet country air and said, "Rose, I hope you're not offended, but I'd like to ask you a question. Your interest in nobility, titles, and ancestry, as an American, I just don't get it. What right does anyone have to a special privilege because four, five, or ten generations ago, a forgotten ancestor was granted a title? And your fascination with these myths and legends; what difference does it make?"

Rose laughed. "That's two questions, but they are

related. The first I would expect from you. America threw off the King and nobility. That's why your Jefferson was so smitten with revolutionary France. Freedom, liberty, and equality. At least you qualify equality of opportunity over redistribution of wealth. But the answer to both lies in our ancient Christian beliefs. Our faith does not devalue tradition. From what I have read and observed, American Christians have a cultural Christianity that mirrors its young, not yet two-hundred-year-old non-conformist religiosity. You come from a young nation that has forgotten church history."

Ike chuckled, "Forgotten? More like we never bothered to learn. Yes, we are a nation of rugged individualists. Read the Bible. It's all we need to know—me and God."

"Exactly. If you read your Bible, you know God blessed King David."

"Yes, a man after God's own heart."

"Right, and what promise did God give to David? What was the reward for his faith? God made a covenant with David that a son of his would sit on the throne of Israel forever..."

"So long as they remained righteous."

"True. And David was not the only one. Recall the promises made to the patriarchs and to the children of Israel. But David makes my point. Was God unjust to grant the privilege of reigning based on David's righteousness?"

"Hmm. I never thought of it that way. Look, I'm no theologian, but wasn't that covenant meant for Jesus Christ the only truly righteous man? By the way, you sound more like your Uncle Hugh than the average Englishman."

"I'll ignore that remark. Of course, we see the promise of Christ now, but Jews applied it to their Kings, and rightfully they did, as even Joseph and Mary were both descendants of David. A promise a thousand years in the making—talk about a tradition! We Brits are an Island people tied to, but always separate from Europe. We are a proud people—an empire—Britannia rules the waves! But now, it's more than our national pride, it's become our survival as a people and our special place in God's sovereignty. That's why the legend of the Grail is so important. Yes, many people have legends—Christian legends. We have Saint Joseph of Arimathea founding our church. It ties us to the very founding of Christianity—here—a safe and fertile ground."

"And your royals and traditions fit into—or it seems to me parrot that tradition out of self-interest."

"Ike, you would be surprised by the royals and nobles who see themselves born into duty. They serve. They are the first to serve in our army and navy. They serve in government and parliament. And remember, only the eldest male retains the title. The younger sons receive no inheritance. They must…"

"They must be placed by their fathers, brothers, and cousins in the best schools and plum jobs. And somehow, the British people accept this, accept being led by weak men like Edward VIII. It seems these traditions that survived Henry VIII's war on relics—these cultural icons are meant to prop up an archaic system of privilege."

Rose sighed. "You don't understand. We need this. Our culture, our heritage, and the glue that binds us are all under attack. We need the affirmation of our worth as a people and a great nation. We need to remember we are connected to God through Christ for a thousand years. Don't you see? We need hope to carry on. But hope is nothing without action. So, Dottie serves, and I dig for evidence—the proof that God was, is, and ever will be sovereign over England."

"Perhaps, what you say is true. Perhaps there is some envy by us Americans—ever separated and forever linked to England. It's like we are the little brother without the inherited title—the second or third son, the cavalier who struck out on his own, successful, comfortable, and still jealous. But I can't stop thinking about the frog in the pot on the stove. You English subjects, like the frog, remain comfortable in your surroundings as the water comes to a boil."

Rose shook her head. "Well. At least we can agree that the water is coming to a boil. Do you want to see what I found, or is it all a waste of time—a bore?"

Ike stopped and looked down. He hadn't noticed Rose had dropped his arm. *Have I misjudged and underestimated her?* "I'm sorry, Rose. It is me who has been the bore. Show me what you've found. I want to understand."

In the musty air of the records closet in the parish office, Rose opened a box of records. "I found this. A letter to the vicar, or better, a reply to his letter from Robert Curtis. It's about the Sword of Saint Peter."

She handed the letter to Ike. "Well, I must say his penmanship is flawless unless he employed a talented servant." Ike began to read:

DAVID MARTYN

Dear Reverend Mister Stone,

I have received your request for custody of the purported Glastonbury Abbey Sword of Saint Peter seized from confessor and priest to Queen Henrietta Maria, the seditious priest Father Robert Philip. While the legend passed down through the Church of Saint Peter and Saint Paul in Churchstanton may be old and of some fidelity to members of your parish, it cannot be connected to the sword once in the possession of the priest Robert Philip. Further, the same sword was proven to be fraudulent upon investigation at Oxford University. The steel blade was not made of Damascus steel, Judean, or Holy Land construction. Close examination determined the sword to be old but of Viking origin. Indeed, the box made for the sword was of more value, and possibly Holy Land construction with Cyprus wood clad in silver with embossed gold crosses overlaid on the cover. This is consistent with relics and supposed ancient objects given by papal envoys as a reward in lieu of gold for the service of the English Catholics acting to restore Catholic rule in Great Britain.

I would urge you and the good Christians of Churchstanton to beware of the pitfalls of relics. Past abuses of misplaced faith: greed in the guise of income generated by pilgrims; money or influence for so-called custodians; trading on the simple faith of the innocent.

In your service,

Robert Curtis

Earl of Montclair

Inquirer General to His Majesty King Charles

"Do you know what this means, Ike?"

Ike's mind was elsewhere. *That old sword box, could it be? The heavy, tarnished, blackened silver with gold crosses. And the inscription, 'The Sword of Saint Peter' – could it be the same? Dad's family stories? Could we be descendants of this Robert Curtis? The clippings—there was a story…"* I'm sorry, Rose. What does it mean to you?"

"It means the Glastonbury Abbey legend—the sword is still out there! The sword, and if the sword, then perhaps the grail is also still out there. Better, they may still be somewhere here, in Churchstanton!"

Ike nodded. "That's true. Rose, if you have the time, there's a legend I'd like to share with you. The story of an American Cavalier."

"Your story, Ike? The Curtis family story? I'd love to hear it."

"Yes. Care to walk with me and listen? I seem to organize my thoughts better when I walk."

Rose laughed. "That's your good English blood!"

Ike looked out the window. "Cloudy. Looks like rain."

"We English are a nation obsessed with walking. We walk everywhere regardless of the weather. And if we are in a hurry, we ride a bicycle. I promise you I won't melt."

Outside, Rose took Ike's arm. "Take your time. I'm happy just to walk alongside you."

Ike sighed deeply, turned, and smiled at Rose. "The story, is, as I recall from my grandfather's telling—Dad never spoke of it—that we descend from English aristocracy. The Royal Governor of Virginia encouraged, recruited really, young men from noble families, educated, ambitious 'gentlemen,' with promises of land and favorable opportunities, to settle and invest in Virginia. With the financial backing of their families, they created an educated upper class to capitalize, guide, and develop vast new lands. Not just farms or plantations, more than tobacco and lumber, I'm speaking of mineral wealth, trade, and everything needed to monetize the abundant land and resources. These elite barons without titles were granted rights to develop and govern the colony. One of these privileged elites was James Curtis, said to be the younger twin brother of an Earl. The story is he established the practice—whether in honor of himself or the family, I do not know—of alternating the first-born names of Earl and Montclair. The Earl inherited with his title control of a Trading Company. Nothing grand, but successful in moving dairy and vegetables from the continent to England. James Curtis was established with twenty acres of land—a requirement to vote in Virginia—a house, wharf, and warehouse in Alexandria, Virginia, and opened a shop trading tobacco for English finished goods."

Rose replied, "That's nothing to be ashamed of. You should be proud of both brothers. The Earl for establishing his brother and James for taking a risk in the New World."

"The whole aristocracy thing didn't sit well with my dad or grandfather. And the story gets worse."

"Slaves?" Rose asked.

"Thank goodness, no. There was an agreement between the brothers that no Curtis would ever own or engage in the slave trade. To their credit, they were strong abolitionists. The problems came later. James couldn't make a go of it in the tobacco trade. There was the problem of competition with established traders, and everything to do with tobacco was heavily dependent on slaves. Not just the plantation slaves, but the tobacco rollers...."

"Rollers."

"That's right. Tobacco was packed into hogsheads—barrels rolled down the roads, 'rolling roads,' to the warehouses and wharves. The field slaves, the rollers, the warehousemen, all the labor was performed by slaves, and James just could not find enough freemen to compete. So, he looked for something else—ship repair. He began repairing the few family ships he struggled to fill. And he convinced some of the crewmen determined to find a new life in Virginia to stay and work. Soon, he found a new opportunity in boat building. Not ships but barges, and eventually canal boats."

"And so began the family calling. Ike, everything you have said so far sounds like a success story. It echoes what I said about the best of the aristocracy in England. I don't see how it got any worse."

"They bought into it—the whole Virginia gentleman, the noble cavalier. They could have gone north, where skill and hard work mattered more than inheritance, and where slavery did not choke off the opportunity of free men of common birth to build a just society. For generations, the Curtis' remained in Virginia, marrying their social equals, having made peace with slavery—not participating directly but benefitting nonetheless, and then there was the church...."

"Ah, your anger with the church and God."

"My problems with God are mine alone. I will not blame

others for what I have done myself. No, I come from a long line of good Episcopalians—Anglicans. James Curtis' grandson, another Montclair, pledged to build churches in Virginia. One was near the Falls of the Potomac River. He was working with the canal company, building and repairing canal boats as well as canal lock gates. More devout than astute, Montclair Curtis mortgaged his house and the business for his mission. Now, I never understood how or why, but his son, Earl, was forced to flee Virginia, having lost his home and business to the Episcopal Church. Yesterday I received a box of letters and clippings from my father. Old and yellowed heirlooms of the past. I haven't gone through them but today, the letter, the silver box of the sword of Saint Peter, well, I've seen it. It's in my father's house."

"And you think answers may be found in this box of letters."

Ike looked into Rose's trusting eyes and whispered, "I hoped you would go through them with me to see if there is a connection. You give me hope that somehow, God has worked something good through their lives, as you say, blessings for generations to come."

CHAPTER 11
TARGET ARGENTEUIL

Arguing that the MI6 mission could impact Operation Oaktree only two days later, Langley obtained clearances for the Oaktree team to attend the photographic analysis briefing for the MI6 mission against the Argenteuil Aircraft factory. One by one, RECON analysis officers briefed in detail the German positions and troop movements in the Paris suburb. After an hour of tedious analysts briefing, it was decided there was no apparent change to the factory's defense status. The lights in the room went on, and without introduction, a man in a drab business suit stepped to the podium. "This is a Special Operations Executive mission. SOE operatives work with the resistance in irregular warfare, sabotage, and assassinations. It's the dirty side of warfare but necessary, nonetheless. SOE will do our job on the ground. We depend upon MI6 and MI9 to give us the best intelligence and to get us in and out. My men have trained hard for this mission. Don't let them down."

Colonel Z went to the podium. "Gentleman, the RECON agrees with the reports from Shepherd and Lady Liberty..."

Val Williams leaned close and whispered in Ike's ear, "An American, Virginia d'Albert-Lake. She can be trusted above all others."

Colonel Z pounded the podium. "Did I hear a name? I will not have the name of a senior officer in Paris compromised. If the identity of Lady Liberty is spoken of again outside this room and without my permission, the offender will spend the rest of the war in the darkest dungeon in Britain. Is that understood? Now, as I was saying, Shepherd's and Lady Liberty's sources within the Paris headquarters of the Commandant of Paris, the Abwehr, and the French Gestapo report no recent arrests of resistance or evidence of heightened interest in the factory. The operation is greenlighted."

Ike stood and said, "Colonel Z, since Flight 545 has provided the RECON and is experienced in agent extractions..."

"We have an extraction plan, Major. But thank you for your offer."

"Yes, sir, but the brief I just witnessed revealed a very fluid enemy troop deployment. I believe the 545 can provide real-time reconnaissance and emergency alternative extraction capability."

"Just what are you recommending, Major?"

"Well, sir, we will have eyes over Normandy anyway, a Supermarine Spitfire. Good range, experienced pilot. I can send him south over Argenteuil and have the Beech Expeditors waiting over the channel."

"Attack aircraft over the target will send the nazis to the shelters. What's one more spitfire?"

"The 545 Spitfire can come in low and slow, extending

range and time over the target—your eyes on scene, and RECON for a wider enemy response. Your attack aircraft will be focused on the factory. Extraction will be at risk. On-scene coordination may prevent another deadly ambush."

Colonel Z nodded. "Make it happen, Major. Group Captain Hastings will provide the frequencies and call signs."

On the ride back to Churchstanton, Ike asked Langley, "The man from SOE? And this American woman in Paris, I'm surprised both Williams and Labrosse know her."

"Yes. Virginia d'Albert-Lake. Runs the Comet Line in Paris. Her husband is in the resistance. His mother is British, and his father is French. He fought with the French Army until their surrender. Williams and Labrosse made their way through Paris with her help. As for the SOE gent, all I can tell you is we call them all the Baker Street Irregulars. Anything more is need-to-know."

Ike squinted and turned to Langley. "The Comet Line? The 'helpers' are unarmed. How can…why rely on a Comet Line helper for intelligence on an armed resistance mission?"

"The d'Albert-Lakes, husband, and wife have been tested and vetted. He's a senior in the resistance, and she is in the escape lines. They play a dangerous game seeking out the informant."

"You mean the traitor."

"As for why a helper and not the resistance team only? The two teams were connected through the *hebergeurs* for the betrayed SOE insertion. The d'Albert-Lakes have been the exception for separation that could not be avoided. We can't undo the past, but the future must be separating escape line operations from armed resistance."

Ike shook his head. "Seems to me the same relationship as MI6 and MI9."

Langley exhaled a plume of blue-gray smoke, tapped out his cigarette in the ashtray, and said, "You're beginning to put things together."

Langley dropped Ike and Dorothy off at the 545 Headquarters. Flight Lieutenant Marley greeted them as they entered. "Major, you are to address the men at the "All Hands" meeting in fifteen minutes."

Ike scratched his head. "I don't recall scheduling an all hands?"

"No, sir. I scheduled it. It's on the Plan of the Day if you read it. It's time you told the men why they are now in Special Duty Flight 545 and briefed them on the mission of the 545. You wanted an Executive Officer; well, it's my job to see your orders and the mission of the 545 carried out. No airman attached to the 545 sees you without going through me, and well, it's your responsibility, not mine, to define our mission and share your vision for the unit."

Ike stared at Marley, then turned to Dorothy. She smiled. "My Number One, or XO to you yanks, is right. Thank goodness I'm not the only one who wants to see this unit operate in proper fashion."

Marley saluted in the palm-out British fashion. After Ike returned with a quick palm-down American salute, Marley said, "Right then, Special Duty Flight 545 will stand for inspection in front of the Hangar at 1400 hours and hear remarks by the Flight Commander." As he turned for the door, he quipped, "Perhaps

Section Officer Barkley can teach you a proper British salute."

Ike laughed. "You're a good pilot, Marley, and I expect you'll do well as XO but don't expect me to give up my citizenship. I'm yank through and through. Get used to it."

"I wouldn't have it any other way, sir."

Ike trooped the line, exchanging comments with the men as he inspected. He made a point of learning the names of the few men he hadn't met, asking them about their duties and their RAF experience. When he finished, he returned Marley's salute. Marley ordered "Parade Rest," as Ike turned to face them. "At ease, men." Ike began. "If you don't recognize the uniform, I'm Major Curtis. US Army Air Corps. Not M. I. Curtis or M. Isaac Curtis, but Ike Curtis to those who know me. And you men of the 545 will get to know me well. It's how I work. I respect the chain of command and expect you to use it. But I like to get my information firsthand when I can. Now, the XO, that is, my Number One, has his way of doing things, and I expect you won't cross him. We need your focus on our mission, not on disciplinary actions. Mission. What is Special Duty Flight 545, and why in hell is a Yank in Command? Most of you knew me as the RECON officer here at Churchstanton. Well, that's why me. RECON is why we were chosen. But a special kind of RECON. You are becoming familiar with new technology, infrared cameras, and film. That, too, is on me, but not the mission of the 545. We have been set aside from the Group for something special, something that will require new skills and tactics.

This is where I'm supposed to say my door is open, but it is no secret that Section Officer Barkley and I are frequently off base..."

Someone shouted, "Aye, off for secret briefings. We're good to go with what we need to know, sir."

Ike smiled. "As you say." Turning to Marley, Ike continued. "So, yes, my door is open when I'm here, but the Number One speaks for me when I'm out."

Ike turned around and pointed at the aircraft in a row on the edge of the runway. "Our aircraft, our tools. Expensive. Hard to replace. But even harder to replace are our pilots. Hell, we can build planes far faster than we can train pilots. And experienced pilots—why they're worth their weight in gold—the true treasure. The 545 is the only unit in the Allied Air Forces solely dedicated to assisting in recovering our downed pilots in Nazi-held territory. So, RECON, yes, but RECON to aid the thousands of brave French men and women escorting our pilots and escaped prisoners of war back here, to England, to rejoin the fight. Primarily RECON, but not only. The 545 will provide agent insertion and extraction flights into France—we'll get in and get out in slow, unarmed, unescorted aircraft. And before you complain, let me remind you that the French 'helpers' escorting our men are unarmed. Hell, even armed, these planes can't put up much of a fight anyway, so stealth and strategy must be our weapons."

Ike paused and looked at the pilots standing in front of him. Each man had proven himself. Ike looked to the men behind the pilots, to the mechanics, technicians, and clerks. "All of you are essential. I know I can count on everyone here. But it's not me you're serving. It's them. Our brothers are trapped in occupied territory—we do it for them. Any questions?"

One of the mechanics spoke up. "Major, we received

sponsons—seaplane floats for water landings. I'd like to set up a shop at a ramp, as we discussed."

"Right. I'll provide that to you. But it begs another question. Security. Everything we do will be on a need-to-know basis. And nothing you do is ever to be discussed outside of this unit. Not in town, not in the mess hall, and not in the Officer's Mess. It's a dangerous game we play. Many of our downed pilots are at risk this very day because of a leak—our men at risk, and brave French and Belgian helpers are dead or in prison. I want every one of our pilots to return. But a leak risks more than our pilots—scores of others in France depend on us exercising scrupulous security. If there is one thing you take away with you today, it is security. Now. get back to work. Tomorrow's mission has all our planes in the air. Pilots report directly to the OPS Room."

Ike walked off. Marley shouted, "Attention." The men smartly came to attention. Marley called out. "Dismissed," and the men returned to their duties.

In the Operations Room, Ike gave the briefing. Pointing to the map, he said, "Argenteuil—an aircraft factory. A joint MI6 - French Resistance target. Our job is RECON and to get our SOE team out."

Marley asked, "Who gets them in?"

Ike replied, "They've been in three days. Parachuted, scouting the factory and the extraction sites."

"Sites, sir?"

"Yes, three designated, so I've assigned the three Expeditors and the Lysander, each to an extraction site. But we'll come to that. Marley, you will need every drop of fuel you can carry. In fact, each of you will top off fuel at RAF Hawkinge. Dover to Argenteuil is 160 nautical miles. I want the Spitfire armed. I know that will reduce fuel, but after an initial raid by two Lancasters breaking off from a mission to Cologne, you will be the only armed aircraft we have. You are there to be eyes first, defense of our team second, and self-defense if needed. I don't want you chasing after targets of opportunity. Our ground team depends on the air raid to send the Nazis to their shelters, where the resistance will plant anti-personnel bombs. They will also detonate explosives inside the factory, destroying all heavy equipment as well as all aircraft. The mission is to leave the factory a total loss."

Marley spoke, "Perhaps a strafing run following the bombing to encourage evacuation?"

"My thoughts as well. I'll leave that to your discretion, depending on what you see. The anti-aircraft gun placements should be taken out, but you'll have to judge for yourself. Now, these are the extraction sites. The Lancasters will bomb at H hour. The H hour plus one landing site is here, a hayfield outside Sartrouville. Expeditor 1 will circle the site and flash the Morse landing signal, K, King. and will not land without the proper reply, P, Pip. The field will be lit with the usual three hand torches. Wheels down at the first torch. No lights until below twenty feet. Then belly light only. That should be enough to put some light on the terrain."

The Expeditor 1 pilot responded. "I'd like to take two passes before H hour plus 1. Won't linger, just wide and slow surveillance. Check the roads for traffic."

Ike nodded. "Agreed. Good idea for the alternate sites

two and three, as well. Site two is here near La Borda; your signal is A, Ace, and the response is Q, Queen. Site three is here, the lawn of a chateau at Le Valmartin, signal F, Freddie, response, E, Edward. Sites two and three will be ordered depending on Nazi ground deployments or delays. Site two is H hour plus 1.5, and site three is H hour plus 3."

A pilot asked, "If they're late, how long do we wait?"

"No more than 15 minutes, but if you see a Nazi greeting party drop a flare to warn our team and return to base. Now, the Lysander, you're to wait at Hawkinge for orders. Resistance will provide a radio confirmation of an improvised extraction plan. Any questions?"

Marley spoke. "Major, we've only flown over Argenteuil and these sites once...."

Ike cut him off, "That's intentional. Our ground team is nervous about leaks as it is. Rightfully, they worry about tipping off the Germans. Paris has not been bombed; this must look like a target of opportunity by returning Lancasters. Paris remains off-limits to the RAF, this operation is not an RAF bombing mission, it's approved as resistance sabotage support. We don't want any French civilian casualties. You've all seen the photographs. Know where the shelters are as well as the guns and factory."

The pilots made notes, and a soft buzz of conversation filled the room. Ike banged his pointer against the lectern. Gentlemen, the H hour is 0100 GMT tomorrow. You are to arrive at RAF Hawkinge to top off fuel by 1800. Flight Lieutenant Benchley, I will ride along with you to Hawkinge. Gentlemen, you have planes to get in the air. Dismissed."

After the pilots left, Dorothy looked at Ike and said, "You're going to Hawkinge, not the mission Operations Room?"

Ike nodded. "You're going to the OPS Room. I want to be in Hawkinge just in case."

"But if the Lysander is needed, there won't be room for you and the team."

"We'll have returned aircraft, refueled, and I want to be able to improvise. Call it initiative."

CHAPTER 12
NIGHT OWLS OVER FRANCE

Ike walked the line of his small squadron as they topped off fuel tanks at RAF Hawkinge. He stopped to talk to Marley in front of his Spitfire. "I won't object if you add more ordnance."

Marley nodded. "I can add a couple of 250-pound bombs. Fuel shouldn't be a problem. Could make an impact."

"Do it. If you can get in low. Try and place them in the offices at the west end of the factory beneath the tower. I want the Nazis out of the building one way or the other. Let the resistance take out the aircraft and factory."

Marley grinned. "This should prove a welcome change from routine surveillance!"

A half-hour past midnight, Ike sat in the radio room at Hawkinge. One of the radios was tuned to the 545's operations frequency. Marley's voice interrupted the static. "Barn Owl, this is Night Owl One. I've completed my first pass. Enemy movements near sites 1, 2, and 3. Repeat enemy presence and movement in all three sites. No enemy movement in the vicinity of the target. Moving to rendezvous with our heavyweight friends."

At 0100 Marley called again. "Lancaster bombs away. Ground personnel making their way to shelters. Explosion. One bomb, now a second and third hit the factory. Several aircraft in front of hangar destroyed. Wide pattern. Most bombs missed. Explosion at end of the field—one gun emplacement destroyed. Two Lancasters safely away. I'm going in. Stay with me Barn Owl."

Ike waited. It seemed an eternity, but only ninety seconds passed. "Barn Owl, Night Owl One, bombs away in a low pass. Two hits on the tower and office wing. Strafed the remaining gun emplacement, climbing. Lots of flak can make another pass, but their fire is closing in."

"Night Owl One, any explosions from the shelters or inside the factory from the ground team?"

"Negative. Wait. Explosions in the factory. And now the fuel tanks. Nothing from the shelters, over."

"Well done, Night Owl One. Hope you got some good pictures for us. Bring her home, refuel, and rearm."

"Roger, returning to refuel and rearm. Expect better film than any newsreel! Night Owl One, out."

Ike breathed a sigh of relief. *He's made it so far. Please, God, get him home safe. What took so long inside? And the shelters remain. Something went wrong.*

At 0150, the Expeditor assigned to site one called in. "Barn Owl, this is Night Owl Two. Completed circuit of site. Enemy pouring into site one from three directions. Repeat, ambush being set, over."

"Night Owl Two, in five minutes, drop a flare over the

center of the site. Take evasive action, circle site and droppings flares as you go. Confirm and return to the barn."

Ike waited. *Is it too much to ask an unarmed light plane to circle an ambush? I have to consider the ground team. But then they must know they're compromised.*

Ten minutes later, the call came in. "Barn Owl, this is Night Owl Two. Flares away. No indication of ground team. Returning to base. Night Owl Two out."

Night Owl Two's sign-off was followed immediately by Night Owl Three. "Barn Owl. Night Owl Three. Copied Night Owls One and Two. Passed over site two. Another ambush. Request orders."

Ike replied, "Night Owl Three at H plus One Twenty-Five, circle site two and drop flares. Don't linger, return to base."

"Roger, Barn Owl, execute warning and return to base."

Ike called the last Expeditor. "Night Owl Four, did you copy others? Over."

"Barn Owl, this is Night Owl Four copied. Will comply, warning flares at H plus 2:55."

Ike did not need coffee to keep him awake. At 0340, Night Owl Four radioed, "Approaching site 3. We got company; a 109 approaching from the east."

"Evade. Turn back. The ground team must know they've been compromised. Make for the coast. Will prepare for sea rescue."

Ike turned to a radioman and said, "Notify air-sea rescue, RECON plane in trouble. Prepare for a channel rescue. Coordinates to follow."

Like all good RECON pilots, Flight Lieutenant Benchley

made a note of possible landing fields while enroute. As the 109 caught sight of the Expeditor and gave chase, the small plane dropped low, looking for safety in the dark shadows of the forest below. *Five more minutes. If I can lose him in five minutes, I have a chance.* The 109 took up position on Night Owl Four's tail. At nearly twice the speed, he would close quickly. The night sky was scattered with clouds. A crescent moon still provided good light to the Nazi fighter pilot. The Messerschmidt closed. Soon, his guns would be in range.

Benchley prayed, "Save me, Jesus." And then the moon slid behind a cloud. The small plane crossed a line of trees, and a small meadow opened in front of it. "Thank you, Lord!" And Benchley cut his engine, turned on his belly light just long enough to sight the ground, and silently dropped his plane onto the meadow. He rolled to the edge, well in the shade of tall trees, and waited. He listened. He heard the engines of the Messerschmitt 109 as it passed over him. He waited and prayed. Forty minutes he waited. He heard and saw nothing. He cautiously started his engine. He quickly sized the field and taxied to the end. Back in the air, he flew low at full speed northwest to the coast. Once over land, he radioed in. "Barn Owl, this is Night Owl Four. I'm over the channel; I'll be home in half an hour. Could use clean pants and a shower."

Ike breathed a deep sigh of relief. "Good to hear from you, Night Owl Four; missed your sweet voice."

"I didn't want to play their game, so I dropped out and took a rest. All's well, over."

"Bring her home, Night Owl Four. A hot shower waiting and a warm bunk with your name on it."

Ike went back to the landline with Captain Langley waiting on the other end. "While you were off, Ike, another report from the SOE ground team. Resistance saw the flares—and knew they were compromised when the Jerries were waiting inside the plant, and one of the resistance was a no-show. They adjusted, took out the welcoming party, and completed the mission. They're already working on another extraction plan. When can you be back?"

Ike replied, "I'll wait here. The sooner they get out, the better. The 545 is better here for now. I've got a plane waiting, and the Spitfire is armed for escort."

"What about the fourth bird?"

"Just reported in. Hopefully, your ground team will solve their security leak before extraction. My men are not equipped against anti-aircraft guns or German fighters. Stealth and secrecy."

"You're preaching to the choir, Ike. Hold on Ike, I'm getting an update… how soon can you get your bird to Poissy?"

"45 to 50 minutes. I've got the Lysander. Just give us 600 feet."

"The Lysander? That wasn't in the plan."

"Initiative. What's the site?"

"A small island in the Seine, Ilot Blanc. Little more than a sandbar."

Ike pulled out the map. "Hold the line while I get my bird in the air."

Ike called the Lysander pilot. "Take off immediately. Course to Poissy. I'll give you the coordinates in the air."

Five minutes later, Night Owl One was also in the air,

racing ahead to RECON the site ahead of the Lysander.

As the ungainly Lysander took off, Ike returned to the phone. "Night Owl Five is in the air. Tell the ground team 45 minutes. Night Owl One is scouting ahead. The signals are H, Harry, response U, Uncle. Standard three lights on the field two hundred yards apart. Wheels down at first light, hand torches only, vertical mount. Let's keep this phone line open until the operation is over."

Ike called his planes in the air. "Night Owl One and Night Owl Five. Coordinates Queen124 Yellow 361."

The pilots unfolded their maps, found the coordinates, and quickly saw the small island across the river from Poissy. Marley in Night Owl One acknowledged first. "Will make a pass before establishing top cover."

Night Owl Five radioed, "Copy One. Will report when I have eyes on the landing site."

Thirty minutes later, Night Owl One called in. "Site is clear. No enemy sighted. Climbing to top cover position."

Another ten minutes passed before Night Owl Five reported. "Barn Owl, have the island in sight. Couldn't you find anything shorter? Tell the ground team no need for three torches just torch one. Giving signal, over."

"Roger, Five, short landing, wheels down landing light only."

"Barn Owl, correct response received. Have three men in sight. Looks like two carrying one. Confirm. One man injured. Repeat, one man wounded. Touching down."

The wheels of the Lysander came down softly in the grass not ten feet beyond the upright flashlight. The pilot feathered the prop while two men struggled to lay a third bandaged man on the floor of the co-pilot seat. Then one jumped in the empty co-pilot seat, and the other crouched on the shelf behind the pilot. Five minutes later, Lysander was in the air.

"Barn Owl, Night Owl Five. Three passengers aboard. Need ambulance for injured man."

"Roger, Night Owl Five, Get him home safe."

This is Night Owl One. I'll keep a close watch over you all the way home."

Ike picked up the phone. "We got them. Three men, one injured. Will have an ambulance waiting."

CHAPTER 13
STARTING OVER

James Langley led the brief at Otterhead House. "Colonel Z sends his congratulations for your efforts on a most successful operation. Production of the Dewoitine D-520, France's best fighter aircraft, has been halted. The factory and all aircraft on the field were destroyed. And thanks to intelligence provided by Emile Dewoitine, safely in the States, the ground team destroyed the special basement bunker, killing the Nazi over-lords and collaborators. Casualties for the resistance and the SOE ground team were light."

Ike interrupted. "Most successful? The resistance was penetrated, and the extraction sites were each an ambush waiting to happen. And tell the dead French and our wounded agent that casualties were light. Most successful? Damn lucky, I would say. Oaktree is two days away. Are we to drop our men into France knowing their lives are in the hands of a compromised French Resistance leadership?"

Val Williams chimed in, "The Major has a point. How can we trust the resistance?"

Langley raised his voice. "Must I remind you that success

is determined by results? The resistance and our agents know and accept the risk. Yes, there was a breakdown. The Nazis knew we were coming. There's always some unknown, some unplanned obstacle. But overcoming obstacles is decisive in any operation. So, yes, most successful. Just as the 545 adapted, overcame three obstacles at ambush sites, and safely extracted our men, it was most successful. Now, let me address the infiltrator. He has been identified as Jean Masson…"

Dorothy asked, "Is he the same man? There were witnesses…"

James Langley replied, "Yes, the traitor to our failed ground team insertion. Likely an alias, but witness reports lead us to believe they are the same man."

Dorothy again spoke for all. "But how?"

Langley stepped away from the lectern. "Bad luck and bad vetting. Masson, AKA Captain Jaques. Claimed membership with resistance in Belgium. Said his cover was blown and moved to France to take up the cause again. Joined the Paris team before his description was widely passed. MI6 thinks Masson believed all the resistance team at the insertion were killed and saw no need to change his appearance. Regardless, his identity was challenged in Paris. The resistance did vet him. Jean Masson is a common name and was unconnected to the alias Captain Jacques he used in the SOE insertion. Despite similarities in age, hair color, and general build, Masson convinced the resistance that he was in Paris when the SOE team was betrayed. Unsatisfied, they tested him. Masson led the attack on a checkpoint for a truck he was told carried escaping allies but was filled with armed resistance fighters. Jean Masson was waiting for a larger target or a deeper penetration. At the factory, Jean Masson never made his planned entry. Armed nazis were waiting. Surprised but not unprepared, the resistance had one great advantage over the defenders: no need to avoid damaging machinery and aircraft. Their grenades and explosives overwhelmed the guards."

Val Williams asked, "Where is this Jean Masson now?"

"Whereabouts unknown. But his description has been passed, and no new recruits are to be accepted until further notice. It's the best the resistance can do. But I would remind you that the French are very good at finding and executing traitors."

Langley looked at his team in the room. "With the infiltration of the SOE insertions and now two MI9 operations, we can no longer be certain that the landing support in Britanny has also not been compromised. I'm afraid Oaktree is postponed until the extent of the breach is known."

Val Williams replied, "We believe there are at least one hundred airmen being hidden—waiting for this operation to bring them home. You speak of risks; Ray and I are two men. They are many and growing in number every day. Have you considered how hard it is to feed and house and clothe this many men? Let alone hide them from the Nazis and their collaborators?"

"Val, I know you and Ray are ready. But it is not just those waiting but the scores, perhaps thousands more to come. And not just our airmen, but the French willingly and bravely who risk their lives—we owe it to them as well."

Ray asked, "How long do we wait?"

BELLS OF REDEMPTION

"It's difficult to run counterespionage in France from England. Weeks, perhaps months. We will use the time to refocus our planning. And one more item, Major, the Hudson we lost last month will be replaced. Two Lockheed Hudson Mark IIIs are being assigned to Special Duty Flight 545. Keep up the good work, and you may become a squadron. Plan on parachute insertions and equipment drops until the situation on the ground is settled. Williams and Labrosse, you will practice—you will become experts at low-level night parachuting."

Langley paused. He picked up a pointer and walked to the map. "Normandy is out, Too many recent operations, too many betrayals. Brittany. Major, I want photographs of every field and meadow in Brittany. I want to know the position of every Nazi road checkpoint, every tank and anti-aircraft gun, every depot and barracks. Concentrate on the coast and ten miles inland. Find every cove, every German patrol boat, and the number in their crews. Oaktree is all about building a sea route to England. We're building a new line with new checkpoints and new leadership on the ground. Val and Ray, no contacts with past helpers, resistance or any MI6 agents. Separate and new. Understood? We've been given time to regroup and replan. Make the most of it."

On the ride back to RAF Churchstanton, Ike's mind raced. "We'll need to get Marley going on the RECON flight patterns. We'll need everything we've got to blanket the Brittany coast with day and night photographs, both high-altitude, high resolution, and infrared. The new Lockheed Hudsons—get the mechanics going on mounting cameras as soon as they arrive—and any mods they require for parachuting.

Their bombing days are over. Then call a meeting of the pilots, no reason not to tell them we've been ordered to RECON Brittany. We won't say why. Their good men, they won't ask. Oh, and send for Sergeant Major Brown, the chief mechanic. I want him to get going on the floatplane conversion. Going to be a long night. I want the 545 to hit the ground running on this."

Dorothy wrote as Ike spoke. "Perhaps Captain Langley can arrange an MI6 intelligence brief on Breton fishermen among the resistance. They may be of help if you intend to employ the seaplane option. And contact the Royal Navy regarding submarines and boat approach lanes."

"Good thinking. Yes, get on it."

Dorothy finished her notes and looked out the window before turning to Ike. "I must call Rose and tell her we won't make dinner and…"

Ike sighed. "Rose. I forgot. I promised her. No, I won't cancel. I'll get the XO going on operational planning with the pilots. That is the most critical and urgent task. You and the XO can set up the others. Tell Rose I might be late, but to keep the kettle on."

Dorothy turned to look out the window again, so Ike could not see the smile on her face. *I think he likes her.* "There's no need to be polite, Ike. Rose will understand. I mean, go if you really want to. Marley and I can handle things after the pilot's meeting. It's up to you."

"No, I promised her, and as you say, I need to trust my staff—good people. Rose would be disappointed; I mean, she has so much enthusiasm for her research. Besides, I always seem refreshed and think more clearly after spending time with Rose and your uncle Hugh, as well."

Dorothy laughed. "Oh yes, don't disappoint Uncle Hugh. Ike, Rose is special. Don't hurt her."

Ike turned to Dorothy. "She is. No. No, I don't ever want to hurt her."

CHAPTER 14
DINNER FOR TWO

It was after dark when Ike knocked on the door to Rose's cottage. The door swung open before Ike completed his knock. A smiling Rose greeted him. "Dottie rang me up and said you'd be late. I hope you're hungry, supper is waiting."

Ike blushed, "You needn't have waited for me. I brought the clippings you asked about. Umm, something smells good!"

"Well, don't just stand there. You can tell me all about them at dinner. Please, everything is ready."

Ike followed Rose to the kitchen. "Can I help?"

"Just sit down. Water, cider, or ale?"

Ike smiled. "Washington State is known for its apples. Cider, by all means."

The table was set for two. Ike sat opposite the kitchen. Rose wore a worried smile as she brought out a steaming bowl. "Stew. We call it 'Everything In It Stew.' It's never quite the same twice. I hope you like it."

Ike nodded. "So everything is subjective?"

Rose chuckled, "That's bad even by English standards. But today, it's minced beef and a little spam, along with cabbage, turnips, carrots, leeks, onions, Marmite, and Dottie's stewed tomatoes over mash. Waste not, want not."

Ike tasted the stew and nodded. "My mom was known to make a close cousin, minus the Marmite."

Rose reached for the folder at the end of the table. "Can I see them, please? I want to know everything about you. Americans are so different, and your family crossed the continent. You must come from pioneers or cowboys!"

Ike tasted the cider. "That's more than apple juice! I should take your cider in trade for my bourbon!"

"We learn to make do, Ike," Rose said as she flipped through the pages. "Do you know there is a journal here, from a Montclair Cutis, dated 1898?"

"That would be my grandfather. He settled in Tacoma before Dad established the ferry in Gig Harbor. Gramps built boats for the 'Mosquito Fleet,' the small steamboats that plied the waters of Puget Sound carrying passengers or cargo. Western Washington is divided by Puget Sound's many bays and inlets. No bridges and few roads. Everything moves on the water. Dad never let Grandpa tell his stories. 'Don't go putin' foolish notions in the boys' heads. They'll do fine standin' on their own two feet.' Grandpa would smile and say, 'Nothin' to be ashamed of. They come from good stock.' Then he would wink and say, 'Don't you boys worry. Someday, I'll write it all down.'"

Ike looked off in memory. "I never did understand why Dad didn't want to hear the stories. Maybe he heard them all too many times before. Hmm. And now he sends them to me?"

Ike sighed. "I didn't come here to sit while you read tall tales. I brought something. The flashlight, that is, if you found any more old vellums."

Rose closed the file. "If you don't mind, I'll save this for later. Finish eating. I do have some more records on vellum. Please, let me try the infrared on them."

Rose cleared the table and returned with a box of documents. She switched off the light and pulled out the first document. Under the infrared light, dark letters appeared. Rose mumbled in Latin as she read, then without looking, she put the page down. "Rents of Abbey lands from tenant farmers."

Ike asked, "Churchstanton or Glastonbury?"

"Good question. It doesn't say."

Rose pulled out another, then a third, "Same document continued. Must have erased a journal and used them in order."

Now Rose was able to quickly scan for the continued document. Seven or eight pages later, Rose said, "Here we go. This is different. Wait! It's a list of relics!"

"From where? Which monastery?"

"I'm reading. Yes! Yes! 'As to the chalice of Saint Joseph, the cup of the blood of Jesus...'"

Ike put his hand on Rose's hand, "What about the cup? Please go on!"

Rose lifted the page and turned it over. She reached for the next page, flashing the light as she scanned. Finally, she put the delicate vellum page down. "That's all. It was the last line; I have to find the next page. It must be here!"

Rose went through each document twice. The continuation page was not there. Ike asked, "The vicarage—are there any more vellums in the vicarage?"

"These are all I found, but there may be more

filed away."

Ike squeezed her hand. "Glastonbury. You must go there. Isn't that where Saint Joseph of Arimathea established the church and monastery."

"The monastery was destroyed. But perhaps the parish church. Can you come with me? Two of us can work faster, and perhaps the parish secretary would be willing to open their records to an American researching his family history."

"I'd love to go. But I don't see how I can get away any time soon,"

"Damn war," Rose mumbled.

"It's the damn war that brought us together." Ike sighed. "That's the first time I've heard you talk about the war. Of all the people I've met, you're the only one who doesn't seem obsessed with the war. When I close my eyes, I see you with a smile on your face, and I imagine you singing merrily as you research through musty files. You bring bright sunshine into a dark world, Rose Osbourne. A woman of passion and determination. How do you do it? How do you exude joy and happiness in all that you do?"

Rose smiled in the darkness. "Joy, yes. Happiness sometimes. They are very different. Happiness comes in moments. Feelings of peace and contentment, time spent with friends and loved ones. I find happiness is temporary. It can be taken away in an instant, just as Charles was taken from Dottie. But joy, oh yes, joy lasts beyond the moment. It keeps a permanent place in the heart. It is knowing, even when happiness has fled, that the connection, the love, remains and always will. I will never surrender my joy."

"Rose, you amaze me. Where do find such deep joy?"

"Well, I didn't find it in a book or in any of my research. It's not about knowledge, it's about love. I feel loved. Of course, Dottie, Papa, and Uncle Hugh love me, but I just know God loves me. To me, faith is trusting in love. I treasure the happy times, but my joy is always with me, just as the love I give and receive never wanes. God is sovereign, so my joy is steadfast.

The two sat silently in the dark, Ike's hand resting on Rose's. Ike patted her hand softly and said, "I suppose we're done with the infrared light for tonight. I really should take it with me. Rose said with a laugh, "We must be certain no spies are about," and she flashed it on and circled the room with its beam. She then tried to hand it to Ike, but the light fell from her hand and rolled on the table; the infrared beam pointed at Rose, illuminating her white silk blouse.
Ike froze for a moment before he turned his eyes away. He grabbed the light and turned it off.

Rose, too, was staring at the beam. She laughed. "It seems you had an eyeful."

Ike mumbled, "I'm sorry, I didn't… I mean… well, now I know how it penetrates Nazi silk camouflage."

Rose said, "Ike, every girl knows that the sun behind her reveals her legs through a cotton dress. Even so, won't wear a slip on a summer beach outing. Don't be embarrassed. I know you are a gentleman."

"Perhaps I should go."

"You'll come again? And bring the flashlight—for the documents, I mean."

Ike stood up. "Of course. Rose, I've been meaning to

ask you…"

"Ask we what? Ike, you can ask me anything."

"I'd like to see you."

"I thought we were…"

"No, I mean, see you not for searching old records. But like a guy sees a gal he likes. Dinner in a restaurant, a movie, a dance, a date."

Rose stood up. "I will count tonight as our first date. But only if I get a kiss good night."

Rose came close. Ike leaned over and tried a gentle kiss. Rose put her arms around his neck and pulled in tight. She moved her hands to the side of Ike's face and held onto his kiss. Neither wanted to let go. At last, their lips separated, and Rose buried her head in his chest. "Yes, I want to see you. I want to dance with you, walk with you, and make memories with you. Ike Curtis, there's already a place for you in my heart."

CHAPTER 15
WILTON PARK

Flight Lieutenant Nigel Marley was briefing Ike on the latest RECON photos of the Brittany Coast when Langley came in. "Making good progress, I hope."

Ike replied, "A bit more than 30 percent. A couple more weeks, and we can paper the mess hall with a 10-mile-wide photograph of Brittany."

Marley began to excuse himself, knowing Langley did not come without need-to-know intelligence for the CO. "I'll brief the men on today' targets…"

Langley interrupted, "Don't go far, Marley. You'll be receiving your standing orders soon. You'll be acting Flight Commander for a couple of weeks. The Major and his adjutant have been ordered on assignment."

Ike turned towards Marley and said, "Give us a couple of minutes, XO. I'll find you shortly in the OPS Room."

Marley nodded and left. Once the door closed, Ike asked, "On assignment?"

"You and Barkley are to report to MI9 Headquarters, Wilton Park, for intelligence, technical, logistics, and procedures briefings and training. Monday morning 0900, you meet with Colonel Z and Colonel Crockatt."

"Colonel Z, I know. But who is Colonel Crockatt?"

"Norman Crockett, Royal Scots. My boss, the head of MI9. Came over from MI6 and SOE."

Ike asked, "What about Oaktree?"

"Postponed indefinitely. The trail on Jean Masson has gone cold. The extent of the damage is unknown. The Abwehr may be sitting tight before moving against us."

Ike sighed. He turned to Dorothy, who was sitting quietly at her desk. "You heard the man. Open-ended orders to Wilton Park. Call the motor pool and arrange a car. Tell them at least two weeks. We can always extend. And ask my Number One to come back. I will need to address the men."

Langley returned Ike's stare. "Right. I'm off to Otterhead House. Must break the news to Williams and Labrosse. We'll talk before you go."

When Marley returned, Ike stood. "I suppose you have a need to know. Barkley and I are off to Wilton Park, MI9 briefings and training…"

Marley shook his head. "Need-to-know that you two are MI9? Worst kept secret in Churchstanton. I mean, it's what we do, isn't it?"

"Right. Well, let's not let it leave the unit. I will address the men in thirty minutes—let them know you'll be acting while I'm gone. Continue the RECON surveys of Brittany. And have Brown install the floats on a Beech Expeditor and the Lysander if you can work it into the schedule. I want the pilots to practice water takeoffs and landings. When you feel they're ready, I want night take-offs and landings. Sergeant Major Brown has the equipment and a hangar at Devonport, Plymouth. We've been given an operational reprieve. We'll make the best of it training."

Sunday morning found Ike in church seated between Rose and Dorothy. Hugh continued his sermon series on prayer. Ike's good mood vanished when his mind got stuck on a single point. Hugh mentioned briefly that one of the oldest and most effective prayers of the church, often included in the liturgy, was the simple line: "Lord Jesus, Son of God, have mercy on me, a sinner." *Mercy, not grace. Seems Pastors like to talk about grace— God's grace, His goodness, blessings, and love. But a prayer for mercy? Kind of puts me in my place. God knows I'm no saint. Who am I to sit between these good women? Mercy. Is that why He doesn't hear my prayers? Can't he see I need mercy? Or do I have a sin problem?*

Rose hooked arms with Ike as they filed out of the church. Walking to the vicarage, Rose smiled at Ike. "You look a thousand miles away. Didn't you enjoy our date last night? Or do you find church tiresome?"

Ike blushed a smile. "No, that isn't it. Last night was wonderful. Our time together makes me very happy. It's just that..."

"What? You can tell me. Please don't say you can't tell me what's bothering you."

"It's my prayers—if you can call them prayers. I don't trust God. I feel he abandoned Linda and me. And the guilt—he won't take away the guilt."

"Ike, I don't expect to be a replacement for Linda. I find

your enduring love as an endearing virtue."

"No, I know I can love you. Linda would want that. You've shown me her memory will always be safe."

"Why don't you ask Uncle Hugh? Despite all else, he has a deep faith and a loving heart. As a widower himself, he is sure to have wisdom in anger with God and overcoming loss."

Ike smiled. "I'll do that."

"Don't wait. I don't want you going off unhappy. I want to see you smile before you leave today."

At dinner, Rose asked, "Uncle Hugh, how do we pray properly? Do we even realize the effectiveness of our prayer."

Ike laughed. "I'm sure Rose's prayer life is fine. She was asking for me."

Hugh nodded. "Yes. We never finished this discussion. C. S. Lewis once asked, 'Do we pray that God will change our lives? Do we pray, asking for things we have no right to? God is immutable. He does not change. That's what makes him God.' Lewis used this example. 'Imagine you are in a small boat coming up to the shore. You use a boat hook to catch the shore and pull. Do you pull the shore towards you, or do you pull the boat to the shore?'

Hugh took a puff on his pipe. "Prayer is not pulling God to our will. It is the aligning of our will to the will of God. This is why we pray. It is a surrender to the will of God and a cooperation with that will."

Dottie asked, "Is it wrong to expect miracles in response to our prayer?"

Hugh shook his head. "No. Of course not. Yet miracles are more likely to come at the beginning of a Christian's walk or before conversion. It may seem counterintuitive, but as the Christian life proceeds, they become rarer. And the refusals, too, are more frequent. This is as it should be. Should not our faith and belief become stronger as we grow and mature in faith?"

Hugh paused and looked into Ike's eyes. "My advice to you, Ike, is when you feel God isn't listening, pray because you feel helpless. Pray because the need flows out of you all the time, waking and sleeping. It doesn't change God, it changes you."

Rose wondered aloud. "But unanswered prayer—I still don't understand."

Hugh replied, "Well, Rose, if the example of the Apostle Paul not losing his faith over unanswered prayer—his thorn in the flesh—does not satisfy you, consider the prayer of Jesus who begged the Father three times: 'this cup to be taken from me,' only to finally surrender to the Father. We have laid all our needs before him in the Lord's Prayer. He has them in hand. Paul prescribed an antidote for all our anxieties when he wrote: 'Finally brothers, whatever is true, honorable, just, pure, pleasing, commendable, excellent, and worthy of praise—turn your mind to these things.'"

Ike sighed. "Guilt is hard to overcome."

Hugh smiled. "Yes. But He can help you pull your boat ashore."

It was nearly 2 PM when Ike and Dorothy set out for Beaconsfield, Buckinghamshire, 150 miles east of Churchstanton, just north of London. Ike gladly let Dorothy drive. He marveled that the nation that ruled an empire never improved its roads.

He muttered as they made their way slowly in a single lane between tall hedges, "I do believe the last good road in England was built by the Romans!"

Dorothy replied, "The road is perfectly safe, why, anything more would be a waste of good land! Don't you worry, we'll be in Beaconsfield before the pub closes. Just keep the map open on your lap."

Ike moaned, "Wonderful! We'll be driving these cart paths in the dark!"

Dorothy changed the subject. "Ike, I'd like to say something about your conversation with Uncle Hugh—about unanswered prayer, which is if you don't mind."

"I don't mind, you were there, go ahead."

"Well, I just wanted to say perhaps you don't realize that God has answered some of your prayers. And they were good answers and more may soon be coming."

"What prayers has he answered?"

"The missions, for one. All our pilots returned safely even when they flew into ambushes—even when chased by Nazi planes they returned safely. You prayed for them—in your heart prayed they would make it, and they did. How many unarmed missions over enemy territory and not a single loss? That's God. And there's more..."

"What else?"

"There's your son, Earl, and your dad and Ole, they're safe, and healthy. They have become a family—there for each other with love and encouragement. Linda would be happy for them. They are blessed. God has blessed them in answer to the deepest desire of your heart."

Ike was quiet. Dorothy waited; a quick glance told her Ike was staring out the window. She knew her words touched him.

"You've won the heart of Rose, a very special woman. You cannot deny she is an answer to prayer—a blessing from God. It's not unheard prayers that burdens you, it's overcoming guilt. God has already dealt with your guilt. He carried it to the cross. It is no longer yours, but his. Let him take what is rightfully his."

Ike mumbled, "I wish He would."

Ike's ability with maps and Dorothy's patience in taking orders delivered them to Beaconsfield in little more than six hours. They enjoyed a hot supper at the inn.

The next morning, Ike and Dorothy were waiting in the paneled outer office when the adjutant's phone buzzed, and the door opened at precisely 0900. The adjutant lifted his head from the document he was reading and said, "The Colonel will see you now."

Lieutenant Colonel Norman Crockatt was seated at his desk. Another man stood looking out the window. "Curtis and Barkley, good that you could come. Major, you've met Colonel Z." Colonel Z did not turn around. "Right. Good work at the 545, but we expect better—with Oaktree on hold, it's a good time to catch up on training, policy, and equipment upgrades. Unfortunate that you did not have the benefit of the full course before joining the fray. There must be no doubt that while Special Duty Flight 545 reports to MI9, war does impose its constraints—your assets will be shared with MI6 and SOE. Your work—your special skills will serve the same, so it need not matter in execution."

Ike replied, "That fact has not been lost on us from the start. We're ready to do our part."

Crockatt continued. "I have set up a crash—excuse the expression, accelerated course based on your field experience. You will focus on enhanced RECON photo analysis, both black and white and infrared. Yes, we've been doing our homework in the lab and the field. Then a full brief on special equipment to be delivered to the field, and new identify friend or foe communications procedures, to be followed by need-to-know intelligence briefings."

Dorothy was surprised to hear herself interrupting. "Colonel, I'd like a briefing on field agent training for avoiding capture, finding support and communication links—and a briefing on the training given our airmen in case of parachuting into Nazi held territory."

Colonel Z turned around and joined the two other officers staring at Dorothy. She took a deep breath and tried to explain. "Familiarity with their training can only but help us better respond, improvise when an operation doesn't quite go as planned—taking the initiative, which can make or break these high-risk missions."

Colonel Z smiled. "We can do better than a briefing. I'll arrange for training and a field exercise for Section Officer Barkley."

Colonel Crockatt spoke. "One last item before you begin. You will notice a large number of German Officers here. They appear to have certain freedoms. You will be cordial and respectful of my 'guests.' They have been encouraged to be open and free to discuss their politics, loyalties, and military achievements. You must trust our method. You are not to discuss your mission but be willing to listen and debate lightly. The discourse should be respectful as two Oxford Dons. My officers are trained in this technique. But if you hear anything significant, please report it to my Number One."

Ike was surprised. "Does it work?"

Crockatt smiled. "Never underestimate the elite narcissism of a senior Nazi—it works like a charm! Given enough time, we may prepare a cadre of Germans to rebuild relations after this war is over." Colonel Crockatt stood up. "Right. You will start with Major Hutton in devices, while I arrange Barkley's field agent training posting. Major Christopher Clayton Hutton, "Clutty," to friends and coworkers, is tasked with devising escape devices for allied soldiers and airmen."

Outside Crockatt's office, Ike flashed a concerned look to Dorothy. "I know you want to understand what Charles has been trained to do, and other airmen and agents as well, but you heard Crockatt—he aims to put you in field agent training. Dorothy, you must be careful. Insist you seek only an understanding. Men like Colonel Z and Crockatt—they don't see you as a person. They can't allow themselves that luxury. You're an asset, only one of many—expendable. Remember the last SOE mission? Losses don't matter so long as the objective is successful."

Dorothy stiffened. "I know what I'm doing. I need to do this. I'll be fine."

Ike shook his head. "Please don't make me be the one to tell Charles that the woman he lived for—the one who made every trial worthwhile, is missing in France. You want to do this for Charles—think what your death would do to him. You are serving—needed where you are in the 545 Churchstanton. Don't be foolish."

Dorothy sighed. "I'll think about what you said."

CHAPTER 16
TOOLS OF THE TRADE

An adjutant found Ike and Dorothy waiting in the anteroom. "Colonel Crockatt suggests you avail yourself of the gardens and wait in the fancy at the end of the lake while your passes are prepared for your visit. Down the stairs, out the back entrance. Straight away, you will see the lake and the medieval castle fancy."

Ike stood up. "Right, the garden tour. They're probably deciding what to do with us. Leighton made it sound like they were anxious to see us."

Their footsteps rang as they descended the marble stairs and turned towards the rear garden entry. "Ike, we are dealing with spymasters. It's always a game. Just play along." Ike pushed the door ahead of Dorothy. "Ike, I know you're a gentleman, but remember, juniors get the door for their seniors."

"Yes, dear," Ike mocked. "Not much of a garden to be seen. Far less grand than Otterhead House and only a little less neglected. So that run-down ruin is a fancy? Looks like bomb damage to me."

"No, Ike. A fancy, it's built to look like a ruin—a private monument to ancient history, like might have been seen on the Grand Tour in Victorian times. Where's your sense of romance?"

"No offense, but London is now full of ruins, and I wouldn't call them fancy or romantic."

Walking around the lake, the path took them behind the fancy. Ike was surprised to see several bicycles leaning behind the back wall. As they reached the steps, a steel door opened in the rear foundation. A man poked his head out and called, "Major Curtis, Section Officer Barkley, this way, please."

They were led down a well-lit stairway descending three flights of stairs, where their escort hit a buzzer and turned a cypher lock. A massive door, as thick as a bank vault, slowly opened, and they entered a top-secret bunker. A young man in a lab apron stood smiling. "Welcome to the works. Major Hutton has been expecting you."

A man past middle age with thinning hair and penetrating blue eyes behind steel rimmed glasses walked impatiently across the room. "Major Curtis, I'm Hutton. Saw your use of infra-red in RECON. Got a bit ahead of yourself, Major. Many projects on infrared, not a top priority, you see, but good initiative, all the same."

Ike scowled, "Not a priority? Tell that to the agents landing in a Nazi trap."

"Yes, quite true in your limited view, and useful, of course. Sent it over to MI6, and photo reconnaissance. But my priority is aiding our men held prisoner or making their way through Nazi territory. Thousands of trained men. We need them. No, we must focus on the big three aids to our men: Map, compass, and food, and if I were to add a fourth and fifth, it would be safe drinking water, then clothes. Oh, we tinker with the odd escape device, saws, knives, signal mirrors, lockpicks, what have you. The key often isn't the device itself, but its packaging and delivery inside the prison or with our airmen. Come, let me show some of our standard issue."

Hutton led Ike and Dorothy to a room where maps were being screen printed on silk. "All of our pilots carry these silk maps. Cloth maps have obvious advantages: easy to fold to small size without creasing; silent to open and refold; easy to hide or wear in plain sight as a scarf or handkerchief. The problem was finding the right ink that wouldn't smear in fine printing—pectin added to the ink did the trick. We have maps of every country in Europe. We can print on both sides. They are relatively small scale, that is, large area so what detail we can show is all important. Rivers are a problem, so safe crossing points are prominent. Railroads are the fastest means of transport to helpers in Belgium or France."

Ike nodded. "Yes, I'm familiar with silk maps. I had no idea of the difficulties you overcame."

Hutton continued. "Notice over here we are working on large-scale maps for specific German POW camps. Much more information to get our men to safe transport. The maps are not the problem—it's getting them to the men. It's really the key to all our escape devices. Most are delivered by mail—hidden in packages from POW organizations."

Ike asked, "Surely, the Red Cross would not allow its work—its neutrality to be jeopardized by escape devices in the aid packages they deliver."

"Quite right. We aren't permitted to put the Red Cross at risk, but we've found the German POW camp commanders somewhat lax in determining the authenticity of relief agencies. They see benefit in rewarding good behavior with relief packages that cost them nothing. So, we simply make them up. The great benefit is that eventually something is found, and the offending non-existent relief agency is banned. We are quite proud of our work at fooling the Nazis. Let me show you a few."

"Here is a map on onion skin paper. Very thin, light, and durable. It can be balled, soaked in water, dried, and flattened without damage. We deliver them inside chess pieces or even dried stuck on the back of playing cards. Games are good vehicles for our devices. Money. Money buys food and railroad tickets. We include real money under the play money in Monopoly sets. Next to games and game pieces, shaving sets have proven successful. We magnetize the blades which allows an escaped prisoner to easily construct a simple compass and include a map in the handle. And then there are small, sealed compasses easily hidden in game pieces, fashioned as collar studs or similar small items."

Dorothy spoke. "You mentioned that some of the smuggled devices are found."

"Quite. We never stop improvising new methods and devices."

Ike asked, "Clothing. Escaped prisoners can't get far in allied uniforms."

"That's where prevention works, and we can benefit from the Red Cross. Look at these RAF flying boots. The leggings are zipped to a lace-up walking shoe. It is a simple matter of unzipping the leggings and cutting away the zipper with the pocketknife carried in the boot. The heel can be opened to retrieve a compass."

Ike had not seen this boot before. "My pilots haven't been issued these boots."

"Hopefully soon. Bomber squadrons are first priority, then fighter pilots and transport."

"No plan for RECON pilots?"

Hutton sniffed, "Looking for submarines? Little need."

Ike's face flushed red. He slammed the boot down, "Mapping Nazi positions, inserting and extracting SOE agents in unarmed light aircraft."

Hutton cocked his head. "Hmm. You make a good point. I'll pass it along to Colonel Crockatt."

Embarrassed by his outburst, Ike asked softly, "You mentioned a benefit of the Red Cross."

"Yes. Uniforms. The Geneva convention permits replacement uniforms for prisoners. Section Leader Barkley, could you remove your blouse."

Dorothy was shocked. Ike smiled. "Blouse—it's your uniform coat, not your shirt."

Dorothy shook her head. "Thank you. I knew that." She unbuttoned her coat and handed it to Major Hutton, who said, "I do hope it's the same as the men's RAF blouse. Yes, good. See here the liner. It's a different color than RAF blue, darker, nearly black. It is removable and easily passes as a civilian jacket. And we do not stop there. Not every allied prisoner can wear an RAF uniform, so we send, or rather include blankets from our relief agencies or add them to family packages. These blankets are made of wool suitable to be cut and tailored into civilian coats. The patterns are even printed on them in invisible ink."

Ike rubbed his chin. "All of this helps once the men are outside the walls but…"

Hutton didn't let him finish. "Iron bars are a big problem. Saws. They need hack saws. The easiest and very effective, is a four and a half inch long saw with a string through a hole at the end. It can be tied to hang inside clothing. We also developed a small blade packed inside a RAF ration tin box Mark II, but the most promising is a Gigli saw. We purchase them ready-made from surgical suppliers. It's a thin, flexible chain-like surgical saw that can be threaded in shoelaces. Does quite well against most metals. And of course, there is the escape knife, a multi-purpose tool and blade delivered in a variety of packages, even sports packages."

Major Hutton led them into another laboratory filled with electrical devices. "We must miniaturize radios. Receivers are straightforward. Its transmitters and aerials that present a challenge. But we make progress. And then there are the requests from SOE. Weapons mostly. Small and large but all unconventional. Can't ignore MI6. They keep a close eye on us."

The gadget master turned and looked Ike and Dorothy in the eyes. "Well, there you have it—at least a taste of what we can do. Any questions before I send you back to my taskmasters?"

"Your number three—food." Ike asked, "You mentioned getting food to the men as a high priority?"

"Right. There I've run against the priorities of the politicians, military and government. Seems they decide the needs of the nation regarding food. So far, money to buy food and SOE money to our French and Belgian helpers is the best we can do. But I haven't given up. We do provide emergency food packs for the RAF. But deploying them in number inside the camps has been severely limited."

Hutton turned to lead them out. Dorothy said. "Excuse me, Major Hutton. I'd like to hear more about typical equipment for SOE agents."

"Your unit is RECON. Your planes need lights to land or mark areas of interest. Did it ever occur to you that flares or even a simple handheld electric torch are prohibited materials in France? Bicycle air pumps that house an electric torch and even a compass are standard equipment, as are cameras hidden in a dozen or more ways. I personally keep a lighter that hides my camera. Why, we've even provided blowguns. What Colonel Z requests, we supply."

A young aide in civilian clothes was waiting when Ike and Dorothy left the bunker. "Here are your passes and endorsements on your orders."

"Why different colors?" Ike asked.

"Major Curtis you are to accompany me to the photo-reconnaissance lab. Section Officer Barkley, a car is waiting at the front entrance to take you to Beaulieu, Hampshire. You are to attend 'finishing school' at Lord Montagu's New Forest Estate."

"Finishing school?" she asked.

"Special indeed. It's the last stop for SOE agent training."

"Dorothy, be careful you don't bite off more than you want to chew," Ike said.

"If it's the last stop, they certainly won't be sending me anywhere untrained. I'm sure it's just the orientation I asked for."

"All the same, be careful what you agree to—sign nothing! And call me."

"I'm sure I'll be back in a couple of days. Good luck with your infrared projects."

Ike finished two weeks of briefings and training at Beaconsfield. Dorothy's call never came. Ike's pressed Colonel Crockatt for an answer. Crockatt stared coldly from behind his desk. "Major, you try my patience. This is all you need to know. Section Officer Barkley remains a member of Special Duty Flight 545 in authorized training status (restricted access). When that status changes, your command will be notified. Good day, Major."

CHAPTER 17
NIGHT AND DAY

Returning to Churchstanton, Ike drove directly to Otterhead House. Langley was meeting with Val Williams and Ray Labrosse. "Major Curtis, good that you are here. We were just discussing the planned insertion site in Brittany. Oh, and don't leave before we discuss Section Officer Barkley's new assignment."

Ike glanced at the detailed photo reconnaissance map on the wall. He had seen it often enough to recognize the chosen field. Turning to Val and Ray, he said, "Would you mind giving a moment alone with Captain Langley?"

Langley smiled. "It's Major Langley now. Why don't you men get a cup of coffee while I hear what Major Curtis has to say."

With Williams and Labrosse out of the room, Ike demanded, "What have you done with Dorothy Barkley? I've heard nothing. She's my adjutant—I have a need to know. What's this about a new assignment?"

Langley smiled. He enjoyed spinning up Ike. "Didn't they tell you? Training at Beaulieu."

Langley chuckled. "Relax, Curtis. She's coming back. Her new assignment is Intelligence Officer. Collateral duty—she will remain your adjutant. Doubling up is common."

"I've been handling intelligence for the 545. Hasn't been an issue. What's changed? What does she need to learn that we aren't already doing? I've sat through everything Beaconsfield had to offer. When will she be back? I don't trust Crockatt or Colonel Z."

"She'll be back when she is ready. Look, Major, think of it in terms of span of control. The 545 is growing. How many pilots, specialists, ground support and staff do you manage? You never seem to miss church on Sunday—what was Jesus' span of control? Twelve disciples—and He was divine. You're not being frozen out or limited. I will withhold nothing from you. You handle your Flight well. Granularity. You direct the operations of your aircraft and pilots superbly. No losses to date. Barkley has proven to be, like you, clever, resourceful and flexible. She is being taught the capabilities and procedures of our field assets. Consider what you will gain having her input on what the field assets can do, how they think and their proven instincts. Remember the Seine extraction—what if comms had failed. Sector Officer Barkley—as an intelligence officer will strengthen your unit and our mission."

"And Colonel Z is not planning on dropping her in France?"

"Major Curtis, anyone in the 545, hell, anyone in uniform may find themselves in France. Your General Eisenhower is planning our invasion. We're taking the fight to the continent. Who knows when 545 crosses the channel?"

Ike sighed. "You're right, of course. So where are we on Oaktree? I see you have the sight. Do we have a date?"

Langley shook his head. "Maybe Barkley can tell us more. SOE is still chasing down the traitor. That's the kind of help she will provide us."

Ike nodded. "I'll let you get back to your meeting with Williams and Labrosse. I must return to the base and see what my Number One has piled on my desk."

Flight Officer Marley greeted Ike warmly when Ike stepped into the office. "Welcome back, Skipper. Any news from the real world?"

Ike smiled. "Beaconsfield is in no way the real word. It's good to be back. What have I missed? Expect there's a pile a mile high on my desk."

"Well, the boys at Otterhead seem satisfied with Brittany RECON photos. The infrared results are improving too, with a little practice. I took the liberty of signing your correspondence 'by direction.' What you need to know is two more aircraft 4 pilots, flight crew and orders for Section Officer Barkley—they're on your desk."

"Lysanders, I hope."

"Yes, sir."

"More planes and crew—hell, that'll take us to squadron strength. Good work on RECON, by the way. Captain, no, now Major Langley is satisfied. You mentioned orders for Barkley?"

"Aye, Sir. Training assignment to Beaulieu. I thought you knew, and Collateral Duty, Intelligence Officer. Been here since the day you left."

That bastard Colonel Z knew all along. He's got his hooks

on Dottie. "Anything on her return to us?"

"No, sir. 'To be determined."

Ike smiled. "Good work, XO. Give me half an hour then we'll take a look at these new aircraft. And I need to get in the air—you choose the plane. Wait. Has Sergeant Major Brown fitted an Expeditor with pontoons yet?"

"Roger. One is at a ramp as we speak."

"XO, prepare to get your bottom wet."

Stepping on the Twin Beech Expeditor's floats brought back painful memories, but Ike pushed them out of his thoughts. "We need data on the sea conditions here. Is the bay protected in all weather?"

Marley shook his head. "Good protection in all but the most severe weather—I'll get you the numbers."

Ike took the controls with Marley beside him. He carefully went through the checklist with Marley and started the engines. The two Pratt &Whitney R-985 450-horsepower radial engines came to life. Ike was pleasantly surprised by the power as he piloted the plane towards the open water. The plane felt solid as it came to speed. Ike pulled back the yoke and the sturdy bird was airborne. "Sure beats the power of the Boeing Model 40 I flew." She lost a little performance in the rate of climb with the floats but rose to her ceiling of 26,000 feet. "Let's see what we've lost in speed," Ike said.

After a while, Marley said, "That looks like all you're going to get. I'm reading 213 mph through the air."

Ike nodded. "Why not get the feel for her, yourself, XO?"

Marley took hold of his yoke. "I've got her, skipper. Where should we go?"

"Guernsey. But stay out of AA range. Just a reminder that we remember who's there."

Marley guided them over the channel until Nazi-occupied Guernsey was in sight. Ike sighed. "God love them. How they must feel—forgotten and abandoned by their nation. No plan to rescue them. They'll just have to wait it out. Take her home, Marley."

As they neared Portsmouth, Ike asked, "Ever put down on the water before?"

"No, sir."

"Well, this will be your first. Damage her, and you explain it to the Master Sergeant. Bring her down easy. Let the floats find their plane. Once she settles in, you can reduce speed."

Back at the ramp, Ike smiled. "Write us up, XO. We are now floatplane qualified."

It was after dark when Ike and Marley returned to Churchstanton. "We might find something to eat in the officer's mess," Marley offered.

"Thanks, but no thanks. I've had a long day. Got a few calls to make and then I'll turn in. See you in the morning, XO."

As Marley headed for the officer's mess, Ike went to his office. He preferred the privacy it offered over the Officer's Mess phone, a privilege of rank. *What do I tell Rose and Hugh, for that matter? Not any easier since I don't know myself. All I have is my worry and Langley's thin story.*

Ike hesitantly picked up the phone and dialed. Rose's

happy voice surprised him, answering after the first ring. "Rose, it's me, Ike."

"Of course it is. I would know your voice anywhere. Good to hear it. You're back. It's not too late. Why not come over? I can throw something together if you're hungry."

"I missed you, Rose. I would love to come over, but it's been a very long day. I gonna crash here?"

"Crash?"

"It's American for fall into bed—I'm exhausted. Look, I wanted to call about Dottie."

"Right. She said you would explain everything. She didn't say much in the letter—not to expect her for a month or two, some kind of training school. I could feel her frustration—says RAF regulations don't permit her to write anything to friends and family. I hear it from everyone with a brother or father serving. By the way, I have another surprise for you. Can you make it tomorrow? I'll cook you something special."

Why does everyone else know more of Dottie's schedule than me? I am her CO! "Tomorrow should be fine. I'm looking forward to it."

"I may even wear my silk blouse. The one that caught your attention."

Ike laughed. "You-re not going to let me forget that are you? Rose, it's good to hear your voice. Till tomorrow then. Good night." Ike stretched out on his bunk and quickly fell asleep.

Sometime later, in the silent darkness of night, Ike awoke, shaking, his brow and hands wet with sweat. Struggling for breath, he gulped air. Slowly his racing pulse retarded, and his breaths grew lighter. *The dream.*

Why, God, do you haunt me? Linda, I'm sorry—so very, very sorry. If you can't forgive me, please give me peace. No, Linda was too loving not to forgive. The seaplane—yes, that's it. It triggered my memory. They say time heals all wounds. Oh, I pray it is so.

Ike sighed and softly prayed aloud. "Lord, God, please, if you are there, if you hear me and love me as they say, let me sleep in peace."

In the dim light of dawn, a scream pierced the silence. "No!"

Ike bolted up from the bed, his eyes wide open, his jaw drooping in fear. "It was just a dream. Another dream. Frightening—different, so real. Is true what they say about it? A premonition? I need to know. Hugh, yes, he's a good man. He's a priest, vowed to keep secrets. I'll ask him tonight."

Ike spent the day with his pilots and ground crew. He inspected the new planes.

Marley explained, "All the planes in the Flight are equipped with RECON cameras. As we agreed, Master Sergeant Brown configured the different models for different roles. The Hudsons, in use by the RAF as light bombers and troop transports, are our preferred plane for parachute drops. The smaller Expeditor, with good room for men and equipment, is the plane of choice for SOE team insertions and extractions. The Lysander, light and nimble, is our rescue plane for stragglers or a single or pair of men requiring immediate extraction. All the planes are now fitted with wide balloon wheels for landing in soft fields and pastures. The Expeditor we flew yesterday is kept fitted with floats for water rescue."

Ike replied, "As always, good work. XO. I know I can rely on you. Pass on my regards to Brown as well."

Ike sighed. "As you no doubt surmised, Operation Oaktree remains on hold. We'll be kept busy with RECON and SOE support missions. Now I need to make my courtesy call on Group Captain Hastings and let him know I've returned."

Hastings saw Ike walk into his outer office and called out, "Ike. Welcome Back! Please, come through."

Ike saluted and said, "I hope Marley has performed well in my absence."

"Sit down, Ike. Yes, Marley is as good a leader and my Number One as he has proven to be a good pilot. Glad you chose him."

"I needed a good man that speaks your language, Group Captain."

"Right. Ike, I don't need to tell you that SOE operations are increasing. And with invasion plans moving to high speed, we're being strained. I'm going to need you more than ever. Notice. You'll know as quickly as I do, but… "

"But the mission may be immediate. I picked up on what you're telling me at MI9. I'll give you all the support I can. Pleasantly surprised by the new assets."

"Believe me, Ike, you'll need them and more."

"By the way, Group Captain, I've heard the 545 has reached squadron strength."

"Not going to happen, Ike. Not saying you shouldn't be recognized as a squadron—just that they prefer to keep you listed as Special Duty Flight—more in keeping with your mission, not to mention lower profile with powers that be. On the other hand, Special Duty Flight designation puts more of your admin and support on my shoulders."

Ike nodded. "In that regard, my adjutant is in training for an indefinite period. I could use some non-com support in the meantime."

Hastings shook his head. "Barkley. No telling when or if they'll release her. I'll see what I can do."

Ike's eyebrows tightened. "When or if, sir?"

"Sorry, just a senior's concern for a young officer. I'm sure it's when."

"I pray you're right. Well, sir, I have a mountain of paperwork on my desk," Ike fibbed. "Need to be on my way."

Ike had managed to put his dream in the back of his mind during the workday, but it came back to him as he drove to Rose's cottage. *How do I handle this? I don't want to tell Rose. Is that fair? Keeping secrets already? Maybe I should let sleeping dogs lie.*

Ike parked in front of the house and, stepping out of the car, paused and looked around. The mid-summer landscape was lush with greenery. He inhaled deeply of the fresh country air. The woods, the orchard, and the clucking of chickens brought back memories of the small farm in Crescent Valley outside Gig Harbor. Thoughts of shelling fresh oysters on the back porch, shucking corn on the cob, and shelling fresh peas with Linda while young Earl toddled about brought tears to his weary eyes. *It's so much the same and yet so very different.*

The front door opened, and Rose called out. "Well, don't

just stand there, come in!"

Ike smiled and walked to the front door. Rose threw her arms around his neck and said, "You're not getting by me without a hug and a kiss."

Rose felt soft and warm in his arms. His doubts and the tension built up over the days ebbed away. After a short kiss, Ike whispered. "Rose, I'm so happy to see you. You're the prescription for all that ails me."

"Come in. Uncle Hugh is here. I hope you don't mind—just for dinner, and then he promises to leave us alone."

Ike called out. "Sorry, Hugh. Didn't have time to pick up another bottle. Next time, promise."

Hugh got up from his chair. "I protest! It is your good company that draws me. Though, I pray you keep your promise for your next visit."

"My good company or a check on my good behavior with your defenseless niece."

"Hey! Who are you calling defenseless?" Rose exclaimed.

Hugh laughed. "My dear Rose, you make his point. Good to see you again, Ike."

Rose sniffed. "Hmm. If I can leave you two alone for a moment, I'll get dinner on the table. I was thinking, maybe a walk after dinner. There's a path through the woods to a pond."

"Ike beamed. "I would love an evening stroll with the prettiest girl in Churchstanton. Rose, if you don't mind, I have something I want to ask your uncle Hugh—as a priest and a vicar, I mean."

Rose turned and saw the strain in Ike's eyes. "Certainly, Ike. Why not step outside to the garden? I need five or ten minutes in the kitchen." *Something's troubling him. He doesn't trust me yet; Does he love me? If he loves me, why keep something from me? Or maybe he's considering marriage—yes. Yes, I would marry him if he asked! It's so sudden, but the war—everyone is in a hurry with this stupid war.*

Outside in the orchard, Ike asked Hugh, "Hugh, you're a priest. What do you know about dreams? Are they premonitions—premonitions of death?"

"Premonitions, Ike?"

"They say if you die in a dream, you will die. Is that true? I read Abraham Lincoln dreamt of his death—he saw his body in the casket days before he was assassinated."

"Why don't you start from the beginning? Tell me what you dreamt that causes so much worry."

"Last night. First, I had the same recurring nightmare. It was watching my wife Linda drown in the airplane. I prayed to God, 'Please put an end to these nightmares! I'm exhausted. Let me sleep.' But I considered this dream after flying a float plane from Portsmouth. First time from the water since the accident. I chalked it up to the memories brought on by flying a seaplane again."

"Seems reasonable to me, Ike."

"Yes, but then I had another dream—so real. I was with Dottie, we were flying over France, a mission—I can't really talk about the mission. But then I was on the ground in France, searching for Charles—I saw him. I had to let him know Dottie needed to find him. He saw me. I couldn't tell if he heard me. Then there was an explosion—I couldn't see for the brightness. When I could see again, I saw myself—my body lying on the ground like a broken doll. A Nazi officer came over and kicked the body, and I began to laugh. Weird, I laughed at the Nazi. I was not dead at all. It was all a joke on the Nazi. I was still alive. And then I realized—no, the body was me. I awoke. Well, am I going to die? What does it mean? And why does God ignore my prayers? It was so disjointed. Does it mean anything at all? And should I share it with Rose? I don't want her to think I'm keeping secrets from here, but then I don't want her to worry. She's so special and sweet. She exudes strength, but there is weakness in any armor."

Hugh stared across the fence. "Well, Ike, not to make light of your dreams, but the fact you are alive puts to bed the old wives' tale that a death in your dream is fatal. Let me ask you a question. Have you ever had faith in God? Was there a time, a moment, when you acknowledged Him as Savior?"

"Now you sound like my dad and a host of Baptist preachers. But to answer your question, yes. As a young man, I felt God's calling, and I prayed for forgiveness and a new life in Christ. I never doubted it. With Linda, too. We both lived like we had faith."

"Ike, Baptists aren't alone in recognizing that God calls to us in love. Christians have believed for two thousand years. He enters in and breathes new life. He gifts us with love and the heart to love Him and our neighbor as ourselves. Perhaps the second dream, the nightmare, is an answer. You laughed at death. God affirmed that you will never die and affirmed your love for Dottie and Charles, whom you never met. A premonition? Perhaps, but it is just as likely missions to France are possible for both you and Dottie. It causes worry. And if I were a betting man, I would wager this training for Dottie concerns you. Her letter was most cryptic."

Ike sighed. "I am worried. I have suspicions, but even I don't know what she's gotten into. What should I say to Rose? I cherish her cheerfulness. I don't want her to worry needlessly, but I know I must be honest with her if we are going to have any kind of relationship."

Hugh nodded. "She's going to learn the truth sooner or later. And honesty can only build a relationship."

Hugh turned to face Ike. With a gentle smile and a nod, Hugh said, "I think we're ready for the dinner Rose has made for you."

The smell of roast chicken awakened a hunger for a real home-cooked meal in his mind. Ike closed his eyes, inhaled deeply, and exclaimed. "Smells great! You roasted a chicken? For me? Is this Christmas in August? Did we win the war?"

"Don't be silly. We raise chickens, Ike. You know that, and when their egg production drops, we eat them. You grew up on a farm, you must know that. It's a balance—an equilibrium that must be maintained."

"It smells so good. A treat we don't get on the base. And I know a roast chicken dinner is special, even on a farm. You're going to spoil me, Rose. Beauty and a great cook!"

"Save your compliments until we taste it."

They sat around the table. Hugh gave the blessing for the feast before them. "Uncle High, do the honors and carve," Rose chimed.

Ike's eyes widened as Hugh placed an ample slice of breast on his plate. "I see celery, carrots, peas, and are those turnips?"

"You mean the swedes?" Rose replied. And there is stuffing with onion and sage. Do try it. And it wouldn't be complete without a good mash."

Ike took a bite. "Just the right amount of garlic. Perfect! It's all so very perfect!"

Rose beamed. "Well, save room for dessert because that's the surprise."

Hugh finished carving and gazed at the plate before him. "You see, Ike, how God has blessed me with two most capable nieces to care for me."

Rose chuckled. "Uncle Hugh, we love you. You are a gift of wisdom and grace, the glue to keeps us all together. Oh, and Ike, I wanted to tell you. While you were gone, I made a trip to Glastonbury with your little flashlight. Well, as one parish secretary to another, I was permitted to research their records. You will not believe what I found!"

Ike looked up from his plate and finished chewing the moist, meaty chicken. "The Holy Grail and Sword of Saint Peter?"

"Don't mock me. Just for that, I'm going to make you wait until after dessert."

Ike smiled and shook his head. "I'm fine concentrating on this meal, Rose."

Rose took a bite and continued. "You didn't comment on my dress when you arrived. Didn't you notice?"

Hugh whispered softly, "Careful, Ike."

"You mean under your apron? But now visible in all its glory? I notice everything you wear, everything about you, your hair, your rose water perfume, the lipstick, and makeup, how your eyes sparkle as you smile—the way you curl that tuft of hair over your right ear, the way you walk and shake your head that bares the nape of your neck, the depth of your blue eyes. Yes, I noticed a gold necklace carrying a single pearl resting above the open top button of your most feminine white silk blouse you wear to tease me. Oh, I noticed. But you do not need the silk blouse, Rose, I am enticed by the very sight of you."

Now Rose was blushing and, for once, speechless. Uncle Hugh coughed softly. "I'm not sure if I should leave you two alone or stay and chaperone!"

Rose finally looked up. "Dessert now or after our walk?"

Hugh replied, "Now, please. Then you two can admire each other alone."

Rose got up. "I have a warm peach pie. The first peaches are in, and I thought, why not pie?"

Ike's eye followed Rose as she made her way to the kitchen. "The old saw says the way to a man's heart is through his stomach, but you go far beyond. You come at me with all the senses, sight, sound, aroma, taste and…"

Rose quipped, "Touch. If you can remain a gentleman, I'll let you hold my hand as we walk."

Ike laughed. "I was going say hugs that warm my innermost soul and kisses sweeter than honey, but then we wouldn't want to give Hugh the wrong idea. We'll stick with the gentleman model for now."

After Hugh's second helping of pie, he wiped his mouth with his napkin and said, "Fully sated, it's time I went home. I still have a sermon to finish, but I think it will wait until morning."

As Hugh rose from the table, Ike cheerfully bid him "Good night."

Hugh stepped behind Rose and gave her a gentle kiss on the forehead. "Thank you, my dear, for a wonderful evening." And then, with a twinkle in his eye, he said, "Victis miserere."

Rose looked up, smiled, and replied, "Cum se submittit."

Ike roared, "Latin! I cry foul! Your English is difficult enough."

Hugh laughed and patted Ike on the shoulder as he left. "Cladem accipere amicus meus."

The early evening stars were waiting for the contented couple as they walked past the garden towards the orchard. Ike reached for Rose's hand. "Remember your promise." She gave his hand a gentle squeeze. "It feels so right. There's a special place I want to show you."

Ike replied, "You mentioned a pond."

"It will be dark soon. The hilltop is perfect after dark. The stars are coming out, just wait."

Ike looked up, "Venus is showing her stuff. And the moon is only a thin crescent."

Rose chatted on, "Every gamekeeper clears the highest hill for the hunt. The game is driven to one of several clearings below that assure the Lord and his guests a successful hunt and a grand view of the estate and manor house. It's all for show. But the best show is the night sky ablaze with stars. Dottie and I would bring a blanket, lay down, and watch for meteor showers streaking across the galaxies. It always reminds me of God's perfect love."

"As a boy, I enjoyed watching the stars from the deck of a fishing boat. No mother's cradle rocked me so sublimely."

Rose sighed. "Was Uncle Hugh any help?"

"Yes, I intended to tell you. I don't want any secrets between us. And Hugh did help. It was a dream I had, a nightmare. I was afraid it might be a premonition. I'll tell you if you wish, that is, if you will risk spoiling a beautiful evening."

"No secrets is a good rule, Ike. I think honesty and trust can only draw us closer."

"Yes, that's Hugh and I agreed. Simply put, I dreamt Dottie and I were flying over France, and then I was alone on the ground in occupied territory. I saw Charles and called out to him. An explosion blinded me. When the smoke cleared, I saw my body lying on the ground. A Nazi kicked the body, and I began to laugh—laugh at the joke on him. I was not dead. But then I realized it was my dead body I was staring at. Then woke up."

Ike paused for a moment. "Hugh thinks maybe God is reminding me of my lost faith, that I have been saved and have everlasting life. And the appearance of Dottie and Charles confirms my concern for them. I didn't mention that I dreamt earlier last night of the recurring nightmare of Linda's death and prayed to God to release me from the dreadful dream. I should be encouraged that my once strong faith, shared with Linda, should be renewed in the assurance that we shall pass from death unto life."

Rose was silent. Ike blurted, "Well, that put a damper on the evening."

"No, Ike. I'm glad you told me. And I'm glad for my Uncle Hugh's wise words. He tells me you are a good man. And I find comfort in a man who knows how to love."

Ike sniffled. He put his arms around her and kissed her. Squeezing her tight, he whispered, "And strange, here, thousands of miles from home, I have found someone new to love. Yes, I can say it. Rose Osbourne, I love you."

The evening passed too quickly, and Ike moaned, "I need to get back to the base." They were content to walk quietly, arm in arm down the path, cherishing just being close. The moon was high overhead when they reached the house. Standing beside the car, Ike gave Rose a good night kiss and opened the door. He stopped, turned around and said, "I'm sorry Rose, you were going to tell me what you found at Glastonbury."

"It can wait, Ike. What I found tonight was far more important."

"We decided to be honest with each other. That means respecting and valuing each other's priorities. Please, it was important to you, enough so that you went to Glastonbury. I want to know."

Even in the dark, Ike could see Rose's eyes brighten. "Well, since you asked, I found a note on the back of a vellum attendance record. I used your infrared light. It mentioned the abbot sent his answer to Bede of Jarrow—a history of the Church in Glastonbury."

Ike replied, "Bede the historian?"

"More than a historian, a monk, a saint in Rome as well as Canterbury."

"It seems to me if the Abbot of Glastonbury Abbey had something to say about the ancient legends, Bede, Saint Bede, would have recorded it."

"That's what others have said, but no one has found Bede ever referencing Glastonbury. So, the question really remains open. Did Bede receive the abbot's letter? Did Bede's reference to Glastonbury get lost or edited? With all Bede wrote about the Roman occupation and the church, his silence is remarkable."

Ike smiled. "It's a mystery. One *we* must pursue."

"You think so?"

"I'm with you 100 percent. Now, I must get back. Good night."

Ike found himself whistling merrily all the way back to the base. When he came to his room, he saw a message taped to the door. "Major Curtis, your presence is urgently requested in the OPS Room. /s/ FLT Marley."

CHAPTER 18
PAYING THE PRICE

Tension assaulted Ike as he stepped through the door. It seemed another full atmosphere of pressure pushed against his head. The teleprinters were clattering. Multiple voices were speaking on phones, and over it all, the squawk box trumpeted the crackled voices of RAF Air Sea Rescue Service crews, alternating between a pilot of a Bolton Paul Defiant circling the channel off Cherbourg and the skipper of a high-speed ASRS Whaleback launch being directed to a recovery site. A voice, the skipper of the boat, could be heard replying, "Aye, proceeding into the minefield now. Can confirm a mine has already surfaced behind us. Perhaps a chance for target practice on our return."

Marley appeared out of the shadows and was soon at Ike's side. "One of our Expeditors. Smithson and Turley. Shot down over the channel. Seems a Nazi night hunter, reportedly a Junker Ju-88 intercepted them. They didn't have a prayer. Our ASRS Defiant sighted what may be a parachute on the water—directing a launch to the site."

"Did I hear they're in a minefield?"

"Aye. It's not a risk to a man in a raft, and the launch is too fast for the mines. At 48 knots, they're safely past before the mine, tethered underwater, out of sight, can surface. If their parachutes were sighted, and our lads are in their rafts, the ASRS launch will fetch them safely home."

Ike stared at the status board and sighed. "Why wasn't I told of a mission tonight?"

A voice replied from behind Ike. "I requested it late. You were not in. I spoke to Marley," Group Captain Hastings said as he stepped beside Ike. "A special drop. SOE operation with the Pat O'Leary Line. Last minute request came from Uncle Claude himself."

Ike stared at Hastings. "All the more reason I should have been notified."

"Major, you've been gone over two weeks. Did you think Flight 545 stopped operating in your absence? Your Number One has full authority to act."

Hastings paused and exhaled slowly before continuing. "Ike, you just got back. Section Officer Barkley is training with SOE. Colonel Z has kept you in the dark. Tonight's mission was a three-person drop. Williams, Labrosse, and a woman. Uncle Claude gave no further identity. I didn't want you to worry when the whole story wasn't known."

"You think it may be Dorothy? She's only had two weeks training. He wouldn't!"

"I don't know. His motives are hard to figure."

"She couldn't be parachute trained in two weeks, not with everything else..."

Hastings sighed. "They landed. It was to be an airstrip

exchange and return. The insertion team was left, but the team to be extracted was a no-show."

Ike's face contorted. "Cobra, the traitor. Another team lost, and a night hunter is waiting over the channel."

"Ike, we don't know that. It's speculation."

Ike shook his head. "The pieces fit."

"A flare. Raft in sight," The launch skipper's voice crackled over the speaker. "One man in a raft. Approaching for recovery."

Somehow, the room became silent. All ears were tuned to the radio. A couple of minutes passed then the voice. "Flight Lieutenant Smithson, Independent Flight 545, safely aboard, No injuries. Smithson reports no sighting of Flight Officer Turley's parachute. Turley last seen bailing from the airplane,"

The pilot of the Defiant's voice came across the speaker, "Have circled the scene half a dozen times. No other parachute or raft sighted."

The command was heard. "Flight Officer Turley missing and presumed dead. Mission suspended. ASRS units return to base."

Ike silently left the OPS Room, walked down the hall to the Officer's Mess, and said nothing to the officers gathered over morning coffee. He took Flight Officer Turley's mug from its wall peg and placed it upside down on a black pennant on the mantle. The conversations ceased, and the now silent men watched Ike as he left.

A small crowd attended Flight Lieutenant Smithson's debrief. Looking tired and haggard, the pilot briefly summarized his mission. "Routine flight across the channel, Turley's navigation was spot on. The airstrip was lighted, torches at the start and three hundred feet. Identify friend signal given and answered correctly. Put down without incident."

A British Major that Ike didn't recognize interrupted, "Flight Lieutenant, you said the proper response for 'friend' was given. There was no indication that the team to be extracted did not show?"

Ike leaned over to Langley and whispered, "Who is he? Haven't seen him before."

Langley replied, "Colonel Z's aide. SOE is in turmoil. You're not alone in fearing it was Cobra's work."

Smithson answered the Major's question. "No, sir. But that is not unusual. The landing site team is independent of the field teams. Standing orders require that we wait eight minutes. Well sir, we got the 'all clear' and landed. The site team was waiting. The insertion team leader deplaned and moved out of sight in the trees. Kept the engine running and waited. Not a minute or so later, Val Williams runs back and tells me the extraction team is a no-show. Tells the woman, the radio operator, to leave the radio and equipment on the plane for now, while he and Labrosse do a quick reconnoiter. I remind him he has six minutes."

Ike asked, "The woman—you say a radio operator, blonde hair, average height?"

Smithson answered, "Dark hair, short, but then the light was bad. Mostly quiet, but I did notice a heavy accent, Polish? Maybe Slovak?"

The MI6 major interrupted. "How did you know she was a radio operator?"

Ike sighed, *Thank God, not Dottie.*

Smithson replied, "Well, Williams said so. Five minutes or so later, maybe a couple extra, Williams comes back. Says, 'no sight of anyone, team or Nazi.' Tells her, 'Grab your radio." Helps the woman unload the rest of their equipment, and then Labrosse comes back and yells at Williams. 'No guide. The guide that accompanied the extracting team and was to take us to Paris.'"

The MI6 man failed to hide his anger. "And what was William's reply?"

"Well. He pipes up and says, 'I know a safe house nearby. Contacts who can get us to Paris.' Seems they were about to come to blows. Well, I step in and say, 'I've overstayed; this plane is heading back. If you're coming, get in.' Williams took two bags and headed for the woods. The others followed. I jump in and turn the plane around. By this time, the landing site team was gone. Took their torches and left. Well, I didn't need them to know the way out, so took off without incident."

Langley asked, "The Junker night hunter, where did he come from? When he intercepted you, was he waiting, circling, or did fly straight to you?"

"Exactly right. Seemed he was waiting at altitude and dropped right on us. I'm sure it was a JU-88. We weren't twenty miles offshore. No place to hide. Flying at a low altitude, good visibility. He dove at high speed. Got us with his first volley. Turley jumped first while I radioed. He may have been hit; I don't know. Said nothing but was holding his shoulder. I looked for the JU-88, then jumped. My chute opened, and I looked around. I couldn't... he wasn't in sight. I tried to find his chute. Nothing. I never saw him again."

Smithson lowered his head and wiped an eye. Hastings calmly said, "Take a moment, Smithson. You did your best. When you're ready, we'll wait."

Smithson sniffed, "I hit the water and deployed my one-man raft. I climbed in and waited. I'm not sure how long—20 minutes? Forty? I heard the low-flying Defiant. I recognized him right away. He stayed with me until the ASRS launch picked me up."

Group Captain Hastings stood. "We're glad you made it back, Smithson. Did I hear Major Curtis say a week's leave? Go home, Smithson. Get some rest."

Ike smiled. "No, Group Captain, I said ten days."

Afterward, on their way to Otterhead House, Ike asked Langley, "Any word on the team coming out? Who were they?"

"Sabotage. Took out a railroad bridge with the resistance. They're safe—for now. They were stopped at the edge of the airstrip and told that their extraction was postponed."

"Postponed? Was this contact identified?"

"No. He used the correct password and response…"

"An insider."

"Yes.

"Cobra?"

"Colonel Z thinks so, or one of his men."

Ike shook his head. "No one got a description of this guy?"

"Seems he held his torch high. No one saw his face."

Ike chewed on what he heard. He blurted out, "Why

warn the team away? Why no Nazi landing party and yet send a Luftwaffe Night Hunter? If it was Cobra, why let two SOE teams escape and down an empty plane?" Ike laughed. "Back home, you need big bait to catch big fish. Do you think Abwehr is arranging their own sting against our Paris agents?"

Langley replied, "It would terminate two lines, the Pat O'Leary and the Comet. Both transit through Paris."

"Yeah. Or maybe someone on Cobra's team is doubling back on him."

Ike rubbed his brow. "Tell me about the mission, Val and Ray, and this, woman, a Pole?"

Langley sighed. "With Oaktree on hold, we can't waste trained men like Williams and Labrosse. State secret, but I'll tell you. Checking security on the Pat O'Leary Line. Rumors are, well, we want to know if Cobra has targeted or infiltrated the line."

Ike exhaled. "Seems like you have your answer."

"No, not yet. We know there is a leak, but we haven't connected it to the Pat O'Leary Line."

Ike asked, "A Polish radio operator?"

"Polish resistance intelligence has established contacts in the Abwehr—very high level. Abwehr is responsible for terminating our escape lines."

Ike nodded. "So, you're telling me Operation Mongoose is on the ground. James, tell me Dorothy Barkley isn't involved in this."

Langley smiled. "Training. She'll be back with 475 in a few weeks."

"I'm no fool. That won't square with me. Your word— nothing will be held back."

Langley took a deep breath, "It's how Dorothy wanted it. Doesn't want her family to worry. Was afraid you might let something slip. Can you honor her wishes? I'll leave that between you and her. After only two days of training, Colonel Z was told she had something special. Two steps ahead of everyone else, and these are clever people. She was sent to Colonel Z for an interview. As I heard it, she has an uncanny ability for analysis—more than analysis, perception, or, better, what Colonel Z refers to as intuition. He wanted to test her, So...'

Ike interrupted. "So, she's not in training. Where is she?"

"Technically. Ike, she is in training and will return as I said. But Uncle Claude sent her out officially as a courier, but more, really. She carried money and instructions to Comet Line leader."

"Where?"

"Dorothy is in Brussels. Her instructions are to evaluate the procedures of the Comet Line in preparation for Oaktree. The Comet Line is the oldest and most successful escape organization. It grew out of the Belgian resistance—large, resourceful, capable and loyal. She carried a letter from Colonel Z requesting full cooperation and promising more funding."

Ike mumbled, "That's just like Dorothy. Don't cause others to worry. Of course, Uncle Claude is right, she sees where things are headed and begins working on a solution on her own initiative. She's never been one to wait for direction."

Langley stared at Ike. "Your concern for Section Officer Barkley goes beyond what is expected of a Commanding Officer. Clearly, it's personal. I need to know, Ike, are you in love with her? Can I trust you two to work together?"

Ike turned and chuckled. "You mean, do I know that she is drop dead gorgeous but doesn't have an ounce of vanity in her? Or that she is kind and understanding putting others first? Or that she is intelligent and capable and a patient listener?"

James Langley laughed. "Surely, she is human, Ike. She must have some fault?"

Ike replied, "The Good Book says we're all sinners, but as for her faults, I've only noted her stubbornness—but some would call that persistence. But as to your question, she's the sister I never had. Love her, yes, but without romance. God knows how she adores her Charles—he is alive, her intuition confirms it. I've never had such a deep trust and friendship with a woman where romance is out of the question. She brought me into her family where I am welcomed and accepted." Ike sighed. "You can trust us to work together, James, simply because I know she cannot be stopped."

Ike sat smiling. *It's true. I love her like a sister. We've become kind of a family. Maybe someday a sister-in-law?*

Langley stopped the car outside Ike's HQ. "I need to drive on, Ike. I'll leave you here."

Ike got out and said, "Right. I've got a letter to write to Flight Officer Turley's family."

Langley nodded. "Your first? They say the first is the hardest. Truth is, they never get easier."

CHAPTER 19
KEEPING SECRETS

Ike was pleased that Rose and Hugh appeared to accept Dorothy's letter of explanation at face value. Their silence made it much easier for him to keep his fears for her safety to himself. Coming out of church Sunday, Rose stopped and said, "I must speak with the sextant for a moment and also Rosalind French. I'll see you outside."

Hugh greeted him at the door, bathed in the noon day summer sun. "Good morning, Ike," he intoned with genuine smile and warm handshake. "You've become quite the regular attender. I hope it is more than dinner with Rose and me."

Ike laughed. "Thanks Hugh. Rose is quite the draw, but I really appreciate your sermons. Your messages and our talks have helped me deal with long suppressed issues."

Hugh nodded. "How's your prayer life? Have you made progress? I don't mean to pry. I heard you pray for the Turley family this morning. That's a name I don't recall."

"Your counsel on prayer has been very helpful, yes, I've come to depend on it. Look, I don't want to interrupt your greeting with your congregation. Can we continue this conversation at dinner?"

"It will be my pleasure. You know, Ike, you can invite others from the base. They would be welcome as well, and I'm sure we can find them home cooked dinners."

As Ike waited for Rose to join him, he was greeted by smiling parishioners, "Good morning Major Curtis," followed by whispers and glances at the approaching Rose.

Rose greeted him with a peck on the cheek. "Thanks for waiting. What a wonderful day! We must take a walk after dinner—only a short drive in the Blackdown Hills, one of my favorite places."

A blushing Ike replied, "A kiss? At church? It seems I'm already the talk of Saint Peter and Saint Paul."

"Let them talk! I'm happy and I don't care who knows it! Come on, I put dinner in the oven before the service."

Hugh poured a couple of drinks while Rose plated their dinner. Ike began, "You asked about the Turleys—the family of a pilot missing and presumed dead. The first from my unit. I had to pray my way through a letter informing them of his loss. To your comment, yes, I find myself praying more—every night, but often through the day. As you mentioned, a few weeks go about prayer pulling you to God. I'm not certain how close I'm being drawn, but I have noticed praying for others somehow brings relief, a peace. It's somehow comforting even if I have no idea if my prayers will be answered. It seems the weight is shifted to God."

Hugh put down his drink and took a puff on his pipe. "Ike, the prescription is having the desired effect. God desires to take the burdens from your heart. And I am so happy to hear that you pray for others."

"It seems when I begin with a simple prayer for my son Earl and my dad, Dorothy and Charles come to mind, and of course Rose and you. I consider the men in the unit, and my mind just goes into double time listing those who need prayer."

"How do you pray for yourself, Ike?"

"That's a hard one. I feel so unworthy. So overwhelmed. It's just a cry for help."

Hugh nodded. "I remember something C.S. Lewis said: 'For most of us the prayer in Gethsemane is the only model. Removing mountains can wait.' We all need saving—often. I'm not talking about your Baptist tradition of once saved always saved—that's redemption. God saves us in many ways—our soul for all eternity yes, but from peril, from temptation and trial, and even from despair."

Ike asked, "Can He save us from ourselves? Your Doctor Lewis has a good way of connecting with those struggling with faith."

"His own struggle is legendary. And he hasn't become complacent. I cannot improve on what he wrote: 'I pray because I can't help myself. I pray because I am helpless. I pray because the need flows out of me all the time, waking and sleeping. It doesn't change God. It changes me.'"

Ike mumbled, "I hope it's changing me as well."

Rose walked in, her mitted hands holding a large platter. "Dinner is served! Sit. While it's hot."

After dinner, Ike followed Hugh to the sitting room and settled into a comfortable chair, his body yearning for a nap. Rose called from the kitchen, "Don't get too comfortable. I'll put the leftovers in the fridge and be right out. Uncle Hugh, you promised to clean up and tend to the dishes. Ike and I are off to Castle Neroche."

Hugh laughed. "She'll feed you but then make you work it off."

"Castle Neroche? I don't recall seeing a castle nearby. I've flown over the area many times."

"Well then, I won't spoil it for her. I will only say it's an invigorating climb."

Rose navigated as Ike drove. "It's an enchanted place, Ike. So much history and the view is doubly rewarding. Why, I can spend hours there, imagining—do you ever wonder about people who lived long ago who shared the same view, whose footsteps you walk in. What would they teach us? Lives lived. Lessons learned, if only we would look at what they left behind."

Rose pointed to the right, "Oh, turn here, on the right. Now, where was I?"

Ike replied, "Imagining interrogating people from long ago."

Rose slapped Ike's shoulder lightly, "Interrogating, Ike? Really? No. Listening and learning. That's what tradition teaches us. We carry down not just knowledge but wisdom—timeless lessons of life."

Ike downshifted. "Pretty steep hill. I'd hate to drive it in the rain. Imagine it gets muddy. Obviously, an old ox cart road."

"Yes, eight hundred and fifty feet high. Too steep for my bicycle. I usually leave it at the bottom and walk up. It's worth the effort. You'll see."

The car emerged from the trees, and the narrow road stopped at the foot of an even steeper grassy hill. Rose jumped out and said, "Grab the blanket. We walk from here."

Ike stepped out, looked around, and commented, "Ah, if I were a poet or a writer, I could pen an ode to the English countryside below; an idyllic landscape covered with a patchwork of woods, fields, and orchards, a tablecloth pierced by the spires and towers of old Norman churches. It is beautiful, Rose. I will say that."

Rose turned to look. "Pierced by spires? Oh no, Ike. They are fruit, long ago sprouted from the blood of martyrs and generations of Christians—seeded and planted to bring us life and faith. Come on, to the top of the castle."

"Castle?"

"Yes, these earthworks are all that remain of a Norman motte and bailey castle, Come along it's only another sixty feet to the top. You'll be able to make out the ringwork and the barbican..."

You'll need to translate. Not in my American vocabulary."

"Barbican. It was a tower or spire over a gate, an outer fortification. It was built by Robert Count of Mortain in the eleventh century. The land was his reward for supporting William the Conqueror. But we know he built on top of an older fortification, going back to the iron age. A sentinel, no doubt, keeping watch over the countryside."

Ike struggled to keep up with Rose as she scrambled towards the top. "Romans, too, no doubt?" He asked.

Rose did not turn around but answered, "No evidence of

them. But the castle played its part in 'The anarchy.'"

"The anarchy? Can you be more specific?"

"In the early twelfth century, King Stephen took the crown due to his cousin, Empress Matilda, or Maude. The civil war went back and forth until the childless Stephen named Matilda's son his heir."

"Not very Christian," Ike replied.

Ike stood beside Rose at the top and gazed. "Hard to believe there's a war going on."

"I come here when I need to put things in perspective. It's like time stands still, and I can think. No, the only sign of war is the planes of RAF Churchstanton."

Rose took the blanket from Ike and spread it out on the grassy crest. "Sit next to me, Ike. I read the papers your father sent. You should read them, too. I know why you're Baptist, and your father and grandfather are so hostile to the Episcopal Church. Nobility runs deep in your family, Ike. And I don't mean your English title—character. It's as if God has blessed your ancestors for their righteousness, which, like King David, has been passed down for generations."

Ike turned and studied Rose. *She never ceases to amaze me!* Rose continued. "It was slavery. He listened to his rector preach against the Baptist Pastor across the street. A passionate defense of slavery and ridicule for the abolitionist Baptist. He watched as the leaders of the Falls Church marched across the street, dragged the Pastor of Columbia Baptist into the street, and hanged him. I can't imagine the cruelty and injustice. That day your great grandfather crossed into Washington DC and offered his services to the Union cause."

Ike's face tightened. Deep furrows cut across his brow. "I never knew."

Rose went on, "He was assigned to the quartermaster corps. He served in the Western River campaigns, procuring steamboats for the Union army. In his obituary, it said he moved his family to Galena, Illinois, a major distribution center for boats servicing the upper Midwest and safely distant from Confederate Missouri and the divided loyalties of Southern Illinois or Kentucky."

Ike found himself asking, "Why did he leave?"

"Railroads. General Grant preferred riverboats during the war, saying, 'It takes an army to defend a railroad, but only a few men to defend a boat.' After the war, that all changed."

Ike nodded. "And they followed the Missouri west, to the land of waterways, Washington's Puget Sound."

Ike inhaled deeply. "I thought you were going to tell me more about the Glastonbury find. It must be more interesting than my family lore. Something about a letter from the abbot to your Saint Bede."

Rose sighed. "I went back but couldn't find anything new. The answer must be with the archives of Jarrow at Durham."

"Durham?" Ike asked.

"Yes, when Jarrow was devolved, the archives were sent to the Cathedral and later the University at Durham."

Ike was lying on his back staring into the sky when he saw Rose sitting up leaning over him. "Her blonde hair, highlighted in strawberry red, fell toward him and framed her face. Her eyes sparkled with anticipation. "Ike, I want to go to

Durham. Come with me. Can't you get a pass for a few days? Please? You're a Commanding Officer. Can't you issue yourself a pass?"

"Well, gee, I don't know. There's a lot going on." Ike fibbed. He was in a holding pattern and frustrated with waiting.

Rose leaned closer and kissed him. "You said you are all in with me on this. If we are to have a future together, we should learn to share each other's interests. It will be fun. Less than a full day by train. I want to be with you. You know I'm in love with you, and you love me. Why, think of it, days, maybe a week together, alone. No chaperone. Oh, Ike, please say yes."

Ike closed his eyes. *I do love her. I want to hold her, squeeze her tight, and never let go.* He sat up close beside her and put an arm around her. "It sounds wonderful." Ike paused.

Rose whispered, "But."

Ike looked into her worried eyes. "But I love you too much to hurt you."

"Hurt me?"

"Let me finish. I'm a soldier. I'm here for the war. There is only uncertainty. I could go down with my plane. More likely, I will be ordered on. We're taking this war to the Nazis. Who knows if I will return? I don't want you to be the girl that tongues wag—'chased after a yank and look how he left her.' You see how Dottie worries for Charles and how we worry for her. Not to mention my family back home. I want to marry you, Rose. But after this war—if I survive, and with the understanding of my son—a boy who has lost the mother he loves. I love you. But I won't risk harming him or you, now."

Rose wrapped her arms around him and pushed him

down on the blanket. She embraced him passionately and kissed him like she had never kissed anyone before. Ike's body screamed, 'Tighter—hold her tighter,' until, at last, they rolled off the blanket and tumbled, arms and legs intertwined, down the grassy slope.

Rose brushed loose grass from her hair. "I'm holding you to your word, Mister Montclair Isaac Curtis. You better come back to me, or I will hunt you down, like, like…"

"Like a long-lost relic in a dusty archive?"

"More like a handsome knight locked in a tower and rescued by a fair damsel."

Ike laughed. "I like your version more."

Ike helped Rose to her feet. "Back home, Rose, we have an expression—'A tumble in the hay.' Always used when innocence is in doubt. How are you going to explain the grass stains on your dress?"

"Me explain? You look like you've been digging trenches! Didn't you have a hat?"

Ike retrieved the blanket and his hat as Rose combed her hair. He got into the car, turned to Rose, and began to laugh. It felt good to laugh, and it felt even better when Rose laughed with him. "Rose, your father named you right. You are the most beautiful flower in the garden. Let's get you home."

Rose sat with her head tilted back, and her eyes closed, drinking in the warm summer air as they drove. Ike asked, "What have you heard from, Dottie?"

Rose sat straight up and turned to Ike. "Dottie, why does it always have to be about Dottie?"

Ike kept his eyes on the road. "I don't understand…"

BELLS OF REDEMPTION

"I've lived my whole life in Dottie's shadow—the pretty one, pure snow-white blonde hair. Perfect figure. Even her teeth are perfect, perfect smile too! She never said the wrong thing—kind and sweet. And the clever one, as well! The perfect Dottie! You have no idea. Every bloke in Churchstanton chased after her. They even asked me to help them. Help them? What am I, a wallflower? And she ignored them all."

Ike replied, "I didn't think she was interested in men before she met Charles."

"She wasn't, but that made them want her more—they thought she was just playing hard to get. And then Sir William found a place at Oxford for Dottie—the serious, studious, perfect one. There was no thought of me."

Rose sighed, then pulled a handful of hair in front of her head. "Maybe it's true. Dottie is regal and tall, like a Greek statue in the British Museum. I'm short, bumbling, with this mousy, dirty blonde hair, no education, and…"

Rose let go of her hair and blew from her face. She looked at Ike with inquisitive eyes. "You don't think I'm thick or trivial, do you, Ike?"

Ike smiled. "I think you're more than clever. You're resourceful and persistent, and even better, you're positive and fun to be around. And I find you beautiful. I think your straw blonde hair, I won't call it dirty blonde, for its beauty, especially with its strawberry red highlights, is simply enchanting, like a prism changing its colors with the light. Your eyes are deep blue, as deep as the well of your soul. Your face shines with exuberance and zest for life. And your figure, well, it certainly catches my attention."

Rose smiled. "You really think so? I want to believe you. You're right! After today, I no longer have any reason to be jealous."

Ike asked, "Tell me, what would you have liked to study?"

Rose smiled. "Why Medieval Literature with Doctor Lewis, of course. But Father would never bring it up with Sir William. One daughter's education was generous enough."

Rose sighed. "Every Sunday, we would listen to Doctor Lewis on the BBC…"

"He seems to be a favorite of your Uncle Hugh."

"Did you know that he teaches Medieval Literature? He's an expert, but most people know him for his fantasy novels and Christian teaching. He sees the connection between Medieval literature and legend and applies it to the Good News story of the Gospel. Stories have power, Ike. Jesus used stories—parables to connect with people. Stories as relevant today as they were two thousand years ago."

"It seems to me your research could teach the famous Doctor Lewis a thing or two about Medieval England."

Rose's face quickly turned serious. "Why did you ask about Dottie? Why ask me or Uncle Hugh? You should know better than us. Dottie has done something. She's at risk, isn't she? What haven't we been told? Now I feel guilty about everything I've just said. Poor Dottie. We're all she has. She's worried sick about her Charles, and she gets no support from her in-laws. They never approved of her."

"Who could disapprove of Dottie?"

Rose shook her head. "The upper class, of course. With

the aristocracy, it's always about marrying well and keeping the family's bloodline blue. Charles is the son of Lord Barkley, Baron of Cawmills. He is the second son, the spare, so to speak. His older brother stayed safely in the War Office in London while Charles risked his life with the RAF. There is a third brother, a younger brother still at Eton. When Charles went missing, his mother wrote to Dottie to say they would move to have the marriage annulled on the grounds it was never consummated.?"

"Surely not? Who could be so cruel?"

"In any eventuality, they don't want her to see a quid of family money. Sadly, Charles left for duty not two hours after their wedding."

"What does Dottie say?"

"She wrote back that a woman never forgets becoming one with her husband, the first and only man she ever shared a bed with. She has not communicated with them since. Now, Ike, you must tell me what you know about my sister."

"Your sister is a stubborn woman but a very brave one and capable. She is helping those who help our men escape the Nazis."

"O Lord, she's over there."

Chapter 20
Groundwork

Rose and Ike out beamed the late August sun as they drove back to Churchstanton. "Drop me off at the vicarage. I must check on Uncle Hugh," Rose said with a contented sigh.

Ike followed Rose into the house to give his regards to his friend. Ike heard the BBC news reader on the radio as Rose called out, "Oh Uncle Hugh, not again!"

Hugh was slumped over in his easy chair, an empty bottle of Bourbon beside him. Rose knelt over and sat him up, taking a framed picture that the sleeping man clung to his chest. Ike asked, "What's he clutching?"

"A picture of Aunt Jane. Too much drink makes him maudlin. He cries himself to sleep. He misses her so."

Hugh stirred, "What? Who? Oh, it's you, Rose. I'm fine. No fussing."

Ike turned off the radio. Hugh saw Ike, and said, "Been listening to C.S. Lewis lecturing us on dealing with loss. Platitudes! The man doesn't know—just doesn't know. Lifelong bachelor. Who has he lost?"

BELLS OF REDEMPTION

Hugh's words cut Ike to the quick and he couldn't shake them as he drove to the base. Ike mumbled to himself, "I can't deal with this now. I need to get to the base."

Ike stopped by the OPS Room across from his office and glanced at the status board. It was clear of any 545 activities. He stepped into the outer office and saw Flight Lieutenant Marley at his desk, bent over a pile of papers. "Hello, XO. Didn't expect to find you here on a Sunday night."

"I thought I would get a head start on next week's schedule and duty rosters."

Ike nodded. "Good man. You haven't seen anything on an upcoming extraction."

"No sir. I've been keeping an eye out for one." Marley looked up. "You're worried about Dorothy, Section Officer, Barkley. She's over there, isn't she."

"Yes, and another team as well. One whose insertion was compromised. I think I'll take a run over to Otterhead House tonight. I'm going to insist you get read in. Hell, you figure it out as it is."

"If you think it will, help." Marley studied Ike for a moment. "You might want to change your uniform, sir. It looks like..."

Ike glanced down at his grass-stained rumbled clothes. "A roll in the hay? Right. Castle Nemoche."

Marley quipped. "Nemoche? It's less than a ruin. There's nothing there!"

"Well, I beg to differ. There is a mount. A very steep mount covered in slippery grass. I took a tumble. All very innocent."

"Well, sir, if the pub rumors are true, you were likely in the company of a Miss Rose Osbourne, Dorothy's sister."

Ike shook his head. "I confess, that is true, but so is the innocent tumble. What else do you hear in the pub?"

"Probably less than the enlisted men. That Major Mickey has sent off Dorothy and now courts her sister."

"Major Mickey, am I?"

"Do you want me to put an end to that, sir?"

"No, let the men call me whatever makes them comfortable. And yes, I am seeing Rose Osbourne. Rose, Dorothy, and their uncle, Vicar Hugh Osbourne, have welcomed me into their family. They include me in Sunday dinner and conversation. But there has never been anything romantic between me and Dorothy. It is a friendship born of shared experience with separation from loss of... Hugh Osbourne is a widower as well."

"You don't owe me an explanation, skipper."

"Nigel, can I call you Nigel? There's something you can do for me."

"Yes, Nigel is fine. Anything, sir."

"You British have a highly structured etiquette, unfathomable to an American. I would like you to encourage men without it seeming to be an order..."

"Yes, sir, encourage them...."

"The parishioners of Saint Peter and Saint Paul would like to open their homes, show some support for the men. If they would come to Sunday worship a good home cooked meal would be provided."

"Yes, sir, you mentioned separation. They wish to share,

hoping their sons and brothers are being looked after as well."

"Yes, I hear their prayers every Sunday, perhaps…"

"I'll put the word out."

Ike smiled. "Thanks. What about you, Nigel? Care to join me next Sunday? Dinner with the Osbournes?"

"Thank you, but I'm no churchgoer. Had my fill as a lad."

"Sounds like a bad experience. I've had my issues as well. Care to tell me about it?"

"Pretty simple, really, and not all that unusual. I was a choir boy who the choirmaster took a shine to. Well, I fought him off and told the vicar. He insisted it was all a misunderstanding and I should never speak of it again."

"Well, I'm no one to preach—had my fill of hypocrites, myself. But Hugh, that is the Vicar, Reverend Hugh Osbourne, is different—genuine. He's a good listener and helpful. He makes it about you and God not what others may think. If nothing else, you're welcome for dinner and some of my Kentucky bourbon." *I hope his condition tonight doesn't mean I've misjudged him.* "Think about it. I'm off to Otterhead House."

"I'll do that, sir. Sure will be nice to have Dorothy back. I had no idea how much of the admin load she carried. Get her back soon, Skipper."

Ike drove up the darkened driveway to Otterhead House. The front face was lit by four large, blackened rearing otter sconces. The guard recognized Ike, saluted, and said, "Good evening, Major. You can park in front. Only Major Langley about tonight. You'll find him in the library."

The library? Ike returned the salute, parked, and clambered up the well-worn honey stone steps. Surprised, Ike poked his head into the darkened room. One desk light cast shadows on the warm wood paneling. A lone figure, sitting behind the lamp was bent over a book. "Langley? That you?"

Major Langley did not look up. "Ike, yes. Come join me."

Ike walked over, pulled out a chair, and sat across from Langley. "Reading? One of Sir William's books?"

Langley sighed. "Yes. The armistice terms of the Great War."

Ike jibed, "That would be 'The War to End all Wars?"

Langley nodded. "Negotiations. The Germans will never accept these terms. A stumbling block." Langley closed the book and looked up. "Good that you are here. I need to brief you on developments."

Goldenrod will not be returning soon. Been extended."

"Dorothy extended? How long? What have you gotten her into?"

Langley took a deep breath and exhaled. "Our Polish friends—a cell in Brussels, bring intelligence from the Abwehr—very senior officers. They want assurances. Dorothy just happened to be in the right place. They're intellectuals—find Dorothy to their liking. She's to get as much as she can—a good faith deposit so to speak. But." Langley paused.

"But their terms?"

"Right. Assurances that a new German government will be recognized. There will be no repeat of Versailles, no reparations, just an armistice followed by mutual withdrawal of forces. They seek peace and a return to normalcy."

Ike's brow tightened. "A new government? They're promising to remove Hitler! You mentioned a good faith deposit."

"Right. They say it's already in the bank—and we have it from another source of one attempt on the Fuhrer's life already."

"Then they're serious."

"Serious, perhaps. But they failed the first time. Can they succeed? Anyway, she's there until... well, until the PM plays his card. Churchill has made it clear he'll accept only unconditional surrender. We tasked Goldenrod with developing contacts with lower-level Abwehr insiders and German Resistance who can help with our escape lines before the high-level talks break down, which this book assures me will happen."

James Langley tapped the book. "Maybe, just maybe, these men will do the right thing regardless of the PM's stance."

"Abwehr? German resistance? And the Poles?"

"Hell, half our intelligence on the Nazis comes from the Poles. Their military intelligence largely escaped west—to Belgium, Holland, and France. By the way, we've heard from Roy and Val. They made it to our agent in Paris. They're doing a little digging on our friend, the Cobra. I don't see an extraction for at least ten days. But, of course, that can change."

"The 545 will continue our RECON, but I'll let Hastings know we should have aircraft available to him." Ike sat back and stared silently at Langley. "I need my Number One read in. Hell, he knows most of it anyway. He's a good man and..."

"Yes, I agree. Tomorrow. Bring him over."

Ike slid back into his chair and stood up. "One more thing. Seems Oaktree and special ops are on hold. I was thinking of maybe taking two- or three-days leave. I want to go north to

Durham with a friend to…"

"You want to go to Durham with Rose Osbourne and rummage through archives. Yeah, go. But I want you to make a stop in Chichester, another Cathedral. More importantly, I want you to meet the Bishop. He'll be expecting you."

That night, Ike sat down at his desk and began to write:

Dad,

This is hard for me to write, and I will need your help with young Earl. I've written about the Osbournes and how they've adopted me into the family. First of all, your prayers for Dorothy, I can't say why, but she is in harm's way. What a capable woman she is! And she has stepped up beyond anyone's expectations. But then, so did Linda.

But it's about her sister, Rose. Well, I didn't think I could love any woman other than Linda, but God has a way of surprising us. Yes, I said God. I believe He hears my prayers after all, though the answers haven't been too clear. Their Uncle Hugh, the vicar, is steering me back to faith. But Rose, well, somehow, I love her without forgetting Linda. And she is extraordinary! Strong and confident like Linda—why I am drawn to such strong women? But they are also so very different. Linda was tall, blonde and very aware of how people saw her. Rose is small, short, that is, petite? Her hair is dirty blonde streaked with red, and oh, how her eyes shine. A gray blue, but full of life and mischief! Not just her eyes— her smile. She radiates joy! Cheerful. I am amazed how good cheer brings patience, understanding, even forgiveness. Good cheer— I'm reminded of all those old Christmas carols. Now I understand the healing power of good cheer.

Bells of Redemption

Dad, I think I love her. She's like the thin pin that plugs the leak in my soul. But not pounded in with force. She bails me out gently, like a bilge stripper, not a 250 gpm dewatering pump. How do I tell Earl? No one can replace his mom, but I believe her warmth and cheer will not be rejected. Help me with this. I told Rose I could not marry without the blessing of my son. And certainly not without my family present. But you know war. I'm a soldier, and the war will move to the continent. I won't leave her as the disgraced mistress of a long-departed yank. Of course, she promises to wait, to search me out and hold me to my word.

What do I do, Dad?

Ike

PS: You never told me why Great Grandpa left Virginia, and why we are Baptist. To think Rose and Hugh are leading me back to Anglicanism—I hope that doesn't disappoint you.

CHAPTER 21
CATHEDRALS

Monday morning a three-day pass was waiting on Ike's desk. "Just fill in the date skipper and you're set."

"I need to make a few arrangements and prepare an itinerary with contacts if you need to get ahold of me—not that I don't think you can't handle it, XO, I know you can. I want to hear if there is any news on Section Officer Barkley. Durham. I need to find an inn or hotel in Durham. And also, Chichester."

"You're covering a lot of territory, Skipper. Durham is a good 270 miles north of London. It's an all-day train ride if indeed you can get there in one day. You'll need a ride to Taunton train station. And then Chichester?"

"Major Langley asked me to stop by Chichester enroute."

"Skipper, Chichester is on the coast, due south of London. Not exactly enroute."

Ike sighed. "Right. I'll need some help with these arrangements. I'm off to Otterhead. Be back in an hour."

Rose was surprised when Ike appeared at the door of

the church office. "Ike! What a pleasant surprise, why are you…"

"Rose, go home and pack your bag. We're off to Durham tomorrow. And when you are finished there, we'll stop by Chichester Cathedral on the way back."

"Tomorrow? Durham and then Chichester Cathedral? I don't understand."

"Well, if the archives of Saint Bede are important to you, the love of my life, they're important to me. And well, the side trip to Chichester is business, but we can make the most of it."

Rose stared, uncharacteristically silent. Ike beamed. "Pack, oh, and I need you to see to train tickets and hotel or inns. Not sure how that's done. I'll stop by this evening—perhaps dinner at the pub, and we can…"

Rose found her voice. "Slow down, Ike. You want me to make arrangements for the two of us to travel to Durham tomorrow? For how long? And find accommodation? There's a war going on. Rooms are scarce. And, and…."

"I thought you would jump at the chance. I've got a pass—if it's too hard, I can cancel…."

"No! Please no! I want to go. It'll work, somehow. But forget the pub tonight. Come to the house. And you can explain all of this to Uncle Hugh."

Ike beamed. "Great! See you tonight, say 1800. I mean 6 pm. I'll bring a bottle for Hugh."

Rose nodded. Ike turned and looked around. "How about a kiss from the fairest maiden in Churchstanton to hold me over until then?"

Rose blushed, "In church? Come here, yank, let me show

you how," she grabbed Ike's tie, pulled him near, and kissed him with great English vigor!

Ike returned at six and knocked on the door of the vicarage. A stern-faced Hugh answered. Spying the neck of a bottle of bourbon peeking out from a paper bag, Hugh scolded, "It will take more than that bottle for me to consent to this romp you planned. Better come in and explain yourself, Major."

Major? He's serious. Ike stepped into the sitting room. Rose was not in sight. "Hugh…"

"It's Reverend Osbourne, Major. Rose is under my oversight while her father is away. Just what are your intentions?"

Ike pulled the bottle from the bag and set it on the table. "My intentions are to let Rose shine. I want to share in her dreams, her ambitions, her life. I want to see through her eyes what drives her passion… perhaps passion is not the right word. Uncle Hugh, yes, I am mad about Rose, but you must believe me, and I have already shared this with Rose, I will protect her reputation. I will not leave her the talk of the village when I depart. Mad is not the word. Love. There, you heard me. I love your niece, and I dream of our future together. I told her—we agree that after the war, when it is safe, when my son can — when everything is proper, then, only then, when it is safe for her, will we walk down the aisle of Saint Peter and Saint Paul. Until then, she will always be safe, honored in my presence, and, well…"

Ike paused. He felt Hugh's eyes boring into him. At last, Hugh picked up the bottle and said, "And Rose told you she would search for you and hold you to your promise."

Hugh sighed, then nodded and, with a smile, said, "I believe you are a man of your word, Ike. This calls for a drink. Rose, bring out a couple of glasses so we can toast your future together."

A beaming Rose bounded like a gazelle from the kitchen with three glasses. She set them on the table, threw her arms around Ike's neck and kissed him. "Never forget, Ike, never forget, if you don't come back to me, I will search you out. You will be mine, and Earl will have a loving home."

Hugh reached into his pocket and pulled out a small envelope. "Here's a letter I wrote to Bishop Williams of Durham. He'll remember me from our days at Cambridge. I would never have graduated without his help. He was first, I was, well, they let me through."

Bishop Alwyn Williams did remember his school chum, Hugh Osbourne. "Hughie? Vicar at Saint Peter and Saint Paul in Churchstanton? A faithful shepherd, from what I've heard."

Ike replied, "He had high praise for you, my Lord."

Bishop Williams smiled, his eyes looking into the past. "Hughie was not the best student, but I could see, even then, that he was what the church needed: a man with a big heart. How he loved people! Someone told me he lost his wife."

Rose nodded. "Yes, my aunt Jane. She and their first child died giving birth."

"And yet he continues."

The Bishop paused and reflected. "How very sad and yet not unusual for God's called servant, to suffer. Well, of course, Miss Osbourne, you may research the archives. Saint Bede's documents are, of course, property of the Bishopric; however, years ago, the wise decision was made for the University to maintain custody on behalf of the church. This facilitates proper care and supervised study. I will provide a note to the library and ensure someone assists you."

The churchman paused and looked over his glasses. "May I ask what it is you are looking for?"

Rose looked at Ike before answering. "I found something of interest in the Churchstanton archives. I'm certain it was overlooked for ages—among a vicar's notes we found reference to Saint Bede's request for history of the early church, and with Churchstanton a close neighbor to Glastonbury—and our local legends...."

"You'll find no reference to the Holy Grail in the archives of Saint Bede, Miss Osbourne."

"No, your Grace, but we hope, perhaps, to find reference of Churchstanton's contribution to Bede's history. It is a very old parish with Roman sites nearby. It would make an excellent contribution to our parish history."

"While I will not stand in your way, it is well accepted that local churches of the later Roman years did not continue after the Roman withdrawal, apart from perhaps a few congregations in Wales. As for Joseph of Arimathea and the Holy Grail, well, it is a lovely legend."

Bishop Williams turned to Ike, and asked, "And why have you joined in Miss Osbourne's pursuit?"

Confusion flashed across Ike's face. Rose replied, "Major Curtis is a family friend. It appears his forefather, Robert Curtis, Earl of Montclair, Lord Inquirer to Kings James and King Charles I also appeared in the archive. I insisted he come along and learn his heritage."

"Montclair? Lord Inquirer, yes, I have come across that name, but I recall the title Inquirer General. Something to do with the Holy Isle of Lindisfarne. Yes. Well, good hunting. Oh, by the way, we would welcome the addition of your note regarding Saint Bede's request for the archives. Hasn't been an addition in years."

Rose shuffled her feet before nodding. "Right, I did not bring it along, your Grace. And though only a fragment remains, it is highly valued in our archives, but I will certainly send you a transcript when I return."

As Ike and Rose left Auckland Castle. Ike stopped to take in the view. "Now, this is a castle. Not like that hill you call Neroche. What's the name of the church behind us? It looks old."

Rose turned and looked. "It's the Chapel of Saint Peter. I read that it was built in the twelfth century. It's the Bishop's chapel."

"Hmmph. And why is the bishop here in Auckland Castle and not in his Cathedral in Durham? It sure looked like a grand Cathedral from the Hotel window."

"This is the Bishop's palace. I don't know why it was moved here from Durham Castle. Probably wanted to get away from the city."

"Some shepherd he was, running away from his flock!"

Rose scowled. "I'm sure there was a very good reason. Do you want to talk about Castles and Cathedrals or help me search the archives?"

"I'm just trying to make sense of this. I've never seen

anything like it in my life. So, there is a castle in Durham, once the Bishop's palace and the Cathedral?"

"Don't worry, you can't miss them. They're right across the river from the University. Now, can we go to the library?"

Driving under the tower clock of the entrance gateway, Ike said, "Good catch when he asked for the Abbot's note. You know infrared technology is a secret. You must never share that document or how we read it."

Rose sighed. "Never?"

"Well, not now. Not while we are at war and the technology is secret. Someday, it will be used for better purposes, peaceful work, even researching ancient documents."

As they drove into Durham, Rose reminded Ike, "Park at the hotel, we'll never be allowed to park near the library—it's on the green—the center of the University. And it's only a five-minute walk."

Ike pulled in front of the Hotel Royal County. "Any chance for lunch before we go? If I know you, you won't leave until the custodian throws you out."

Rose sighed. "All right. But not the hotel dining room—it will take too long. We just passed a pub. There it is, not a hundred yards, the Half-Moon Inn. Much quicker, and much more affordable."

Fortified with a mediocre shepherd's pie—there was a war on—the couple walked briskly across Palace Green to the Durham University Library. Rose handed a librarian the note from Bishop Williams. The young woman quickly read the note and looked up at Rose. "Please wait here, Miss Osbourne, while I speak with the Head Librarian. An escort will be provided at once."

As the Librarian hurried off, Ike mumbled, "It's good to have friends in high places. But be sure you can use our little red torch out of sight of peering eyes."

Soon the Head Librarian appeared with two assistants. "Miss Osbourne, this is Miss Thatcher. She will show you to the Saint Bede collection. Please give his Grace our best regards."

Rose smiled. "I will do that Miss, Miss…

"Mrs. Hawkins."

"I will gladly report to Bishop Williams on the assistance I receive. Now, I have much research to do and so little time."

"You heard her, Miss Thatcher. Make sure they have everything they need."

Miss Thatcher proudly commented as they walked. "This gallery is the main reading room. It was originally the Cosin library, founded by Bishop Cosin in 1667. The University Library was permitted use of the library when it was founded in 1833. Since then, the roof has been raised to permit this grand room. The library has been expanded with a two-story porch and the reception area where we met. The University assumed full custodianship of the combined libraries a few years ago. Very exciting! The portrait panels you see above the bookshelves were painted by Jan Baptist van Eerssel in 1668. The Saint Bede collection is only available to scholars or, of course, by request of the bishop. It is safely locked away in a vault. I must insist nothing be removed from the collection."

They followed Miss Thatcher down a narrow corridor of locked doors. Near the end, she stopped, chose a key from a large ring, and unlocked the door. She turned on the electric lights and stepped into the small windowless room. "Saint Bede's collection is boxed by date. There is an index catalog here at the desk. You open a box here at this desk. When you are finished with a box all contents must be redeposited and the box returned to the shelf before another box can be opened. Nothing leaves this room. Is there a year you wish to begin with? Or perhaps you want to search the catalog first?"

Rose replied, "Saint Bede's call to the churches for the history of the Romans in Britain."

Miss Thatcher flipped through the card index. "The first mention is contained in box 23, row four, shelf 3. Come, I'll show you."

The librarian led them to the shelf and pulled down a box tied closed with a purple ribbon. "Here we go. Now, before you open it, please record the number and today's date and sign your name. Do this for each box."

Rose quickly completed the log entry, picked up the box, and undid the ribbon. The interior of the box was lined with a patterned material, perhaps linen, to protect the documents from the chemicals in the cardboard box. "Can I touch them?" she asked.

"Right. Gloves. I didn't mention gloves. There should be some here. Ah, yes. One pair. Only one of you should handle the documents."

Rose put on the gloves. *Vellum! Perfect!* Ike, I'll read, and you can take notes. Oh my! We left the notebooks in the car."

Ike shook his head. "The car is at the hotel!"

Rose turned to the earnest young librarian. "Miss Thatcher, any chance you could loan us a notebook or two?"

Rose lifted the first document and began to read the Latin script. Miss Thatcher sighed. "I really shouldn't leave you alone."

Rose did not lift her eyes from the document. "The bishop will certainly vouch for us. You have his letter."

Ike interjected, "If it would make you feel better, lock us in while you go back for the notebooks. We'll be your prisoners until you return!"

The young librarian rubbed her chin. "I am supposed to assist you, I suppose…"

Ike repeated the offer. "Go. Lock the door if you must. Just don't forget us."

"I suppose so. You really don't mind? I'll be back in ten minutes."

Miss Thatcher left closing the door behind her. They listened as the key turned the lock. "She will come back," Rose assured herself.

Ike asked, "If there is a letter here, you should not need the infrared."

Rose set the first document down and picked up another. "You're probably right. But it hasn't been found yet, so perhaps…"

"Hasn't been found yet? More likely it doesn't exist…"

Rose's eyes flashed. "It must!"

Ike continued, "Or perhaps they didn't recognize it for what it was."

"Or the monastery was short of funds and reused the velum. We don't have time for this. Just give me the torch."

Ike reached into his jacket pocket and pulled out the

small khaki flashlight with the red lens and silently handed it to Rose. She turned it on and pointed it towards the top document. "Just as I suspected! Written over." She quickly pulled out document after document, each revealing a second Latin text beneath in fading black ink. "They are all on scraped vellum!"

Ike peaked over her shoulder. "Anything worth reading?"

Rose sighed. "No. These are just routine practice sheets from the scriptorium. But they prove something important may be hidden."

Ike looked at his watch. "Right. Time. Why did you start with this box? The letter from the abbot would be at least a year, maybe two later."

Rose snorted. "Who's the archivist here? I'm looking for the request. Did it go to his bishop first and then to others? The archbishop of York? And then where? And how were the responses to be collected? It must be in this box."

Rose mumbled in Latin as she quickly went through the pages. "Yes! A petition from Bede to the Bishop requesting permission to query the churches and parishes of all of England to record the history of the realm from the Roman days until the present. And it is witnessed and approved by the Abbot of Jarrow. We must set it aside for notes when Miss Thatcher returns."

Rose kept staring at the delicate letter. "To think Saint Bede held this very document in his hand. His quill dipped in an ancient ink well nine hundred years ago penned these words, and I hold it in my hand."

Ike mumbled, "Yes, but this document is plain to see. It

must be in the catalog. Why not look for Bede's warrant in the catalog and save us some time?"

Rose blushed. "You're right, of course. Look for the answer and then the responses."

Rose found the reply cataloged, to be found at the bottom of the very same box. Pulling it out she read and interpreted. "As I suspected, it was quickly forwarded to the Archbishop of York who immediately sent instructions to the dioceses in the north and forwarded with a strong recommendation to the Archbishop of Canterbury for action in the south and west. Each parish priest was asked to provide, with the help of local Abbots, what local history he could. Royal history would be provided through Canterbury aided by the Privy Council and the King's Chaplain."

Ike asked, "Does the catalog list each response? Does it organize them in any way?"

Her answer came quickly. "By Bishopric. Churchstanton is a parish of Bath and Welles, box 25."

Ike ran to retrieve the box. "You start with this box while I return the last."

Rose reluctantly returned the letters to the lined box. *Oh, to spend hours, days, and months going through these archives. What a glory to hold so rich a history in my hands.*

Her thoughts were interrupted by the sound of a key in the lock. Hinges creaked, and the door opened. Miss Thatcher was back with notebooks, pens, and two more pairs of gloves.

Rose greeted her. "I hope you don't mind. We returned box 23. I checked the catalog and saw box 25 should contain what I am looking for, if it exists."

"Well, I suppose that's alright."

Rose quickly went through the box. The top document was a letter from Bishop Lyfing. "He writes that all his parishes and abbeys have responded. They're all here, Ike. Now let me find Churchstanton."

Rose kept digging and reading. She got to the bottom, set the last page down, and turned to Ike. "It's not here. Nothing from Churchstanton and nothing from Glastonbury."

Rose reread the letter from Bishop Lyfing. "Yes, it clearly says all replied."

Ike said, "But he does not say all are included. Could he have held them back? He must have. What do we know of Bishop Lyfing?"

Miss Thatcher replied, "There are records of all the bishops and abbots as well." She went to the catalog and quickly shouted. "Box 1, of course."

Miss Thatcher quickly retrieved box 1 and found an index of Bishops. "Here it is. Bath Welles, Bishop Lyfing. Previously Abbot of Chertsey. Bishop of Bath-Welles 998 through 1013 when he was consecrated Archbishop of Canterbury."

Ike replied, "Archbishop of Canterbury? No doubt politically astute and well-regarded by the king. I'm not saying he wasn't a good man and faithful priest, it's just that...."

Rose was mumbling. "Let me remember, the turn of the eleventh century—Danish invasions, Chertsey is in Surrey—Anglo Saxon. Yes, he would have crowned Cnut—a Danish conqueror, King. Perilous times, Ike. He led the Church through very hard times."

Miss Thatcher interjected. "It says here his birth name

was Aelfstan. An Anglo-Saxon name. Elf stone. He was given his name Lyfing or Darling when he entered the abbey."

Ike sighed. "It doesn't appear you're going to find what you're looking for here."

"No. London. How do I get access to the archives of Lambert Palace? Perhaps a note from Bishop Williams? But before we go, Miss Thatcher, Seventeenth Century—Lindisfarne—can you take us to the archives?"

"Certainly."

Ike looked at his watch. "It's getting late. I'm sure Miss Thatcher needs to get home on time. Why don't we return in the morning?"

CHAPTER 22
LIGHT AND DARK

It was late. Ike and Rose stepped out of the library into the dark night. The moon and stars were shrouded in clouds. The green and the streets were empty. No streetlamps marked their path. No window signaled a warm hearth and refuge from overwhelming darkness. Even so, Rose slipped her hand into his. With her free hand, she switched on the little, red-lensed torch and pointed it toward the ground. "Good to have in the blackout. At least until our eyes adjust."

As she spoke, the gray-black sky cracked, and the darkest black was painted with bright, cheerful stars. The crack widened as the clouds withdrew their foreboding blanket. A quarter moon soon appeared floating above them. Ike felt the tension ebb like a falling tide. "I think this is the best moment of the trip. Not that today wasn't rewarding. It's just that it's good to be walking beside you—your hand in mine. It's peaceful—I could forget there is a war. Just you and I...." Ike's voice trailed off.

Rose squeezed his hand, pulled herself close, and leaned her head against his shoulder. She sighed. "I've never been so happy. Oh, Ike, promise me it will always be like this. You and I, together beneath a starry sky—apart from every worry and fear,"

Ike stopped, wrapped both arms around her and kissed her. "I can promise you this, I will always cherish this moment—our moments, our time together. I will remember how soft you are against me, how your hair tickles my nose when I smell the nape of your neck, how your lips beg to be kissed, and how your eyes swallow mine and draw me deep inside your soul."

Rose looked up into Ike's eyes. "Is it real, Ike? Is this what love feels like? Is it forever? Oh, please tell me this is forever!"

"Real? Oh, yes. And I will hold onto it forever."

The two walked on in silence, content with the love that bound them. They came to the hotel. Ike wondered aloud, "Do you think the dining room is still open?"

Rose quipped, "I will insist they find us a quiet, lonely spot."

Ike laughed. "One thing I know, no one can say no to Rose Osbourne, why...."

The peace was broken by rumbling thunder. The night air reverberated with steady, rhythmic booms. A doorman unseen in the shadows of the darkened entrance called out. "Better come in. No telling if a kraut overshoots his target or has an errant bomb. Quickly, if you please, sir and madam."

Bombs, Ike thought. *The clear sky brought the Luftwaffe!* "Where? How far?"

The doorman replied, "By the sound of it, Sunderland. The shipyards, no doubt. Not fifteen miles east. We here in

Durham have been lucky so far. Surprising, what with the mining works nearby."

Ike muttered, "Sounds like they're coming this way."

The doorman replied, "Aye. Some nights, if the wind is right, you can hear the fighters goin' after them over the sea and the crack, crack, crack of the coastal artillery guns. Tonight, it's Sunderland. It could just as well be Shields or Newcastle. The sad truth is they won't stop the works. The ships will be built, the ports are still open. It's the sad sots who live there killed in their beds, blown apart at their supper table. Hundreds, maybe thousands. Aye, they pay the price. The clouds, only the clouds, keep them away, and even then, they may drop their bombs in frustration, hoping to kill any on whom they fall."

Ike and Rose stood at the door in silence. "Right, better ye be getting in. Have a hot meal and a good night's rest." He held the door open and smiled as they went in.

Ike followed as Rose chose a table in the corner of the empty dining room and sat quietly as they waited for service. "You're worried about Dottie," Ike said softly. "The bombs brought the war back to you."

Rose looked up with hopeful eyes. "Is it wrong to be happy—to forget the war for a time?"

Ike smiled. "I think God gives us moments of happiness, reminders of love, to help us through the troubles. I'm no preacher, but it seems to me that good times and bad times come jumbled together as if they are at war with each other. They are a reminder that we live in a troubled world, but even in the darkest night, God lets his stars sparkle in the heavens as a reminder."

"Just a reminder?"

"No, I think it is more of a promise that he is there. He cares and will, as his prayer assures us, deliver us from evil."

Rose's eyes brightened. "You remind me of something Uncle Hugh said. It was the Sunday after the miracle of Dunkirk. He preached on Daniel, well, Meshach, Shadrach, and Abednego, Daniel's three friends in the fiery furnace. He said, 'God comes to us in the fire. He did not come before the fire but in the fire. He is with us when we need him, in our troubles. Not just before, not preventing, but enduring. Better than enduring, protecting—saving. Those three friends of Daniel had faith. They trusted God. Even if God did not save them, they proclaimed their faith. The Lord was their God and Savior. Do you think Dottie remembers? Oh, I pray those who did not make it off the beach of Dunkirk and the good people under the bombs that fell tonight—I pray they knew the peace of his presence."

"He gives us strength when we need it, not always before."

Ike reached across and took her hands into his. "Tonight, these past weeks—how much stronger are we knowing we are loved? He has given us each other."

The waiter came over. "Good evening. The kitchen is about to close."

Ike nodded. "Well, I'm hungry, so anything filling."

"Something hearty, then. We are known for our game pie. Tonight, it's turkey and Ham, and we have a hearty pea and ham soup."

Ike looked to Rose, who nodded. "Bring them on! Enough for two and two good ales."

As the waiter walked away, Ike said, "Now, tomorrow. What exactly are we looking for?"

"Why Robert Curtis, of course. You heard the bishop. Somehow, Ike, your ancestor is tied to the Holy Isle of Lindisfarne. There is something about you—your return to England. It's like a recovery of your ancestry, a return to duty, a noble cause."

"I'll grant you that fighting Nazi Germany may be a noble cause, but I'm no knight of the Round Table on a great quest."

Rose laughed. "Let's see what we find tomorrow, my shining knight."

The morning drizzle did nothing to curb Rose's enthusiasm. As they scurried along beneath a shared umbrella, Rose cheerfully commented, "After the library, we must visit the Cathedral."

"It does look grand. Nothing like it where I come from."

"The building is impressive—a wonderful expression of Norman art and architecture, but I'm talking about the chapels—one to Saint Bede and one to Saint Cuthbert, founder of the abbey at Lindisfarne. You'll learn more about him today."

Miss Thatcher greeted them at the front desk and led them to the Lindisfarne archives. Rose spoke up: "Yesterday, Bishop Williams mentioned references to an Earl of Montclair, Sir Robert Curtis. We would like to see any, really, all references to him."

"Not a bishop or abbot. Let me see if he is cross-referenced."

Miss Thatcher's fingers moved swiftly through the box of index cards. "Here's one. Captain Robert Curtis, cross-referenced to the archives of Bishop Neile of Durham. I'll get the box."

She was back in a moment. Flipped down through the documents and pulled out a ledger. Following her finger as she speed-read, she said, "Here it is. Received a letter from Archbishop Abbott granting a preferment with emolument to the *priest* Robert Curtis. Vicar of the hospital, orphanage, old people's house, and workhouse in Berwick-upon-Tweed. 150 pounds a year paid by the Holy See of Canterbury. Father Curtis, also Sheriff of Cawmills and Captain of the Royal Cawmills Cuirassiers, will call upon the Bishop of Durham, who is charged with his spiritual and clerical oversight."

Rose shouted, "A Priest? And Sheriff?"

Ike shook his head. "And Captain of Cuirassiers, I might add."

Rose mumbled, "No title. He was a commoner."

"Makes me like him more," Ike replied.

Miss Thatcher turned the page. "It's attached to another report. Yes, this one concerns Lindisfarne. "Sergeant Aidan Lilburn, Royal Cawmills Cuirassiers, returned a Lindisfarne Gospel recovered by Captain Robert Curtis, stolen and held by the papist and traitor, the Reverend Doctor Fitzhugh, found in the possession of Harold Percy, keeper of Alnwick Castle."

Miss Thatcher turned to a note that was included by an archivist as Rose asked, "Is there more?"

"There is a note that the recovered Lindisfarne Gospel is in our collection along with the famous four Gospels penned by Bishop Eadfrith in about 715. The gospel recovered by Father Curtis was also quite early, well decorated and included old

English word-for-word translations from the Latin Vulgate between each line."

Rose chimed, "In the collection? Can we see it?"

"Yes, of course. But there is another mention of Robert Curtis. Bishop Neile noted that Father Robert Curtis knighted Sir Robert, was made Earl of Montclair upon agreeing to marry a ward of the king, Lady Eleanor Montclair, and declared the King's Lord Inquirer, all in reward for saving the King from assassins and capturing his assailants."

Ike said softly, "He earned it. He earned his title."

Rose reached for his hand. "There is a love story here. His agreed marriage to Lady Eleanor. I just know, somehow, it was a love match."

Miss Thatcher added, "His preferment came from the Archbishop of Canterbury. Most unusual. There must be much more to his story." She picked up the next page and read to herself. "There is more here. Correspondence from Bishop Laud of London, he followed Archbishop Abbott as Archbishop of Canterbury. Hmm. He was no friend of Sir Robert Curtis and questioned his allegiances and fitness as a priest. It is well known Bishop Laud feuded with Archbishop Abbott. It seems Sir Robert was a friend of Archbishop Abbott. Bishop Neile defended Sir Robert, admitting Father Curtis befriended and supported non-conformists, Scottish Kirk Presbyterians, Lutherans, and Calvinists; nevertheless, he was faithful to the Church of England and well known for his good works to widows, orphans, and the infirm. His tenants were said to be partners in his trading company. He was well regarded for providing food to protestant refugees of the 30-year war on the continent, though some feared he brought too many German refugees to England. Oh, and here is an account of the wedding—a double wedding! Yes, his lieutenant, oh, this seemed a scandal!"

"Scandal? Let me see that." Ike said.

Taking the page, he read. "Here it is, married at Berwick-upon-Tweed alongside a former sergeant and reputed smuggler Edward Barkley, now Barron of Cawmills. It says King James gave him the Curtis family title taken from the traitor Sir Geoffrey Curtis, redeemed by Viscount Berwick, Lord James Curtis…"

Ike looked up. "Barkley? Rose, did you say Dottie's in-laws are the Barkleys? Baron of Cawmills?"

Rose was stunned. "Yes, well, Charles' father is Baron of Cawmills."

Ike laughed. "So much for their blue blood! A reputed smuggler! He would've done well on the Washington coast during prohibition."

Rose shook her head. "But obviously a friend of Sir Robert, enough that they paid to redeem a family title only to grant it to Barkley."

Ike read on, "Barkley's wife the widowed wife of a gamekeeper—strange friends for a Lady, a ward of the king. Miss Thatcher, where could we find more information on Sir Robert?"

Rose laughed. "So now you're interested!"

Miss Thatcher replied, "As a Lord Inquirer, there should be palace archives in London. And then, Archbishop Abbott's archives are at Lambeth Palace. And I suspect, as a Lord, more might be found in the archives of Parliament. Of course, the family would have the most complete history."

Rose reminded, "Miss Thatcher, you promised to show us the Lindisfarne Gospels."

"Yes, if you are finished, Major? Let me lock up here. I will take you over."

Could I really be a descendant of an Earl? A priest, soldier, and spy? Curtis is a common surname, even so. He set the letter back in the box. "Right. Of course. The Gospels. Lead the way."

Chapter 23
Das Lamm

Ike adjusted the window shade against the bright morning sun. He inhaled deeply the scent of her hair as she slept cuddled alongside him, her head resting peacefully on his shoulder. The rhythmic swaying of the railcar on the tracks provided a false sense of peace. *How lovely she looks—innocent and vulnerable. How like a child. I've never seen her asleep before. Her energy! I thought she could never stop. Last night was wonderful. Almost magical. We talked—it was about nothing and everything, But I haven't had a more enjoyable time since, well, since....*

Ike carefully leaned over and kissed the top of her head. *I had to laugh when she came down this morning. She both smiled and yawned her way through breakfast. It was a late night, nearly dawn, before we went to our rooms. Not even strong coffee (at least they called it coffee) could bring her to full consciousness. But I love her just as much asleep as awake. I like her beside me, feeling safe. Yes. I want to protect her; to know she can trust me. I must protect her.*

The railcar shook as the wheels screeched, passing over

an uneven rail. Jolted awake, a weary-eyed Rose whispered, "What was I saying? Oh, yes. We must go back north. Lindisfarne. You must see it." Rose looked up at Ike, "What? That smile. What's so funny?"

"I could count your breaths by the wisp of hair you blew away with each breath."

"You think I was sleeping? I was just resting my eyes."

"Well, after an hour, they should be well rested. It's okay. It was a late night, and I'm just happy to have you beside me."

Rose straightened up, stretched, and yawned. "Are you sure we can't spend some time in London? We must change trains anyway. There's so much we could learn there, so many unanswered questions."

"Another time. I promise. I'm worried about Dottie and others as well. I need to get back. And I agreed to meet someone in Chichester. We will have one more night, but we must get back."

"You're worried too? Why don't you call in and see if there is any news?"

"Rose, you know they can't give operational information over the phone. I'm sure you can find something to do. I'm meeting a man under the cross. He said I would know it when I see it."

"Not at the Royal Sussex barracks? Who are you meeting?"

"Never mind. There must be a Cathedral or something historic in the town."

"Yes, it was once a Roman city, and it is famous for its

ancient church and cathedral and Saint Richard. I'll take you to the cross. It is a five-hundred-year-old covered market gate over the intersection of four streets."

Rose pointed to the cross as they stopped in front of the hotel. Ike nodded. "Hard to miss." He looked at his watch. "I'll be back for dinner."

Ike walked into the market and spotted a newsstand. He chose a paper and said softly, "You wouldn't have change for a dollar? Not a shilling or pence left in change."

The vendor quickly took the bill, slipped a note on top of the paper and said, "Give this address to the hackney driver."

Ike nodded. "What about my change?"

The man smiled. "Sorry, not a shilling or pence left in my pocket. Good day, yank."

The taxi driver dropped Ike off in front of a small stone cottage behind the Bishop's Palace. His knock on the door was immediately answered. "Major Curtis, I presume. Please, come through. He is expecting you."

Ike followed the young man down two flights of stairs, through an underground tunnel into the Bishop's Palace. "Please forgive the informality, but not all visitors want to be seen coming or going."

"And that goes for the Bishop, himself, from time to time, I suppose."

His guide silently led him up into a small room. "Please wait here. I'm sure it won't be long."

Five minutes later, a tall, thin man with graying hair, wearing the simple clerical collar of a priest, entered the room. He extended his hand and said, "You must be Major Curtis.

George Bell. I'm glad you could find time to see me."

Ike rose. "Your Grace…"

"George. Please, and your given name?"

"Ike, well, it's really Montclair. Montclair Isaac, but it's a long story."

Bishop Bell smiled. "Ike it is." He sighed. "I'm hoping you can help me. James Langley suggested we speak. You're the one with the airplanes. There is someone we must get out—out of Germany. He's in grave danger. Done his best, more than one in his position should ever be asked."

Ike replied, "You're talking about an extraction—from Nazi Germany? A high-value politician? Why come to me? This sounds like an MI6 operation."

"High-value person, yes. But not a politician. And though I have a good relationship with MI6, my friend is a trusted source in the Abwehr, but some of my views—solid Christian views questioning the morality of area bombing, taking the life of civilians—many women and children, well, I find it reprehensible, unchristian and barbaric. I know the Luftwaffe is guilty, but is Hitler to be our standard? So, let's just say MI6 is too public, too political…"

Ike couldn't help but interrupt. "MI6 too public? They are the most secretive…"

"MI6 does nothing that has not been approved at the highest levels of government, the Prime Minister and many others, stubborn, all of them."

Ike sighed. "And you think I can do what MI6 refuses."

"James Langley thinks that MI9 is not MI6 and that your little squadron flies unwatched by the higher levels. He reminded me that American Officers were perceived to, how should I put this, to play loose with their standing orders. Being results-driven, a certain latitude is given for seizing the initiative."

Ike snorted. "I think the word you're looking for is cowboy. We're a bunch of cowboys with no discipline."

"Not my choice, Major. I'm sure a successful operation requires a great deal of discipline."

"Tell me, who do you want extracted and from where?"

"His name is Dietrich Bonhoeffer, a theologian. But let's call him 'the Lamb' Foolish enough to leave safety in the United States to return to Germany and fight against Hitler. He's in Berlin. But where the extraction takes place is something you will arrange. We can expect some mobility. He has traveled, most recently to Sweden."

"Sweden is neutral! Why doesn't he return there."

"Too provocative. He is Abwehr working for the resistance. We believe he is being watched, as are others in his cell. A silly matter of poor accounting. He would be a fugitive, held by the Swedes, unable to leave, and well, Sweden hasn't been hospitable to refugees from the Nazis. No, he must disappear from inside Germany or Nazi-occupied territory."

"Just one man, no family?"

"As you say, family as well. No wife or children, but his mother and father and his sister and brother-in-law, also in the German resistance, also Abwehr. His brother-in-law recruited Dietrich into the Abwehr for his protection."

"You call him Dietrich. It's personal. You are close to him."

Bells of Redemption

Bishop Bell nodded. "Yes. He is a friend. A good Christian brother. He put his life on the line, as a Christian, to fight Nazism by cutting off the head of the snake. He and others in the Abwehr have helped us—with solid intelligence and we lead them on with hollow assurances of help and promises our government will never honor. Personal, yes. But it is the right thing to do, and you can see that MI6 will not do it. Their hands are tied by government ministers. Let the good perish along with the bad, a small price to pay in this ugly war."

Ike sat silently. George Bell was wise enough to let the Spirit of God move in the heart of the American officer sitting across from him. Ike looked up and said, "I will need more to go on. An extraction will require precise planning and extensive coordination."

"James Langley will see that you get what you need. Who knows, Ike, perhaps God has called us to this time and this work."

The Bishop stood up. "Let me give you something, Ike. It will help you understand Doctor Bonhoeffer, to see a brilliant mind joined to a willing heart. It's a book he wrote." He took a book from his desk and handed it to Ike. "'The Cost of Discipleship.' Dietrich is willing to pay the price."

Ike took the book, turned it over, and read the synopsis on the back cover. "'When Jesus calls a man, He bids him come and die.' Let's pray it doesn't come at the hands of the Nazis."

That night at dinner, Ike asked Rose rhetorically, "How do they do it? How do men offer up the lives of other good men in their belief in the greater good? How far will they go? How many deaths are too many? Nigel Marley told me Britain allowed the sinking of the RMS Lusitania liner filled with innocent people during WWI rather than tip their hand they had cracked the German Navy code. How do they sleep at night?"

Rose looked compassionately at the man she loved. "Something happened at your secret meeting. Something has brought this horrible war bearing down on you. What did he say? I know you can't tell me secrets, but I want to help."

Ike smiled and handed Rose Bonhoeffer's book. "Homework. I am to read this book."

Rose stared, dumbfounded.

Ike sighed and looked away. *Dottie is doing their dirty work. Gathering intelligence from brave Germans risking their lives to stop this war. She is passing on false promises to men whose fates are almost certainly sealed.*

Ike's first stop after dropping Rose off at home was to Otterhead House. He stopped by the OPS Room and read the board. No new OPS schedules for Oaktree or Mongoose were posted. Ike knew that didn't mean things weren't happening, only that no new operations were scheduled from headquarters. The action remained with the teams in France.

Ike stepped across the hall to Major Langley's office. A light rap on the open door, and Langley looked up from his desk. "Ike! Come through! Close the door behind you."

Ike entered, shut the door and sat down. Langley continued, "Now that your wanderlust has been satisfied, you can get back to work."

Ike replied, "Nothing new on the board. What have you heard from Dorothy?"

"Goldenrod is safe. Excellent agent, a natural. Doing splendid work. Getting far more from the Krauts than they intend to share or even know they give."

"So, she continues to string them along. They are risking their lives to help end this war."

"That's a little harsh, Ike. Aren't we all at risk in war? Goldenrod is performing as ordered. It takes a great deal of discretion and finesse to carry on negotiations before…"

"Before they learn, they will receive nothing in return."

"Not so. Their information will be used to end the war, just not as they plan."

"How far do you expect her to go? Does she know she is just stringing them along? And what happens to her when they learn it is all for naught?"

Langley fidgeted with his good arm to find a pack of cigarettes in his jacket. "I've warned you, Mic, about the dangers of a personal interest in agent Goldenrod." Langley stopped to tap the end of his cigarette on the desk before putting it in his mouth, fumbling with a book of matches, and finally lighting it. A simple task made difficult with one arm. He took a drag and put the cigarette down in an ashtray. He leaned back and said, "You need to have more faith in her. She spends evenings at the opera, symphonies, and best restaurants. Her days at the art museums and galleries. She reports she is treated with the respect due a lady. She sees their intention to present themselves as cultured, thinking, and civilized men, not the monsters the press would have you believe."

Ike replied, "All the same, I hope you have a solid escape plan for when the time comes. What about Val and Ray?"

"In Paris now on the trail of Cobra. Nothing yet. We may need to extract them soon. Hearing some concern their tactics may be a little too aggressive."

"Any extraction in France runs the risk of drawing Cobra. If Williams and Labrosse are as noisy as you suggest, they would be tempting targets."

Langley nodded. "Right and we must use that to our advantage."

Ike shook his head. "You're using them as bait?"

"They are there to find Cobra, one way or another."

Ike stared at Langley, *what makes a man this cold?*

Langley took another drag on his cigarette. "You met with our handler in Chichester. Can we help him?"

Not Bishop Bell, our handler? Just another agent tasked with handling, gaining information from an enemy contact. Ike nodded. "He makes a compelling case. Berlin—that's a long way in a small, unarmed plane. If he can come west, get closer. But from what I heard, he would be missed very quickly and expected to go west. An extraction would be dicey with the Gestapo in hot pursuit. And the problem multiplied when you consider the others, his family."

Langley agreed. "No one said it would be easy. Planning. Time. We still have time on this one. I want this one, Mic. Work your magic. I want it to happen. Give me something to take back to Bell. See what we can work out."

Ike was outside the door. The sound of parking lot gravel crunching under his feet was the only sound in the still and peaceful air. *Langley is high on helping Bishop Bell, or is it Bonhoeffer? He is risking his career on this, going against MI6. Or is*

Bells of Redemption

MI6 unhappy with the minsters? Someone cares about a German pastor and theologian. It has to be a good sign. I wonder when Kut will get back from the States? Could we send Bonhoeffer and his family east? East to our friends in the Czech resistance?

CHAPTER 24
NIGEL

Nigel Marley was at his desk, bent over a pile of folders when Ike came through the door. "We could request another staff adjutant," Ike said. "You're my best pilot. I need you in the air."

"Welcome back, Skipper. I get my flight hours in like everyone else. But an adjutant doesn't know our flyers like I do. Somethings I must do myself."

Ike stopped in front of Marley's desk. "I'm not carrying my load. I need to spend more time here with you."

"Skipper, you do just fine in keeping the brass off our tails. We all have a job to do."

Ike sat down. "I just came from Jim Langley's office. Says everything is smooth going for Dorothy, Val, and Ray. What's he not telling me?"

"We've been busy with RECON for the US 8th targeting Belgian war production. The results have not been good. They've been going in high, too high. Look, I know they're new, but we've been at it awhile. No bombardier can be on target at altitude. Two days ago they went after an auto factory outside

Brussels, now building planes. One, maybe two bombs on target from an entire squadron. No damage. How many tons fell on innocent Belgians? Reports of civilian death toll near a thousand. Who do we risk? Our airmen, or civilians?"

"Dorothy is in Brussels."

"She is safe. But our Belgian friends are not happy, and the Germans, well, they're tightening the screws. The Abwehr negotiators are getting anxious. Smooth? Hardly. As for Val and Ray, we're to pull them back. It seems they are making too much noise. The French don't like the attention they're getting. Working their extraction now, trying to second guess what Cobra may know."

"We shouldn't be hard on Langley. He treads a fine line with MI6. Seems there's a price to pay for our operation of rescuing downed flyers. The MI6 insertions and extractions are only the tip of the iceberg. He wants us to extract a German pastor and his family, Abwehr no less, from Berlin of all places."

"Berlin? Has he gone mad?"

"Seems MI6 has its hands tied, so they whisper their wishes in his ear. Some theologian—his handler believes he is being watched, and his options are limited. East. Do you think we can send him east to the Czechs? Strong intel and resistance operation. We would need to refuel. Stay remote, away from ports, cities, and industrial centers."

Marley scratched his head. "You want to fly small, unarmed planes halfway across the Fatherland? That kind of operation would require coordination in theatre, a lot of planning."

"We have some time. I was thinking north via Norway.

Not too many Nazis up there yet. Solid resistance, isolated landing fields. Then drop down East of Berlin. Maybe float planes? Give it some thought. If only Kut were back. I'll stop by the Czech squadron and see if they have heard from him."

Marley sighed. "I spoke too soon when I said welcome back."

"It seems this mission was my price from Langley for my short excursion."

"Right. Miss Osbourne, it seems you two are the talk of Churchstanton. The cowboy Yank and the quirky but pretty parish secretary."

Ike smiled. *Quirky?* "She has her charms."

"I'm sure she does. By the way, I've decided to accept your Sunday dinner offer. I need to meet your young lady."

"Great! I'll let them know."

Sunday morning, Nigel Marley rode with Ike to Saint Peter and Saint Paul Church. As Ike turned his staff car into the car park, they saw men piling out of three camouflaged British military lorries. "That would be our lads," Marley said.

"Our lads?"

"Off to church and a home-cooked meal. No worries. Reverend Osbourne is expecting them."

Ike turned and stared at Marley, who smiled and added, "All volunteers, with a little encouragement as you asked."

Rose was waiting at the door. She greeted Ike with a peck on the cheek and took his arm. Ike flashed a boyish grin and said, "Rose, this my XO, or Number One. Flight Lieutenant Nigel Marley. Marley, Miss Rose Osbourne, Dorothy's sister."

Rose smiled. "Good morning, Flight Lieutenant Marley!"

"Nigel. Please."

"Welcome, Nigel. Are you the one to thank for this wonderful turnout?"

The bell calling the faithful to worship began to toll. Rose smiled at Nigel and tugged Ike's arm. "Come. The processional is about to begin. You will sit with us in the family box."

They made their way up the aisle as the procession began behind them. Rose picked up the Book of Common Prayer as the cross led the procession past them. She opened it to the proper page and handed it to Ike. Nigel bowed as the cross passed. Ike joined the hymn, singing softly but growing stronger as Rose chimed in. Then, Nigel's voice rose beside him, strong and clear in perfect pitch. *The man can sing!* Nigel never glanced at the book. It was clear he had sung this hymn many times before.

Nigel repeated the liturgy perfectly from memory. He sang the responses and hymns beautifully, listening intently as Hugh climbed the pulpit to preach. "I want to welcome our brave brothers from RAF Churchstanton. God bless you for your courage and service to our nation. I ask that you wait after the service, where you'll be introduced to parishioners who are eager to take you to Sunday dinner."

Hugh looked down at the open bible on the pulpit. Pausing briefly, he began. "Brothers and sisters, I want to share with you some thoughts on John's Revelation. We continue to pray for an end to this war. We pray for loved ones and, like our friends from the airbase, all our troops, but I am often questioned if this terrible war is the beginning of the apocalypse

John's vision describes. Let me say there are clear lessons here for us most appropriate to our circumstances. For the past weeks, we have concerned ourselves with prayer, how to pray, and whether our prayers are heard. We have struggled to make sense of unanswered prayer, so it is most fitting that in chapter five, verse eight, John writes concerning the heavenly throne of Christ: 'And when he had taken the scroll, the four living creatures and the twenty-four elders fell down before The Lamb, each holding a harp, and golden bowls full of incense, *which are the prayers of the saints.*' Are our prayers heard? More than heard! They are burning incense before the throne of our Savior! A Holy incense, whose recorded purpose before this time was to cleanse the temple! Prayers of the saints—of sinners the like of us, an incense before the Lamb who was slain. Think about that the next time you pray!

What a wonderful picture of victory John paints. Revelation is the perfect bookend to Genesis. How they mirror each other! The Genesis creation story's account of light— before the sun, moon, and stars, our world was lit by God. And how is the new heaven to be lit? By the glory of God. In Genesis, we see the creation of the waters, the deep, a fearful place of unseen creatures, storms, and tempests. In Revelation, we see a crystal sea, calm as glass, where there is no fear, no pain, no storm, and no tempest. Peace is celebrated in timeless praises sung to our God and Savior."

Hugh looked out over his congregation before continuing. "But Vicar, you ask, the tribulation, Armageddon, the battles, the four horsemen, it's all so terrifying. Yes, John saw the wrath of a righteous God spilled out on Satan, his demons, and the lost, lessons not to be ignored. So, let me answer the question: Is this war the beginning of the end? Friend, the end times go back to the day Christ arose. I agree with many Church Fathers who argue that the present age, the Age of the Church, is the last days. This morning, I want us to look at who John addressed this letter to—seven churches in Asia Minor, and what we may learn from them. Throughout the ages, much ink has been spilled into speculation regarding these churches. But the most obvious and, I believe, the most pertinent is that John addresses the historic churches in the named cities. Isn't that what Paul did in his letters to the churches in Rome, Corinth, Galatia, and Ephesus? Are Paul's letters to these churches any less authoritative teachings to us?

So, what do we know of these churches? They were believers living through a time of severe persecution by Rome. They knew tribulation, pain, and suffering. They witnessed Rome's demand for soldiers, slaves, crucifixions, and unfortunate live bait to be thrown to lions and bears for the amusement of Rome's masses. John's letter challenged them as they struggled to survive a hostile world. He begins with Ephesus, a church we know through the Apostle Paul. John shares the words of our Lord Jesus, who says: 'I know your works, your toil, and your patient endurance, and how you cannot bear with those who are evil… I know you are enduring patiently and bearing up for my name's sake, and you have not grown weary,'"

Hugh looked out and smiled. "A very favorable beginning—'But I have this against you that you have abandoned the love you had at first. Remember therefore from where you have fallen; repent and do the works you did at first.'"

Ike glanced at Nigel. He saw his jaw drop before he lowered his head. He heard him sigh as he sat silently.

Hugh continued. "Now, I encourage you to read these letters on your own. They are short. You will find similar praise and challenges. But just a couple more passages instructive for us today. 'And to the Angel of the church of Philadelphia write: 'The words of the holy one, who has the key of David, who opens, and no one will shut, who shuts and no one opens. "'I know your works. Behold, I have set an open door which no one else is able to shut. I know that you have but little power, and yet you have kept my word and have not denied my name… because you have kept my word about patient endurance, I will keep you from the hour of the trial that is coming on the whole world, to try those who dwell on earth. I am coming soon. Hold fast to what you have so that no one may seize your crown. The one who conquers I will make a pillar in the temple of my God.'"

"And finally, he writes to the church of Laodicea, 'I know your works: you are neither cold nor hot. Would that you were either cold or hot! So, because you are lukewarm… I will spit you out of my mouth. For you say, I am rich, I have prospered, and I need nothing, not realizing that you are wretched, pitiable, poor, blind, and naked. I counsel you to buy from me gold refined by fire, so that you may be rich, and white garments so that you may clothe yourself and the shame of your nakedness may not be seen, and salve to anoint your eyes, that you may see. Those whom I love, I reprove and discipline, so be zealous and repent. Behold, I stand at the door and knock. If any man hears my voice and opens the door, I will come in to him and eat with him, and he with me. The one who conquers, I will grant him to sit with me on my throne, as I also conquered and sat down with my Father on his throne. He who has an ear, let him hear what the Spirit says to the churches.'"

Hugh closed the Bible on the pulpit and asked, "Two doors, my friends, the open door never to be shut or the closed door upon which Jesus knocks waiting for you to open. Doors to a heavenly throne. Doors to a new heaven and a new earth where God intended his people to walk from the very beginning in Genesis. The fulfillment of his plan in creation. The steps to the door are painful, but the reward is eternal. So it was for the seven churches, and so it will be for us. We do not know the day of his coming, but he tells us to prepare and that we are not alone in trial and tribulation. We can endure in the power of His Holy Spirit. Now let us come to His table in remembrance, to be refreshed in the hope of our salvation."

Nigel's head was bowed. Ike caught a glimpse of him wiping a tear from his eye.

When it was time for their box to go forward for communion, Nigel stepped out and back to allow Ike and Rose to go forward to the altar rail. Returning to his seat, he changed his mind and found a spot next to Ike. He kneeled and crossed his arms. Declining the elements, Ike watched through the corner of his eye as Hugh stopped in front of Nigel, placed his hand on his head, and whispered a blessing. *I don't know Nigel at all. I work closely with him. I trust him completely, but I don't know him. There is something inside him, beneath his good cheer and competence.*

After all the RAF airmen were paired up with parishioners and off to homes for Sunday dinner, Ike and Nigel joined Rose and Hugh at the vicarage. Ike presented Hugh with a bag. Hugh smiled. "Two bottles! Right. Thank you indeed! This calls for a drink."

Ike laughed. "One is from me and the other in appreciation for the men—and with my Number One, Flight Lieutenant Marley, we may put a heavier dent in your ration."

Hugh laughed. "Welcome, Flight Lieutenant…"

"It's Nigel, please, and I am happy to be invited."

"You're always welcome, Nigel. Call me Hugh. I hope Ike didn't twist your arm getting you here. Where are you from, Nigel? Any family?"

"North, near Manchester. A wife and daughter. She's three—my little girl." *I had no idea he had a family. What a fool I've been,* Ike thought.

"They must miss you very much. One quick drink and then we must go to the table. Rose is in the kitchen. This should be of great interest to you, Ike. A taste trial."

Nigel looked at Ike, who replied, "Dottie, that is, Dorothy usually does the cooking."

Rose was unusually nervous when she brought the hot baking dish from the kitchen and set it on the table. "I had to improvise on the ingredients. I'm not sure how they will work together. Oh, I also baked bread, in case the pie is too thin."

Nigel nodded. "It smells delicious. It seems every home-cooked meal is an adventure. My Millie tells me there is never a recipe for what's available. I say it makes meals fun. And there is nothing fun about eating on base."

During a lull in the dinner conversation, Ike asked, "Hugh, we've talked about my issue with the church. I mean, I love Saint Peter and Saint Paul—in the past—how do you—how should we, help good people who have been mistreated by the church, church leaders?"

Hugh sat back, tapped his lips with his napkin, and said, "Ike, that's one of the most difficult problems in ministry. When, as I say, bad Christian leaders happen to good people, there are two wounded people: the parishioner who was wronged and the leader who wronged him. The sad truth is the leader who wronged someone else is more likely to receive help. Everything favors him. He is vested in the church and less likely to refuse help, while the wronged parishioner is slow to receive or may never receive acknowledgment and help. My fear, and I have seen it happen, is that the wronged parishioner blames the church or, even worse, God."

"Why not blame the church?" Ike asked.

"Yes, of course. It's an easy target. Too often, complaints are ignored, understated, or covered up. Some church leaders think they need to protect the church and discourage disclosing what happened. Can you imagine? They think God, the Church, the Body of Christ needs our protection! It's upside down! The church is a community of sinners. Everyone one of us. We come together to worship and serve—to become disciples of Christ, striving to overcome our sins. It is the church that needs God's protection, and thankfully, we have it."

Nigel concentrated on his food as Hugh finished.

Ike nodded. "Okay, then what should be done?"

"The Bible says the person wronged should confront the other…"

Ike interrupted, "A child, young person, or, say, the wrongdoer was in high authority?"

Hugh continued, "It should be reported to the minister, or in the case of the minister, his bishop. There can be no healing without justice, repentance, and forgiveness. There must be accountability. Only Satan wins if a child is ignored. An injured child will either feel guilty—somehow it was his fault a terrible thing happened or reject the church and walk away from God."

"And then there is no hope."

"Ike, there is always hope. God is not blind. He cannot be mocked. His Spirit moves. It may take some time, but God has a way of assuring the hurting that He loves them. He sends friends, a loving spouse, or uses some event to rekindle the flame that never expires."

Rose looked at Ike. "Linda did that for you Ike. She loved you and put you back on the path."

Ike smiled. *Linda. Yes—until I killed her. Is God giving me a second chance with Rose? But it is Nigel who needs help now.*

Ike looked up and said brightly, "Sorry, Nigel. I didn't mean to get off on a boring tangent. I enjoy my talks with Hugh. But I must say, old man, to sound very British, you sing like an angel! What other skills are you hiding? Is there anything you can't do well?"

Nigel just smiled.

Ike asked, "When was the last time you took leave? Tomorrow, I want to see a request on my desk."

CHAPTER 25
ESCAPE

A waxing moon was still low in the sky when Ike and Nigel left the vicarage. A relaxed and talkative Nigel remarked, "Jolly good time. Glad I came. I'm happy for you, Skipper. Rose is swell, and so is Hugh, er, Reverend Osbourne. Not stuffy at all and, well, seems to have a good heart. Wise and funny, too. I like him. Happy to tag along anytime you ask, though don't want to be a third wheel between you and Rose. How did you get your hands on two bottles of American bourbon? I need to know your source."

Ike smiled. "Some secrets I keep to myself. You were able to keep up with Hugh. I hope you didn't drink too much. I want to make a stop at Otterhead House."

"Too much? No. I'd say just right. I feel good. Though a bit lonely for Millie and Penny. Say, Skipper, you weren't serious about a two-day pass, were you?"

"No. I'm serious about a four-day pass. Make it happen. And Penny better be your little girl."

"Aye. Penelope Sharon Marley. The sweetest little angel ever to come down from heaven."

"Don't fall asleep on me, Nigel. Look alert when we see Langley."

Ten minutes later, Ike nudged the snoring Nigel and said, "Can you do this, or should I leave you in the car?"

Something clicked in Nigel's brain—duty. "I'm good. Let's go."

When Ike saw Langley in his office, he said, "You've become predictable. You're always here on Sunday night."

Langley looked up. "Who are you calling predictable? I've been waiting for you. We must move quickly on a hot extraction."

"Val and Ray?"

"Seems the Abwehr showed up at their door. Luckily, they were warned moments before. The resistance is complaining. They're bringing too much heat. The good Lady Virginia d'Albert-Lake has them. But they just cost her a good safe house."

Langley stared at Nigel. "Good that you're here. We'll need an armed escort on this one. We can't be coy about it. No time for multiple locations. We name the field and go right in."

"And Cobra?"

Langley sighed. "We assume Cobra will know and be waiting with Abwehr and perhaps more. Hence, the firepower. If we don't take out Cobra, we can at least bloody his nose. An SOE team and French Resistance will be on the scene as well, acting as clean-up."

"When?"

Langley replied, "You saw the moon. Tomorrow night, if possible. Tuesday night, if you must. Don't lose the full moon.

Weather should be good."

Ike looked at Nigel, then turned to Langley. "Right. In and out under fire with close air support. We'll make it happen. I'll pass the landing site to you by 1100. Not one used by SOE."

"Good. I know I can count on you. I want to give just enough time for Cobra to act but not enough for him to bring in big guns. And you can expect German coastal defense will be looking for you. Likely a night hunter as well. They missed Val and Ray at the safe house. They'll be angry about it."

On the drive back to Churchstanton, Nigel said, "I'll start with the landing site. One never used before, limited access, one way in and out where we can force their hands on the ambush site, yet good cover for Williams and Labrosse. Rain. It rained today in Paris. Clearing is not expected until tomorrow afternoon. I'm worried about mud. I assume you want the Lysander and a short field."

A sober Nigel looked out the window at the moonlit countryside. "I guess that pass will have to wait."

Ike kept his eyes on the narrow light beam ahead. "Four-day pass on my desk as directed, Number One. I want you on your way by 1600 tomorrow."

"Skipper, I appreciate what you're trying to do, but you heard Langley, ground support. The Spitfire is the only armed bird we have. And no one flies her but me…"

"I'm qualified."

"No offense, but have you ever fired her weapon? Do you know how to find a landing site at night? You need me on this one."

Ike made a quick glance at Nigel. "You're right. I won't

put men's safety in my hands with my flying experience. I was thinking a couple of Hurricanes. Night hunters from the Czech squadron. They're good pilots, and their Hurricanes are better armed. Your Spitfire gave up half its weapons to make room for cameras. You're left only with basic self-defense guns. I want more firepower. I intended to check on Kut anyway. I'll call on Group Captain Hastings first thing. Now it's his turn to pay back our support of the Eighth Air Force."

"Kut?"

"Flight Lieutenant Kuttelwascher, ace…."

"Yes. Eighteen kills. Isn't he…"

"Hero's tour in America, I want him on the Berlin extraction—if he gets back. Look, Nigel, I know you're good. I'm just saying, why not let a couple of better-equipped Hurricanes take this one? There will be other firefights." *And you'll live to hug your Millie and Penny one more time.*

"Flying night hunter is one thing. Navigating to a tiny strip is another."

"The way I see it, both take a lone wolf to pull off. In any case, my mind is made up."

At RAF Churchstanton, Ike told Nigel, "Get some sleep. I want a clear head when choosing the site. I'll check in with Hastings at 0800 before joining you in the OPS Room."

Group Captain Hastings looked up when he heard Ike knock on his door. "Come through, Major. You haven't come to volunteer your unit—it would be a first. So, what is it you want?"

"Now, Group Captain, have I ever turned you down? But as you say, I could use your help. May I close the door?"

Hastings pointed to the chair. Ike closed the door, sat

down, and said, "Rather urgent. We have two MI9 agents we need to extract ASAP. Stirred up the hornet's nest in Paris and overstayed their welcome."

"An extraction? Isn't that your everyday operation, Ike?"

"Oh, I can put down a Lizzie to pick them up, but there's a problem."

Hastings nodded. "Somehow, I think your problem will become mine."

"We expect a hot extraction. They've been compromised. We've been hunting a leak. A traitor in the resistance—Cobra. Our men were one step ahead of an Abwehr arrest. I need ground attack support at night in an unlit field near Paris. My Spitter is lightly armed—the cost of fixed cameras. The plan is to make lemonade out of this lemon."

"You're using the extraction as bait."

"They will know. We don't know how they know, but they will, so I figure two Hurricanes standing by once the Jerries open up. We expect Cobra to be waiting with the ambush. With luck, it will be his last licks. In any case, we bloody his nose. I could use two night hunters, experienced Czech pilots. Thought you might carry water for me with the Squadron Leader. I'd like to meet him. Truth is, I want to check on Kut as well. We have something in the pipeline that calls for Kut's special skills."

An hour later, Ike found Marley in the OPS Room bent over a RECON map of France. Three sites near Paris were circled. "Three possible sites? Let's run through them," Ike commented, ignoring pleasantries.

Nigel Marley sighed. "They all present problems for us, but I just can't find any better close to Paris. Did you get your

Hurricanes? Don't settle for the old Mark I. Even with eight browning .303 machine guns, they don't pack enough punch to take down a Bf 109 let alone do any good against an armored vehicle. All the .303 is good for is putting tracer fire forward for the cannon."

Ike bent over the map. "Two Mark IIs. Agreed to outfit each with two 250-pound bombs, eight RP3 rockets, and two .79-inch Hispano Mk II cannons. They're more than able to make an impact. Now, talk me through these sites."

Marley nodded. "Let's hope their firepower is there when we need it. Our little Lysander will need all the protection she can get. Site 1, here to the west, provides the best landmarks. The Hurricanes should be able to navigate there with the least trouble. It is also the most exposed. The Jerries can choose between three ambush sites, which have several ingress and regress routes. Site 2, slightly to the south, is an abandoned dirigible aerodrome not used by the Nazis. Limited access, old concrete, and dry gravel runway, no issue with a muddy field, but the clearing is wider than we would like."

"It gives the Hurricanes plenty of room to come in low."

"And it gives the welcoming party excellent target sighting."

Ike circled the site with his finger, looking at the surrounding terrain. "Tell me about the third site. This one up north."

"Right. To begin with, it's awfully close to d'Albert-Lake's Chateau. Not sure we want the Nazis nosing around up there. It is the tightest field. Barely long enough for the Lizzie. Thick woods for the resistance to operate from. Also, the least accessible, perhaps some risk of our team and the Nazis encountering each other enroute. And while it restricts the Nazi ambush to this one side—to the east is a marshy pond—there is a high risk of mud in the field if today's forecasted rain is heavy. How good are these Czechs?"

"They've been fighting the Luftwaffe longer than the RAF has. They may not have Kut's 18 kills, but they're good. Site 3, high risk, high reward against Cobra."

Nigel stood up straight. "I'll chart the route and flying time. We'll need a rendezvous point for the Hurricanes."

Ike replied. Send the coordinates of site 3 to Langley ASAP. He'll release the messages. What time should we post?"

"0200. The skies should be clear. Plenty of night to get there, still good moonlight. Enough time for a firefight and home before dawn."

Ike gave a solid pat on Nigel's shoulder. "I've called a pilot's pre-brief for 1300. Once we have a green light from Langley and the final weather report, we'll have a final OPS Briefing here 30 minutes before the Lizzie flies. Gives you time to pack a bag."

"Skipper, why not…"

"Call me in the morning from Manchester. I'll let you know how it went."

Just before midnight, Night Thrush One, a black, ungainly Lysander, took off from RAF Churchstanton, heading east for the coast of France. Fifteen minutes later, Night Thrush Two, a second Lizzie took off. The two small planes flew separate courses between known German coast guns and watch stations. The seasoned pilots knew to avoid Dieppe in the North, where thousands of Canadian troops died in a disastrous raid the month before, and Grand Camp Maisy, where the Germans were constructing a large coastal defense complex. Luftwaffe night hunters were the greatest threat. The two light planes crisscrossed the French countryside toward a rendezvous point.

Night Owl One and Night Owl Two followed an hour later. They too, split up and made their way east to the rendezvous. The flight plan was for Night Thrush One to go into the landing site first, make a pass, and watch for the signal light while Night Owl maintained its position above. Night Thrush Two was to stand by in case Night Thrush One was hit. She was to wait for the Hurricanes to pacify any resistance before a second landing was attempted. Despite speaking only broken English, the Czech pilots were seasoned inflight communicators.

Langley, Ike, Hastings, and the Czech Squadron Commander listened as the planes checked in. The silence was broken when a Czech voice screamed into his radio. Night Owl Two. Luftwaffe night hunter—I'm under fire. I'm hit. I think I'm hit. Diving in a roll. I have control. Looking. Looking. I see a hole in the fuselage. I see the cloth blowing. It went through, a cannon round, no explosion. He can't match my turn. Coming up behind him. Just a little more, come on, just a—I have him, I think, yes, I have you, bastard. Steady now…hit him. Smoke, he's going down. No chute. A Bf-109. I see the splash. You can keep your fast and sexy Spitfire, I'm alive because I'm in a maneuverable, wood and cloth Hurricane. Thank God we now have the .79-Hispano cannons."

Ike mumbled. "It was over so fast."

The Czech Squadron Commander replied, "Not when it's

you in the cockpit."

Fifteen minutes later, all four planes checked in within a minute of each other, "At Rendezvous. Proceeding to site." One voice continued. "Night Owl two taking high cover. Weather clear, visibility good."

Not another ten minutes passed before the radio crackled. "Night Thrush One making my pass. Ground lights lit. Identify friend signal given and acknowledged. Going in."

"Drawing fire, drawing fire. Small arms fire. Aborting landing. Going around. More fire. Where are you, Night Owl?"

"Turn right, Thrush One; stay low over the forest canopy. I'm coming in."

"Night Owl One, I confirm a hit—personnel carrier. You're on target, Wait, a second emplacement 100 yards to the right, anti-aircraft guns. They're all yours. I'm climbing out of view."

"I have the second emplacement in sight, rockets first— letting go bombs. Bombs away, I'm coming around for another pass. I'm drawing small arms fire. Anti-aircraft emplacements quiet. Preparing for a strafing run. Any company on top, Night Owl Two?"

"Just me and Night Thrush Two."

"After this run, I'll climb to cover and let you back up Night Thrush one landing."

"Roger, Night Owl One, trade places."

"Night Thrush One, on approach. I'm down, crap! Mud! I will need help turning her around. I need some dry ground for takeoff."

Three minutes later, the radio squawked, "Two

passengers aboard. Powering up for takeoff. Pray I don't bog down again. Hear small arms fire coming from the woods. Nothing coming our way. Believe it's the resistance finishing the job. Come on, come on, just a little more. Little Lizzie don't fail me now. Please, Lord. Please, oh, please. Yes! We're up and clear. Night Thrush One returning to base."

"Night Thrush Two returning to base."

"Night Owl One escorting Night Thrush One and Two home."

"Night Owl Two, top cover. Returning home. Request scrap paper and tape handy."

Ike picked up the mic and called, "Night Thrush Two, is there any chance you're bringing home a couple of picture postcards of the French countryside?"

The radio crackled, "Better than that, Major Mic. Have the local newspaper: black and white and red all over."

CHAPTER 26
AFTER ACTION REPORT

Ike was asleep the minute his head hit the pillow. The moon was low in a black sky when his right hand clenched into a tight fist. His sleeping body trembled. Quivering lips mumbled in reply to the unheard voice in his dream. "Ike, how's your fuel?"

"Nearly full."

"Great. I need you to take a look at something for me. Old-growth forest. You should be able to get there and back. Here's the coordinates."

Ike checked his map. "Right. Just outside Paris."

Linda smiled. "Paris? I've always wanted to see Paris."

Ike put a finger over his lips. "Shush. You're not supposed to be here, remember?"

"Setting course. I'll contact you when I'm over the Paris woods."

"So much water," Linda commented wearily."

"That's why they call it an ocean. We're nearly across."

"Will we be able to see the Eifel Tower soon? What a sight! And the Arc de Triumph will be lighted, I'm sure."

Ike's sleeping body jolted up from the bed before falling back, limp. "We've been hit! I never saw him. A Messerschmitt 109 from behind. Look, you can see him passing in front. I'm pulling the stick with all my might. I can't bring the nose up. Brace, Linda. Brace for the water."

Ike was in the water. There was Linda beside him in the cockpit. Her eyes were wide open. Her blonde hair swirling around her. The water in the cabin was red with blood. Ike unbuckled his seat belt and struggled with Linda's. Her lifeless body floated placidly in the cold water. At last, Ike pushed his feet from the floor, and he sped upward through the torn cockpit overhead to the surface of the sea.

A life raft popped out of the plane, and he clambered into it. He stared into the night sky and closed his eyes to the horrible images in his mind. The raft rolled gently in the calm waters. He did not know how long he floated. He opened his eyes and saw a small boat approaching. A calm voice called out, "Take heart, you're saved. Are you alone?"

"My wife, Linda, she didn't make it."

"We'll get you into the boat, and we'll look for her."

Ike crawled over the gunwale. "I watched her die. She went down with the plane."

"How terrible! We'll still look."

The boat circled the waters for several minutes. The sea was empty. There was no sign of the plane, a life raft, or Linda."

The lifeboat coxswain said, "Nothing. Let's get you back to Churchstanton, Major. My name is Rose. You're going to be okay."

It was midmorning when Ike awoke. He stumbled to the

sink, washed his face, and shaved. *I promised to call Nigel. I owe it to him. First thing when I get to the office. Then I need to see the RECON photos from last night. I should let the pilots and crew get some rest. We'll do the debrief at 1300. That should work. I'll let Langley know. That dream. Lord, when will they end? Why am I tormented?*

It was strange to enter his office and not see Nigel or Dorothy working. He was alone. He sat down and dialed the contact number Nigel left. A woman answered on the first ring. "Hello."

"Mrs. Marley, this is Major Curtis, is Nigel there?"

"Oh, Major, yes, let me call him. Thank you for giving him the pass. Here he is."

"Skipper, how did it go last night?"

"We got them out and bloodied the Jerry welcoming party. I haven't seen the pictures yet, but the pilot reports were good."

"So, everyone made it back safely?"

"It was a bit of a nail-biter. One of the Hurricanes had a Bf 109's cannon shell pass through the fuselage—it didn't explode, and the Czech shot him down. Plenty of ground fire, but it was left for our French friends to mop up. Val and Ray are back safe."

"Glad to hear it. Any word on Dorothy?"

"You mean since yesterday? No. But I'll try to pin Langley down when I see him at the debrief. How's the family?"

"Very happy to see me. Millie thinks you're the greatest—demands I thank you."

"Well, you enjoy them. I just called to let you know—like

you asked."

"Thanks, Skipper. But before you go, I just wanted to say, how do I put this? The Czechs, the others—they have families too. I know what you're trying to do. You can't save us all—you can't give everyone another goodbye. It's going to be a long slog. We know it. We're prepared for it."

Ike sighed softly. "Right. But I can help some, if only a few, for a while. You give your girls a hug for me. I want to hear all about little Penny when you get back. Goodbye, Nigel."

Ike had barely enough time to put together the photographs for the mission debrief before the pilots, Langley, Hastings, and the Czech Squadron Commander, arrived. Williams and Labrosse were the last the last to stroll in. Ike stood to the side of the screen, which displayed the bombed emplacement with the mangled carcasses of two trucks and two-wheeled guns.

"Good afternoon, gentlemen. This photograph sums up what I have to say. You are commended for successfully completing a challenging mission. As you can see, you destroyed two trucks and two guns. Reports from the French confirm 24 Jerries dead and one civilian. No Germans are believed to have escaped. The guns were heavy duty anti-aircraft, Flakveirlings, or Flak 38, 4-barrel auto canons firing .79-inch caliber rounds at 450 rounds per minute. Fortunately, it appears they were waiting for the landing and for Val and Ray to show themselves and their French helpers. Our infrared photos show a ten-member French resistance spread out across the field on the edge of the marsh. They know their business."

Ike paused and changed the picture before continuing.

"Now, as to friendly casualties…none. Havel, I'm afraid we have been unable to confirm your kill. We have listed it as probable. We will keep it open for now in case any coast watcher or intelligence can confirm it. But good show! Your squadron continues to lead the way here at Churchstanton. I'm told your plane has been repaired, 'taped over as you say,' and is back in service. Questions?"

Ray Labrosse asked, "One civilian but no friendlies? Has he been identified?"

Ike replied, "You mean, was he our traitor, Cobra? We don't know. No identification was found. The body was burned. He was identified as a civilian by his shoes and some clothing parts. We can deal in probabilities. A French civilian in the company of the German welcoming party tipped off by Cobra. It seems a strong probability to me. But then, Cobra may not be a single person. Time will tell."

Val Williams spoke out. "The bastard is dead. We got the son of a bitch. I know it. I'm ready to go back. You with me, Ray?"

Langley stood up. "Thank you, Major. May I add my congratulations to all here and our support on the ground. Bloody good work. You're dismissed. Val and Ray, a word with you in Major Curtis's office right now."

In Ike's office, Langley asked Ike to sit beside him and commanded Val and Ray: "Stand at attention. You two created this mess. You have risked the lives of SOE agents in Paris, the French Resistance, cost us a safe house and risked the lives of how many pilots and four planes with your blundering in Paris. Oaktree is indefinitely postponed. I have every right to send you back to your units if they would even have you…"

"But sir, we got Cobra," Val replied.

"Don't speak unless you're told to speak. For once, try listening! Now, I'm sending you back for refresher training. And if I get one bad report or word back regarding either of you, you're history. Do you understand?"

Ray replied, "Yes, sir. Refresher training, sir."

Val started to say something, but he caught the fire in Langley's eyes. "Refresher training, sir. Yes, sir."

"Good. Now get out of here while your orders are prepared."

After Ray and Val shuffled out, Langley turned to Ike and said, "It couldn't have worked out any better. Our boys brought the heat and ferreted out Cobra. Odds are we got him."

"So, you sent them in as bait to begin with? That's all they are to you?"

Langley peered at Ike. "I sent them in to find Cobra, and it looks like they did. They're determined, resourceful, capable men. I counted on them being the bold, risk-taking men they are. The qualities I needed…"

"As bait."

"Yes, if that's what it took. But after this, they will know to be careful where they tread—to follow orders. Now, I need them to change and adjust. When I send them back, they will work alone, not depend on or put at risk our French friends. If Cobra has survived, he will be a greater threat to Oaktree."

Ike shook his head. "You gave them no encouragement."

"There's a time for encouragement, but now I want a

little humility. Oaktree will be a far greater challenge."

Ike was quiet. Langley got up to leave. Ike said, "Speaking of challenges, how long will you leave Dorothy in Brussels? She's hardly a hardened asset, and the recent bombings are bringing new heat to the Belgian resistance."

Langley smiled. "She is keeping her Abwehr friends in line."

"They haven't given up with the delays? They don't see you are stringing them along?"

"She has them focused on the problem of arranging the escape of their families."

"She must know you have no intention of extracting them or their families. She does know?"

"Dorothy, like all of us, knows only what she needs to know. Good day, Ike."

Chapter 27
London Hard Apple Cider

The sun set early in late October, that is on the few days it broke through the ever-present gray clouds. Ike steered his car around a rusty lorry backed against Rose's garden gate. The flatbed carried three full and one half-full crates of apples. Two young women wearing the three-quarter-length tan coats of the Land Women were emptying bushels of apples as Ike hopped out of his staff car. Rose stood next to a gray-haired man with a clipboard behind the tailgate. She called out. "You're just in time! Our work is about to begin!"

Ike wandered their way, eyed the truck and the young women, and replied, "Looks to me like you're about done. Seems you left the hard work to these land girls. I didn't know you employed anyone."

Rose gave Ike a peck on the cheek. "No, we don't have the work. They work for our neighbor, Mister Hillcroft. He's good enough to bring them here for the apple harvest. He supplies the labor, trucks them to market, and we split the sales price."

Turning to the old farmer, she said, "Mister Hillcroft, this is my friend, Major Curtis."

Hillcroft extended his hand, "Heard a lot about you, Major Curtis. Well, time to get these apples to market, wouldn't be prudent driving these roads after dark. I'll settle with you tomorrow, Rose. My regards to the vicar. Good evening, Major."

Hillcroft walked to the gate and whistled. Soon, the two young women appeared carrying orchard ladders, which he tied down on the flatbed beside the apple crates. The girls jumped in the truck and Hillcroft drove off in a cloud of black soot and dust.

Rose recognized Ike's puzzled look. "He's not a bad bloke. Seeing you made him the most talkative I've seen him in years."

"Talkative? You mean his unwillingness to lend a hand? Seems he let the girls do all the work."

"They're volunteers, city girls safely out of the bombings. He pays them 28 shillings a week and takes half back in room and board. Less than the going rate for a farm worker at 38 shillings a week, but then, the men have all been conscripted, and for what, private's pay? Hardship upon hardship! If it weren't for a good garden, we'd all starve."

Ike stammered, "I fear bringing it up, but you mentioned, 'our work?'"

"Right. We must gather all the ground apples. Can't be sending them to market. It would get us blackballed. We need to get them in before fox, deer, rats, or rot get them. Cider. Uncle Hugh is a master at making good hard cider."

"Well, I'm glad Hugh has found a calling! That saves me from pressing duties."

"Very funny. Not everyone has an American friend with access to good bourbon. Hard cider is what gets many good folks through. Now, once we gather the apples, you will replace Dottie in the kitchen when I can the vegetables. We won't make it through the winter without them."

Rose picked up a burlap bag and tossed it to Ike. "We can't waste the light, and Uncle Hugh frowns on us working on the Sabbath."

Ike swung the gate open to allow Rose to pass through in front. "After you, Rose"

As she passed, he said, "Well then, you'll be too busy to go to London with me next week."

"London? Next week?" Rose slung her bag at Ike. "Take that, Mister. Leading me on like you did. When do we leave? How long can we stay? I have the letter for Lambeth Palace."

"Are you sure, Rose? I wouldn't want to be responsible for Hugh being deprived of his canned veggies."

Ike took one look at the ground beneath the trees and uttered, "We'll be here all night."

It was a gloomy London morning when Ike dropped Rose off in front of Lambeth Palace, the official residence of the Archbishop of Canterbury. The Palace included historic chapels and offices. Rose was expected. She had an appointment with the archivist. She gave Ike a peck on the cheek and jumped out of his staff car. "See you for supper. Drinks before dinner at 6. No excuses! Don't be late."

Ike nodded. "I'll be there. Happy fishing," and he drove off. A short drive across the Thames and he was in the heart of

London. He navigated his way to 54 Broadway and parked in front of the Minimax Fire Extinguishing Company. He showed an attendant his pass and left his keys. Upstairs, he waited outside the office of Colonel Z. A half hour passed before the mahogany door opened, and half a dozen men filed out. The adjutant called to Ike, "He'll see you now, Major."

Claude Dansey looked up as Ike entered. "I'm a busy man, Husky. What is it you want that Langley can't deliver."

The spymaster made no motion for Ike to be seated. It was going to be a brief meeting. Ike was to the point. "An Abwehr operative in Berlin. Extraction. I require an experienced pilot, Czech, special skills…"

"Berlin Abwehr? I don't need to know—we have never had this conversation."

"Yes, understood. I need help arranging access to Flight Lieutenant Kuttelwascher, the only man for the job."

Colonel Z put down his pen and looked at Ike. "Kuttelwascher? He's in America,"

"I know that, sir. He should be back, and, well, I'm told he will not be rejoining the squadron. I thought…"

"His combat days are over. He'll be reassigned, likely training officer duty."

"Yes, but for this mission. The asset I'm to extract can't come west—being watched. My plan is to send him east to Decin…"

"Czechoslovakia?"

"The Germans have a large garrison supporting Abwehr operations against the Czech Resistance. A perfect cover for an Abwehr agent. From there, it's an easy trek to a small, short field in the mountains east of the Elbe."

"A long flight over Nazi Germany."

"Six hundred thirty miles as the crow flies. Round trip within the range of a Hudson. We would send them over southern Norway and then south to our friends in Oland Island, Sweden. A contingent fuel stop, if necessary, though we would fit extra fuel tanks. We feel the uncontested air space is relatively safe. Kut is from Svaty Kriz, right in the target extraction zone—intimately familiar with the area and the German positions. He has the right stuff."

Colonel Z tapped his finger as he cast his glance across the room and out his office window. "It could work." Turning back to Ike, he continued. "When do you move on this extraction that I've never heard of?"

"Soon, I hope. Perhaps within a month. It hasn't been finalized, but the asset is in danger."

"Kut won't be back until after the new year at the soonest. He's quite the attraction over there. You'll have to find yourself another pilot, Major. You've spoken to the Czech Squadron Commander, no doubt. Who does he suggest?"

"Well, they have another ace, Josef Frantisek, but he's about to be pulled as well."

"Another ace. You are very picky, Major."

"I'll take that as a compliment. Seventeen kills most of them in four weeks of flying night hunter."

"I'll see he is made available. If he survives. Have Langley keep me informed on this mission, and remember, we have never discussed this. Isn't it time for your walk in the park? Good day, Major."

Ike turned to leave but stopped and asked, "One more thing, sir. Agent Goldenrod, when is she returning? I need her at Churchstanton."

Colonel Z was writing at his desk. Without looking up, he said, "Good day, Husky."

Ike exited the building but did not go to his car. He walked down Broadway to the corner, turned on Queen Anne's Gate, crossed Bird Cage Walk, and entered Saint James Park. His mind raced as he walked. *He knows I'm meeting with Bishop Bell. I wonder if he has met with him as well? Can this distancing be merely politics? He knows everything. I know nothing. Well, I do know he wants this extraction to happen. But why?*

George Bell was waiting. He sat quietly on a bench, scattering birdseed to hungry sparrows. Ike sat down next to him. "Can't all seeds be ground into flour for bread? Or is only the English countryside hungry?"

The Bishop of Chichester put his hand in the paper bag on his lap, withdrew a few more seeds, and scattered them. He replied softly; Jesus said: 'Are not two sparrows sold for a penny? And yet not one of them will fall to the ground outside your Father's care. And even the very hairs of your head are numbered. So don't be afraid; you are worth more than many sparrows.'"

Bell looked at Ike, smiled, and said, "I'm about my work, the Lord's work, feeding sparrows."

Ike found himself nodding. "Your German pastor, he is worth more than a sparrow? And the lives of pilots and brave resistance fighters? Why? Why does Colonel Z want him out, even against opposition from ministers? I'm told even the

Prime Minister?"

Bishop Bell said nothing. He just spread more bird seed.

Ike took a deep breath and continued. "How soon can he be ready? He'll need to get himself to the Czech border town on the Elbe, Decin. There's an Abwehr office in the Nazi garrison there. Trains run from Berlin to nearby Dresden. The Czech resistance will deliver him to the landing site. We can accommodate him and four others. I need two weeks."

"He's not ready. Unfinished business, he says. He'll like the plan. He has sent friends, relatives—Jews to Switzerland, but that line is being choked off by the Nazis. When he says not yet, you must realize he returned from safety in America—this is his calling."

His grace took another handful of birdseed and spread it in front of his small, feathered flock. "You have no idea how hard it was for my friend, Dietrich. Such a gentle and compassionate man. It is one thing for rational men to rely on Aquinas or Augustine to justify in their minds, a just war. But a pastor, one who loves his flock. To enlist as a soldier and fight the evil in his own homeland—well, it is no easy thing. A decision, once made, is not easy to abandon. I can only appeal to him that this is but a transfer in his ongoing campaign. But as for the Prime Minister and I, we are captive to our past words and messages. The Prime Minister cannot be seen as granting any quarter to Germany, even German civilians, while London and our great cities are bombed. I campaigned against the area bombing of German civilians, even presenting a bill to the House of Lords. You know what came of it? I am ridiculed in a song by Noel Coward..."

Ike looked up, "Noel Coward? A song."

"Don't Let's Be Beastly to the Germans. Very clever. It goes:

"Don't let's be beastly to the Germans,

When our victory is ultimately won,

It was just those nasty Nazis who persuaded them to fight,

And their Beethoven and Bach

are really far worse than their bite.

Let's be meek to them,

And turn the other cheek to them,

And try to bring out their latent sense of fun.

Let's give them full air parity,

And treat the rats with charity,

But don't let's be beastly to the Hun."

Churchill loves it. I heard he asked for three encores on first hearing it. My efforts have cost me—will cost me in my ministry, yet I am my friend's handler for Colonel Z. I know the Prime Minister will never give the Abwehr what they request in return for their help, yet I continue in this charade, hoping that at least God grants me eyes to see him safely out of Germany. He has a fiancée, a young woman. Doesn't he deserve some happiness in life?"

"Your friend, and yet you keep the decision from him."

"I rely on the proverb: 'Faithful are the wounds of a friend, but the kisses of an enemy are deceitful."

"Is Colonel Z a friend or an enemy?"

"I believe Colonel Z is neither friend nor enemy. He sees only an end goal. In this case, my friend Dietrich is low-level in the Abwehr, but he will be made an example of what England can do for its friends. I will find peace in pastor Bonhoeffer's rescue."

Ike stood up to leave. "Then you must convince him to move soon. Every extraction gets harder than the one before."

Rose was beaming when Ike greeted her in the hotel dining room. He bent over and kissed her gently. "Looks like one of us had a good day. Did you find the letters to Bishop Lyfing you were looking for? And solve the mystery of the Sword of Saint Peter and the Holy Grail? Tell me they are waiting for us to dig them up in Churchstanton."

"And you promised not to mock me, remember?"

Ike sat down across from her. She didn't wait for his answer. "I was shown Archbishop Lyfing's papers. It's quite extraordinary to see the Primates' archives. But, no, I didn't find what I was looking for. But I have by no means come to the end of the road. There are other records, or maybe more among the Occulta Sunt."

"Occulta Sunt? Sounds scary."

"It's Latin for secret things. They are records, letters, and documents of past Archbishops not to be released. Archivists aren't allowed to open them. Only the Archbishop can permit access. He alone can read them and decide if they can now be made public. I put in a request, of course."

"Sounds like it may be a while. So, why the bubbly smile I see?"

"I found something else. Even better. Your ancestor, Robert Curtis. Archbishop George Abbot wrote much about him. They're going to make copies and send them to me."

"Really? You must have charmed them."

"Your Robert made quite an impression. The Archbishop wrote he was determined to mentor and encourage a remarkable young priest who became a soldier, spy, and Lord Inquirer. Abbot believed Robert was called by God and uniquely gifted in his work. He was inspired by his genuine kindness, humility, and compassion. A man who chose his friends well. He wrote of God's choosing such a gentle person to become a soldier, a warrior for justice, yet benevolent in his treatment of the widows, orphans, and victims of an unholy world war tearing apart Christ's body, the church. Why, he even wrote that Robert took in the widow and children of a would-be assassin he captured. He heard the man's confession and prayed with him as he led him to the gallows."

Rose paused. "Can you imagine? A good priest—I think of Uncle Hugh—someone gentle and loving, being called to such a life? As a soldier, expected to kill? A spy? How can God expect such men to do such terrible things?"

Ike sighed. *How indeed?* "I imagine because justice should always be tempered with mercy. Men should not enjoy war, killing, or bringing others to judgment. God chooses carefully where good men should serve."

A waiter came to the table. "Can I get you something from the bar while you look over the menu?"

Ike piped up, "Something stronger than an ale tonight."

The waiter said, "A hard cider, perhaps? Our whiskey is only what the patrons leave. No telling what's really in the bottle."

Ike was confused. "Only what your patrons leave?"

"Oh yes. Good whisky is hard to come by these days. We allow patrons to open what they bring, but they must leave the bottle when they depart."

"They agree to this?"

"We wait until they open their bottle and then point out the sign over the bar. Our regulars are accustomed to the practice, hence a witch's brew of liquors."

Rose laughed. "Two hard ciders."

The waiter returned with two bottles of hard cider. Rose took one look at the label and scoffed. Truly dreadful. Do you know, Ike, that this was made from concentrate? Only 35 percent juice. The rest is water, sulfites, and preservatives."

Rose took a taste. "Made from only tannic varieties. Dry but without crispness and subtle flavors. Uncle Hugh would never drink this."

"With my bourbon, he has no need."

Ike signaled to the waiter. "Is this the best you have?"

"It's what we carry. Very little crafted cider makes it to our distributor."

Ike smiled at Rose and replied, "If you could find a superbly crafted hard cider—we're talking about 100 percent juice, a perfect blend of tannic and flavorful apple varieties—could you sell it at a premium? I mean, for those who desire real country hard cider?"

"I'm certain our manager would entertain such an arrangement, sir."

Rose pounced. "We'll speak with him after dinner."

CHAPTER 28
THE ABWEHR STRIKES

On December 2, 1942, Ike was in the OPS Room with Marley, planning a parachute supply drop supporting an SOE operation in Belgium. One of Langley's men interrupted them. "Major, a car is waiting. You are to come with me now."

Ike stared at the young, rated man. "Not so much as a 'your presence is requested, sir?' No salute?"

The man saluted. "Major Langley insisted there is no time for pleasantries. He said to be blunt, and you would respond immediately."

Ike nodded. "I leave this with you, Number One. Something tells me we need added precautions on this one. Stay until I return." Turning to the rated man, he said. "Otterhead House, I presume? Let's go."

Led to the OPS Room in Otterhead House, Ike was surprised to see Airey Neave, Langley's counterpart in the London MI9 headquarters. Neave was well known among escapees from Nazi Germany for his escape from Colditz Castle in Saxony, not far from the Czech border. Recruited by Uncle

Claude, he was responsible for Britain's support and execution of the Comet Line and Pat O'Leary Line for escaping Allied airmen. He called the shots on the planned Oaktree Line as well.

Langley immediately welcomed Ike. "It's good that you could come, Ike. You know Airey. Sit down, please." He continued while Ike found a seat. "Bad luck. It seems all of Brussels is found out. Abwehr, with many police and Wehrmacht soldiers, is rounding up our Belgian friends. Comet Line leadership is falling like a house of cards. Over a hundred we know of, and the arrests continue."

"What happened? What about safeguards? We're doing a drop outside Brussels tonight."

Airey Neave replied, "Change in plans, Major. An extraction instead."

Please tell me we're extracting Dottie. "Can I assume it's Goldenrod?"

Neave ignored the question. "A random ploy. Abwehr shopped a couple of English-speaking Nazis looking for an escape. They were taken to a safe house, the Marechal family home, about a week ago. We've suffered penetrations in the past—it's going to happen, but this—yesterday they arrested Baron Jacques Donny, aka Father Christmas. He was the Comet Line Treasurer—disbursing the money we provide. Torture yielded its rotten fruit. The leadership, the entire Brussels operation is compromised."

Langley interjected, "Thankfully, Deedee was not in Brussels. She is near the Spanish border with a dozen of our airmen. The most experienced and accomplished helper, she will be able to rebuild."

Ike asked, "The extraction—who? Where? A hot extraction?"

Neave replied, "Right. Couriers and our Brussels team if they can make the site."

Neave noted the uncertainty in Ike's eyes and continued. "As good as she is, Andre de Jongh—I'm certain the Abwehr now knows Deedee's name—insisted on independence in operation. She refused our offers of radios. She knows transmitters always bring the Jerries looking. Couriers. Most of her information was delivered in person to the British Consul in Bilbao or at the final stop in Gibraltar. But we supplemented communications through couriers. Since things got hot, we have shuttled couriers, but the team has been grounded, and now we need a larger airlift."

Ike asked, "How many?"

"Eight if we get them all. We don't know if they all remain in contact. There has been a breakdown—always an inherent difficulty in courier communications, meeting dates, and places, and, well, no one knows who is being watched. And then there was last night. Our extraction failed. The Jerries were waiting. Our plane was hit—one man dead. The good news is the Nazis jumped the gun. Went after the plane early, our people had time to make an escape."

Ike shook his head in frustration. "Had time? You don't know if they made it? And SOE doesn't bother with cameras; too much weight, you say. Abwehr knew the landing site. How was it chosen?"

"It was chosen beforehand and communicated by the previous courier. Evidently, someone caught up in the Abwehr dragnet. And tonight's landing site?"

"Your choice. Our last team carries a radio."

"They would be crazy to transmit. We must put down in a new site. One that no Belgian ever supported. And there are too many for one plane. Multiple sites have the advantage of partial success in case of compromise, but…"

"But complicates getting our people to the right site. It's your call, Major."

Ike tapped his fingers nervously. "And SOE, what will they be doing?"

"Supporting you. First, a diversionary attack miles away. Looking like a SOE commando raid and an armed landing team to secure your site."

"No offense Airey, but I'd prefer air cover and ground attack support from the Czechs."

"You'll have it."

Ike summarized, "Belgium near Brussels undergoing a massive manhunt for local helpers aiding…wait, how many airmen are still in hiding—trapped in their safehouses? How many will your teams deliver?"

"We're leaving them in place. We can only hope not all will be arrested. We can't risk any more traps. Shouldn't be too many anyway. As I mentioned, "Deedee had recently left with a contingent. So, there you have it. Get to work, Major."

Ike turned to Langley. "How did you communicate with Goldenrod? Courier? The same couriers that support the Comet Line?"

Langley nodded.

"Our Brussels team—that tells me that she is also being

pulled. What would stop our Abwehr friends from turning on her? They can't be seen as collaborating, they must know they are being led on. Tell me she will be there."

Langley sighed. "If she makes the site, she will be extracted."

Airey Neave got up to leave. Ike grunted. "One last question: how will we relay the site, time, and signals?"

Neave replied, "BBC will broadcast our instructions at 2000 tonight. I want your planes to touch down at 0200. The team will have 6 hours to make the site."

Before midnight, a black Lysander, followed by two black Expeditors, climbed through the low clouds into a clear night sky lit by a half-moon. Ten miles from the English coast, they descended into the top of the cloud cover, hiding from Luftwaffe night hunters and Nazi coast watchers. Half an hour later, four Hurricanes of the Czech Squadron departed RAF Churchstanton. Somewhere over Belgium, the Hurricanes sped over the slow Special Duty Flight aircraft. The radios were silent. But the crews on the three small planes shared one common fear: the low ceiling would prevent them from finding their landing site or, worse, not sighting the signals to land safely.

Ike's plan was bold and daring. Something none of the pilots had done before after dark. Ike determined to take maximum advantage of the diversion and chose one site that was close in and easy for all team members to find. Close-in was high risk and high reward. He determined to be close enough to the diversion to draw any nearby Germans away from his landing site but far enough to give him time to get in and out before the

Jerries redeployed.

The lowly Lysander approached first. Coming towards Brussels from the southeast. The small plane dropped out of the clouds at 300 feet. The city was brighter than he expected, even with a blackout. Coming upon the site and preparing to circle, he saw bright flames and fiery explosions ahead of him. He saw the Hurricanes dive upon a castle, the old Saint Giles prison near the city's center and only a couple of miles from the landing site. The four Hurricanes supporting Belgian resistance fighters took out the main gate and destroyed the waiting prisoner transports. Saint Giles was the first stop for the captured Belgian helpers. They were processed and either held for immediate interrogation at Saint Giles or driven 15 miles north to Breendonk Prison, in truth more a concentration camp staffed by German and Flemish SS. The atrocities committed at Breendock had become well-known throughout Belgium. It was the perfect target.

Ike smiled at what he saw from the co-pilot's seat. He picked up the radio and said, "Night thrush one, ceiling 300, splashdown light lit. going around."

The small plane circled the large man-made lake in Bois de la Cambie Park, a finger of the Sonian Forest bringing greenspace into the center of Brussels. Ike signaled the letter 'H' as he passed over Robinson Chalet on Robinson Island near the north end of the lake. Immediately, the letter 'Q' flashed back. "You're clear to land Night Thrush 2, Night Thrush 3 standby in cover."

Minutes later the float-equipped Expeditor splashed down into the lake and taxied to the Island dock. Six people scrambled on board, and four minutes later, the plane was roaring back down the lake. "Your turn, Night Thrush 3," Ike said as the first Expeditor disappeared into the cloud cover. Minutes later the second Expeditors splashed down and taxied to the dock. "How many do we have, Night Thrush 3? Do we have them all?"

"Three souls, Night Hawk one. No one waiting. Taxiing out."

Ike replied, "Will standby for five. Night Thrush 2 and 3, do you have Goldenrod aboard?"

"Night Hawk 2, no Goldenrod."

"Night Hawk 3, no Goldenrod… hold… team lead reports Goldenrod a no show. Repeat, Goldenrod a no-show."

Ike turned to the pilot. "Put her down. We'll wait at the dock. Give her ten minutes."

"That's not the plan, Major. We've been lucky. Why push it?"

"Then drop me, I'll call in with the handheld."

"Major, it has no range. You're not thinking this through. Exposing yourself! This plane! You preach risk and reward. Let's go, we can return another day. You pulled it off tonight, and you can do it again."

Ike sighed. *She chose to stay. A no-show. She knew, but she chose to stay. It's her. Stubborn to a fault! Dottie, God save your hard-headed, stubborn hide.* "You're right. Take us home."

Ike left the pilot and unit debriefing to Nigel Marley, and he drove to Wilton Park for the SOE debriefing of the extracted mission team. The de-briefing brought Colonel Z and Airey

Neave from London. Number one on the spy master's list was how bad it was in Brussels. What remains of Comet Line's leadership and strength?

Colonel Z questioned and reassured. "How did Abwehr penetrate and execute so widely in one sweep, and how quickly can we rebuild? What leaders remain? Know this—we will rebuild!"

A Czech agent replied, "Abwehr's penetration was easy. It only took one arrest. Comet Line helpers came together early before a disciplined cell structure could be formed. Friends and neighbors knew each other, trusted each other—and talked with each other so that sources and leaders were well known. Andree de Jong knew this and did her best. She instituted strong measures to prevent an arrest—the ban on radio communications is a primary example. Prevent detection at all costs. But once penetrated—once inside, a large number became vulnerable. It is a lesson we earned early in Czechoslovakia."

Neave followed up. "Mademoiselle de Jong was not in Brussels. It will not be safe for her to return. Who remains to take her place? How many helpers remain? And airmen, how many airmen were swept up? How many remain hidden in Brussels?"

"Andree left with seventy allied airmen in three groups. If they are on schedule, they should be at or across the Spanish border. I'm not aware of any airmen remaining hidden in Brussels. They got out in time. As for rebuilding. There are upwards of seven hundred Belgian helpers in the cause. Yes, Comet can be rebuilt properly in a more secure cell structure. As for a leader, I would look to Nemo…"

Neave whispered to Ike, "Jean Greindl. He took oversight from Andree's father, Frederic 'Paul' de Jongh, who has traveled to Paris to coordinate with the French."

The Czech continued. "Nemo remains at risk. He, too, is well known among the helpers."

Ike interrupted. "Goldenrod—what has become of her? She worked with you on the Abwehr negotiations—was she given word of the evacuation?"

A second Czech nodded. "Yes, we were together. We left at the same time, each going a different route to the park and rowing across to the island and Chateau Robinson. It is very well known in Brussels. A very good choice, too. She never arrived."

Ike continued, "You're Abwehr contacts—they gave you no warning? Any word on their whereabouts? Have they fled? Have they abandoned the negotiations?"

"Sir, Goldenrod asked the same questions. We received no warning. I cannot answer to what has become of them."

"You were close to her in Brussels. Did she give you any indication that she was searching for these answers?"

"Goldenrod kept herself separate. I, we did not know her safe house. We signaled our meetings through hanging laundry. I do not know her relationship with Nazi officials. It was well known—she was often seen in the company of senior Nazi officers—there was talk—gossip, concern that perhaps…"

Colonel Z interrupted, "Concern she flipped?"

"She was comfortable in their company—that was the concern."

Airey Neave, "Would not a good agent appear comfortable in the company of one she seeks to compromise?"

"Of course. I only say there was concern."

Ike asked, "What senior officials?"

"Roland, our Abwehr senior contact spent much time with her. She partied even with the Military Governor, General von Falkenhauser. Though the General saw many people. To his credit, he kept his promise not to arrest Belgian Jews or require them to wear a star of David so long as order was maintained. Brussels was safe for Jews unless arrested as resistors—then he could no longer protect them from the SS."

Ike whispered to Langley, sitting beside him. "Could General Falkenhauser be privy to his Abwehr negotiators?"

"If he was, it has blown up in our face."

The Czech leader finished, "We are anxious to return. We are more helpful in Belgium or France than here in England. We must continue our work. Rebuild for security, yes, but return soon."

Colonel Z began to wrap up, "Well said. We shall see to it. Your work must continue…"

Ike interrupted again. "One last question. Goldenrod was sent to negotiate with Abwehr conspirators, but did she show an interest in our airmen? Ask about English bomber crews?"

"I do not know. She did ask to meet Andree De Jongh. It was arranged."

The meeting broke up. Ike sat alone thinking. *Which was it, Dottie? Maintaining the Abwehr connection or a private search for Charles?*

CHAPTER 29
RESETS

Ike knew he had to stop by Saint Peter and Saint Paul. Hugh and Rose needed to know what happened. Hugh was in his study. Rose was digging through the archives, collecting vellum parchments for further examination under Ike's infrared flashlight. Ushered into the drawing room, Ike insisted each take a seat. "I have news from Dottie, that is, of Dottie," Ike stammered. He nervously wrung his hands and sighed. "I'm afraid it's not good news…"

"Something's happened to Dottie," Rose screamed. "No! God would never let her be hurt."

Hugh reached across and took Rose's hand. "There now, Rose. God will never abandon Dottie. He loves her and knows how much we love her. Let's hear what Ike has to say."

Ike bowed his head. "Last night we extracted our agents and teams from Belgium. Dottie was supposed to be among them. We know she received the instructions. We know she started out with others, but… well, she never arrived at the rendezvous. She had time. More than enough…"

"Never arrived? What happened? Where is she?"

Ike waited. "It was a large group. Two planes landed and loaded. I waited in a third in case more arrived. I waited for stragglers—far longer than normal. It was a miracle of God that we recovered everyone and made it back safely."

"Not everyone," Rose snapped.

"No. I asked about her—each of the planes. I wanted to land and search for her, but. But it was too dangerous—unfair to others. She had time—she knew…"

"You left her? You left my sister to be captured or killed? How could you? How could you be so heartless—after all she has done—we have done for you. It's your fault. You got her involved in this spying of yours. It wasn't enough that Charles was missing, but now Dottie is too. Get out! Get out! I hate you!"

Hugh went to Rose and put his arm around her. "Rose, that's not fair. Ike cares. You know he does."

Ike mumbled. "I'll show myself out."

Rose screamed. "Don't come back. I never want to see you again!"

Sunday Ike woke to a bleak winter morning. He washed, shaved, dressed, and walked to the Officer's Mess for a cup of coffee. He did not sit down. He took his cup and walked across the dead winter grass to HQ toward the small three-room office labeled 'Independent Flight 545.' As Ike reached for the door, he heard the bells. They stopped him in his tracks. He thought of the first time he heard them call. He remembered the ringers and the passion they brought to their calling. His mind's eye saw Hugh, in his robes, a cincture knot in the simple rope belt around his waist. He remembered Hugh turning and smiling at him as he passed. He felt the warmth of his smile and the truth of his teaching. He longed for that truth. He yearned for comfort and assurance of God's mercy. But he could not return. Rose would be there.

A truck backfired as it started. Across the field at the Czech barracks, young men, far from their homeland, wearing the uniform of the RAF, piled into the truck. They were off to church. Not Saint Peter and Saint Paul. They were Catholic. They were given use of a private chapel in an old manor house. A Polish priest who learned a few West Slavic Czech words said mass. The bells of Saint Peter and Saint Paul rang their final call to the faithful. *I come, Lord, I come. Perhaps it is better not to understand the words of men—good men that they are—I need you to know, I come.*

Ike walked briskly to his staff car and followed the truck. He waited for the young men to file in before he followed and slipped into a seat in a rear corner. *Can you hear me, Lord?* The Latin mass was unintelligible, but the priest's gestures and the responsive voices to the liturgy spoke to him. *Holy, Holy, Holy. You are Holy, God. All powerful. Creator of heaven and earth—worthy to be praised.* Ike bowed his head. It bobbed lightly as he prayed: *God have mercy, Christ have mercy, Lord have mercy on me a sinner. I know, oh Lord, I know you hear me. I need you, and I worship you.* Ike laughed to himself. *I don't need to understand their words. God is being praised and worshipped. That is enough—I come to worship.*

The fall of the Comet Line was still being evaluated when more bad news reached London. Andree de Jongh was captured on the Spanish border. Intelligence reported she was betrayed by a farmer whose field she crossed with her band of airmen. Langley shared the bad news at Otterhead House. "Comet Line is dead. Brussels leadership has scattered. Abwehr is advancing along every root, stem, and branch of the line. And, it is with great regret, that I report that Comet's inspirational leader, the brave and intrepid agent Dede, Andree de Jongh, has been captured along with seventeen of our airmen."

Langley paused as gasps and side comments swept the room. "Please, troubling though it is, let me continue. Nemo has gone to ground. The work in Belgium is frozen. In Paris and all of France, the Pat O'Leary Line struggles to stay one step ahead of Abwehr agents. Cobra, dead or alive, his impact continues. For the first time, Abwehr has us on our heels. Our numbers returning have dropped. Our men, if they escape, can at best be hidden—and wait. But the safe houses available are full. New safe houses are hard to find. Food and clothing are difficult to provide. We have money but diminishing connections. Our couriers are targeted. God only knows the toll our helpers are paying. They fight without arms. Young women, mostly—teens, students, but also doctors, police officers, farmers, shepherds, yes, even nobles…"

Langley paused and tapped the podium. The room became silent. The steely-nerved young officer was not known to let his emotions get the better of him. "Oaktree must proceed immediately. But it must be revamped. We will continue with the plan for sea escape routes. Speed. Speed them to the coast. Much faster, shorter, and eliminate the risks at the border. But… hear me loud and clear, Val and Ray, No contact with Comet or Pat O'Leary Line leadership. None. No trips to

Paris. Stay away from Belgium. Ray, you will be the communicator. Radio. There will be no couriers, no landings, no air extractions. Parachute in and parachute additional supplies on my authorization only. There will be no BBC-coded broadcasts of your arrival or position. You must find your safe houses and establish the lines to the coast for beach extraction. I'm counting on your experience. You both escaped. You know how the lines are supposed to work. Ray, your French is sound, but remember your days at the Sorbonne and hide that dreadful Canadian accent. We'll drop you in with bicycles, a few days of food and two radios. Then it is up to you. You have the best training in the world. Can you do it?"

Val jumped to his feet. "It's about time! Are we ready? We've been waiting for this from the day we landed back in England. Ready, damn straight, we're ready, right, Ray?"

Ray Labrosse nodded. "We'll have to be on the move. The Jerries are getting damn quick at triangulating radio signals. We need short-coded sequences—bursts, really. Thirty seconds and out. And I hope, if it's not asking too much, put us down near a known safe house. And I mean safe. You get us situated, and we can make this happen."

Ike asked, "You're asking an awful lot, eliminating landings. Risk to them and their equipment. No couriers—you heard Ray's concern with radios. We've had great success with insertion and extraction."

Langley shook his head. "Ike, you've had great luck. I'm not questioning the skill and achievements of your men. But landing sites require coordination and coordination has brought compromise. There will be no compromising this operation."

An hour later, riding back to Churchstanton from Otterhead House, Ike told Langley, "You're sending them in despite what happened. It's too soon, the risk...."

Langley was uncharacteristically short with Ike. "Too soon? Is it too soon for our men trapped? Is it too soon for the helpers and resistance who put their lives at risk? Too soon? Did Williams or Labrosse say it was too soon? No. Rather, pray Cobra is eliminated, but regardless, Oaktree goes forward in two weeks. Did you miss what I said? Comet Line and Pat line are not enough. Oaktree will provide another, faster escape route by sea from the coast of Brittany—we have commitments from the Royal Navy of gunboats and commandos to expedite the extractions. Consider the time saved and the reduced risks. How long to get to the Spanish border? To cross the Pyrenees? And then hope to find a ship to anywhere with connections to England. And if not Spain, where? Sweden is no help. Switzerland is safe, but it means sitting out the war. What other alternative? The far away coast of Yugoslavia? Yes, it's been proposed. A few escapes have succeeded. It's not the answer, only longer, slower, and more dangerous. No. Even once the Comet Line and Pat O'Leary lines are rebuilt, a safe route across the channel is our best hope."

Langley pulled in front of RAF Churchstanton Headquarters. "I'm off to Wilton Park. I must choose a safe house. I'm thinking SOE—resistance—unconnected with Comet and Pat O'Leary lines."

"Mixing apples and oranges now? You know there isn't the best relationship between them."

"You heard Ray. Just get them situated, and they'll be on

their own. I'll keep in touch."

Ike jumped out, went into his office, and shut the door. He didn't even get his coat off before Marley wrapped on his door and entered. "Skipper, this can't go on. You can't hide in here like some desert hermit. The men are asking questions. You haven't made the rounds. They think you've lost confidence in them. You spend more time with Czechs than the 545."

"You know that's not true. You're the XO. Straighten them out."

"I don't know, it's not true. Leadership comes from the top. Look, I know it's about Dorothy. You didn't want to leave her. You had no choice. And believe me, if you landed and things got hot—someone killed or injured—you and your leadership would be destroyed forever."

"That's enough, Nigel. I care about all the men and all of those working for us in the occupied territories."

"Do you? Then start acting like an adult."

"Finished?"

"Aye. But one more thing. Rose. I heard about your visit. Hugh called on me. Seems you won't accept his calls. Rose will recover. Funny how that happens when you love someone. But Hugh wants to remind you that Saint Peter and Saint Paul Church is more than Rose. It's Christ's church. His body. As a member of the body of Christ, your presence is about worshiping God in community—even I understand the communion of saints. The same God that has kept you and our men alive. You dragged me there, and I'm glad you did. It's time you ended your little pity party and recover your strength—what is the verse, 'God is my strength and my redeemer.'"

Ike stood there and said nothing.

"Put on your coat, Skipper. We're going to the hangar and the ready room."

On the way out, Ike said, "Two weeks. Val and Ray parachute in in two weeks. No more landings. No couriers. They'll have bicycles. Ray will have two radios and couple days food. Langley is looking for a SOE safe house to drop them in. God help them."

Marley asked, "No news on Dorothy?"

"Not yet. More bad news: the Comet Line Leader, young Andree da Jongh, was captured along with seventeen airmen on the Spanish border... you know, Nigel, I'm convinced Dorothy is okay. She decided to stay—whether for the mission or to find her husband, Charles, I don't know. But she is one strong-willed woman."

CHAPTER 30
SIDE TRIP

More than a week passed before Langley returned to Otterhead House. At a hastily called briefing, he announced. "Oaktree has been paused. All insertions and extractions are on hold. The situation on the ground is too unsettled. The right people have commenced a counter-intelligence operation of our contacts with Comet Line, Pat O'Leary Line, and their connections with resistance cells. The old leadership continues to fall like dominoes. Nemo has been captured. The early patriots were too well-known across functions. The pyramid of cells was formed too late to be effective. It will take some time to assess the current risk and establish a viable leadership structure. We need to know who can be trusted. Ike, I will need some specialized recon, and there will be some drops. Wait in my office. The rest of you are dismissed."

Groans of frustration filled the room as the staff left. Alone, Langley said, "I need a pilot for an agent extraction. As far as anyone knows, it's a photo recon mission. One man. Belgium. He will set his own lights and be unescorted. Just our man and your plane. No ground support—no resistance or helpers. Find a field away from Brussels, perhaps west, near the French border. Fast in and fast out. Speed and secrecy are all you have."

Ike didn't mince words. "Didn't I just hear you say so no one can be trusted? And I'm supposed to send a plane and crew in there naked? Speed" In a Lysander? Secrecy with Abwehr breathing down the neck of every friend on the continent? How do we communicate with this guy? Semaphore?"

"I know. That's why this conversation is private. We're bringing in an MI9 agent, Albert Ancia. He's been on his own. Don't you worry about comms. That's my problem. Trust me, solved. I want Marley. He can be trusted—has nerves of steel."

Ike shook his head. "No one I would trust more. But he has never made an extraction landing. First time, naked, only with luck, one light, one man? No. You ask me to trust you, well, when it's my pilots, you must trust me."

Langley nodded. "Fair enough, twelve-hour notification. Needs time to travel from Brussels. Oh, one other thing. Bishop Bell has been in contact with the pastor. No date imminent."

"Whoever coined the phrase: 'Hurry up and wait, sure got it right for this business.'"

Ike paused. "This Belgian, Albert Ancia, he's that important? And he wasn't on the evacuation flight."

"Colonel Z's call. He's the future, Ike."

Ike and Marley studied the RECON maps of the Belgian French frontier. They needed a location an easy bicycle ride from a train station. An isolated, dark field miles from a German garrison or anti-aircraft emplacement. The Dieppe airspace had been avoided since the Canadian fiasco. "Behind Dieppe. It's close—on the border, and empty," Ike said.

"How far behind? Train stations. Ypres?" Marley offered.

"Too large, slow getting away from the town and farms. Same for Lille."

"Handschoote is very isolated, but it is across the border. It means risking another border check of papers."

Ike shook his head. "Haringe and Roesbrugge. Here on the Yser river. Just before the border crossing."

Marley turned his eyes toward Ike. "It's open country and behind Dunkirk. The coast is still thick with Jerries."

Ike nodded. "Twenty miles. I'll take those odds. Good open landing field for a single man to find and to light. Fast in and out. No worries about getting off quickly—taxi in any direction."

Marley grunted, "I'll say open. Not a tree for miles…so long as he is not followed."

"The Abwehr is arresting on sight, not following. Interrogations have given them the names they seek. If he shows, I believe he'll be on his own. Now, pilot. I think Smithson. He's proven himself. I'll sit in the second seat."

Marley stiffened. "You? Again? What are you trying to prove? Wait. This is about Dorothy."

"I have a few questions for our Belgian friend—MI9 recruit. I don't trust Colonel Z to invite us to any debrief. Give the coordinates. Instructions for a man on a bicycle. I want two lights on the field 300 feet apart at 0100. Hand torch, identify signal is Yoke, countersign Zebra."

The Lizzie crossed the French coast fifteen miles south of Dieppe, shrouded in scud clouds. The plane began a wide circle back towards Dunkirk. The coastal rainy scud clouds gave way to a low ceiling of four hundred feet. The Yser River formed the border between France and Belgium. It meandered slowly to the sea. Ike called out as they approached the hills on the French side, the highest reaching just over five hundred feet. Smithson piloted across to the Belgian side, and they skirted unseen in the low clouds with the few farmers below asleep in their beds.

When Ike's dead reckoning placed them over Roesbrugge, he told Smithson to drop out of the clouds for a look. The dark sky made the fields of grain and grass appear as dark as the sea. Ike checked his watch 0058. They continued towards the coast. Then a light appeared off to the right. A second, a short distance beyond. Smithson banked the plane for a flyover. Ike reached for the signal lamp and flashed 'Yoke' one long, two short, one long. Instantly, he recognized the countersign, two long followed by two short flashes. "I read Zebra. Put her down."

The Lysander landed on the short, dead stubble of a wheat field. The ground was firm beneath the fat tires, and Smithson taxied to a lone figure who ran forward to collect the landing light. Ike threw open the door and motioned for the man. We'll taxi to the other, come on."

A young man, panting from running and flowing adrenaline, ran up and tossed a small bag to Ike. Ike stood in front of the door and said, "Looks like we have company." The man turned around. Three sets of headlights were driving quickly up the road along the field. "Abwehr, I saw them waiting at the station. I slipped under the train. I left the bike and ran. Help me in."

Ike smiled. "Figures. First, tell me about Goldenrod; she didn't make the extraction."

Confusion contorted the man's face. "I am to say nothing until I am officially debriefed."

Ike blocked the door. "First, you answer my questions, then we go. Gunfire. Do you want to wait for your friends?"

"Yes, yes. I will tell you. She chose to stay."

"In Brussels? And MI9 left her?"

"No, no, please, I will tell you all. She is safe. Please."

Ike stepped aside; his right grabbed the man's shoulder, and his left grabbed his belt. Lifting, Ike tossed him in the rear before climbing into the cockpit. "Let's go, Smithson. I think it is safe to leave the landing light."

As the small plane climbed into the clouds, Ike asked, "You were saying Goldenrod is safe. I want to hear it."

Ike caught the bewildered look in Smithson's eyes as he turned to question Albert Ancin. "Safe, you say. Where?"

"Goldenrod was determined to accompany a helper, called Lilly. Lilly, a leader of the guides from Brussels. She goes to warn the guides and the safehouses from Brussels to Paris. Goldenrod insisted she go along to learn the protocols and procedures. Goldenrod did not tell the others to be evacuated lest they try to dissuade or compel her."

"You say they are safe."

"Abwehr has not arrested them in Belgium. We know. They must be in Paris. No one is to return to Brussels. It is not safe. Nemo is arrested, and Franco now leads, but he is in hiding."

"Colonel Z knows this?"

"I cannot say. I have been in hiding since I received my orders to England. I have not left an attic outside the city for days. I was lucky. Nemo came with my orders hours before he was arrested. Brussels is a deathtrap."

Ike sighed. He offered his hand to the shaking young man. "Welcome to freedom. Just a small matter of avoiding the shore guns and any Luftwaffe night hunters. You'll be fine."

Ike turned to Smithson, "Isn't that right, Flight Lieutenant?"

Smithson stared. Ike responded. "What? I would do the same for you and any man in the unit. We leave no one behind. But we'll keep this between the two of us."

"Aye, Skipper. Heading home."

A Staff car sat darkened in front of the 545 Hangar at RAF Churchstanton. As the Black Lysander taxied to the hangar, Ike watched the red glow of a cigarette visible in the car. *That will be Langley, anxious to get his new charge to Wilton Park.* Ike turned around and said to the nervous Belgian behind him. "Welcome to England. Wait where you are. I'll get the door for you and a light so you don't trip."

Ike and Langley stepped out simultaneously. Langley ground his cigarette butt into the ground. Ike spoke first. "Albert Ancia. He's in one piece. Abwehr showed up as we left. Cooperative fella. Tells me Dorothy is safe. Says she left Brussels the day of the extraction in the company of a guide code-named Lilldy...."

Langley interjected, "That would be Michelle Dumon, their most talented guide."

Ike continued, "They set out to warn the guides and *hebergeurs* down the Comet line. Believes they are in Paris now."

"That is good news…"

Ike talked to him. "Ancia received his orders from Colonel Z while in hiding. If Ancia knows about Dorothy, for certain, Colonel Z knows. And what about you, James? Did you know?"

Ike sighed. "No. You are not one to leave a man behind. You're in this because you're human."

Langley reached for a cigarette. Ike struck the match for him. "Thanks. For the record, no. Uncle Claude holds his cards close to his chest."

"Well, I'll give you a heads-up. The Colonel will not be happy that I encouraged—make that compelled—Ancia to come clean. He said Colonel Z ordered him to say nothing to anyone until he was officially debriefed. I held the plane with Abwehr in full charge until he agreed to talk. You might consider Uncle Claude's reaction during your ride to Wilton Park tonight. But all-in-all, a good night."

Ike opened the door to the plane and helped Albert Ancia out. "Here you go, my friend. I'm afraid your travels aren't yet over this evening. This officer will see you safely to Colonel Z."

The next day, Ike found Hugh Osbourne alone in his vicarage study. "Ike! Good to see you. Please, come and sit down. I've missed our chats."

Ike stood in the doorway. "I'm not here for a social visit, Hugh. I just came by to say we have news of Dottie. She left Brussels with one of our helpers and made for Paris. She is believed to be safe. I am working on better communications with her. But I thought you would want to know. And please tell Rose for me. I know how she worries."

"She's over in the Parish Office. She would be glad to hear from you."

"No, I've got to get back to the base."

Hugh sighed and put down his reading glasses. "Come to church on Sunday, if for no other reason than to praise God and thank him for our answered prayers. You belong, Ike. Your family is here. You are loved, and the body never functions as well when a member is missing."

"I'll think about it."

"God bless, Ike. See you Sunday."

Back in his office, Ike sat down to a pile of paperwork on his desk. Marley was thorough and organized. Documents requiring his signature were paperclipped inside folders, open to the signature page. Most were routine, but those the XO thought Ike should read contained a note: 'Skipper, you need to read this. M.'

Ike worked his way through the pile until he came to an unopened envelope. Ike recognized the handwriting at once. A letter from home. Ike tore it open and read:

Son,

Hope this letter finds you well. Little Earl, Ole, and Marge say hello. I cut out an article from the Tacoma Tribune that might interest you. I was surprised to receive a special invitation to an event over in Seattle near the old float plane launch you used. Surely you recall. That neighborhood has changed. Cheap houses atop the land everywhere you look, if you get my drift. Anyway, an allied war hero, an Ace pilot, was giving a speech. So, I went out there. His English was hard to understand, but he was something, all right. Insisted on shaking my hand and saying what a fine son I had. A Czech fella says he knows you and asked about your family. His name is Karel Kuttelwascher, name sure sounds German to me, but no worse than Eisenhower. Well, the long and short of it was I invited him to dinner in Gig Harbor, and he said yes! Well, you could knock Ole, Marge, and little Earl over with a gaff pole. A real live war hero! He came out and insisted on helping cook. Fed him fresh Salmon and crab, but he did things with potatoes, cabbage, onions and beets I've never seen. Even talked me into a beer. A real blessing, son, knowing you're doing right by your country and doing right by good people from all over the world. Says he will look you up when he returns.

We're all praying for you, son. We miss you and love you. I got your letter with the pictures of Rose. Earl says she is pretty. He also says he is getting better at hitting the curve ball. As always, when are you coming home?

Love, Dad

Folded into the letter was the front-page article: 'Allied Ace visits the Puget Sound'.

Ike went to church on Sunday. He waited for the bells to finish their call to worship and the processional to begin before he found a seat in the back pew. Head bowed and eyes closed for prayer, he felt the air move, and he smelled the sweet aroma of Rose as she slipped in beside him. His body tingled as she slipped her arm inside his, and her fingers wove into his. How much he had missed her! How pleasant it was to have her beside him again. He did not lift his head for fear the tear in his eye might be seen.

CHAPTER 31
DROPPING IN

James Langley stopped by Ike's office on Monday afternoon with his now weekly report on agent Goldenrod. After Langley took Ike's complaint to Colonel Z, who reportedly listened non-plussed, a report on Dorothy was provided every Monday. Ike nodded when he heard Dorothy had returned safely from the Spanish border with Michelle Dumon. "Good news on two accounts. Dorothy, safe and gaining experience, of course. But the regularity of the reports tells me SOE has solved their communication problem."

James Langley sighed. "Not really. Our radio operators rarely last a few weeks before being captured. The nazis have mastered triangulating quickly. We're just too slow in our transmissions—the code needs to be faster and shorter—and the antennas—we need better, shorter antennas. The time to stretch them out and recover, unseen. We are losing good people, often young women, far too quickly."

Ike looked up, his eyebrows arching in concern. "Really? Then where, how the regular reports?"

"The Free French. And that presents a whole different

problem for Uncle Claude. SOE must rely on the French, which means cutting them in for British SOE support in France, where he would rather not. Be sure De Gaule is using this to pressure Churchill and Eisenhower. Most of the surviving French Intelligence, their BCRA, don't ask me what the French name is—now works for the Free French. Headquartered in Paris, it's the Mithridate Network. It's one of the issues I wanted to discuss with you today. Colonel Z is asking, well, directing, payback. He wants to add French agents to our Oaktree drop next week."

"Next week? We're finally greenlighted? Great! Hey, the more the merrier. I guess I should ask how many."

"Too many for a Lysander or even the Expeditor. How many can you cram on a Hudson?"

"Gear. How much gear? And it needs to be handled by a parachute crew."

"Ray and Val will have two radios, two bicycles, and backpacks. Our French brothers, three, perhaps four, will be traveling light."

"I don't see a problem, James. What other nuggets are you holding back?"

James smiled. "High value, high risk. Word is out that Armand will be on board."

"Armand?"

"Leader of the Mithridate Intelligence Network in Alencon, Normandy. He must make it. Pray there is no leak, no penetration. There is nothing the Abwehr or the SS Waffen would not do to capture him."

"Well, there's nothing like bringing a little heat. I don't

see a problem at my end. I'll get busy on the drop site."

"That's another thing. Mithridate Paris will choose the site."

Ike squinted. "Can I, at least, plan on escort and cover?"

"I'll pretend I didn't hear that. I guess that about wraps it up. I'm off to the SOE Operations Room."

Ike smiled. "Whose bailiwick is this? Remind me that MI9 is not part of MI6. Or are we just Uncle Claude's obedient lap dog."

"Later, Mic," and Langley was out the door.

March 20, 1943, was a cold, gray day. The calendar may have anticipated spring, but the skies over England and France were darkened by low clouds and blurred by whirling snow flurries. Ike shook his head in frustration. "There's nothing here. Just one faint infrared hit. It could be anything. It might be one of the guide lights, but it's well off-target to the left. It's pointless to post a photo. All we have to go on is the crew's report… post it anyway. I'll question them."

Marley nodded. "Nothing's come across the wire yet. Just the pilots…"

"I want every man on that plane in the room. Perhaps between them, we can piece something together."

Half an hour later, the 545 Operations Room was filled. Langley stood at the back and listened. Ike stood at the podium. The lone gray-black RECON photo of a dim red light illuminated the screen. "That's all you brought home. So, I have a lot of questions this morning. MacDonald, you're up. Give me a blow-by-blow on the drop."

BELLS OF REDEMPTION

Flight Lieutenant MacDonald, pilot of the Lockheed Hudson, stood up. "Yes, sir. Skies were clear over the channel as predicted. Kept low. If the Luftwaffe was there, I never saw them. We lost the moon 15 miles inland. Dead reckoned navigated to our turn southeast of Paris, steadied up on compass course 325, as planned, and dead reckoned for the Forest of Rambouillet. Dropped down to find the ceiling. Caught only one short glimpse of the ground from 200 feet. Possible sighting of the Ponds of Holland…"

"Possible? MacDonald? Did anyone on board confirm the lake? My God, its straight as an arrow and long. Two lights, one at the southeast end and one at the causeway at the other end. There isn't a larger target within fifty miles of Paris!"

MacDonald turned and looked at his fellow crewmembers. "Yes, sir. Big. But no sir. It seemed flat and black—water or field, I don't know for sure."

"Was it before or after the RECON photo was shot?"

"Sir, the cameras were firing the whole time of the approach, so I couldn't say."

"Continue."

"Yes, sir, I climbed to 400 feet, and we dropped the equipment. Two chutes. Both opened. Assuming we passed over the Grand Pond, I made the left turn to 270 compass, and the men parachuted. Everyone cleared. All chutes opened. Continued on 270 to the coast and headed home."

Ike nodded. "Sergeant Farnsworth, you were at the door. What did you see?"

"Like the Flight Lieutenant said, sir, we were in the cloud cover. Flurries too. But I did see all chutes open."

"Not even a glimpse of the ground? No lights?"

"No sir, just black sky with gray snow and the whites of the parachutes as they opened right away."

"MacDonald, did you run through alternatives with your co-pilot?"

"Pilot Officer Jeffries can speak…"

Jeffries stood up. "Aye, sir, I asked if we should make another pass. Mister MacDonald replied, 'We have a probable sighting. Any turns would only take us farther off course,' the ceiling, the flurries—Major, it wasn't going to get any better."

Ike stared at the young man. "Take your seat, Jeffries."

Ike paused. "You men did your best." Ike looked at his watch. "It's been ten hours, and we have no confirmation that the five men we dropped are alive, captured, or dead. But I know you did your best. I would have done the same. Dismissed."

As the room emptied, Langley made his way to Ike. Ike shook his head. "Follow a large arrow to one small field in a heavy forest, and they couldn't find it."

Langley nodded. "Val and Ray are survivors. If anyone can make it, they will. As for the French team, well, they'll have friends looking for them."

Ike sighed. "It's been ten hours. You would think Ray would have made radio contact by now. Oaktree has been one setback after another."

Langley clasped Ike's arm. "It all comes down to initiative. Not something that can be trained. Val Williams has it in spades. I'm heading over to the SOE Operations Room. Maybe they've heard something from Mithridate."

Ike mumbled, "God forbid they keep us in the loop."

The following afternoon, a light knock on his door prompted Ike to reply without looking up, "It's open. Come through."

James Langley cleared his throat. Ike looked up to see Claude Dansey standing before him. Ike rose and said, "Colonel Z, please take a seat. What can I do for you, sir?"

Colonel Z and Langley sat down. Dansey said, "Langley reminds me I owe you an update. I know you're a busy man, so I thought I would stop by. They're all safe. Mithridate reports a meeting with Val Williams. Quite extraordinary, really. Rough drop. Both radios were damaged and a bicycle as well. But Val pedaled his way to a helper he remembered in Paris, Yvonne Le Rossignal. She took him to their mutual friend, Elizabeth Barbier, where Armand was also waiting. Seems MI6 SOE and MI9 can't help but work together. Armand sent Val to Jean Lanlo, his man at Saint-Quay-Portrieux, to set up a base in Brittany. Both Val and Ray Labrosse are on their way."

Ike sighed as he nodded. "That's good news. So, at last, Oaktree begins."

Colonel Z smiled. "There's more. Goldenrod. She has left Paris with Lilly…"

"Michelle Dumon," Ike added.

"Right. Their best. That young woman can charm, cry, or smile her way past any German policeman. They're off to the Chateau de Bourblanc in Brittany. The Countess de Mauduit is housing scores of airmen in the Chateau under the very eyes of the Jerries who visit her regularly. Another American. She should be useful to Oaktree."

Ike smiled. "More good news. Thank you, sir. We at the 545 will give it our best, sir."

Claude hesitated, "That's not the only reason I came. You've become the nagging wife I can't ignore. It's your damned humanity, Curtis. You insist on putting names and faces on our work. It's so much easier with numbers. The greater the number, the greater the good. It's damned hard not to be brought down by faces, real people. But I'm glad you're here to remind me that they matter. Every single one of them. Someday, when our victory is won, I will be glad I struggled to know each one we lost had a face, a name, a family, and a legacy for their life sacrificed for the greater number—those who follow. Only my dear wife and the stubborn Yank sitting at this desk keep that small flame flickering."

After Dansey and Langley left, Ike couldn't concentrate on work. He needed to take it all in, to savor the hope and joy that flooded in. *I need to see Rose. To tell her the good news. No, I can't—later.* He found himself walking towards the Officer's Mess. Unconsciously, he made his way to the coffee urn, took his cup from the pegboard, and filled his mug. He stared absent-mindedly at the bulletin board. He didn't hear Group Captain Hastings walk up behind him. "Wing party, Friday night. You should come. Bring your girl, Rose, isn't it?"

"I never go to these things. You know that. Put on a happy face and drown your troubles in drink."

Hastings shook his head. "You'll never change. All the same, you won't want to miss this one. Trust me. This time, come. Bring Rose, celebrate. Didn't I hear you've received good news? There will be a special guest. Kut Kuttelwascher will be there."

"Kut? Back here?"

"Kut and his pretty English bride, Ruby could teach you a thing or two. They know how to live through this war. My quarters 1900 Friday."

Rose was ecstatic. "Dottie is safe, and you want me to go to a party, with the officers and their wives? At the Group Commander's house? They requisitioned the largest manor in town for him! Will there be dancing? I've always wanted to go to a dance! I've only danced with Dottie, but I want to try. Yes, I want to dance with my handsome officer gentlemen! Friday? What will I wear?"

"Rose, you would look good in a burlap dress."

"If that was a compliment, I missed it, mister."

Ike grimaced. "Right, let me try again. You're beautiful—no matter how you are dressed, there's no hiding the beauty of my Rose. You're resourceful. I trust you to find the perfect outfit. So, you'll come? I'll pick you up at 7."

At 6:55 Ike rang the bell. Rose shouted from inside. "I'm up here, Ike. Come up and tell me what you think."

Ike bound up the stairs two at a time. Rose was seated in front of a small vanity mirror applying lipstick, the only makeup she used. She turned around, brushed her hair back and said, "Well? Is it better than burlap?"

"Wow!" was all he could muster. Rose was resplendent in a navy-blue dress with a tight bodice accented in small white stars and a plunging decotage. A matching navy skirt fell in wide pleats from her narrow waist down to above her ankles. A small but tasteful pearl necklace encircled her neck.

"It's a party, not a royal ball. And, your dress, its, well, it's..."

"It's what, Ike? You don't like what you see?"

"I like it very much! We can skip the party, and we can just celebrate here alone."

Rose laughed. "Now, that's a compliment a girl likes to hear! But you're not getting off that easy. It comes with a white lace jacket. But I'm glad you're jealous. It was Aunt Jane's. I'm bigger on top. Dottie helped me tailor it for her wedding, though it's still a little tight. Now, if you're done gawking, we can go."

Group Captain Hastings met them at the door. "Welcome, Ike. Glad you could make it. This must be the famous Rose Osbourne who snagged our only eligible Yank. Welcome Rose. Please, there are drinks at the bar. You'll find Kut and his lovely bride, Ruby inside."

As Rose walked by, Hastings gave a smile and nod of approval to Ike. Kut called out to Ike. "Mic! You made it my friend! Finally, we are together again! This is my lovely wife Ruby and who is this beautiful young lady I see?"

"Kut, Ruby, meet Miss Rose Osbourne, my date."

"More than your date, Mic, from what I hear." Bowing to Rose and kissing her hand, Kut continued, "It is a great pleasure to meet the special lady of my good friend. I have been waiting for this day since I first saw your photograph in the Curtis house in Gig Harbor, Washington. You must tell me Mic, Harbor I know, but what is this Gig? But I digress, you have a good man—he comes from, we Czechs would say—dobry peoplr, in English, good people. People of the earth."

Ike and Rose had the same thought: *Rose's/my picture in*

BELLS OF REDEMPTION

Dad's house? A very good sign! Kut continued. "I was telling Ruby about my visit to America. What a country! Beautiful and so large. One can scarcely imagine so much space. You must tell me, Mic, so big! How does one find their way across. It's a different place, a different world than Europe. Good people but they just don't understand what is happening, but they begin to see. They are coming and in strength. So many factories turning out airplanes and tanks and ships. Hitler and Tojo will never stand against such a wealth of factories. It is won, I tell you, the war is won."

Ruby took Rose's hand. "Kut, you and Mic have much to catch up on. Let me take Rose. She needs a drink, and I need girl talk."

"Of course, my love, go. I will chat with my friend."

"Out of earshot, Ruby said, "Has it started? The looks, the whispers behind your back. It will. It doesn't matter that they love us, that they are good men, war heroes. They are foreign and that makes us, well...the favorite topic of the village gossips."

Rose's jaw dropped. "No, I mean, I didn't know or just didn't want to see it. Surely, you have friends—Kut is a charming man."

"It's hard. You need to decide if you can deal with it. Oh, family will stand by you—at least to your face. Friends? Well, you'll quickly learn who they really are."

Rose took a breath. "But it's worth it—the love."

Ruby replied, "Yes. Yes, it is. But love? I do love him, so very, very much. But the war—it does something to them. Kut is kind and thoughtful and loving. But at night I wake up and he is sitting in bed, wide awake but not with me. He is somewhere else, some hell of this war. Somewhere, in the depth of his soul he is on fire, burning—driven. I guess that was the price of battle."

"Ike tells me that Kut has been assigned training duty—a command no less."

"Yes. He sees young men that are bound for combat, knowing most will be dead in a few months. To him it is worse than going himself."

"Ike never talks about his duties. He only talks about keeping track of my sister, Dottie, who is stuck in France. I never ask him. Am I wrong? What should I do?"

"You're not wrong. You can only be there for him. Love him, it's his only salvation."

At the other end of the room, Ike mentioned to Kut, "I know you're supposed to sit out this war in semi-retirement teaching young kids to fly. But I have this mission—extracting a German pastor from the Czech border. I know, but hear me out, he's German resistance. He was safely in America teaching, a scholar of some repute. He went back and penetrated the Abwehr—he plots the murder of Hitler and reports to MI6. He's under suspicion. Good people, if not the people in power want him out alive."

"Where?"

"I was thinking, send him to Decin, the German garrison, from there into the hills east of the Elbe—your country. Czech resistance will be on board. A Hudson. Stops in Oland, Sweden, SOE maintains a secret base on the Island."

"I will do it. Yes, yes, of course. We will talk more of this, my friend. Finally, a mission. Now, where are our ladies? What would we be without them? Hey? Beasts, yes, we are beasts without women to love us."

CHAPTER 32
BRITTANY SPRING WARMING

ke greeted Langley as he entered the Operations Room at Otterhead House for the weekly Oaktree brief. "I see congratulations are in order, Lieutenant Colonel." Ike gave him a salute. "Shouldn't I salute? Wouldn't want to tire your good arm."

Langley returned his salute and smiled. "Thanks. Ike. We count on you Yanks for our daily humor. Find us seats in the front. I know you'll speak your mind, and I don't want an audience. Airey has the brief. You'll find it enlightening."

Ike's interest was piqued when Airey Neave addressed the radio problem. "Communications remain priority one. Mithridate is our only option, and they have made clear their security concerns. Val's many contacts with French and resistance operatives, as well as new hebergeurs and helpers, strain the security protocols of our only remaining links. Our sources in France suspect Mithridate itself may be penetrated. Our last report confirms that Val has established himself in Saint-Quay-Portrieux with the French local agent, Jean Lanlo—Lanlo has been tested and is trusted. Many recently downed airmen have been rescued and hidden by locals—my analysis—London is surprised by the broad support of the French citizenry to accept extraordinary risk in rescuing our flyers. Two days ago, an American B-17 crew was rescued and were immediately taken to Val in Saint-Quay-Portrieux. While this is welcome news, we are concerned that the number of evaders is exceeding the helper's resources to house, feed, and clothe…"

Ike whispered to Langley, "Let me guess, coordinating with the Admiralty is laborious and slow. Let me put something together. A coordinated airlift using all my assets, why I've proven float planes work—the estuary is perfect for the Lysanders and Expeditors—and nearby fields for the Hudsons. Start with the high-priority pilots—I hear a spitfire pilot was rescued last week the day he went down, and that American B-17 crew. They're still healthy and could return to duty at once. Go back to Val. Ask the number of high priorities he recommends."

James stared ahead. "We'll talk later. You need to hear what Airey has to say. London calls the shots."

Nieve was still briefing. "His latest estimate exceeds one hundred evaders awaiting transit near the coast of Brittany. Whatever the logistical problems facing Oaktree, the mission has been very effective in locating and organizing the evaders for travel to England. London has called for an airdrop of another radio for Ray Labrosse and cash to pay for the black-market purchases of food, clothing, housing, and guides. The Admiralty is providing a radiotelephone for beach-to-boat communications. Other general items include bicycles, maps, and sundry related equipment."

Ike couldn't hold back and interrupted. "One moment,

Airey. You just told us the numbers are exceeding the support infrastructure. Would London be open to a partial airlift from Brittany—high priorities. The 545 could put together a coordinated floatplane and landing field extraction. We could handle upwards of thirty in one operation. It would relieve the bottleneck while the Admiralty plans their sealift."

Ike felt Langley's eyes bearing into him, but he did not turn his gaze from Neave. Airey replied, "I can see the merit of your argument, and as always, the services of the 545 are valued. However, London is firm that the success of Oaktree will be met in the establishment of a beach-to-boat-to-sea route from Brittany. The operation you are proposing, I feel confident in saying, would be viewed as a risk to Oaktree's intended purpose. The German response would be immediate and overwhelming."

Ike muttered, "So, I'm to shut up and wait."

Airey smiled. "I wouldn't put it so harshly, Ike. There are many players in this operation with their own concerns and priorities. Let's just say that your initiative in contingency planning may come in handy at some future time."

Langley whispered, "Colonel Z recognizes diplomatic skill in the placement of his people."

Airey continued. "My last point is the security of Mithridate, which I touched on earlier. While MI9 has been searching for Cobra, other events—we can't accept coincidence as causation—suggest Cobra or a wider cell has penetrated the Free French Intelligence and our Mithridate connection. Lacking any other communication options, we must proceed cautiously with contingency wherever possible. It's a deadly game we play.

As we speak, both Comet Line and Pat O'Leary line agents and helpers are being arrested and interrogated. Security. I can't emphasize it enough. Questions? Oh, one more thing before questions: If you're a praying man, say a prayer for the French citizens. Not just the dedicated resistance but the farmers and villagers, women and young people, who have so much to lose. They will prove to be our greatest strength in Oaktree."

Afterward Airey joined Ike and Langley in Langley's office. Airey's mind remained focused on the brief. "London truly is amazed. I can't give names or specifics, but since Val and Ray dropped in and somewhat clumsily made their presence known, we had mayors, police chiefs, railroad ticket masters, butchers, grocers, doctors, the entire cross-section of the countryside step up to help."

Airey sighed. "But…"

Langley completed his thought. "But in a new and wide net, everyone talks. Just when MI9, SOE MI6, and Free French Intelligence are being linked, Gestapo and Abwehr informants are sure to penetrate Oaktree. It's a security nightmare."

Ike interjected, "Exactly why we can't wait for the London committee to get its act together. Time. We must move quickly."

"You're preaching to the choir, Ike. I'm sure Airey and Uncle Claude are pushing as hard as they can," Langley replied.

Ike sighed. "Sorry, Airey. I'm sure you are. Tell me, any news on Goldenrod?"

"Goldenrod is being sent to Val, Ray, and Lanlo. She will connect the countess and the remnants of the Comet Line with Oaktree. The Chateau is the largest safehouse in the area. Any additional space is welcome."

"How long can you leave her there? She isn't trained for this kind of heat."

Airey's eye bored into Ike. "She is as determined to stay as you are to pull her out. We're all expendable. As always, we do what's best for the mission."

Ike nodded. "Message received. I only remind you that sometimes we—the mission must do what's right by the agent in the field."

Airey replied, "Colonel Z admires your zeal, Ike. But don't overplay your hand. Oh, one other thing. The Colonel requests you see Bishop Bell. There's been a development. London, this week."

Ike returned to Churchstanton. Nigel Marley stopped him as came through the door. "How did it go, Skipper? Any news that you can share?"

"Here's a question for you, XO. What do you call a horse designed by a committee?"

Nigel smiled. "I'm sure I'm about to learn."

"Ike replied, "A camel. And an operation planned by a committee is a fiasco. If you can pull yourself away from your desk, come through. Oh, first get someone busy on travel arrangements. I need orders, the staff car, and accommodation for one night in London this week. What's the schedule look like?"

"Thursday looks best. Unit your visiting?"

"Room 900. Make it happen."

"Yes, sir, MI9. And Skipper, a couple of care packages from home are on your desk."

Ike had his coat and hat off before he reached his desk. Two large boxes awaited his inspection. Ike didn't need to read the return address. They were clearly from home. He pulled out his old pocketknife and cut through the string and paper. Opening the first box he removed the letter and smiled down at his loot. "Marge Olson, you're a saint! Rose will love this, and so will I."

Just then, Marley came through the door. "Is this a good time? I can come back later."

"No, perfect timing. Sit down. It seems Val Williams is a master at collecting evaders. He has one hundred airmen, including the crew of the B-17 shot down two days ago and a spitfire pilot less than a week in France."

"That's good news, isn't it?"

"Great if we can get them out. He also has broken every security barrier between MI6 SOE, MI9, and Mithridate, hell, all Free French Intelligence operations. It seems every Frenchie, women and children included, is getting into the act. God bless their bravery, but no one knows who to trust. Abwehr and the Gestapo will surely penetrate his network. Dorothy is going to the coast to help out. She's connecting Oaktree with the remnants of the Comet Line through a local countess. She always did punch above her weight. Langley claims she won't leave until Oaktree is up and running, or my guess, she finds Charles."

Nigel nodded. "Seems we need to act quickly."

"My thoughts as well. The Admiralty is one hold-up, but I suspect the Free French, and the politicians all have a hand in it. I recommended a full-on airlift—one event, Lysanders and

Expeditors with floats, and our Hudsons on one, maybe two fields—figured we could ease the overcrowding by thirty or so—high priorities—pilots. Got turned down flat. Airey Neave gave a little wiggle room for us to bottom drawer a contingency plan."

"I'll get right on it. I'm assuming Saint Quay-Portrieux."

Ike shook his head. "I pray the Jerries are never as good as you. Next week, I'll stay here, and you can tell me what will be briefed."

"Thanks, Skipper, but you've taught me how to think. Float planes, a clever twist, will need an estuary. I'll have the orders on your desk in the morning."

"Good. Now, I need to make a delivery in town,"

Ike took a box under each arm and was out the door. Parking at Osbourne Cottage, Ike could see Rose working in the garden. Rose heard the car pull up in the gravel, stood up and brushed the dirt off her slacks. "Ike, you're just in time to give me a hand with the potatoes."

Ike left the boxes in the car and walked to her in the garden. "Maybe a kiss will persuade me to help." Her quick peck didn't satisfy him. "I'm going to need more than that." Before he could say another word, she wrapped her arms around him and gave him something to remember.

"Now, only because I don't want you to soil your trousers, you will cut the seed potatoes while I plant. Aim for three eyes on each piece, but at least two."

Ike looked at the long row of freshly turned soil. "You've been busy. Let me guess. After the potatoes, you're planning on turnips, onions, beets, and carrots. All good hardy root vegetables that thrive in a cool climate. And then there will be the apples."

Rose corrected him, "You forgot the carrots and peas."

"Yum, I love your carrots and peas. Oh, and no doubt cabbage. But it's still a little early for them."

"Did you come here to tell me how to tend my garden, or is there something else you want to say? Start cutting those potato eyes. I'm all ears, mister."

Ike picked up the pail and began to pare. "Two reasons. First, I'm off to London on Wednesday night. Hope to be back Thursday night. Second, I've got something for you—a care package from my mother-in-law, Marge. But I'll save that until we have the potatoes in. And there's news. Dottie is safe. She is in Brittany doing great work. Look, Rose, there's no easy way to say it, but I've been told your sister is too stubborn to come home."

Rose took a handful of the potato nuggets and buried them in the loamy soil. "Doesn't surprise me. She's looking for Charles. If anyone can find him, she can."

Rose looked up. "I gave it to God long ago. I just trust Him. Somehow, I know she's going to be okay—You're going to have to move faster, Ike, if you want dinner before dark."

Ike went to work cutting the seed potatoes. Rose bent over planting and asked softly, "You'd search just as hard if it was me, wouldn't you, Ike? I'd never give up on you."

Ike nodded. "Yes. Yes, of course, I would, but I can't help worrying about her. I feel responsible, and, well, I don't think I could handle the guilt if anything happened to her. But knowing you trust God somehow makes me feel better."

The April sun had just dropped below the horizon when they finished. Ike went to the car and retrieved the boxes. He set them on the kitchen table while Rose pulled dinner from the oven.

When she came out, Ike explained. "Marge is a gardener and a great cook. Our climate back home is also cool, so I asked her what else besides root vegetables do well in a short, cool summer. Seeds, proven seeds she swears by and instructions. You, my dear, are about to expand your game! You can put every bit of that good English earth to use. She recommends green beans, lentils, winter squashes, pumpkins, celery, spinach, broccoli, cauliflower, rhubarb, and my favorite—sweet corn. I know it does best with warm summer sun, but this variety was bred just for the Pacific Northwest—plant it in long rows at the top of the hill so the wind pollinates it. Marge plants spinach between the corn, and somehow, they protect each other. Imagine, corn, fresh on the cob. It will melt in your mouth.

And here, she has melons and tomatoes—cucumbers and zucchini. I know what you're gonna say: your dad was an estate agent—some of these do best in a greenhouse. Well, a glazer will be here to replace the broken panes and get the old greenhouse back ship shape and Bristol fashion. Sweet melons this summer and red, ripe, juicy tomatoes!"

Rose was busy going through the seed packets. "I don't know anything about some of these. Where do I start?"

Ike gave her the letter from Marge, and she began to read.

BELLS OF REDEMPTION

Dear Rose,

I'm looking at your picture as I write this letter. I see a sweet, loving face. Ike has told us so many wonderful things about you that I feel I know you already. Anyone who has captured his heart is nothing less than a blessing from God. Everyone here in Gig Harbor feels you are already family: you, Dorothy, and Uncle Hugh. Now, I know some of these vegetables are not typical cool weather plants, but if you start them indoors or in a greenhouse and you tend them right, you'll find they'll do just fine. Ike tells me that he hasn't seen some of these in England, so I've enclosed some recipes and canning tips. We couldn't survive out here without our garden, so I feel a kindred spirit. There's plenty of time until harvest, so please write if you have any questions. Or just write to say hello. And one last request—don't let him miss church. Remember, no excuses! God isn't through with him yet.

Love,

Marge Olson

PS: Young Earl says green beans aren't like sweet peas. You eat them pod and all—cooked, of course.

By the time Rose put down the letter, tears were streaming from her eyes. She leaned over and hugged Ike tightly.

Ike showed his pass to the sentry in front of the War Office in Whitehall, London. Reading Ike's orders: Major M.I Curtis, MI9 Room 900, the sentry handed him a note that read 'Duke of Cambridge Equestrian Statue, 0915.' Ike walked across Whitehall towards the Horse Guards parade. Soon, George Bell stepped beside him. "It's a good morning for a walk, Ike, though I find Major Crockatt's delight in cloak and dagger a bit tiresome. Shall we walk to Whitehall Gardens?"

"Good morning, your Grace…"

"George, please."

"Lead the way. I'm all ears."

"I'm afraid my friend has been arrested. He's in Tegel Prison in Berlin."

"You did not need me to come to London to tell me this. You haven't given up on him."

"Quite. I've heard from his mother. A godly and most enterprising woman. Her brother is General von Hase, Military Governor of Berlin. The General has visited Deitrich in prison and expects him to be released. He tells her his arrest came about from a discrepancy in accounting, not suspicion of treason."

"His uncle is a general? You trust this man?"

"Career Wehrmacht, no friend of National Socialism. My point is we must be prepared to act quickly once he is released. He may never have another chance."

"The plan is drawn. He is to travel to the Nazi garrison at Decin. From there, he will be guided into the Czech hills. I have the airplane, the pilot, the route, and the stops arranged. I ask for several days advance notice."

Bishop Bell breathed a sigh of relief. "What should I relay to Paula, that is, his mother?"

"Nothing until I tell you. Why risk any more suspicion? And contact me directly next time."

They had stopped at an overlook on the Thames River. Bishop Bell raised his right arm and pointed. "That's Lambeth Palace. So many great men. Spiritual giants walked those halls. Our national pastors—too many martyred."

Ike replied, "Kings. They couldn't learn to bend their knees."

Bishop Bell reached into the pocket of his raincoat. "I have something for you." He handed Ike a book. "Read this. It will make sense."

Ike took the book and read the cover. "The Cost of Discipleship by Dietrich Bonhoeffer." He turned it over and read the headline from the back dustcover. "I remember this. Langley mentioned it. Who could forget 'When Jesus calls a man, he bids him come and die.'" Ike opened to the title page. It was signed under a note: 'To my good friend, Bishop George Bell, a man willing to lay his life on the altar for Jesus.' "This is your copy. It must be special to you. I can buy a copy."

Bell shook his head. "I know it—I know the man. His memory will always be with me. You read it. Please. We cannot let this man die."

CHAPTER 33
REGROUP

The lights never went out in the Ops Room in Otterhead House. James Langley appeared omnipresent. When Ike walked in, Langley acknowledged him immediately. "Good, I need your advice on a drop site. Money, repair parts for Ray's radio, and a radio telephone for the boat operations. Val Williams has expended all his cash reimbursing the safe house *hebergeurs* from the broken Pat and Comet lines housing our airmen. He has gathered sixty priorities to date, and more are known to be in the area. He has moved thirty-four to the Chateau. The countess has arranged to purchase food. But the Chateau is being watched by the Germans."

Ike nodded. "I thought Ray was still in Paris. The radio is the first priority. Here, this field is outside the XVth arrondissement. It's been an option for some time. Never used. The cash, radio, and repair parts—when do we go?"

"Tomorrow night."

A week passed when Langley briefed Ike. Mithridate is losing patience. They threatened to cut any further cooperation with

Oaktree. Ray hasn't connected. His radio remains out of commission, likely the antenna. I want you to send a Lysander overhead to see if an airborne receiver can pick up the radio telephone we dropped him. It's all about timing."

Ike squinted, "You want an unarmed Lysander lingering over Paris during a transmission being tracked by the Jerries? Paris under intense heat?"

"We'll make it short. It's worth a try. Think of the flexibility it will provide if it works."

Ike scratched his chin. "Ray's a radio operator, not a messenger or courier. Mithridate wants nothing to do with him. Val and our evaders are camped out in Brittany. Send Ray to join Val in Saint Quay Portrieux. We haven't transmitted from that area. The German response will be less practiced, and we'll get a better idea of the radiotelephone signal range for the Admiralty. Get him on the beach if you can. Hell, there won't be a long antenna to de-rig in a hurry. Come back to me when Ray is ready."

"You're right. Let's get him out of Paris. After this last setup, if we still need Mithridate, we'll use a French courier. Thanks, Ike. You do know more than infrared photography."

Ike piloted the Lysander over the Brittany Coast, his radio tuned to the designated frequency. At 0111 Ike turned up the volume. A loud squelch of a broken voice overcame the droning noise of the engine. Ike reduced the squelch and listened. A voice to be certain but still not clear. "How far are we from Ray's position?"

Marley let the soft red beam on his map light fall on the chart. "Less than twenty miles, skipper. Could it be the altitude?

We're over eight hundred feet."

Ike brought the plane down in a spiral to 500 feet directly over Ray somewhere on a beach below the cliffs of Brittany and tried the volume. Labrosse's French Canadian accent was unmistakable: "272"—static—"4"—more static—"esti…"—static again. Ike tried the squelch and lost all sound. Ike asked, "Give me the altitude on the cliffs."

"Marley shook his head. "428 feet. We can't chance anything lower."

Ike replied, "I can fly seaward of the face."

Marley replied, "Not in this visibility."

Ike spoke into the mic. "312, 312, 312," and waited. There was no reply. "312, 312, 312." Still no reply. Ike changed the frequency. "Night Owl One, no joy, returning to base."

First thing in the morning, Ike went to see Langley. "Ray's portable radiotelephone won't cut it. Did anyone even bother to test it before it was air-dropped? We need to get him one that we know will work—he will need range out to sea and overhead."

James looked up and shook his head. "Not going to happen, Ike. The Admiralty just put a hold on the amphibious operation until fall. They're unhappy—say the night is getting too short, not enough cover of darkness by their calculation."

Ike replied, "Val has over sixty ready to go, and more are showing up every day. We can't leave them there until October or November."

Langley nodded. "Right. We do it the old-fashioned way, over the Pyrenees."

Ike muttered, "Damn Navy. If it was sailors, they'd show more interest. Damn interservice bullshit—RN white hats are sayin' screw the RAF."

Langley sighed. "Ike, give it a rest. The Royal Navy is having it tough too. And you won't see them walking away from a sinking ship. We'll get them out."

Ike paced the perimeter of Langley's desk. "My plan for thirty. It's ready to go. Sites, planes, comms, and even the script for the BBC. Say the word, and Marley will have it in your hand in minutes."

Jim Langley watched Ike as he marched wild-eyed in front of him. "You haven't heard it all. Val's gone missing—his second run to Paris—leading them out eight at a time. The group never arrived. Mithridate has picked up intel from Abwehr of eight evaders arrested. Did the Abwehr get lucky? Or was it another leak? If I were to green light your air mission I would be risking thirty evaders in one swoop. Not just evaders but the entire Flight 545. A trap that would take us out of our mission for months. So, no. Give it a rest. Do your job. And be thankful it's not your decision."

"Val captured," Ike moaned. "Oaktree is in shambles." He stood there staring at the floor. "You're right, of course, about the risk. Operation Mongoose is the real failure. There is a Cobra, and he is on to us." Ike sighed. "Right, Jim. You know where to find me. The 545 will stand by for orders."

Ike headed for the door. Langley called after him. "Aren't you going to ask about Dorothy, Colonel Z's Goldenrod update?"

Dorothy! How could I forget? Will I fail her, too? Ike turned around. "I'm all ears."

Langley smiled. "Resourceful agent. She has taken it upon herself to connect our injured and recuperating evaders to the Oaktree Line. We've long known that injured airmen are being cared for—hidden away in monasteries, abbeys, why, even hospitals, under the eyes of the Jerries—well, they couldn't be expected to walk across the Pyrenees. But a boat lift, well that is doable. Agent Goldenrod is taking inventory and prioritizing plans to move them to the Saint Quay-Portrieux *hebergeurs.*"

Ike nodded. *Recuperating. A reasonable scenario for Charles.* "Yes, with a successful Oaktree, a sealift makes sense for the injured. But if they can't walk, can they fly again? I mean, low priority, I'm glad we want to get them out, back to England, good treatment and family—but the mission priority—trained pilots to get back in the cockpit…"

Langley patted the folded sleeve of his missing arm. "Surely you heard of Group Captain Doug Bader? Ace? Commands the 161 at RAF Tangmere. Legless. Can't keep him out of the cockpit. The 161 is wholly dedicated to SOE. They're the first chair. In Uncle Claude's eyes, the 545 plays second fiddle. They handle the nastier side of our mission. Connected to the Baker Street Irregulars—Dorothy has made the right call. We need to get them out. They're willing and able."

That evening, Hugh was at the cottage when Ike stopped by. He was helping Rose in the garden. He was bent over a wheelbarrow, pitchfork in his hands. "What's she got you doing, Hugh, spreading manure? What does that say about a preacher?"

Hugh stood up and brushed off his knees. "Seems she has me over a barrel. I like to eat. Almost as much as I enjoy a good bourbon."

Ike laughed. "I should have figured you're getting low. Sunday, I promise."

Rose laughed. "Uncle Hugh has always been clear about his priorities." Her face turned serious. "News of Dorothy? Is she okay?"

"Yes. Safe, well, considering where she is and what she is doing—searching out the injured and recuperating allied evaders, hidden away in monasteries and abbeys—planning on getting them out."

Rose nodded. "As we all know, searching for Charles. If he's alive, and God knows we believe it—she'll find him."

Rose paused. "You don't look well, Ike. Something's troubling you."

Ike sighed. "I say Rose is safe, and that's true, but the mission, well, seems we've hit a wall—failure after failure and now, delays. Watching it fall apart, knowing you can't—hopelessness. Job. I feel like Job. Beset in disaster. I mean, not me personally, but those around me—people I care for, they're bearing the brunt—and I watch—helpless to stop it."

Hugh walked up and put an arm around Ike's shoulder. "You chose the right man to identify with."

Ike gave a sad laugh, "Blame it on my Baptist upbringing. There's a Bible character for every occasion. His complaints, Hugh. I don't get it. Oh, I know how the story ends—his praise, his restored wealth, and his new family—but his friends, the ones condemned by God—I gotta say, from where I'm sitting, some of their arguments make sense. And honestly, Job's complaining—how is he a model of righteousness? I get the pain. I don't get the model for the rest of us."

Hugh replied, "You ask the right questions…"

Rose interrupted, "I know why. Job stayed true. It all makes sense, Ike. Job's complaints—they were prayers. God wants us to pray. He can handle our fears, worries, and, yes, angry complaints. Job stayed. Job stayed with God even when he was getting nothing in return. Ike, get angry with God; that's okay. But know him, know who he is—what he can do. Tell him, yell at him. But stay with him because you can be certain he will stay with you. Be Job. Stay. Know the end of the story—God does hear. He will answer. God will reward."

Hugh pulled Rose close and squeezed the three of them in a tight hug. "Ike, God has given you a gift in this very special woman. Praise and honor him. I'm going to miss her so very much when you take her away. But I know she will tend another garden, and oh, how bountiful it will be."

Take her away? I never thought about that. Can I take her from her family? Is that fair? Will she come?

The next morning, Ike rose tired from a sleepless night and faced the man in the mirror. Slapping cold water on his face, he stared at his image. "Okay, God. I'm angry. Angry and confused. You want me to talk, I'll talk. Yeah, I know you're there. You've always been there. Linda convinced me and now Rose tells me the same thing. So, listen, I'm waiting. I'm not a patient man. I want to know. I want answers—real answers—solutions. I'm on you day and night from here on in."

Bells of Redemption

Entering the office, Ike stopped in front of Marley. Without so much as a good morning, Ike asked, "Number One, have you noticed we don't really know what's going on? I mean in theatre. What do we know for certain? All we get are reports from intelligence, filtered, I'm sure, by Colonel Z. And what is his source? Cryptic messages from Mithridate. We don't see anything. Even our drops, insertions, and extractions are made at night. We fly in cloud cover and land in blackness. We think we're calling the shots—doing something. But we see nothing. What is there to see from the cockpit of a Lysander at night? It's all second-hand information. Hearsay—inadmissible in a court of law. For all our efforts, we're just being told a story."

Marley replied, "We hear the radio chatter. That's real and Ray's voice. You know Dorothy and Ray were there. He's okay. I'm sure what we're getting is good. All the connections are made. The teams are on the ground waiting when we land. It's good. Skipper, what's really on your mind?"

"It's Oaktree. Failures and setbacks. I see Cobra, his head up, hood spread, his tongue tasting the air for our scent, and his eyes, watching, planning his next strike. What became of Mongoose? Isn't anyone out to kill that snake? They got Val. Captured. Oaktree is in shambles. And then there's Dorothy— you haven't heard the latest. She's collecting our wounded airmen squirreled away in Abbeys and Monasteries and, yes, French hospitals—arranging their boat lift to England. They're letting her stay. Yesterday, the Admiralty delayed the beach operation until the fall. The nights are getting too short, they say. You can be certain she will stay and keep searching for her husband Charles. I need to save her—save her from herself."

"Skipper, I'm behind you one hundred percent. You know that, but you need to know, yes, your vision is clouded. You are far more effective here than you ever could be in the fog and confusion and lousy comms that and Dorothy, everyone in Oaktree faces in France. I have a cousin; she's blind—can't see a thing—but she hears everything, feels what no one else can feel, and her senses, well, she perceives more than anyone I know. Maybe being blind—not seeing is a good thing. Think, perceive, and act. You're a man of action—we've all seen it. Do it blind. It draws on your strengths. And Dorothy is a big girl—smart and resourceful. She's doing what she needs to do. Save her? You can't stop her. Better to support her. But in the end, she, we, all of us are just one among thousands fighting for something we believe in. You can't let your fears for others get in the way."

Ike nodded. "Did I say good morning? Everything good at home—the wife and little Penny? You've been blessed, Nigel. Treasure them."

"Thanks, they're well. And good morning to you, Skipper. The folders on your desk need signatures."

CHAPTER 34
GENERAL ALARM

On the sixteenth of June, a heavy fog settled over Churchstanton. Ike made his way from the 545 Office to Otterhead House. Langley had called and said cryptically, "Ike, you need to get over here ASAP." As soon as possible still meant slow in visibility of less than 30 feet. Ike's mind raced as his car crawled. *He could've at least given me a hint. Dorothy? God, I hope not. Protect her, Lord—yes, I'm talking—praying to you. New mission? Not happening in this weather.* The car pulled in front of the war-weary mansion, and Ike jumped out. He yelled to a sentry inside the door. "Where's Colonel Langley?"

"Ops Room, Major. He's expecting you."

"What's up, James? Nothing is getting off the ground in this fog."

"They're cutting through the resistance and the escape line like a scythe through a wheat field. Mithridate signaled a General Alarm. A May Day would be more appropriate, but there isn't anyone who can rescue them. One last broadcast, and they went silent. We're still trying to get a handle on the situation. It remains sketchy. Here's what we've pieced together. Paris is penetrated. The Jerries set up a mouse trap at 72 rue Veneau, home of Elisabeth Barbier...."

Ike interrupted, "Don't recall ever hearing the name or address before."

"You haven't. It's on blackout outside Room 900. She's the gatekeeper in Paris. The apartment is the Free French Intelligence's peephole."

Ike asked, "You mean like the door to a prohibition speakeasy?"

"That's the analogy. But if you get past her, it's an open doorway to all operations in Paris, hell, in France."

"Crap. And the Jerries have Mademoiselle Barbier? Hell, she's in for a rough time of it."

Langley shook his head. "No. She was tipped off and has gone to ground. But they've nabbed several agents already. It's SOP for the French, our people too—can't wait for messages or couriers, go to the peephole to secure contact."

"Oaktree?"

"That's where Val went for help after the drop, and Albert Ancia, or Armand, the French agent, dropped with him. Also, the delivery point for the cash. It's well known to operatives, but even with the best imaginable security, it was too well known."

"Dorothy and Ray."

"Many times."

"Do they know?

"Not sure. Look, we believe the French are pushing the warning out as quickly as they can. They know their vulnerability. That's why the General Alarm. We just don't know when Mithridate will contact us again."

"Well, at least we got them out of Paris before this. Sounds like Cobra finally went for the fatal strike."

Langley sighed. "That's only half the story. Abwehr is conducting a sweep in Brittany. A dozen agents, *hebergeurs*, guides, helpers, and we figure about twenty of our evaders have been arrested. They also arrested the Countess Betty de Maudit at her Chateau du Bourblanc..."

Ike shouted, "Tell me they didn't get Dorothy!"

"Dorothy and Michelle Dumon are making a circuit of the abbeys for the boatlift of the injured evaders. The Jerries searched the house and missed thirty-four airmen hidden in a crawl space between floors. A house servant was able to hide their shoes and boots while the countess bought time talking to her arresting officer."

"So, Dorothy is safe."

"As far as we know, but..."

"But what?"

"Three of the arrested in Brittany were doctors. We can only hope there was sufficient warning to move their patients—our men."

"And stop Dorothy from walking into a mousetrap."

Langley was tapping a pencil on the map laid out before him. "It's not just Cobra. It's too much at once. There must be another infiltrator."

Ike asked, "Could be one man—he's had months to compile his list."

Langley shook his head. "The Jerries don't work that

way. Methodical—SOP requires the traitor to put eyes in the house and the person to be arrested—no wrong addresses, no wrong guy. Oh, he may be shielded from view, but he's there. No. We have another snake—Adder.

"Well, which is which?"

Langley looked into Ike's eyes and said, "Maybe we'll know that once we've chopped off their heads."

Langley paused and said, "Right. Not the clarity we would hope, but I thought you should know. Now, our response. We're pulling our people—as many as we can from Paris. The orders will go out tonight—the next good moon. A Lysander, choose the site very carefully. Never been used before."

"Just Paris?"

Langley nodded. "Just Paris—most network connections, highest risk."

"What about Brittany? Oaktree—it's in shambles."

"We're still awaiting a decision. But we do know Ray will stay. Someone must keep on top of the 90 or so evaders still hidden there."

"And Dorothy?"

"If she can get to Paris, I'll make certain we hold a spot for her on your Lysander."

"Only one plane."

Ike, it's not my decision. The risk. But yes, only one plane."

Ike nodded. "Okay. One plane. You mentioned waiting for a good moon. Plenty of light now. Full in less than a week—six days. We have two weeks of good moonlight. But my men can handle whatever we have."

"The team in France will need time—Dorothy will need time—to find her and get her there. Five days? Six days? The full moon gives everyone the best chance. Give me the site I'll give you the day."

Returning to his office, Ike was surprised to see the back of a civilian sitting in the waiting room. Marley stood as soon as Ike opened the door. "Major Curtis, you have a visitor…"

The man stood and turned to face Ike, "Good morning, Ike. I hope you can spare a few minutes with a friend. The help we talked about."

"Bishop Bell, your Grace, yes, of course. Please come right through." Ike opened the door of office and stepped aside to let the bishop go first. "If I knew you were coming…"

"I didn't mind waiting. I have other business here in Churchstanton, church business—I thought I stop by and catch you here."

Bishop Bell sat down. "I have news—news from Berlin. Most excellent news, indeed. But I will need your help. Pastor Bonhoeffer's escape is arranged! He can walk out of the prison, virtually any day now. The guards—yes, the guards call him pastor. He is free to walk about the prison and minister to prisoners and guards alike. He is a modern-day Saint Paul or Saint Peter! The jail cannot hold him! Even his guards know he is a man of God!"

Ike's surprise stretched his face. "And you need me…"

"Right. Getting out of the prison is one thing, out of Germany, well, our plan, Czechoslovakia."

Ike replied, "Without his Abwehr credentials, Decin is out. Dresden. It's close to the border—a large city—good rail service. The resistance should be able to guide him."

George Bell smiled. "My thoughts exactly. Already in the works. Can you have your plane, your contingencies ready in five, six days at the most?"

The same day as Paris? "I have a pilot, the best. And the arrangements with Sweden. But, yes, we can be ready."

Bishop Bell smiled. "Good! I will pass the word. Do you know that the guards planned this escape? They have a workman's uniform sized for him waiting in a closet. When we give the go-ahead, pastor Bonhoeffer will change into it and walk out the front door. Paula, his mother, will meet him and take him to the train station. God has planned great things for this man. Have you read the book? Read it. See his heart for God. He will challenge you. We are created for good work—not pleasure. True reward in life is overcoming challenges— overcoming self is the first and greatest challenge."

Ike found himself smiling and nodding in agreement. Somehow what he heard made sense. Ike got back to business. "I'll need new RECON photos for my pilot. And passwords and codes of our friends in the Czech resistance, can they make the pickup in Dresden? Who chooses the landing field? I'll need more, and soon. Is Colonel Z still pulling the strings?"

Bishop Bell nodded. "Claude Dansey will be expecting you. He'll give you everything you need."

"Claude Dansey? Not Colonel Z or Uncle Claude? You must see a different side of him."

"As Bishop, I'm a member of the House of Lords. It provides some prerogatives. He is a decent man. Hard decisions."

Ike nodded. "London calls. The sooner the better."

Standing up, George Bell said, "I'm off to the Church of Saint Peter and Saint Paul. I have a letter from the Archbishop of Canterbury for the parish secretary." He winked at Ike, "I understand the young lady is a close friend. Would you like to come along?"

Ike stood. "She's being given access to Bishop Lyfing's records? There's something you should know."

Bishop Bell replied, "Not to worry, historians have been through them many times. She won't find any deep dark secrets."

Ike said, "Sit down. She might. I know you are bound by the State Secrets Act, so what I am about to tell you is covered by the act. You see, quite by accident I discovered that infrared light, which we use in reconnaissance photography—it was quite by accident, you see, well, under infrared light vellum, any ancient parchment, that had been scraped for reuse—it seems the original reappears under the light. Rose has found records in Saint Peter and Saint Paul parish archives and at Durham as well that have remained hidden for centuries."

George Bell cocked his head and replied, "If what you say is true, she, you may have unlocked the greatest archeological and historical find in years. And imagine, all this historical potential sitting safely in our vaults."

Ike nodded. "Unfortunately, Bishop, this application of infrared technology cannot be made public until after the war."

"Yes, I see. You're suggesting I withdraw the invitation or prohibit the use of infrared light. At least she could see the written response of interest to her, but she won't find the answers she's seeking."

Ike replied, "Or, perhaps, someone cleared by the State Secrets Act could accompany her. I'm sure any new information she finds could be freely shared with the archbishop, so long as the method is withheld. It occurs to me that if the information has been hidden this long, waiting until victory over the Nazis is not unreasonable."

Bishop Bell said, "I believe his Grace, the Archbishop, would be keen to learn what treasure sits within the archives. Yes. But not a word to your young lady until it is arranged. I will deliver the letter but tell her she will be accompanied in accordance with protocol."

Ike drove Bishop Bell to the church. Rose's bicycle stood against the half wall leading to the door. As they started for the door, Rose approached from the vicarage. "Hello Ike, and, and, good morning, Bishop…"

"George Bell of Chichester. Good morning, you must be Rose."

Rose bowed, Uncle Hugh, that is, the Reverend Hugh Osbourne, our vicar, is in the garden. I'll take you to him."

"It's you I've come to see, Rose. I have a letter…"

"Me? Please, come into the vicarage. Tea, let me offer you tea. A letter for me?" Rose noticed Ike standing silently beside the bishop. "You know each other?"

Bishop Bell smiled. "We've come to know each through a mutual friend. You can thank Major Curtis, his friendship helped bring about what I am about to give you."

Rose's smile radiated unbounded joy. "Lambeth, you brought a letter from Lambeth Palace. Oh, this is wonderful!

Into the house at once, let me wash my hands and face and get the tea going. Ike, you know the way, show Bishop Bell to the sitting room. Uncle Hugh will want to hear this as well."

Ike led George Bell into the vicarage as Rose ran to the garden. She could be heard calling. "Uncle Hugh, Uncle Hugh, come at once. Bishop Bell of Chichester is here. He has a letter from Lambeth Palace."

Once tea was poured and Rose seated, George reached into his pocket, pulled out a small envelope and handed it to Rose. She took it and gazed at the wax seal stamped with the crest of the Archbishop of Canterbury. Hugh chimed in, "Open it Rose. We're all as anxious as you."

Rose slid a letter opener under the seal and slowly cut it away preserving the image intact. She slipped the page from the envelope and read:

To Miss Rose Osbourne, Churchstanton
Greetings,

It is with great fondness and affection I consent to your request to review the archives of Archbishop Lyfing held at Lambeth Palace. It is my sincere hope that your inquiries into the long traditions of Saint Peter and Saint Paul Church in Churchstanton and indeed all Great Britain are fruitful. The archivist at Lambeth Palace will be expecting your call.

May God Bless your endeavor
/s/ Wm Temple
The Most Reverend and Right Honorable,
William Temple
The Lord Archbishop of Canterbury

Rose jumped up, ran to Ike and gave him a kiss. "I'm so happy. The note, it is in his own hand. He took the time to write to me! It's all so amazing! When can we go? Soon. Say we can go soon. Are you so very busy that you can't take a few more days off and come with me?"

Ike's eyes brightened. "Rose things are getting busy, but it so happens I'm off to London tomorrow, or the next day. If you can arrange it. But I can't stay. I need to be back here. There is a war—and Dottie—don't get your hopes up, but we hope to bring Dottie back soon."

"Dottie? Dottie coming home? I knew you would look out for her. But London, just get me there to get started, please. If I need to stay, I'll be fine on my own. But I want you with me when I enter Lambeth—a special memory—we're doing this together."

Ike turned to George Bell, "Is tomorrow too soon?"

Bell smiled. "Reverend Osbourne…"

"Hugh, please, your Grace."

"Hugh, may I use your phone?"

CHAPTER 35
HIDDEN IN PLAIN SIGHT

Rose was surprised to see Kut Kuttelwascher waiting in the car when Ike picked her up. "Squadron Leader Kuttelwascher, it's a pleasure to see you again. Are you going to London as well?"

Kut smiled. "Good morning, Miss Rose. Yes, Major Mic and I have business in London. If I had known you were riding along, I would have invited Ruby to keep you company. She remembers you fondly."

Rose climbed into the car. "As do I. We had a nice talk—girl talk, you understand, but her advice—I felt it helpful."

Kut turned to Rose, his face serious. "You would do well to listen. Ruby is a very wise woman. One who understands a man at war. She is a great gift from God—my encourager. She puts aside her fears—she knows there I things I must do. Can you do that, Miss Rose? Can you encourage when everything in your heart tells you the risk is too high? It is only for a time. Yes, when it is over, I will repay her."

Rose glanced at Ike who listened in the front seat. "She spoke of the cost of love. A cost beyond romance and longing."

"Good. Be strong. Be patient. Major Mic is a good man. He will be a blessing too, someday." Kut turned to Ike, "So, tell me, Mic, does the Colonel know I come? He will not like it."

"He has no choice. I only do what he himself is doing to the…"

Rose asked, "To who? Who are you two talking about?"

Ike started the car. "Never mind."

Ike drove Rose to the front of Lambeth Palace. Kut whistled. "A palace, Miss Rose. Your friend lives in a palace?"

Rose replied, "Oh, no, Kut. This is Lambeth Palace, the London home of the Archbishop of Canterbury. I've been invited to research the archives—history of our village."

Kut looked puzzled, "Archbishop of Canterbury? Your English pope—or is the king your Pope? I've heard how your Henry VIII made himself head of the Church in England."

Rose laughed. "No, the King is not our pope. Yes, he is head of the Church of England, but his role is Defender of our Faith, not a religious teacher or bishop. Nor is the Archbishop of Canterbury a pope. He is the first among equals of all the bishops of the Anglican Church both here and in the empire. And there can be no criticism of our church in Europe, Kut, as you will recall since the days of the reformation, counterreformation and throughout the thirty years war, it was accepted regarding Kings, and Princes, the doctrine of 'his rule, his church.' So, if it was good enough for the Hapsburgs to declare Roman Catholicism their state church, then it is equally just for Henry and the Kings of England to establish an Anglican Church."

Ike interrupted, "Which only goes to show the arrogance of kings and princes. Why not let the people go to the church of their own choosing—according to their conscience?"

Kut nodded. "Rose, between you and Ruby I may learn what it is to be English."

Ike mumbled, "And I choose to believe God hears the prayers of his faithful, whether Catholic or protestant."

As Rose jumped out, Ike called after her. "I will try to meet you here later today, after the meeting. If not, I will meet you for dinner at the hotel."

Rose came to the window and gave Ike a kiss. "Come back here. I will be too excited to leave. Dinner can wait." Turning to Kut she said, "Goodbye, Kut. Please, join us for dinner. And I hope to see you and Ruby again. Soon. We must make it soon."

Colonel Z scowled when Kut entered with Ike. "I don't recall asking you to bring a friend."

Ike smiled, Colonel, this is the pilot for the mission, Squadron Commander Kuttelwascher. Born and raised in western Czechoslovakia, he knows the area, and the has the skills...."

"Yes, Kuttelwascher. I thought we agreed on the other Czech. As I said before, he's a bloody war hero. The government would object if they knew."

Ike countered, "That was because we didn't know Kut would be back in time. And it's my understanding they object as it is. Isn't the plan to ask for forgiveness after the mission rather than permission before? He's the best man for the job. He'll make it happen."

Colonel Z placed a pointer on a map. "The Czechs have recommended this site. A narrow field on the backside of the mountain. Just short of a thousand feet. I have photos as well."

Kut bent over the photo. "Yes, I know the place. Remote. Good, if they can get there undetected. Good air approach—the gap through the ridge, here. Yes, they have done their homework. I come through the gap, fly between the ridges, make the pickup and I'm out before the Jerries are the wiser. Low over the Baltic to Sweden, wait for the all clear, and back to England. Yes, I will do it. When?"

Claude Dansey handed Ike a folder. "Here are the signals and the BBC Broadcast codes. Everything is there."

Ike nodded. "Just make sure the Czechs get him there on time from the Dresden Station."

Kut replied, "Have no worries, my friend. We Czechs will do our part."

Ike asked, "You know these men—the Czech resistance team?"

Kut slapped his back. "They are Czechs. They will succeed."

Colonel Z stood up and examined the two men standing in front of him. "Right. There you have it. Five nights from tonight. Good luck gentlemen."

Ike replied, "Five nights—the same night as the Oaktree pull-out. You must know Paris, Brittany, the French Resistance BRI, it's all in shambles."

Colonel Z looked Ike in the eye and said, "I am quite familiar with Oaktree and the situation in France. Five nights from tonight. You have your orders."

Ike stared. "You are using Oaktree as a diversion to the Czech mission. We know there are leaks, Oaktree has been compromised, but the Germans would not—it's not the Germans, you are worried about, but SOE and official MI6 reports to the ministers. It's unsanctioned. You're going out on limb for this German pastor. Why do so many want this man rescued?"

Colonel Z went back to his paperwork. "I'll expect a full report via James Langley after the mission de-brief."

Outside, Ike said to Kut, "You heard Rose, I'm to meet her at Lambeth Palace. We can meet for dinner at the hotel later. Should I drop you there?"

Kut shook his head. "No need, my friend. I am off to shop for my dear Ruby. You enjoy yourself—be a part of her excitement while you can. I'll call after dinner for a night cap together."

When Ike arrived at Lambeth Palace, he was surprised to be led to the apartment of the Archbishop. The elderly cleric rose to greet his new visitor. "Welcome, Major Curtis, Rose, Bishop Bell, and I are having the most interesting discussion."

Ike walked over to Rose and gave her a kiss on the cheek. "Is it all that you hoped for, Rose? Did you find answers in Bishop Lyfing's papers?"

Rose smiled. "Answers yes, but not what I was hoping for, but that does not mean...."

Ike turned to Archbishop Temple and said, "Your Excellency, Rose is a most persistent woman, I hope she will not become a pest."

"Ike! Rose protested. "I'm not a pest!"

William Bell laughed. "Miss Rose Osbourne will always be welcome in the archives. Especially if she brings her new archivist's tool."

Ike replied, "I'm sure Bishop Bell has shared our concerns with its use, but with your assurances of secrecy, Miss Osbourne could visit from time to time for a head start on what you may believe to be the most promising documents. So, Rose, what did you find?"

Rose sat down again. "It seems that Bishop Lyfing was a kindred spirit to our C.S. Lewis. He was sympathetic to deeply held legends for their devotion—a common man's desire to understand and find reality in his faith. The bishop, who later became Archbishop himself, wrote to Bede discouraging the scholar from recording events not thoroughly documented and attested by chronicles of the time. Perhaps that is why Bede's work does not address the first Christian—likely a Roman, to carry our faith to Great Britain. His letter with Bede's acknowledgement is among the documents. But there is more. Bishop Lyfing did not object to the placement of relics in the churches. I was surprised to learn nearly every church sought a relic for its altar as a reminder of what the saints, believing forefathers in our faith, sacrificed for our Christ."

Ike nodded. "We all know where the veneration of relics took us."

Bishop Bell commented, "Relics were collected for nearly a thousand years before the abuses of Rome. They were approved by the early church councils. It proves that any good device of man can be abused."

Archbishop Temple spoke. "Regarding the Holy Grail, Archbishop Lyfing questioned tying the accounts of Joseph of Arimathea to the Arthurian legends of the Holy Grail. He was sympathetic to permitting pilgrimages to small local abbeys, in the age of pilgrimages, as practical for the poorest among us. But he encouraged the Abbots to remind the pilgrims that the blessings of the cup comes not from the cup but the wine, the blood of Jesus shed for us sinners."

Rose nodded. "Archbishop Temple was about to provide an example of how such an elaborate legend could take root—how it can capture both our hearts and minds."

William Bell nodded. "I was going to say, if I believed Saint Joseph of Arimathea did come to England from Jerusalem—a long journey to the ends of the empire, I think he would need to carry all his wealth with him. He would have sold all that he owned and carried it as jewels. Perhaps even setting his jewels in a chalice. The chalice would be set aside for the sacraments, but also as his wallet, selling a jewel as he needed money. When the jewels were expended, the gold chalice could be sold. In this way Saint Joseph went about the Roman settlements making disciples. And soon other Christians joined him from Rome and churches spread throughout Roman England."

Ike replied, "Until the jewels and the gold were gone. It is a plausible theory."

The Archbishop replied, "And as you and I fit reality into a story, that's what the legends have done for others."

Rose replied, "And why Doctor Lewis calls the miracle of the Gospel, where legend—the reality, and the facts merge into the truth. The only truth that captures God's will and revelation to us who believe."

Ike asked, "All of these Roman ruins. Is there any proof

of a continuous church in England? One going back to the Roman occupation if not to Saint Joseph?"

William Temple sighed. "A case may be made for the church surviving in Wales, but if any Britons were converted, they died out with the withdrawal of the Romans. Certainly, the pagans Britons were no friends to anything Roman. But God did not abandon our Island. He sent a Roman Christian, Saint Patrick, to Ireland to establish a vibrant church among the Irish who returned the favor sending missionaries the likes of Saint Aidan to Lindisfarne and, to Cuthbert, Eadfrith and Eadberht to relight our path to God. But that's another story."

Rose whispered, "And you are tied to that story, Ike. There's more to tell you about that."

Archbishop Temple rose from his chair. "I have asked my housekeeper to set places for you. I would be honored if will stay and sup with me tonight."

CHAPTER 36
RECONNAISSANCE AND ANALYSIS

Ike and Marley sat in the OPS Room staring at the photos. Marley took a pointer and said, "Look closely, if you flip through the photos this motorcycle is following our bird. And not just in this run, but every mission this week. And there are tracking trucks parked near each target site. They're waiting for us but not with anti-aircraft guns, they want us to show our hand for the extraction. They want to set a trap—the team and the plane."

Ike nodded. "Cobra—he knows about the extraction, but the site hasn't been released, so he has focused on our RECON for an early indication. I hope Langley knows what he is doing. The broadcasts are individualized for each agent, but if Cobra has compromised the BRC French Intelligence and resistance support, or learned just one of the intended receiver's code, the team will walk into the trap. Time—how much lead time will he give the team? Has he gathered them all close to the site? Is Dorothy safely in Paris? He tells me nothing—security, yet he has us fly all over the Paris suburbs."

Ike stood up, walked to the screen and said, "Lay them out for me. Mark the motorcycles and tracking trucks. I'm going to see Langley at Otterhead House."

James Langley looked up as Ike entered his office. "I've seen the RECON photos. And no, the extraction will take place on schedule by SOE assets."

Ike walked over and opened the file in front of Langley. "Here, flip through. Motorcycles following the route of our birds. And tracking trucks. No anti-aircraft. They're reconning our recon. Cobra knows we're coming for our people and is planning a trap."

Langley replied, "Yes. You confirm what we hoped and planned. He doesn't know the site—no one does. It's our best, only chance of success. And when the site is chosen, only the team members will know. Not the resistance or even the Free French Intelligence."

"They will wait without protection from the French?"

"That is their best protection. No leak unless it is one of our own team members. And we're willing to take that risk."

Ike continued. "Time—they must be able to move quickly before the Jerries can respond. That means you must preposition them close to the extraction site. How—with Mithridate on the run, how do you know they've made it—or even know if they know?"

"We're confident…"

"You don't know? Dorothy was last known to be in Brittany chasing down evaders in abbeys and hospitals—without comms support. All you have is hope, no assurance."

"As I said, we're confident. Ray will not allow her to be left behind."

"But Ray *is* being left behind. And his comms are a joke."

"Look, Ike, everyone on the ground in France knows the situation. They have each other's back. Trust them. Do you have anything else for me?"

Ike sighed. "No. I just hate being left on the outside. There is one other thing. From what you tell me, our RECON has been a diversion. Your whole plan is based on one plane in an unsuspected location, but you ignore one significant risk. Getting that plane safely to the site. All it takes is one good Nazi night hunter, one lucky coastal watcher, and our people are stranded. Let me send up a standby, loitering, just in case. Hell, I don't need the rest of the plan now. But just in case, we have a second chance."

Langley laughed. "You're a persistent SOB. Yes, I'll give you that."

Ike smiled. "Thanks. Now, I need to know how many souls we are lifting. I need the right plane."

Langley replied, "Six, if they all show."

"Right. Too many for a Lysander. A Beech Expeditor, smaller than the Hudson. While we're at it, have you given thought to top cover? A night fighter? Just sayin' and I will be in your OPS Room for the mission."

"You're welcome to the OPS Room. I'll be at Wilton Park."

Ike cocked his head. "They are being tight asses on this one."

BELLS OF REDEMPTION

Mumbled words shattered the silence. Heavy breathing and shouts were heard but unseen in the black darkness of the night. "No! He's on us! We're hit! No power, we're going down. Brace, Dottie, brace for impact. Head between your knees, hands, and arms over your head. I'm trying to pull us level. Once we hit, out as fast as you can. Open the window, you won't be able to open the door. Any way out. Brace! Brace! God save us!"

A loud groan echoed in the small room. Again, Ike was in the cockpit of a small plane underwater. Beside him, blonde hair flowed in the current. A woman's body floated serenely beside him. When his soul could endure the dream no more, he screamed, "No!" and awoke in a heavy sweat. *Oh, Lord why do you punish me with these horrible dreams?*

The evening in Rose's cottage with a warm meal set before him, Ike shared his dream with Rose. "Why does God haunt me? The dream—Linda's hair, her lifeless body. I thought I was past it. You said, stay with God. Argue and shout but stay. To what end? I don't know his mind, his will. Why?"

Rose came from the kitchen and wrapped her arms around Ike's neck as he sat. "There is an old saying that God never wastes a hurt. Our pain, if we stand by him, just trusting, our pain brings a blessing. The stories of the martyrs tell us the greater the pain, the greater the good and the blessings that followed..."

"It didn't work out so well for the martyred."

"No sarcasm. I'm serious. Ask them in heaven, I'm sure they're humbled by God's reward and their victor's crown. But your past dreams were sometimes different—maybe brought on by your fears or doubts."

Ike nodded. "Yes. In this dream, Dottie was in the cockpit bedside me."

Rose offered, "That's your fear. You are worried about her and feel guilty that she is in danger, just like your guilt for Linda. It wasn't your fault. It's a farewell—you need to let go. Give it to God."

Ike turned around and wrapped an arm around Rose. "Yes, it was different. The blonde hair reminded me of Linda, but was it Dottie? I never saw her face. And then something gave me a shove and I was propelled to the surface in a beam of moonlight. And as I rose, I saw the bottom of a boat directly above me. As I broke the surface I saw two hooded figures in the boat. But just as I gulped in a great breath of air, I awoke. I woke up not recognizing who or what I saw."

Rose pulled out the chair next to Ike and sat down. She took his hand in hers. "I've been praying for you, Ike. I pray because I love you, but also because God has his hands on you. I don't know why, but deep down I know he has called you to him and his service. Every dream, you're saved. He's telling you he has more planned for you. I can't explain it, but I have this peace that all will be well."

Ike sighed. "I wish I had your faith."

Rose kissed him. "If you are done yelling at God, maybe it's time to acknowledge who he is and give him the praise he deserves. Indeed, as the Almighty, all creation cannot help but praise him! For me, praise opens my heart and mind and ushers in my love and adoration. As I come closer to Jesus, I find my fears, worries, and doubts fall away."

Ike was silent. Rose pecked his cheek again. "Eat while

it's still warm. Didn't you say something important begins tomorrow?"

Kut Kuttelwascher was waiting in Ike's office at 0800. "Good morning, Mic! I want to be over the North Sea when it gets dark. It is good that we go over everything one last time. I want to go over the codes. Short. Once over the sea, only German. One letter and one number. I don't want to be tracked. And the pass go at Oland Island."

Ike replied, "Right. First stop RAF Sullom Voe, Shetland Islands, for fuel. That will put you north, above the entrance to the Baltic. You will fly across southern Norway. The coast is rugged and sparsely populated. The SOE has been successful running boats back and forth to the Norwegian Resistance. They have a good handle on the German positions. Past the coast and southeast across Norway to Oland Island, Sweden. From there, across to Czechoslovakia. Six hundred miles to Shetland, when do you leave?"

"I would like to depart immediately. Give me time for a warm meal at Sullom Voe while they refuel—a little rest and time for mental preparation before I begin the cat and mouse game with the Jerries."

"Your plane is fueled and ready to go." Ike stood and offered his hand to Kut. "Good luck my, friend. Come home to Ruby."

As the two shook hands, the door opened, and James Langley stepped inside followed by Bishop George Bell. Langley turned to George Bell and said, "Have you met Squadron Commander Kut Kuttelwascher? One the RAF's top aces."

Bell bowed slightly and replied, "It's an honor. I've read so much about you and your many victories."

Ike said, "Kut is about to leave. He has a long flight ahead of him."

Langley replied, "That's why we've come." He turned to Kut and said, "I'm afraid your mission is canceled. You can stand down."

Ike's "Canceled?" and Kut's "Stand down?" were simultaneous.

George Bell pointed to chairs. "Perhaps we should sit down. Yes, it's true. I insisted I tell you myself. We were foolish to think Pastor Bonhoeffer sought freedom. You see, he refuses to leave his flock. A good shepherd never abandons his sheep."

"Prisoners? And his guards?"

"His flock all the same. We should have known. He had freedom in America but came back to fight Hitler."

Ike sat down his face twisted in unbelief. "But he must know they will find him out. He was Abwehr. Gestapo will connect the dots. You said that there have been plots…"

"Three—just from among his friends. But the information he provided us—Churchill will not release it yet…"

"Information?"

"Proof. Photographs, logs, statements. The Jews—they are not being sent to work camps—they are death camps. Mass extermination. Doctor Bonhoeffer and his brother-in-law, Hans Dohnanyi, want the world to know, and the German people to know the evil and gross inhumanity of the Nazis."

Ike continued, "He must know they will execute him. It's only a matter of time before they find his evidence."

Kut was listening silently. "He is doing what is right. A true man of God. He speaks of sacrifice. But tell me, he has a family. They were to come. Surely, they can be rescued."

Bishop Bell shook his head. "No. No one will leave Berlin. They accept their fate trusting in the mercy of God."

Ike mumbled, "What was it he wrote? 'When Jesus calls a man, he bids him come and die.' Who can live to that standard?"

Bishop Bell replied, "Only someone God has called and prepared."

Nigel Marley watched James Langley, Bishop Bell, and Kut file out of Ike's office. "What was that all about? Was that a bishop?" He asked.

"Kut's mission to Czechoslovakia was just scratched. Yeah. Bishop Bell. Kut was to extract a German Pastor and Abwehr member working for our side. His guards arranged his escape from a Berlin prison, but he refused to go. He believes God called him there to shepherd his sheep. Sounds crazy, I know—but, if you knew the whole story—well, God bless him. But we have more urgent matters. I saw Langley last night and got his okay for a backup plane for the Oaktree extraction tonight. We'll need an expeditor—who's up?"

Marley reached for the duty roster and read, "Pilot Officer Martinson."

Ike sighed. "Turley's replacement. He's pretty green."

Marley replied, "I can ride with him if you like. Hell, we were all green once."

"I've got something else for you. I want your spitfire flying high cover against night hunters. As much arms and ammo as you can have ready."

"Night hunter? Langley agreed to this?"

"He didn't say no. And have a Lysander ready for me."

"What are you thinking, Skipper?"

"Hell, I can't even get an invite to the OPS room—Wilton Park—I figure I'll watch on scene. We've too much invested in this. I won't say we missed any precaution."

"Dorothy—we'll get her out. We must."

Ike stared at his XO for a moment, then said. "Those are the orders. Make them happen. And I want you in your rack after lunch. Rest. I need you sharp tonight."

Chapter 37
Leave No Man Behind

Ike was finishing lunch in the Officer's Mess when James Langley walked in. "A word, Major. I'm off to Wilton Park." Ike followed Langley to his staff car waiting at the door. Langley opened the door. Ike got in the back. Once inside, James said, "SOE has placed our man, Major Suttill, code name Prosper, in Le Mans. He has established secure communications apart from Mithridate. All our evacuees have been notified. Vaubezon, a chateau and farm outside the city near Ancinnes. Prosper is establishing a drop zone for the Resistance. Make sure you have enough fuel. Hour Zero One Thirty. Get us some good pictures of the area if you can. We never had this conversation. You're acting on your own initiative."

Ike replied, "Thanks, Jim. I'll see to it that no man is left behind."

After midnight a lone black plane of Special Squadron 161 lifted off from RAF Tangmere, home of MI6 SOE air operations outside Chichester in West Sussex. Minutes later another black Expeditor from the 545 took off from RAF Churchstanton. Waiting high above the French coast Nigel

BELLS OF REDEMPTION

Marley looked down on the clear moonlit sea. His spitfire cruised easily making lazy circles over the crossing zone watching for the two expeditors and any Luftwaffe night hunters.

It was shadows on the sea that alerted him, first one, and not far behind a second. Black shadows on a golden sea. Two small planes were making for France. Marley's spitfire began a slow circling descent, his eyes looking about for any telltale sign of the Luftwaffe. Then out of the corner of his eyes, he spotted a third shadow following behind the first two. He continued his descent and came down above and behind the trailing plane. His right thumb instinctively found the trigger button atop the stick. He identified the plane as Lysander and reached for the radio switch. With a smile in his voice he said, "Good morning, Skipper. Got you sighted in. Our birds are making for the rendezvous not ten minutes ahead of you. So far, so good. I'll leave you here and catch up with them."

Ike was startled, "Where are you, Marley?"

"Why on your tail, of course. You're leaving a good shadow in this moonlight."

"Now that you've had your fun, don't let them out of your sights again."

"Been quiet up here, but I'm moving along now. If you're going to linger, be careful. Frankly, I think you're less visible over the countryside. I'll catch you on the return, Night Hawk out."

Once the two Expediters crossed the coastline north of Caen, Marley breathed easier. "No more shadows for a night hunter to pick-up. Just ground watchers reacting to the sound of aircraft engines."

From his vantage high above Ancinnes, Marley saw a

flashing light on the ground. *There's the landing confirmation; he should be touching down soon.* Suddenly, white tracer rounds shot across the sky behind the first Expeditor as it attempted to land. Flames burst from the engine of the small plane. Marley hit the throttle and dove for the attacking aircraft. *How did I miss him? Where did he come from? I've got you. Steady.* Again, the night stillness was broken by machine gun fire. Seconds later, the landscape was bright with a red and white ball of fire as a twin-engine Messerschmitt Bf110 night hunter crashed and burned. Marley was on the radio. "Owl one hit but landed. Jerry night hunter downed. Making overflight of our bird for assessment."

Marley was interrupted by Night Owl One. "Landed safely, but this bird will not make it out. Friendlies present, over."

"Night Owl One, stay put. This is Night Owl 2 coming for the pickup. How many souls waiting?"

"Seven, one on a stretcher and the two of us. Over."

Ike turned on his radio. "Night Hawk, is the cover secure now?"

"Cover is secure, but headlights on the road. Company is coming in a hurry. Breaking for strafing run to slow them down."

"Roger, Night Hawk, buy us time. Night Owl Two, put her down and load who you can. I'm only ten minutes behind you. I'll take the stragglers. Over."

"Already down, Night Leader. Will make it quick."

Five minutes later the radios crackled. "This is Night Owl Two, taking off with tight quarters, crew plus seven. Gear and two still on the ground."

Ike replied, "Be right down. Is Section Officer Barkley aboard?"

Ike waited. Moments later came the reply. "Night Leader, confirm we have a Flying Officer Barkley aboard, the man in the stretcher, over."

Charles? Not Dottie? She must be still on the ground. "Roger, Night Owl Two, get them back safe. We'll finish up here and provide top cover on the way home."

Marley's voice cracked. "There are more coming on two other roads. Suggest you make it fast, Skipper."

Ike's Lysander touched down, and he taxied toward two figures silhouetted by the burning Expeditor. They ran to his plane as he spun it around. Machine gun fire tore through the tail as Dottie and the co-pilot of Night Owl One jumped in. Marley made another strafing run as Ike's small plane climbed to altitude. He swung south, avoiding Caen, looking for a clear path to safety.

Entombed in his small room, darkened against any light by heavy blackout curtains, Ike tried to sleep. His body was willing, but the torment in his mind fought against any restful peace. The dream began as it always did in the cockpit of his floatplane. His tired and anguished voice pierced the blackened silence. "Brace, Linda, brace. There is a debris field ahead. Large deadheads. I can't get her back up or avoid it. God save us!"

Again, he was in the water, trapped in the cockpit, Linda beside him. His eyes turned to her. *God save her, please! She is here. I can see her blonde hair flowing brightly in the dark water. Radiant even. White? She is wearing a white robe, like her choir robe, but so much brighter. And a golden sash. Singing. I hear her singing. Yes, how much she loved to sing—the old hymns and anthems. Even at home, while she did her chores, she sang. She is turning—her face—it's too bright, even in this dark water I must squint my eyes. Beauty—far more incredible than I remember. She is wearing a tiara; no, it's a crown of gold. But her face, oh, the love in her eyes—and peace. I don't see her lips move, but I hear her singing—the song reminds me of the chorus from the Messiah, 'Blessing, and honor, glory and power, be unto Him that sitteth upon the throne and unto the Lamb, forever and ever. Amen.' Yes, I remember. She sang the Messiah every Christmas. She's coming to me. My Linda is alive, and she's coming to me....*

It was midafternoon when Ike arrived at the Church of Saint Peter and Saint Paul. Rose's bicycle was propped against the gate of the vicarage. Ike went to the door and knocked. Hugh answered. "Ike! Come in. We just heard from Dottie. Isn't it wonderful! Praise God Charles is home safe. She never gave up. She knew—she trusted God, and she knew."

Hugh led Ike to the sitting room. Rose ran to him and hugged him tight as Hugh continued. "Safe, in an abbey all that time. A Doctor risked his life—an amazing doctor. Poor Charles—badly injured—broken ribs, a pierced lung, a broken leg, and a broken back. Surgery after surgery but the prognosis is good. He can now move his arms and legs, fingers and toes— just a matter of time. He is healing from the last surgery and then rehabilitation, but he will walk again. He will recover. Oh, praise God for his mercy endures forever!"

Rose kissed Ike and said, "Dottie's faith fed my faith. As she trusted, so did I. You must believe, Ike."

Bells of Redemption

Ike smiled. "When I got into my car at the base today, I believed there is a God, but my doubts persisted. But when I got out of my car at your door, well, I no longer believe—I know! I know God! Yes, it's more than a mere belief in God. I know him. He lives in my heart—his Spirit speaks to me and tells me I am his child, a beloved son."

Ike laughed. "The world is in shambles, but I know it's not ours to destroy. God is sovereign. I have peace. He brought comfort—more, he brought joy! Oh, such joy in my soul. Let me tell you about a dream I had this morning. Please sit, I must tell you."

Ike began, "I've shared with you my nightmare. Well, it began the same way, but oh, how quickly it changed. Linda—my angel, Linda, she was there beside me, resplendent in glory, singing praises to God. She's alive. She came to me—yes, she sang, but she never said a word. She came to me in heavenly glory and placed her hands on my waist. She looked up, so I looked up and a beam of light from her face shone on the bottom of a boat—my rescuers, my salvation. She gently but firmly shoved me towards the boat. And when my head broke the surface, I saw you. Rose, Dottie, and you. Hugh, you lifted me from the water and as soon as my feet touched the deck, the boat was gone. I was standing at the altar of Saint Peter and Saint Paul in my dress blues. To my right, the pews were filled with the good parishioners of the parish. To my left sat Dad, Ole, James Langley, Group Captain Hastings, Colonel Z, and all the men of the 545. Looking down the nave, I watched as young Earl walked up the aisle beside Marge Olson, followed by Nigel Marley and Dottie, who took Best Man and Bride's Matron positions. Then the organ music became louder, and I saw my beautiful Rose in a magnificent dress proceed up the aisle with you, Hugh, in your finest robes. Walking behind Rose, guiding her wedding gown train, was Linda. I awoke with such joy. I had to come straight here and share it with you."

Rose was crying. Hugh said softly. "I have never seen such a strong calling of a man. Ike, God has called you to a purpose. He placed you here. He sent Dottie to your office. He brought you to us—and Rose. He has healed your wounds, forgiven your doubt, and blessed you with love. All the men you worked to rescue, your determination to save Dottie—all the time, it was your salvation being worked out. You say you know God. I say, Amen! To know God is to know and do his will. He has renewed your spirit—prepare and fortify yourself, Ike. His calling will require more strength than you can muster—it will require trusting in his strength."

There was a loud knocking on the door. Hugh rose to answer. A young American officer stood there with Nigel Marley behind him. "Good afternoon, sir. I am looking for Major Curtis. I was told he may be here."

"Ike," Hugh called. "An American officer is here, looking for you."

Ike went to the door. "Are you Major Montclair Curtis?"

"I am."

The lieutenant saluted and said, "Major, General Eisenhower sends his compliments and requests your presence at Allied Headquarters. The matter is of some urgency. The General requests you accompany me immediately."

"Right. Let me get my hat. I'll be right out."

Back in the sitting room, Rose ran to Ike, wrapped her arms around him, and kissed him. Come back to me, Ike. You must come back."

Ike kissed her again, "Before the wedding—yes, trust God, he has brought us together."

Rose smiled and then quickly ran through the door and across to the church. Ike offered his hand to Hugh, who grabbed him and gave him a bear hug. It has been my great pleasure."

Ike wept. "My pastor, my shepherd, and my friend. Keep me in your prayers."

Ike wiped his eyes, picked up his hat, and left. Marley was standing outside. He saluted Ike and then offered his hand. "Come back to us, Skipper. We need you here."

Ike nodded. "Nigel, you're damn good Number One, a true leader and a damn good friend. You haven't seen the last of me."

Ike walked to the car. The lieutenant opened the rear door for Ike and closed it behind him. The young man went around to the driver's door and settled in. As he started the engine, the bells of Saint Peter and Saint Paul began to toll. Ike rolled down his window and spoke. "Lieutenant, what do you hear?"

"Church bells, sir."

Ike nodded. "What are they saying?"

The lieutenant turned around and said, "Saying, sir? I don't understand."

"It's a hymn of praise to God, thanking him for his work of salvation—Jesus saves, Lieutenant, Jesus Saves." *Lord, I'm staying.* "Drive on, Lieutenant."

Ike began to whistle as the words of an old hymn, a favorite of his father, played in his mind: *Stayed upon Jehovah, hearts are truly blessed. Finding as He promised, perfect peace and rest.*

Ike smiled and waved at Rose as she ran out of the church. *Yes, I'm stayed on Jehovah.*

Lord Jesus, where are you taking me?

ABOUT THE AUTHOR

David Martyn retired from a career in the Maritime industry and lives in Gig Harbor, Washington (nicknamed *The Maritime City*) with his wife Karen. David writes Christian fiction.

David's historical fiction series, *The Robert Curtis Mysteries*, take place during the 17th Century Thirty Years War (when the Church was at war with itself) and the lead up to English Civil War. These mysteries include: *Called Into Service, Soldiers of the King: the Bramshill Affair,* and *Lords and Ladies: the Banqueting House Plot.*

His Biblical series of novels, the 'Hall of Faith' series, include*: The Praise Singer: a Disciple of Melchizedek, The Oak of Weeping: the Story of Isaac, Deborah, and Rebekah, and The Epistle: a Story of the Early Church..* David also wrote a pocket novel, *Huldah and the Last Righteous King,* and a collection of short stories, *A Light in the Darkest Night.*

David's short stories can be found in Blue Forge Press anthologies: *Unconditional: Ten Stories of Enduring Love, Unnerving: Volume 2,* and *Unnerving: Volume 3.* A complete listing of David's works can be found on the website: blueforgepress.com